GALVESTON '44

B.W. PETERSON

ISBN: 978-1-7356049-0-9

SWIFT HOUSE PRESS
7380 S. Eastern Avenue, Suite 124-216
Las Vegas, Nevada

Galveston '44

Chapter 1

Sheriff Sam Baker pulled his squad car to a stop along the sand-dusted seawall. A family of four, wearing bathing suits and carrying brightly-colored towels, waved to him as they walked past. Sam waited until they disappeared down the concrete steps leading to the beach before he took the metal flask from the glove compartment and took a good pull of whiskey.

He looked out over tea-colored waters of the Gulf, past the horizon, to where he imagined foreign lands might start. But movement much closer to this shore captured his attention—two merchant ships about a mile apart steamed towards the port.

Sam grabbed his binoculars and got out and pulled his sweat-soaked tunic away from his back. White summer clouds tinged with gray drifted over the merciless sun and cut the glare from the churning surf. He raised the binoculars. Four more ships appeared and filled the gap between the first two. Convoys like this had started to appear a year ago after German submarines had sunk more than fifty freighters since the war began. The end of 1943 had seen a drop-off in attacks, and this year none had been lost to the Nazis.

The cruiser's radio squawked. Sam jumped. He wasn't used to the damn thing yet, and didn't like being personally tethered to headquarters. He reached into the car and grabbed the corded microphone.

"Station One," he said. "Come in, base."

A woman's raspy cigarette voice broke through the radio static. "Sheriff Baker?"

A moment passed as she fumbled with the mechanics and muttered to herself. He waited patiently, glad no one was around to hear.

"Station One, come in please."

"I'm here, Grace. Did you forget to release the button?"

"Yes, sir. I just can't get the hang of this dang thing." She drew out every other word like Southeast Texas rhyme. *Dang thang.*

"It's a new world, ain't it."

"I'm too old for anything new-fangled, Sheriff. Maybe you should get somebody younger in here."

"Afraid not. The deputies would be too distracted by somebody younger."

Silence followed on the other end. "Are you sayin' I'm past my distractin' days?"

"You're never too old to bother somebody, Grace."

"I'll have to puzzle on that a minute, Sheriff. In the meantime, I got a call from Wayne over at Madam de Sousa's place."

Sam pictured Phyllis de Sousa's white, three-story house—one of the classier cathouses in town.

"*Deputy McRae,*" he corrected. Grace tended to act motherly to the young deputies. "Deputy McRae better not be enjoying their services."

"Sheriff, I doubt if Deputy McRae would—"

"That was a joke, Grace."

"Oh, I'm glad to see you're back to jokin'."

Sam waited, hoping Grace would take it as a sign she should return to the day's business.

"Also, Claire called," Grace said. "She asked for you to call her."

The noonday sun burned through the clouds. Sam fanned himself with his hat. "Duly noted."

"I may be out of line, sir, but shouldn't you be with your wife today? It's real quiet around here and—"

"Are you forgetting something, Grace? About Deputy McRae?"

"Oh, I almost forgot. He arrested a john that hit one of the, well, the ladies over there at Madam de Sousa's place."

"Is she hurt bad?"

"Apparently not."

Static from the radio hissed in his ear. He spoke louder. "What's the problem? Why not just bring the man in?"

"He said there's extenuating circumstances." Grace slowed down her drawl even more to pronounce *extenuating*.

"Like what?

"He just said Deputy Eilers is also there."

Grace let that bit of information hang in the air. Sam read it as Wayne's code for saying Eilers fucked up somehow. Again.

"Is that all McRae said?"

"Just that the perpetrator is a one-legged fellow."

"One-legged?"

"That's what he said."

"I'm on my way."

Sam climbed into the squad car and started it up.

A one-legged man misbehaving in a cathouse, and Deputy Eilers probably fucked up in the line of duty. He hoped it would take his mind off his son.

Galveston '44

Chapter 2

Sam slowed the squad car as he neared Phyllis de Sousa's whorehouse. The two deputies stood in the shade with the perpetrator sitting with his back propped against a pine tree. Deputy Eilers stood a little apart with his arms crossed over his chest. *Almost fifty years old and still pissin' in the wind*, Sam thought.

Two scantily-clad women sat fanning themselves on the wrap-around porch of the three-story, colonial house. A crowd of onlookers stood halfway into the street.

Sam climbed out of the car, and the crowd moved back to the curb.

Deputy Wayne McRae nodded in greeting. "Sir." Wayne's voice was calm and controlled, as usual. Whether the situation was under control or fluid and tense, he never appeared ruffled or anxious. Only twenty-one and already twice the lawman Deputy Vernon Eilers thought he was. Wayne was tall and clean cut. It was no wonder his daughter was attracted to him.

Eilers stood a good six inches shorter, with a beer belly that protruded over his gun belt. His gray-flecked moustache bristled in all directions like a well-used scrub brush. Sam thought it to be representative of his general dissatisfaction with most everything. He held an unspoken grudge against Sam because seventeen years ago the town's powers-that-be passed him over as the new Galveston County Sheriff. Instead, they greased the wheels for the election of a younger man—Deputy Sam Baker.

"Sheriff," Eilers said, acknowledging his superior's

7

arrival. His tone suggested something needed to be discussed and settled. Preferably to his satisfaction.

The one-legged man looked up at Sam with a contrite expression. His pitiful appearance—greasy hair, tattered clothing—matched his hangdog mug. One leg was long and skinny and its foot wore a well-travelled shoe. The other leg extended only a foot or so from his hip. The extra cloth from his pants leg was pinned around the stump. At his side lay a pair of wooden crutches.

The man wiped a thin stream of blood from an angry knot on his forehead.

Sam fanned himself with his hat. He noted that Eilers' eyes darted over to his fellow deputy, probably angry with him for calling Sam to the scene. Deputy McRae appeared unruffled by the conflict with the older lawman.

"Who was first on the scene?"

"That would be me," Eilers said, sighing. "I got a call from Grace that somebody assaulted one of these goddamn whores." *Hoo-urs.* Sometimes Eilers sounded like a cowboy from one of the Western novels Sam liked to read.

"Let's keep our opinions to ourselves, Deputy."

Eilers pursed his lips like he'd tasted something sour. "I arrived as the perp was running out the door. I grabbed him and pulled him back inside."

"Stop," Sam said. "How can a man on crutches run?"

"He was fleeing, Sheriff. I had to physically stop him."

"Is that how he got that knot on his forehead?"

"I had to take control of the situation. Any of us would've done the same."

No, Eilers, Sam thought. *Only you would have a problem subduing a one-legged man.* Sam turned to Deputy McRae. "Where did you come in, Deputy?"

"I got a call from Grace as well, Sheriff. I was in the

vicinity so I swung by to see if I could assist."

"What did you see when you arrived?"

"I saw Deputy Eilers standing over the suspect with his boot on his chest," Wayne said. "The ladies were shouting at him to let the man breathe."

Eilers faced McRae. "They were interfering with the arrest of a suspect, goddammit. You didn't see the whole—"

"Address your comments to me, Deputy Eilers," Sam said.

Eilers crossed his arms over his chest. "Well, I got plenty to comment on."

"You and I *will* have a discussion."

Sam wondered how long it would take to find a replacement for Eilers and get the new man trained. It just might be time to turn the deputy out to pasture. But he'd hate to do it—a fifty year-old man might have trouble getting new work. Sam told him to go back into the house and get ice for the man's forehead. "And ask nice."

Sam watched Wayne's eyes follow Eilers to the brothel. To the young man's credit, he didn't smirk or display a look of vindication. If anything, his expression was one of pity for his fellow deputy.

Sam and McRae went over to the prisoner. "What's your name, fella'?" Sam asked.

"Stanton Flowers, sir. I'm terribly sorry for the trouble I caused today, Sheriff." The man spoke with a southern drawl, in a voice that suggested education and culture. "This was totally out of my character, and I deserve to be punished. I've never been a violent man. Other than the war, of course."

"What war would that be?"

"The Great War. World War I, they're starting to call it now."

"Is that how you lost your leg?"

Flowers unconsciously touched his stump. "In the Battle

9

of Bayonne. Cannon shrapnel."

Memories and images Sam thought he'd buried long ago rushed back. In another time he'd seen countless soldiers that looked like this man—dirty, missing a limb. "*I* fought in the Battle of Bayonne."

"I hope you came out all right, sir."

Sam was reluctant to admit he'd never been wounded despite seeing friends shot to pieces right next to him. He'd been cut by shrapnel on a few occasions but never seriously enough to take him out of action.

Eilers brought ice wrapped in a towel. Flowers pressed it to his head. Sam sent the deputy over to keep an eye on the growing crowd. He turned to Wayne. "You questioned this man?"

"Yes, sir. He told me one of the working girls inside refused to take him upstairs. He got upset, and when he grabbed his crutches from her one of them hit her on the face. Then Eilers arrived and allegedly punched him on his head." Wayne pointed to Flower's forehead. "As you can see."

"Is that right, Mr. Flowers?" Sam asked.

"That's the gospel truth, Sheriff. Your deputy had that look on his face like he was going to kill me. He turned to the young lady in question and called her the vilest of names."

"Where the hell was Madam de Sousa when all this was going on?" Sam asked Wayne.

"She's not here. Otherwise, she would have come out with her derringer and put a stop to all this."

Sam looked up at de Sousa's bordello. "Keep an eye on Mr. Flowers, Deputy."

Chapter 3

Sam walked through the open door of the bordello. The smells of stale smoke and cheap perfume permeated the room. Women in corsets and various underthings sat on red velvet couches and chairs. The atmosphere was charged, as befitting the aftermath of violence.

"Who's the lady that got hurt?" Sam asked. The women cast quick glances at one another but stayed silent. "Come on, now. I got to know whether to charge that man with assault."

A young woman with thin red hair and pink-rouged cheeks was urged forward by the other women. Sam beckoned her to join him by the corner window. He pulled the thick drapes aside. A ray of sunlight caught the pink mouse under her eye. Come tomorrow it would turn black. "Does it hurt?"

"It don't hurt me much, Sheriff," the girl said. "Tell you the truth, I've had worse than this."

"What happened?"

"The man was upset because I wouldn't take him upstairs. But it wasn't on account he didn't have but one leg. I did a one-legged man before but he was real clean. When I gave this'n here today his crutches, he grabbed 'em so hard one hit me in the face."

"It wasn't intentional?"

"No, Sheriff. He said he was sorry, and then he sat down and put his head in his hands. I thought he might be crying, but he never looked up until the deputy arrived."

"The older deputy?"

"Yes, sir."

"What did the deputy do?"

The woman hesitated, looked off.

"It's all right," Sam said. "This is just between you and me."

The woman had just gathered herself to speak when outside Sam heard the sound of cars skidding to a hard stop. He pulled the drapes wider—a black Ford now blocked the squad cars.

He ran outside. Four large men were trying to lift Flowers from the ground while McRae and Eilers held him down. Sam grabbed a scar-faced man by his leather vest. "What the hell are you doing?"

The man tried to pry Sam's hands loose but couldn't. "Mr. Romano said to take this asshole away."

As if on cue, a black Cadillac slid to a stop. A huge block of a man with only one name—Drago—jumped from the car and hurried towards them. The big man wore his trademark sport coat which hid the handgun he always carried. He was followed by a short, stocky man with thinning hair dyed a deep black. Vince Romano's presence—and his menace—transcended the size of his large bodyguard.

Across the street, the arrival of Galveston Island's dominant mob boss kicked the crowd's chatter up a notch.

Romano stopped inches from Sam, his face bright red, ropy veins in his neck throbbing. His black eyes, however, looked up at Sam with dead calm. "What the fuck are you doing, Baker?"

Sam towered over Romano. He could see down into Romano's shiny scalp where thin streaks of gray hair had escaped the dye process. Romano was vain and tried to camouflage his fifty plus years of age, most of which were spent bending people to his will and expanding his criminal enterprise.

"I could ask you the same thing, Vince," Sam said.

Romano pointed at Flowers, who was now shielded by the deputies. Drago hovered over them as if he might make a grab any second. The other men stood by ready to help. "This man fucked up in my whorehouse, and we're taking him away."

"This is Phyllis de Sousa's place."

Sam knew that if Vince and Drago took Stanton Flowers into their possession they'd teach him a severe lesson, no matter that he only had one leg and was down on his luck. No matter that he had served his country and paid a huge price for it. Flowers would serve as a warning to anyone else who might get out of line in one of Romano's joints.

"Where is Phyllis de Sousa?"

"How should I know? I bought her out, and she's gone."

Sam waited for Vince Romano's expression to betray him but his liquid black eyes revealed nothing. In Sam's years of observation, he could rarely tell when the mob boss was lying or not. Sam eventually came to a certain conclusion: Vince Romano believed his own lies.

"I'm going to have to look into that, Vince."

"Stay out of my business, Sheriff."

"I'll need to see a bill of sale."

"You know what you can do with your bill of sale."

The festive crowd across the street had grown substantially. They clamored for blood. Anybody's blood. They were witnessing a power struggle and would report the winner and loser to their friends. Soon the whole town would know who had backed down. Sam had played diplomat in the past and had given in to Vince Romano over minor territorial disputes. But not today.

Today he just didn't give a damn.

Sam beckoned Romano to step further from earshot. But the mobster—always aware of appearing to be the alpha dog—circled around and made Sam walk to him.

Drago stepped closer but Deputy McRae blocked his path. The two men locked eyes. Deputy Eilers stood in front of the other three men.

Sam bent down to level his eyes with Romano's. He kept his voice down but found himself hissing. "You are not taking this man away today, Vince."

"Sam, when we leave here in one minute, that piece-of-shit will be going with us."

"He's a veteran of the Great War where he lost his goddamn leg." Sam pointed at the house. "The girl in there barely got hurt."

"Doesn't matter," Romano said. He nodded at the raucous crowd. "Those fuckers out there need to know you can't damage the goods in my cathouses."

"He'll spend the night in jail just like any lawbreaker."

"No," Romano said. He started to turn.

Sam grabbed him by the wrist. "*I* said no."

Vince looked down at Sam's hand and back up at him in disbelief. "You've got about five seconds to let go of my fucking arm before Drago gets real upset."

Sam felt a jolt of readiness rip across the muscles in his shoulders. It was the same involuntary reaction he'd had as a boxer when the first bell rang. And as a young soldier when the order came to charge.

"Five seconds? That's more than I need."

All the air seemed to vanish from the whorehouse lawn. Everything seemed to slow down. The chatter from the crowd dimmed. The edges of Sam's vision blurred. By contrast, the man in front of him snapped into sharp focus.

Romano's expression of dismay guaranteed that he took Sam at his word. "You sure you want to cross this line?"

"I just did. Here's what you're going to do. You're going

to tell your men—including your yard ape there—to get in their cars and wait for you. Then I'll let you leave."

Vince's face twitched like he'd been slapped. "You've really gone downhill this last year, Sheriff. And you got whiskey breath today."

"Good observation."

"I know what your problem is. You think you're the only one who lost a son in the war."

Sam was prepared to take Romano's best shot, but it hit him where it hurt most. What the gangster didn't know was that it pushed Sam closer to a reckless state that scared even him.

"Go ahead and get your goons to leave," Sam said. "I don't have all fucking day."

The menace in the mobster's face faded. Now they were just two guys talking. "After all I've done for you," Romano said.

"You haven't done shit for me."

"Maybe not as much as I did for your father."

"What are you talking about?"

Romano prodded him in the chest with his free hand. "You ended a family tradition."

"I won the election for sheriff when he died," Sam said. "That's our family tradition."

"That's when you should have taken me up on my offer to partner."

"I said no. I wouldn't be your lap dog."

"But your father didn't say no, He *was* my lapdog."

"Bullshit."

"He took me up on my offer because he was a lot smarter than you."

Sam's anger threatened to flare. "My father was *not* corrupt."

"Let's just say he did little favors for me."

"Like what?"

"He let me know when the Texas Rangers were about to raid my casino or one of my gambling joints. He ran people out of town that tried to muscle in on my business. And I made sure to return the favor."

Sam caught movement out of the corner of his eye—Stanton Flowers lay back on the grass, holding his stump and grimacing in pain.

"You're lying, Sam said. "My father was a great sheriff. He had a good working relationship with the Rangers."

"Oh, sure. I told him not to rock the boat, so it would look like he was a straight up guy. Sheriff Jim Baker was good at his role."

"I'm starting to regret I didn't shoot you a minute ago."

"The truth hurts, Sheriff," Vince said. "So I'll spare you the messier things Jim did for me."

"Where did all this dirty money go, then? We were comfortable, but we weren't living high off the damn hog, either."

Sam saw Drago take a step towards them. Deputy McRae's hand settled on his gun holster.

"Maybe I shouldn't tell you how he spent his blue money," Romano said.

"I don't want to hear you slander my father's good name with some bullshit story that's impossible to check out. You make an accusation, you'd better be able to back it up."

Romano smiled. He was enjoying Sam's uncertainty. "Jim's money went to his *chilla*."

"Chilla?"

"You need to get out more, Sheriff," Vince said. "That's what the Mexicans around here call their mistresses. Sheriff Jim's money went to keep his young whore in style."

Sam felt his immediate surroundings—the white whorehouse, the half-dozen men surrounding the one-legged man, the caustic gangster whose wrist he now gripped—spin around and reorder themselves into a world different from a moment ago.

"He wouldn't do that," Sam said. His denial of Romano's claim sounded less forceful than he'd intended.

"Go ahead and ask her. Hell, you might even know her."

Sam thought back to his home life with his mother and his older sister, Missy. His father was often gone, but then so was Sam. Enforcing the law in Galveston County was demanding. He remembered his parent's relationship as being respectful and deferential to each other, but not affectionate. As a kid he had thought that was normal. But as an adult he had learned differently. His and Claire's relationship was often affectionate but sometimes heated. Only in the last year had it become distant.

"All right, I'll bite," Sam said. "Who is she?"

"Alma Rodriguez."

Sam repeated the name—somehow it rang a bell, but it was a common name in Southeast Texas.

"She was a lot younger than your father. Long black hair, black eyes."

"You just described a million Mexican women, Vince."

"Kind of tall for a Mexican lady. She was what they called high-spirited, but I thought she was just fucking crazy. She had a big laugh you could hear a block away."

"It's possible my father visited a whore, but he didn't take money from you."

"Why don't you go ask her, Sam? She's still in town." Romano's expression was smug, triumphant. "You fucked up today, Sheriff," he said. "Now people in town are going to think you're my fucking puppet, just like Sheriff Jim was."

Vince pointed to the whorehouse. "Instead of butting into my business, you're going to be busy trying to deny that you're on my payroll."

"Why didn't you pull this bullshit when I rejected your offer seventeen years ago?" Sam demanded. "Why now?"

Romano shoved his face closer to Sam's and bared his teeth. "Because you threatened me, you son-of-a-bitch." He pulled his arm free and signaled for his men to follow. Drago took his icy stare away from Deputy McRae and fixed it on Sam.

Romano and his men jumped into their cars and roared away. Their exhaust settled on the street. The crowd quieted.

Most of them would say Sam had prevailed, but he knew better.

Chapter 4

Sam stood on the covered porch of the small stone cottage. He took a deep breath. He turned to watch the yellow taxi ease off from the curb and drive away. Sam had paid the cabbie, Gus Josie—a man who knew almost everything about everybody in town—for the information that brought him to this unassuming house. For such a personal matter, he had avoided using any of the deputies.

True to his usual skill and efficiency, Gus had found her in the late afternoon. "Easiest three bucks I ever made," he said when Sam paid him. "She's been put out to pasture, Sheriff," he added. "Too many young'un's available."

With Gus' words in mind, Sam expected to see a woman—especially one who had relied on her looks and her body to earn her keep—worn out, used up. But that image didn't fit the woman who opened the door to Sam's knock. Yes, time had etched a few lines into her face, but her brown arms, exposed by a sleeveless white blouse, were slim and toned. Her untamed black hair hung freely down her back. Her equally black eyes regarded Sam with wariness.

"Well, Sheriff, what took you so long?"

Alma Rodriguez opened the screen door, and he walked in. The small house was orderly and clean, and the smell of cooked food wafted from the kitchen. Alma lit a cigarette and watched him, the smoke drifting up languidly from her full lips.

From the kitchen came the scraping of a metal utensil on a glass plate.

19

"*Mijo*," Alma called.

A young man with closely-cropped hair, perhaps in his late teens, walked into the living room. He wore the light tan uniform of a U.S. Army Infantryman, and the upper sleeve bore the single stripe of a buck private.

"Have you met Sheriff Baker?" Alma asked.

"Honored to meet you, Sheriff," the young man said. He gave Sam a firm handshake. "I'm Johnny Rodriguez."

"My pleasure, Johnny. Just out of boot camp?"

Johnny nodded. "Yes, sir. Shipping out tomorrow." His brown eyes lit up with the eagerness of an untested recruit.

Don't go, Sam wanted to tell him. *Don't break your mother's heart.* Instead, he said, "Give 'em hell, son."

Johnny saluted smartly. "Sir. Yes, sir." He kissed Alma on the cheek. "Thanks for lunch, Mom."

The screen door closed behind Johnny as he left. Alma turned to watch him walk away as if she were fixing him in her memory.

"He'll be all right," Sam told her. "The Normandy invasion has Jerry on the run."

Alma gently pressed her cigarette out in a clay ashtray. She watched the dying stream of smoke as if it could tell the future. "I was sorry to hear about your son."

Her condolence, coming as it did as they were both thinking about *her* son, caught him off guard. Before he could mumble his thanks, she said, "The house is mine, you know. Your father made sure my name was on the title. *My* name only."

Sam waved her statement off with a sweep of his hand. "It's your house."

He wanted to ask her about his father, to try to understand him better. What had he been like with her? More passionate than with Sam's mother? Did he give her jewelry and other gifts that should have gone to his mother? Did he talk about where he got the money to buy her the little stone house?

But he'd learned what he wanted to know. His father had lived two lives, and his second one, the one with the once-beautiful and wild Alma Rodriguez, had been funded by the dirty work he did for Vince Romano.

* * *

Sam sat in his idling squad car as it baked in the mid-afternoon sun. His hand felt too heavy to reach for the gearshift or even the whiskey flask in the glove box.

Gus Josie had dropped him off after his visit to his father's *chilla*, as Vince Romano had called her. Sam had looked out the window the entire ride back, unable to look Gus in the eye. The cabbie, usually talkative, remained silent. Sam figured he probably knew Sam had just discovered the secret life of Sheriff Jim and Alma Rodriguez. Why else would he visit her without his squad car?

Gus had been around during Sheriff Jim's reign—he would have known, yet he'd never said anything to Sam. Sam appreciated that. Given a choice, he'd prefer to live under the same illusion he'd held ever since he'd worked as a deputy under his father's command.

Even back then, Sam had been a good detective. Why hadn't he discovered the reason for his father's long absences from the family? Vince Romano knew where he'd spent his time and his dirty money, yet had kept it like an ace up his sleeve for twenty-some-odd years. Was it just this morning that Romano had threatened to spread rumors that Sam also worked behind the scenes for the benefit of the mob boss?

The names of people who Sam wanted to prepare for that lie flooded his mind. His wife and daughter, of course. And he would huddle with Arin Haugen, Galveston's chief civic leader and the town's richest man. Haugen was often able to dissuade the gangster from acting in a manner that would damage Galveston's reputation as a safe place for tourists to satisfy their most basic urges.

He needn't warn the powerless mayor, and the chief of police *was* working for Vince.

Then Deputy Wayne McRae sprung to mind.

Sam radioed the jail and Grace, in turn, radioed Deputy McRae to meet him at the seawall. Wayne was waiting for him when he pulled up. As he climbed out of the cruiser a brisk breeze blew in from the Gulf and ruffled his uniform pants legs.

Sam's grim expression alarmed Wayne. Sam figured his first thought—understandable for a young man in love—was that something had happened to Sylvie.

"She's fine," Sam said. Then he asked Wayne if he thought his boss took money from Romano for favors rendered.

"Hell, no," Wayne said. "I've never seen you give that son-of-a-bitch anything other than a hard time. The way you made Romano back down today should tell people you aren't on the take."

Sam warned him that he might hear rumors to that effect soon.

"Anybody tells me that, Sheriff," Wayne said. "I'll straighten 'em out real quick."

Tension eased from Sam's shoulders for the first time since that morning's dustup with Romano. Sweat from his brow dried as the steady breeze made the afternoon tolerable.

He and Wayne leaned against his cruiser and looked out at the sunburnt tourists frolicking in the churning waves. He'd started the day off right here with a stiff shot of whiskey, thinking of his only son who lay somewhere in far-off Italy. Killed by Nazi artillery fire, they had said.

A part of him accepted the Army's notice-of-death: *We regret to inform you...*

But another part of him rejected the notion that his big, fearless boy could have been vanquished by some fascist army hell-bent on exterminating an entire race of people. Until his remains were identified and sent back to him and Claire, Sam's gaze would continue to drift to that distant shore in search for his son.

Sam was sure Wayne's mind was on Billy on this day, the anniversary of his death. They had become fast friends when Wayne came to Galveston to become Sam's newest deputy. He had passed Billy's rigorous scrutiny and started dating Sylvie. Sam and Claire accepted him like a member of the family—as a possible son-in-law—and their frequent dinners together were lively affairs. Billy and Wayne had traded good-natured barbs, and Sylvie had added a few of her own.

They had all gone to the bus station to see Billy off to boot camp. His son, barely eighteen, was nearly giddy with the prospect of following in his father's footsteps and fighting the resurgent German military.

"We'll get them for good this time, Dad," Billy had said with a confident nod. He and Wayne were alike that way—certain of their beliefs, sure of their actions.

When they waved goodbye to Billy as he stepped into the bus, Sam thought he'd detected an expression of envy in Wayne, a look of regret that he wouldn't be able to follow his gung-ho friend into battle. He'd been rejected to serve because a spooked horse at his family's ranch had fallen on his leg and fractured it in two places.

Now, a year later, Sam and Wayne stood together—each man silent in his own thoughts—and looked past the imaginary horizon to the troubled shores of Europe. On the anniversary of Billy's death, Sam wondered how his right-hand deputy felt about not following his best friend into battle. Did he feel guilty that he hadn't joined him to fight Hitler's army? Or, was he relieved to be alive and in love with a charming and lovely girl? Did he ponder the possibility that God or Providence had prescribed him a debilitating injury—one that kept him from the war—so that Sylvie wouldn't have to suffer another crushing loss?

Sam wasn't a man who gave much credence to thoughts of things you couldn't touch or see. But if God in his secret plan had sent one young man to salve the wounds of a family grieving the death of another young man—then he would thank Him for the deliverance of Wayne McRae.

And curse Him for the taking of Billy Baker.

Chapter 5

Sam stepped into the dark house. He took off his gun belt and laid it on the hutch drawer. The only sound was the soft whir of the ceiling fan.

From the hallway came the clattering of small claws on the wooden floors. Little Rags, a dirty-white cloud of dog fur with pink protruding gums and white crooked teeth, scampered up to Sam and sniffed his hands for a possible treat. Finding none, he snorted his disappointment and hustled back into the rear of the house.

"Nice to see you, too, Rags."

Sam knew by the dog's retreat into the inner sanctum that either Claire or Sylvie were home. He was merely a poor substitute in their absence. Sam followed on Rags's heels as the mutt disappeared inside the guest room. Claire's thin arm reached out and closed the door.

She hadn't come out to greet him, and the sound of the door closing reverberated into the hallway.

Bad sign.

He knocked lightly on the door. From inside a radio played a mournful Billie Holliday song. "Claire, I need to talk with you."

"Why didn't you call me, Sam?"

Damn, he thought. With the dustup with Vince Romano and the visit to Alma Rodriguez, he'd forgotten to call her. No doubt she had wanted to be with her husband on this day of remembrance. Even if, as usual, he would have been reluctant to say much. "I'm sorry, Claire. Open up, and I'll explain."

"It's too late for that," she said.

"This is important."

"Later, Sam. Please." Her voice sounded strained, like she'd been crying. Better to wait.

Sam went into the kitchen. He poured a glass of whiskey and set it on the stone countertop. He knew he'd fucked up. He hoped he could count on her forgiving nature one more time. She'd had to roll with the punches for the entire span of his career as a lawman. The life as a sheriff's wife hadn't been her first choice, but she'd tolerated it with minimal complaint.

Sam took a sip of whiskey and tossed the rest in the sink—he didn't want to be drunk when he talked with Claire. Besides, he knew that liquor wouldn't ease his apprehension over Vince Romano's threat to spread rumors that he owned the sheriff.

Nor would it wash out the bitterness he tasted since learning that his father *had* been in the gangster's pocket and that he had betrayed his mother's loyalty for years.

No, there was only one antidote for the tension that gripped him like another layer of skin.

He took off his tunic and walked out the back door.

* * *

A chorus of cicadas scratched out their nightly song as the last slivers of sunlight lit the tops of the pine trees.

Sam strode to a wooden shed looming in the dusk. He stepped inside and lit a kerosene lamp. The light flickered and illuminated the rusty rakes and shovels that hung on the unpainted walls. A lonely hammer lay on the dusty workbench.

Sam rarely touched any of these tools—for him the only purpose for the shed was a heavy punching bag that hung from

26

a thick chain wrapped around a ceiling beam.

He pulled on his boxing gloves and jabbed lightly into the leather bag. He threw easy straight rights and combinations until the first drops of sweat dripped from his forehead. He punched harder. A straight right hand. A thunderous left hook. The bag swung back and the chain screeched in protest. Shovels and rakes rattled against the walls. Warmed up now, he let loose, throwing non-stop combinations and his signature right hand.

At first the explosive sounds coming from the leather bag masked Claire's knock at the door. Sam usually felt irritated that she wouldn't just open it and talk with him. But now he welcomed the chance to make amends.

She stood in the murky light, as serious a look on her face as he'd ever seen. She wore red lipstick and earrings that matched her red hair. Except for the strain in her face, she looked beautiful.

"Mosquitos are out," he said. He led her into the house.

In the kitchen, she turned to face him. "Sam—"

"Claire, I'm so sorry I didn't call you back. I should have been with you today, but let me tell you what happened and I think you'll—"

"I've already heard what happened," Claire said. "You had a confrontation with Vince Romano at a damn whorehouse. There's talk all over town—people say you got physical with him."

"I was keeping him from taking a defenseless man away so they could beat him up. The guy lost a damn leg in the Great War."

"Did you threaten him?"

"I laid down the law."

She shook her head in dismay. "By threatening a gangster who has more guns and men than you do and less restrictions

27

on using them? Now he has to save face." The last time she'd been this distraught was the first few weeks after they'd been informed of Billy's death. "You've changed, Sam. You used to get your point across to Romano more diplomatically. Maybe you take chances now because you don't care what happens to you anymore."

Sam's bare chest rose and fell from his workout. Claire's accusation made him skip a breath.

"That's crazy," he muttered.

"You haven't tried to come to grips with Billy's death and you won't. We're not enough for you, Sylvie and me."

"We don't even have his damn remains back." Sam glowered. "All we got was a goddamn notice from some Marines come knocking on the door."

"That's the day you started to blame yourself."

"For what?"

"Because you knew how goddamn horrible war is, and you didn't try to get him to wait until he was drafted. But most of all, Sam…" Claire's voice broke and she paused. "most of all, you blame yourself because you weren't there to protect him."

"You must be reading tea leaves. I never said anything like that," he protested.

"That's because you won't talk about it with me."

He looked over her shoulder into the guest room where three suitcases stood lined up. Rags lay next to the first one, whimpering because he knew—like Sam now realized—that his mistress was leaving.

"Where are you going?"

A tear dropped down her cheek. "I'm going back to Dallas."

Her words rang in his head but he couldn't make immediate sense of them. He felt naked, exposed. Sweat poured down his bare torso. The boxing gloves felt as heavy as lead. "For how long?"

"I don't know, Sam. You can call me if there's an emergency. I'll be at David and Jeanne's."

"Otherwise don't call. Is that it?"

"Give me some time."

Someone knocked at the front door.

"Come in," Claire called.

David Whittington, wearing his customary three-piece suit, walked in.

"Hello, Sissy," he said. He looked at Sam—shirtless, wearing boxing gloves—and shook his head slightly. His and his family's long-held disappointment that Claire had married a former boxer-turned-lawman was confirmed once again.

"David," Sam said, "You wanna give us a damn minute?"

Whittington pulled his gold pocket watch from his vest. Dallas bankers ran on a tight schedule. "Why don't I just grab the luggage." He walked into the guest room and came out with two suitcases. Rags followed him, his whimpering bordering on a child's cry.

A host of emotions ran through Sam—anger and abandonment chief among them. He was caught between the desire to beg her to stay and the impulse to spit out something cutting. But she'd been patient with him and had accepted the life of a sheriff's wife despite her misgivings. And how could he strike back? She never looked as dear or as beautiful to him as she did in that moment. "Claire, this thing with Romano will pass."

"I hope so." A single tear dropped from her eye. "I love you, Sam. But I won't watch you die."

By instinct gained from twenty-three years of marriage, he stepped forward to comfort her. Claire stepped back and swiped at the tears on her cheeks.

Claire was through talking. Sam stood mute, struck by the

image of sand slipping through his fingers.
    She hugged him briefly. Then she was gone.

Chapter 6

A welcome breeze rustled through the oak and pine trees populating the All Saints Cemetery. Not even noon yet and the air was hot and steamy. Sam spotted his mother's marble gravestone first. Her epitaph read, *Beulah Lynn Baker. Born 1876, Died 1932. Devoted Daughter, Wife and Mother.* Sam thought, *nothing more need be said.*

His father's grave lay next to hers His inscription read: *Jim Quinton Baker. Galveston County Sheriff. Born 1874. Died 1928.* If it proclaimed him to have been a devoted father and husband, he'd have to return with a hammer and chisel and chip away the falsehood.

Sam fanned himself with his hat. He remembered how his mother had never complained about his father's long absences or let on that she knew anything about his infidelity. Did she know he was a dirty cop? Did she know he worked behind the scenes to benefit Vince Romano?

How could she not? Sam wondered. She not only had a quick mind, but it seemed to him and his sister, Missy, that she could merely look into their eyes and tell if they were lying or up to no good. Sam bent and pulled a few of the weeds that covered her grave. He'd have to press the management to better maintain its appearance.

He wondered where he would lie someday in the family plot. There was room for everyone, including Billy, if they ever got his remains back from Italy.

Then a thought struck him that almost made him sag. If he and Claire couldn't somehow find their way back to each

31

other, would she prefer to be buried in the Whittington's large plot in Dallas? Would Sylvie want to join her mother? These thoughts left him feeling unmoored. The grass-covered ground in front of him rolled like a wave. When it receded there was only room for three people. Him and his parents. The last thing he wanted now was to be laid to rest next to his father. He would instruct the caretakers to be buried on his mother's side.

He put his hat on and walked unsteadily across the gravel path. In the past he'd come away from a visit to his parents' graves with a sense of peace. Now he felt like a stranger—an impostor—lay next to the cherished wife and mother he had betrayed.

Sam reached the parking lot. A colored man watched him from in front of the squad car. *The caretaker,* he thought. Just the man to talk to about cleaning up his mother's grave. As Sam stepped out of the cool shade of the trees, he could see that the man's erect posture and raised chin might rule him out as someone who cleaned gravesites. He stood about five-eleven, Sam guessed. Maybe six feet. Probably late twenties. His shoulders and chest filled out his white shirt, and his neck was thick and sturdy.

But it was his intense focus on Sam that made him think the man might have a bone to pick about the arrest of a friend or relative. Or, a diatribe about how the Negro in general was treated unjustly by the police and the courts. That particular complaint had only been voiced to Sam a couple of times, and only recently at that. He wondered if it was the start of something.

"Sheriff Baker," the man said. He shook Sam's hand. "My name is Henry Jackson."

"How can I help you, Mr. Jackson?"

"I want to inform you of a situation that you may or may

32

not have knowledge of."

Here it comes, Sam thought. *I falsely arrested his brother or his cousin.*

The easy way the man had with language showed he possibly had education. He could even be a lawyer sent down from up North to lodge a complaint against him or one of his deputies. Sam had heard of that happening to the police department in Houston.

"I witnessed the confrontation you and your deputies had with Vince Romano and his associates yesterday at Madame de Sousa's place."

"Is that right? Which side were you rootin' for?"

Jackson's expression remained stoic. "Beg pardon?"

"Just a little joke. Carry on."

Unamused, the black man continued, "I'm aware of law enforcement's need to protect confidentiality, but I want to know if you questioned Mr. Romano concerning the whereabouts of Phyllis de Sousa."

"You're right, Jackson. That's privileged information."

"Fair enough, Sheriff. But would it not be reasonable to assume that nothing good has come of Madame de Sousa?"

A line of cars with their headlights on entered the cemetery and crawled past them. Sam shielded his eyes from the glare reflected from the black hearse's windshield. A woman in the second car fanned herself with her pillbox hat. Not even noon and the June sun beat down mercilessly. Sam hoped that for the sake of his survivors he would be laid to rest between November and March, not during the hellish Texas summer.

"That's pure conjecture," Sam said. "Besides, what law enforcement assumes about Phyllis de Sousa is none of your business.

"Oh, but it *is* my business, Sheriff. I'm dealing with a

33

similar situation."

"You telling me you own a whorehouse, Mr. Jackson?"

Jackson frowned. "No, but my sister does."

"What's her name?"

"She's known as Madam Peaches."

"Never heard of her."

"That's unfortunate because Vince Romano has."

An image flashed into his mind of the gangster as he bragged the day before about having Sam's father in his pocket. "What does Romano know about her place?"

"Enough to want to hijack it. Just like he did with Madam de Sousa's joint."

"De Sousa has a classy cathouse. Why would he want to take over a...?"

"A nigger joint? Is that what you're trying to say?"

"If you want to put it like that, Mr. Jackson, then yes," Sam said. "I happen to know that Romano doesn't speak too kindly about people with your skin color."

"He doesn't, but what he *does* like is the color of money."

Jackson was correct—the mobster's obsession with money defined him as well as anything. With the exception of what he lost to bookies, he held onto it with an iron grip. He particularly liked to bet on boxing matches and frequently solicited Sam's advice on upcoming fights. *I've been out of that game a long time,* Sam always told him. *All I know is they're going to beat the crap out of each other.*

Romano had finally quit asking, but added Sam's failure to help him beat the odds to his expanding list of resentments.

"So, what makes Madam Peach's place so appealing to our friend Romano?" Sam asked.

"It's profitable. And it's, to use your description, as classy as Madam de Sousa's."

"Do you bring johns over there, Mr. Jackson?"

The man's forehead pulled together above the bridge of his flat nose. "I'm no pimp." His dark brown eyes flared with anger and something more—a dignity bordering on fierceness. "I provide security at my sister's place."

"You throw troublemakers out on their ass."

"It rarely comes to that."

"So let me guess. Romano came to your sister and demanded protection money."

Jackson nodded. "He sent that big, scar-faced gorilla."

"Drago?"

"No. But plenty big."

"He scare her?"

"My sister doesn't scare."

"What did she tell him?"

"It's what I told him," Jackson said. "We wouldn't pay him a damn cent for protection and we weren't interested in selling."

"Romano wouldn't want to hear that."

"No, it didn't go over well with this gentleman."

A young couple walked by—the woman carrying a bouquet of flowers—and said hello to Sam.

"He couldn't go back to Romano with his dick in his hand," Sam said. "He'd have to get rough."

"He tried."

"What'd you do?"

"I threw him out on his ass."

Jackson spoke with a contained anger and, Sam thought, an acknowledgement of the gravity of his actions. Next time—and there would be a next time—Romano would send Drago to go along with the scar-faced man. Show him how it's done.

The mourners from the funeral procession had gathered around the open grave. The preacher's prayer floated out on the hot wind but its message died before it reached Sam and the black man.

"You know you put a target on your own back, don't you?" Sam said.

"I'm not going to allow what happened to Madam de Sousa to happen to my sister."

"You should have just reported it to me."

"You wouldn't do anything to help a Negro madam."

"I'm sworn to enforce the laws of Galveston County."

"You didn't even help Madam de Sousa, and she's white."

Sam realized that Jackson had put him in the position of defending himself. "I didn't know there was a problem there."

"As you stated, you're the law. You should have known that—."

"Look," Sam said. "I'll talk to Romano about your situation."

"Talk?"

"You heard me. In the meantime, don't step on anymore damn rattlesnakes."

Sam turned to walk to the squad car. Jackson said, "There's another situation you're not aware of, Sheriff."

Sam wanted to get out of the heat, but he turned back to face the Negro. He was gratified to see that small beads of sweat now dotted his forehead. "Make it quick."

"Your daughter is seeing Dominick Romano."

The name eluded Sam for a moment until a picture of the young man snapped into place. He was Vince Romano's son from a former marriage. Newly arrived in town, Romano had already installed him as manager of his nightclub, the Indigo Palm. Sam had only seen him once when Dominick—sporting a beautiful young woman on his arm—had disappeared into a posh restaurant.

"Bullshit," Sam said. His daughter didn't date gangsters, even if they had sleek black hair and leading-man looks.

36

Sylvie had her pick of any young man in town. Why would she be interested in someone who routinely broke the laws that her boyfriend, Deputy Wayne McRae, was sworn to enforce?

Jackson looked at his watch. "If we hurry we can see them."

"They're together right now?"

"Soon."

"Where?"

"The courtyard at St. Paul's church," Jackson said. He pointed at a beat up '36 Ford. "We'll go in my car so they won't spot us."

"How do you know all this?"

"I see them there every day."

"Every day?"

"Precisely at noon."

Sam leaned against his squad car but the heated metal made him pull back. "Your story gets more, what's the word? Fanciful. It gets more fanciful all the time." Sam scrutinized the man's face for signs of deceit or evidence of a con, but found no obvious tell. No detectable truth, either. And he sure wasn't going to be chauffeured in an unknown Negro's car. Anyone's car for that matter. He wouldn't break protocol and put himself in a situation where he didn't have control of the means of transportation. Or the destination.

Besides, in the unlikely event that she became involved with another fella, Sylvie would break the bad news to Wayne. She wouldn't double-time him. Her integrity was on the same high level as her looks.

"I'm going to pass on your kind offer, Mr. Jackson," Sam said, opening the cruiser's door. "I suggest you get out of this damn heat."

As Sam pulled away, the young Negro stood stock still, his chin held high and his expression unreadable.

Galveston '44

Chapter 7

Business district denizens scurried along the sidewalks seeking a quick lunch. Sam sat in his unofficial surveillance car—a white '38 Ford in serious need of a paint job—and kept his focus on St. Paul's Catholic Church. Sam had never darkened the doors of the old church but he liked the solidness of it. Most of it built from huge blocks of white limestone striated by black veins. As a testament to its fortitude, the structure had survived the devastating hurricane of 1900 with minimal damage.

Sam pulled his big straw hat over his forehead as a clump of citizens approached, shielding their eyes from the sun. He shared their discomfort. He was baking inside the car like a burnt pot roast.

He looked at his watch. Ten minutes past noon. Neither Sylvie nor Dominick Romano had appeared in the church's tree-shaded courtyard.

He began to relax. His sensible daughter would not be interested in a gangster's son. She had a growing relationship with Deputy Wayne McRae, a young man who had won her hand over several suitors because of his confidence and charm. Sam and Claire considered his character and integrity to be on par with Billy Baker's, and that was saying something.

Another ten minutes passed. Sam fired up the engine. Before he could drive off, someone rapped lightly on the passenger side window. It was the Negro.

Jackson.

Sam sighed and pointed to the backseat. Jackson climbed in. Sam looked at him in the rearview mirror, searching his unreadable face for acknowledgement of the bullshit he had put Sam through. "It's past noon, my friend. Where are they?"

"She's late," Jackson said. "The young man in question is waiting for her."

The sun broke through the clouds, and trees and plants seemed to rise to meet its rays. Sam focused on a narrow gap between the hedges and saw a young man with black hair sitting on an iron bench, his arm draped over the back like he owned the place.

Dominick fucking Romano.

"Here she comes," Jackson said.

Sam didn't see Sylvie until a group of merchant seamen parted to watch her hurry past carrying a wicker basket. A drunken sailor made as if to follow her, and his shipmates laughed.

Sylvie's face shone with an excitement Sam hadn't witnessed much in the last difficult year. She paused at the arched door to the church and looked around before entering.

"See that?" Jackson said. "She checked for unwanted eyes."

Sylvie walked into the courtyard. Romano stood, smiling. She held the picnic basket in front of her, laughing. She said something that made him laugh, too.

Sam was reminded of Dorothy and her basket in *The Wizard of Oz.*

"Girl knows how to make an entrance," Jackson said. Instead of gloating about the meeting actually occurring, Sam caught a note of regret in the man's tone.

Sylvie and young Romano both wore white—she in a sleeveless dress and he in a crisp shirt open at the collar. Romano took the basket and set it on the iron bench between them as they sat.

Sam couldn't remember a time when Sylvie was this excited to see Wayne. "Do they always wear white?"

"No, but they always dress nice. They aren't taking this thing lightly."

Me, either, Sam thought. Dominick ran the Indigo Palm, for Christ's sake. The nightclub was known not only for the top-flight music acts playing there, but as a place where mob guys brought their mistresses.

"How the hell did you discover this?" Sam asked.

"I keep my eyes open."

And you think I don't? Sam wanted to say. But the reality was that Jackson and not he had discovered that someone other than Wayne McRae was courting his daughter. Someone Billy Baker would have firmly discouraged from even coming close to his little sister.

Sam felt himself wanting to wake up from a long slumber, wanting to come out from under the black cloud he had hidden under for the last year. He had missed things. And this was a big one. Just when tensions were at their highest ever between him and Vince Romano, their offspring had become engaged in what looked like a mutual attraction.

Claire would be alarmed by this. Galveston's dominant mob boss repulsed her.

Sylvie took sandwiches out of wicker picnic basket and handed one to Romano.

Sam had seen enough. "Mr. Jackson, I appreciate you tipping me off to what's going on here," Sam said. He took a few bills from his wallet and held them out to the man.

The Negro ignored them. "If you'll dissuade Vince Romano to back off my sister's joint that would be—."

"I told you I would talk with him."

"Only you can prevent something serious from happening,

41

Sheriff."

"Something serious already happened. You got physical with one of Romano's men, now they're obligated to teach you a lesson."

Jackson's face remained stoic but Sam saw the resolve in his brown eyes. "You have a good day, Sheriff." He checked the surroundings before climbing out of the car.

Sam looked at the courtyard one last time. The only element of their flirtation he could take heart from was that their greeting had only involved a handshake. No hug, no kiss. Maybe she just found young Romano interesting and had no intention of beginning a real romance with a gangster.

Sam would cling to that hope but he knew his daughter well. He knew when she was enchanted and excited.

Regrettably, that time was now.

Chapter 8

Sam entered the dark house and listened for signs of life. Little Rags scampered out and jumped against his leg. The dog hated to be alone, and since Claire's departure Sam had learned he did, too.

The house had always been a beehive of activity. Billy and Sylvie and their friends filling the house with their youthful energy and noise. Claire would feed them homemade cookies and sweetened lemonade, sometimes cautioning them to tone it down if Sam came home with a troubled expression.

How he wished for that ruckus now. How he wished for a reversal of the losses that had emptied their home. First Billy, then Claire.

Now Sylvie. His daughter was at home less and less and seemed to be flirting with the young manager of a nightclub owned by his mob boss father.

Rags followed Sam into the kitchen where he poured a generous shot of whiskey into a highball glass. He spoke reassuringly to his anxious friend, but Rags's eyes remained fixed on the front door, hoping one of his mistresses would open it. "I know how you feel, buddy."

Sam downed the whiskey in one swallow. And poured another.

* * *

On the nightstand the phone rang—shrill, like a fire alarm. Sam rose slowly from the depths of a troubled, whiskey-soaked sleep. He checked the other side of the bed, forgetting that Claire would not be next to him.

He fumbled for the phone. "Baker," he said. His voice sounded rough, dry.

"Sheriff Baker, this is Deputy Turner." Sam pictured the baby-faced deputy as he sat at the front desk of the jail. The lonely night shift of manning the new station-to-station radio.

"Go ahead, Deputy Turner."

"Sheriff...," Turner stopped. Sam detected something held back in the young man's voice that made Sam sit up on the edge of the bed.

"Sheriff," Turner went on. "I just got a call from Deputy Eilers. He said Deputy McRae has been shot." Turner's voice rose at the end of his statement, as if asking a question, or to express some doubt. As though he were pleading with Sam to tell him it wasn't true. "Deputy Eilers says McRae was shot in his squad car."

Sam stood unsteadily. Blood pounded his head. "Where is he?"

"Old Pelican Road. About a quarter mile south of the Thomkins cutoff."

Sam dropped the phone. He pulled on his boots and strapped on his gun belt. Bile rose bitter in his throat. He lurched into the bathroom and threw up in the toilet.

He hurried to the living room. He had his hand on the doorknob when he heard soft footsteps padding behind him.

"Daddy?" Sylvie stood in the dark hallway with a white blanket wrapped around her. Her short black hair was barely mussed, and her large olive eyes were opened wide with concern. "What happened?

Sam had scrambled out of the house in the early morning hours many times before. But Sylvie had never before emerged to ask him why he had to scramble out before dawn in a wrinkled uniform. Caught off guard, Sam almost blurted what Deputy Turner had said, that Wayne McRae had been shot. Her boyfriend of several months might now be dead.

"Go back to bed, sugar," Sam said, his voice still sounding like sandpaper on concrete. "I've got to take care of something. Won't take long."

She didn't move. His commands no longer worked on her. Not even from her imposing father.

"We'll talk a little later," he said. He wouldn't tell her until he saw with his own eyes that it was true. Let her have a few hours more of innocence before she heard that another young man in her short life had been wounded or killed.

Sylvie moved out of the shadows. The moonlight caught the certainty that something had happened that would affect her deeply. He could see in her face the same reaction that Claire had during these early morning emergencies—the same expression of concern for him and the same dismay as to why he wanted to perform a duty like this. "Is someone hurt?"

"Get some sleep. Maybe we can have breakfast later."

He opened the door. He had to go. She grabbed his arm, tears already in her eyes. She knew, somehow she knew. "Who is it, Daddy?"

He pulled his arm back and ran.

Galveston '44

Chapter 9

Sam floored the squad car's gas pedal. Telephone posts flashed by on the dark rural road. The siren wailed like someone crying. The lone cherry top on the roof flashed red, even though there was no one on the road at this hour to heed the warning.

He pushed the cruiser into a controlled slide around a curve, straightened out and was upon them. The gray outline of uniformed men stood motionless in the road like frozen sentries.

Headlights from a parked car illuminated a cruiser jutted up against the thick shrubbery that demarked the side of the road. The squad car looked like it had already started to decompose and the swamp on the other side would soon claim it.

Sam slammed on the brakes. He slid to a stop with his lights pointed at Wayne's car. He jumped out and ran his flashlight over the scene.

Deputy Eilers stood over Deputy Gilbert Robicheaux, who sat in the road with his hands covering his face. His shoulders shook as he sobbed. He and Wayne had been great friends.

"Deputy Robicheaux," Sam said. "Are you hurt?"

Robicheaux looked up, startled to see him. "No, sir."

"Then get up."

The young deputy rose on shaky legs. He looked down the long dark road, purposely avoiding Wayne's car. The full moon illuminated his receding blond hair and the shiny scalp below. That was something Wayne teased him about—

premature baldness in a man barely twenty-one. Robicheaux, in turn, made fun of Wayne's prominent Adam's apple. On and on it went.

"Where's your hat, deputy?"

"In the car, sir."

"Put it on. You're on duty."

Eilers shook his head. "Prepare yourself, Sheriff. He's shot up real bad."

The last of Sam's hopes crumbled and blew away in the sticky Gulf breeze. Eilers searched his eyes, challenging him to see who was stronger. Sam met Eilers' gaze until the older man looked away.

Sam braced himself, walked to the cruiser and shined his flashlight inside. Wayne lay on the front seat with his head against the passenger door. His hands were tucked under his chin, as if he were merely sleeping. Blood covered his face, glistened wetly in his hair.

Sam's legs nearly buckled. Whiskey-bathed bile rose once again in his throat but he swallowed it down. He wasn't going to throw up in front of Eilers.

"Dear God," he whispered. More of an accusation than a prayer.

He turned to Deputy Robicheaux, who stood in the middle of the road, his jaws clamped down to keep from crying. Or screaming. If he did either, Sam feared he would join him.

Sam pointed at the dilapidated bar set back fifty yards from the road. The windows were dark. The rusted shell of a car sat parked in front. The paint on the wooden sign that proclaimed it as the Thirsty Pelican had been bleached white by the searing Texas sun. Its clientele were hard drinkers who, if they weren't too drunk, could be serviced in the parking lot by rough trade whores on their way to obsolescence. The last stop for the whores *and* the drunks.

48

"Deputy Robicheaux, go pound on the door and see if anybody is in there. Keep your gun ready." Sam didn't think the killer would hide in such an obvious place but the young deputy needed something to occupy his mind.

"Yes, sir," Robicheaux said, his voice weak and crackly. He walked across the road, his boots crunching against the white seashells in the deep parking lot.

Sam walked around to the other side of the squad car. He pushed through brambly shrubs that ripped the skin on his arms. He shone the light inside from the open window. He could see that Wayne's legs were curled up on the front seat, not on the floorboard. That struck Sam as odd. If he'd been shot from the driver's side window his feet would be on the floorboard and his legs pinned by the steering wheel.

Unless, mortally wounded, he had tried to crawl away from more bullets. Sam hoped to God he hadn't suffered long.

He swept the rest of the car with the torch and found Wayne's hat in the backseat.

"Deputy Eilers," Sam called. Eilers answered back and Sam was surprised to see him standing beside him.

"Did you or Deputy Robicheaux disturb anything in the car?"

"Sheriff, I opened the door with my handkerchief and leaned across Wayne to check for a pulse. There weren't none."

"Who called it in?" Sam asked.

"Deputy Turner said it was a man. Fella wouldn't leave his name."

"What time?"

"About three a.m."

Sam's checked his watch. Almost four. It would be light soon. He didn't know if he preferred that or the darkness that enveloped them and made this seem like a bad dream—a nightmare where the young man he hoped to someday call his son-in-law had been shot up to the point of barely recognizing him.

Another squad car braked to a hard stop. Deputies Garza and Stubbins climbed out. They started to walk to the car but he sent them and Eilers to comb the ground for bullet casings or other evidence.

He flicked on the flashlight and trained it on the backseat—Wayne's hat rested at an odd angle. He lifted it with the torch and found a pistol lying underneath. Sam knew the gun—a Police Special—was Wayne's. But he had assumed it would still be in its holster, which Wayne was lying on.

He pulled out his handkerchief and lifted the gun and smelled cordite. The gun had been fired.

A picture formed in Sam's mind: Wayne had been shot with his own pistol. Then his hat placed over it for some illogical reason—it wouldn't hide the gun for long, so why do it?

He tried to picture the other possibility–that Wayne had fired his gun at his attacker, or attackers. But how could he have put the gun in the backseat and placed his hat over it after he was shot?

The first image, of someone shooting down at him with his own weapon—the horror of it—formed again even as he tried to repel it.

Sam returned the gun to its resting place in the backseat. That's when he caught the glint of fresh blood on the lower side of the backdoor. Blood also lay darkly on that part of the seat. Wayne had either been shot back there or placed there after he'd been shot. But there were no bullet holes in the seat or in the door. And why put him in the front seat after he'd been shot?

He looked for shell casings in the car but there none. Wayne had been shot with his own gun, but not in his own car.

Sam shone the flashlight behind the car where a short stretch of tire tracks veered sharply from the road and left an imprint in the damp ground. The car had been braked hard and left as far off the road as possible. What he wanted to know more than anything in his life was who the fuck had driven Wayne's squad car. And where did he go after he pulled Wayne, a sizeable man, out of the backseat and placed him in the front?

He either ran off or someone picked him up. Sam looked down the desolate road. He tried to imagine another car disappearing into the darkness.

Eilers returned. He shook his head. "We didn't see nothing on the ground, Sheriff."

Sam beamed the light back on Wayne. He felt a need to remember him as he now lay, so that the image and his rage would fuel the fiercest search for justice he'd ever undertaken. It was personal now.

Sam flicked off the flashlight but the full moon reflected off an object from inside Wayne's clasped hands. With his handkerchief, he pulled out a round, metal object from between Wayne's fingers. It was bigger, thicker than a silver dollar. When he held it to the moonlight a skull-and-crossbones image, crudely etched into the metal, glared back at him.

The killer had left a calling card.

Galveston '44

Chapter 10

Footsteps echoed from across the parking lot as Deputy Robicheaux walked back from the bar. He stopped in the middle of the road, reluctant to venture closer to where his good friend lay. "Ain't nobody there, Sheriff. I pounded on the doors and looked in all the windows. I hope I wasn't out of line but I kicked in the backdoor and looked around."

Sam was glad the young deputy had taken some initiative and maybe took out a little grief and anger on the bar's door. He showed Robicheaux the skull-and-crossbones medallion.

"You ever see Wayne with this?"

The young deputy studied the sinister object. His expression turned troubled. "No, sir. I never seen nothing like that before."

"Sumbitch put it there after he shot him," Eilers said, his voice rising in pitch. "Had to of."

"Neither of you breathes a word about this," Sam said. "I'll show it to the other deputies in due time. Understood?"

Sam made them swear to it because he didn't trust Eilers to keep his mouth shut.

Headlights pierced the dark road as a car approached. It stopped. Clyde Hermann, a slender man with gray hair stepped out. He carried a black medical examiner's bag. Hermann's expression was grim, but then Sam had never seen him look any other way. Whenever Sam caught himself complaining about the difficulties of being sheriff, he only had to think of what Hermann had to do.

"Is it true?" he asked Sam.

Sam nodded. It was now time for him and the deputies to step aside and let Clyde do what he could for Wayne.

In the distance came the mournful wail of an ambulance's siren. Finality was setting in just as the first glow of dawn appeared in the eastern sky.

The effects of last night's whiskey tried to pull Sam down, but anger and grief kept his mind whirling. He took a deep breath and emptied himself of all that pained him—the loss of the two young men—Billy Baker and Wayne McRae—who had meant the most to him.

He opened himself up for answers. Anything at all.

Did Wayne stumble onto some crime and get surprised by superior numbers? *Possibly*, Sam thought. But Wayne McRae was a careful and capable lawman, even for one so young.

Was this a revenge killing? Again, anything was possible, but Wayne had never mistreated any prisoner or citizen in the time of his service. If anything, he bent over backwards to be respectful and helpful. Still, the crude medallion with its symbol of death made his murder seem vindictive and deliberate.

Sam ran through his mind the history of Wayne McRae's all too short life as he knew it but couldn't recall any conflicts he'd had with anyone, until he got to the pissing contest over the one-legged man at the whorehouse. Wayne had stepped in front of Drago, and the two men had exchanged hard looks. But no punches had been thrown, no guns had been drawn.

The main event had been waged in private when Sam threatened to shoot Vince Romano rather than surrender a beat-down, one-legged war veteran to him.

Had Romano settled the score by killing the deputy Sam was closest to, the one his daughter was dating? It was something to consider, but on the face of it he had to question why Romano would further stir up the hornet's nest. He knew

Sam would turn over every stone in Galveston County to find the man who had killed one of his deputies.

And to protect himself and his organization would require Romano to expend resources and manpower, and that would cost him money. Vince didn't like to spend money. He only wanted to make it. The inevitable headlines about a cop killing would slow the tourist trade, which meant less visits to Romano's whorehouses and casinos. Which, again, meant less cash for him to stuff under his mattress, or wherever the hell he stashed it.

Sam had to think that Romano was too level-headed for that. His public persona was that of a friendly provider of gambling and flesh to citizens and tourists alike. Would he rock the boat for revenge of this magnitude? Sam's intuition told him no.

As the ambulance slowed and wound its way through the squad cars, another theory came to Sam: a rival gang—maybe one from out-of-state—had killed Wayne to put heat on Romano and attempt a takeover of the Free State of Galveston's lucrative rackets.

He knew that possibility could develop but the only outside organization to try that had been during his father's tenure as sheriff. Romano—maybe with Sheriff Jim's help—had put a brutal stop to it.

Sam ordered the deputies to continue combing the area for evidence.

He looked back at the Wayne's squad car for inspiration but for now he had run out of suspects. He walked to his cruiser and opened the door. A last thought struck him, the name of someone who would benefit from killing Wayne McRae.

Dominick Romano.

Galveston '44

Chapter 11

Sam closed the door to his office and sank into his chair. It was the first time he had been alone since the phone rang in the early hours and woke him from a dead drunk. He closed his eyes but couldn't block out the cacophony of distressed voices coming from the outer office. Nor could he erase the disbelief and grief on the many faces gathered to deal with the murder of a popular Texas lawman.

He'd had to send poor Grace to the house. She broke down every time she answered the phone or radioed one of the deputies.

A tenacious reporter from the *Houston Post* had called demanding an interview with him. *Houston? Don't they have enough murders there to feed their lust?* The press there continuously painted Galveston Island as the sin capital of the country, even bawdier than New Orleans or San Antonio. Even more unchaste than the new, glittery Las Vegas, built by the mob from nothing on the sands of the Nevada desert.

Sam acknowledged the reporter's right to an interview but he wasn't eager to let any journalists write about his vomit and blood-stained uniform.

Someone knocked lightly at the office door. Sam told them to enter. Deputy Robicheaux handed him a steaming cup of coffee and left. Sam had spoken with him earlier, encouraging him to come back from the dark place he was stuck in. He would need time to fully accept that his good friend would never again be there to tease him about some exaggerated shortcoming.

Sam dialed the house, hoping to speak with Sylvie, *needing* to speak with Sylvie. The phone rang endlessly. He hoped to God she wasn't with Dominick Romano.

He rubbed his forehead as loss and anger mixed with the emerging hangover. He ran the scene from the lonely stretch of road over and over in his mind. He kept coming back to the same dead-ends. Deputy Eilers was no help as a sounding board. Sam had detected a touch of triumph in the deputy's shallow eyes because the killing had puzzled and staggered Sam to such a degree.

Eilers would get the axe when they caught Wayne's killer. But for now he needed all hands on deck.

He had sent two deputies to spell Garza and Stubbins at the scene of the murder. Deputy Turner was interviewing the nearest neighbors to the Thirsty Pelican, although they were few and far between. Deputy Stubbins would question the owner of the bar, Orville Sessions, when it opened in the afternoon.

The phone on his desk rang and startled him. *Sylvie,* he hoped.

He snatched up the receiver. "Sheriff Baker."

"Hello, Sam."   It was Claire. She had entered his mind during the dark chaos of the day, knowing she would have to be notified, but wanting Sylvie to do it. Resentment at her leaving him rose up to join his grief. He pictured Claire sitting in the large dining room of her family's estate where the maid would have served her breakfast.

"Hello, Claire."

"Is it true, Sam?"

"Yes."

She sobbed. When she spoke again, her voice quavered like someone speaking underwater. "How is Sylvie taking it?"

"I called the house but she doesn't pick up."

"I want to come home and help you with the arrangements and everything."

"The McRae family will take care of the arrangements."

"You'll need to say some words about Wayne at the service. I can help you with that."

"I've got words," he said, louder than he'd intended. "I've got plenty of goddamn words."

"You don't sound good, Sam. I want to help you."

"Everything is under control, Claire."

"Sam..."

"I've got to go."

He hung up.

Galveston '44

Chapter 12

Sam walked past the jail cells that lined either side of a narrow corridor and out the back door. The mid-afternoon heat hit him like a furnace but he was glad for the fresh air and the escape from the ongoing turmoil inside.

He climbed into his squad car and fired up the engine. Deputy Garza swung the iron gate open and ordered the curious onlookers to move back.

A large woman pushed against the deputy and pointed fiercely at Sam's car. It was his older sister, Missy. It had completely slipped his mind to call her, and she was probably pissed about it. She adored Wayne, often hosting him and Sylvie for one of her seafood dinners. Sam and Claire had often joined them. She had doted on Billy, too, and was crushed by his death, so much so that Sam had avoided her and her emotional reminder of the loss of his son.

Sam pulled his hat down over his eyes. He started to drive through the gate and past his sister. He had almost succeeded when she jumped in front of his cruiser. He had to stop.

Missy put her hand on her hip and gave him the disgusted look that he remembered from their childhood. He got out of the car.

She hugged him tight. He could feel her tears on his own cheek.

"Trying to avoid your big sister. Shame on you."

"I'm sorry, Missy." He started to make the lame excuse that he hadn't seen her but how could he miss an aggressive woman who wore her trademark multicolored dress and stood taller than most men. When they were kids she had protected him from the older boys until he passed her in size and could not only take care of himself, but her too.

Her round face screwed up tight with grief and shock. "I just can't believe it, Sam."

Sam just shook his head. There were no words sufficient to express his simmering rage over the loss. All day long he'd heard the standard expressions of grief, just like when Billy died. Well-intentioned words, but feeble in the face of profound loss. "He was very fond of you, Missy," Sam said. "He loved your cooking."

"Lordy, that boy could eat."

Sam smiled for the first time that day. Missy handed him a piece of paper from her dress pocket. "Sylvie came over and gave me this note for you."

Daddy, I called all day long but couldn't get through. I'll be at my boss' house. Can you please come over?

At the bottom of the note she'd written an address.

"Boss?" Sam said. "When the hell did she get a job?"

Missy jabbed a hand to her hip. "At least two weeks ago, Sam. You should be keeping up with your daughter a little better."

He tried to think back to the last time they had talked—other than the rushed conversation this morning—but his mind wasn't yet capable of remembering anything that had occurred before Wayne's murder.

"She works in a hair salon," Missy said. "She's learning to be a stylist."

He realized even more that he was losing her. But she wasn't his only loss. "Claire left me, Missy." Had it only been a couple days before? It seemed a lifetime ago.

"Sylvie told me," Missy said. "You're a good man, Sam, but you just can't bottle up everything inside and still be part

62

of a family."

Sam nodded, already regretting that he'd hung up on Claire. He needed her now, but this wasn't the first time he'd stood in his own way of accepting what was good for him. He had a notion to tell Missy about their father, about the young mistress he had supported all those years. But he held off—she had enough to deal with today.

He hugged her again. "I'll see you soon, Missy."

She smiled and pointed at Sylvie's note. "Go see your daughter."

Galveston '44

Chapter 13

Dark clouds had gathered all afternoon, turning the sky a deep purple. A strong wind snapped small branches and blew dry leaves across the road.

Sam drove his squad behind Gus Josie's taxi as it turned on yet another street and went deeper into a rural area he'd never been in. They passed houses set back on large lots that grew scarcer the further they drove.

Gus pulled to a stop. Wearing his customary black fedora, he slid over to the passenger side window. He pointed at what appeared to be a jungle of trees and shrubbery. "The house is back in there, Sheriff."

"I don't see a mailbox. Gus. How would you know this is the right place?"

"I'd bet a pretty penny this is it."

Sam looked again. A small twinkle of a light appeared through the greenery. "Okay." He made a circular gesture. Gus turned around and pulled alongside him. Sam held out folded bills to him. "I appreciate it, Gus."

"Not today, Sheriff. I knew Wayne, too.

"*Especially* today, my friend."

Gus accepted the money. "I'll use it for flowers at the funeral."

"One other thing. I want you to keep an eye on Dominick Romano. See if he's leaving town or hiding out somewhere."

Gus looked at him a long moment as Sam's request registered with him. "You suspect him for Wayne?"

"It's just a long shot."

"You got it, Sheriff." Gus tipped his fedora and drove off.

Sam found the narrow driveway and drove down its winding path. Overgrown tree branches scraped the sides of the cruiser. He hoped one wouldn't break the car's cherry top. He saw Claire's Chevy, and his heart skipped a beat before he realized that Sylvie was using it.

He cleared a clump of trees, and the house—built of cedar and stained a deep rust color, came into view. The porch railings were made from thick tree branches and gave the place the look of a hunting lodge.

Sam climbed out of the squad car as Sylvie burst from the front door and ran into his arms. He held her tight as she cried.

She looked up at him with an expression of pain and disbelief that he'd seen from her only once before—when they received notice of Billy's death overseas. It broke his heart that she had suffered two tremendous losses in one year, and he was powerless to rectify them.

"Daddy, I called the jail over and over, but I couldn't get through. I needed to talk to you so bad."

"I called the house several times, sweetheart. I wanted to talk with you, too."

"I was at Missy's. Then I came over here. I love my aunt, but she wouldn't stop crying and wailing."

Sam was glad she hadn't run to Dominick Romano's arms. Maybe she thought it wouldn't be proper to seek solace from a new suitor when the former boyfriend—so recently the man in her life—had been killed. Or, did she suspect the gangster's son had something to do with it?

She would have to be questioned about anything Romano might have said about his competition, Wayne McRae. This wasn't the time, however. He would have one of the deputies interview her. Another question would also have to wait—had Wayne died thinking he was the only man in Sylvie's life or had she given him the bad news right before he left on his last patrol? He hoped to God not.

He caught a quick flash of someone at the picture glass window. "This is your boss' house?"

"Her name's Laura," Sylvie said. "She was a friend of Wayne's too."

"Everyone was a friend of Wayne's."

Fat raindrops fell out of the darkening sky. Sam turned his face to meet them, hoping to be cleansed of all he'd seen and felt this long day.

"Daddy," Sylvie said. "Mom came by the salon the morning before she left. She was upset."

"What did she say?"

"She needed to get away for a while. I asked her why, but she didn't want to talk about it right then."

She left because she was weary of being a sheriff's wife, he wanted to say. *Afraid she'd become a sheriff's widow.*

But what else could he do? He didn't know any other way to live except to fight. His father, Sheriff Jim, who had until recently been the person he admired most in the world, had instilled that in him.

It's a tough world, son, was his constant reminder. *You best learn to fight.*

And so he had.

"I guess her patience with me ran out."

Galveston '44

Chapter 14

Sylvie led them through the front door and into the living room. High cathedral ceilings and a stone fireplace maintained the house's feel of a country lodge.

Sam longed to lie on the plush leather couch and sleep forever.

"Laura?" Sylvie called.

They walked into a bright kitchen where an iron pot simmered on the stove. The aroma of seafood gumbo filled the room. Sam's mouth watered. He realized he hadn't eaten anything since the night before when he had scarfed leftover beef into his mouth in between shots of whiskey.

Sam was caught off guard by the woman who walked into the room. He guessed her to be in her early thirties. She was dressed in black pants and a red blouse. Both were understated but flattered her figure. Her blond hair hung straight to her shoulders. She wore no makeup, no lipstick. The only jewelry was a simple ring on her right hand. Sam had expected the owner of a beauty salon to be older and wear an elaborate hairstyle. But she didn't need anything extraneous to make her what she was—pretty in a clean-cut, natural way.

"Daddy, this is Laura Stevens," Sylvie said.

"My pleasure, Laura," Sam said. They shook hands. Hers was warm and strong

"Sheriff Baker, I'm so sorry," Laura said, in a slight English accent. "Wayne was a lovely guy."

"How did you know him?"

"He'd come by the salon to see Sylvie. He was always

joking around, making everyone laugh."

"That was Wayne," he said. "He kept the mood light at headquarters, too."

"You look exhausted, Daddy," Sylvie said. "Sit down."

Sam sat at the kitchen table, and weariness fell over him like a blanket.

"Are you hungry, Sam?" Laura asked.

"I could eat something, if it's not too much trouble."

Sylvie stared at his tunic in horror. "Is that blood on your shirt, Daddy?"

"I scratched myself on some bushes," Sam said. He showed her the jagged red lines on his arms. "It's my blood." He hoped she wouldn't ask about the blotches of vomit mixed in with it.

Laura set a large bowl of steaming gumbo on the table. He took a bite and closed his eyes with the taste of it, his need for it. "It's damn good. Thank you."

She brushed his back lightly. "Take off your shirt. I'll clean it for you."

"Don't bother, Laura."

Laura pulled the tunic tight to get a better look at the stains and the wrinkles from the night of sleeping in it. "It's a disaster."

"And it smells," Sylvie said.

"Maybe we'd better," Sam said. He unbuttoned the tunic. "My other uniform is dirty, too."

Laura held it at arm's length. "We may have to burn it."

They laughed...and laughed again when Laura brought him a leather jacket that barely covered his bare torso. "You've got boxer's shoulders," she said.

"How did you know that?"

"Oh, I've heard all about you from this one," she said and nodded at Sylvie.

"That's just something we told her and her brother so they'd obey us."

"Oh, right," Laura said. "As if the sheer size of you wouldn't scare a child."

He was charmed by her slight British accent and her sense of humor. He asked her about the beauty salon, and she and Sylvie laughed about a fussy woman whose hair Sylvie had cut the day before.

They talked about anything other than Wayne until Sylvie started crying. "It's wrong," she said. "It's just so wrong."

Sam laid his arm over her shoulders. Laura came around to the back of her chair and hugged her from behind so that they were all connected by touch. The combined smells of the two young women, something like vanilla and roses, mingled with the rising steam from the gumbo. If he could, he would stop time and stay in this soothing cocoon forever.

As soon as he left Laura and Sylvie's comforting presence his rage would return. He would resume the manhunt for the killer of Wayne McRae with the skeletal staff of deputies available to the sheriff's department.

And now they were one man down.

Galveston '44

Chapter 15

Sam ran through the hard rain and unlocked the front door. Rags padded out and snorted his displeasure—poor guy had been alone all day. Sam waited to see if he'd run out and piss, but he took one look at the wet grass and decided against it.

Sam scooped the dog up and walked out to the backyard and into the shed. He lit the gas lantern and tamped down the flame. Rags lifted his leg and pissed on a corner post.

"A man's got to go when a man's got to go," Sam said.

He pulled on his heavy bag gloves. No way could he sleep now. Laura's gumbo had helped fortify him. Rage had trumped exhaustion and burned in his veins. He didn't bother warming up. His first punch, a hard right cross, exploded into the heavy bag and rattled the chain. He threw a left hook and followed up with rapid combinations.

It all flowed naturally as he pounded the bag like he had when he was twenty years old and fighting as a pro. His mind floated free of thought until his arms began to tire. He wasn't twenty after all.

His defenses broke down. He couldn't block out the image of Wayne lying all shot to hell in the front seat of his cruiser.

He wondered if Billy had looked like that when the Germans killed him—bloody and almost unrecognizable. He thought of them both, and they blurred together, two young men killed decades before their time. His arms burned but grief drove him to keep hitting the bag. Tears finally fell, blurred his vision. Two more punches, and his arms dropped to his side.

He was done boxing, but not crying.

The door rattled. *Probably a gust of wind from the thunderstorm,* he thought. But it swung open. Laura stepped into the flickering light as gray sheets of rain fell behind her. Her blouse was sopped and clung to her curves. She stood just inside the shed as the leather bag continued to swing on its chain.

He wiped at the tears on his cheeks with a glove but it was obvious he'd been crying.

Her forehead pulled together in sympathy. "I wish there was something I could say, Sam."

"That's okay, Laura. I don't have any words, either." His voice sounded rough.

She pulled his uniform shirt from a plastic bag. "It's clean. I just hope it dries by morning."

"I'll hang it under a ceiling fan," he said. He took it from her. "Thank you so much, Laura. Wayne's parents will be here tomorrow andw, well, thanks."

"Least I could do, Sam. Let me know if there's anything else you need." She turned to leave.

"Don't go," he said. He didn't want to be alone. Sylvie had gone to her Aunt Missy's, and he was afraid he'd choose whiskey to keep him company. "Come in for some coffee."

She walked over to him and brushed the hair off his forehead with her fingers. "You need a haircut."

Her touch felt comforting. "Do you know any good stylists?"

"I just happen to know one. You have some scissors?"

"I think I can scare some up." He dialed the lantern down and the flame died. He grabbed the uniform shirt and picked up Rags. They ran through the rain and into the house.

Laura shivered and wrapped her arms around her wet blouse. Sam brought her one of Claire's. She turned around

74

and took off hers and her bra. Her back was lean and narrowed down to meet the beginning flare of her hips. She turned and looked down. She'd only been able to work the bottom buttons of the blouse, leaving her full breasts framed by the thin material. "Did you pick this one on purpose?"

"Try another one?"

She smiled. "You wouldn't arrest me if I left it like this, would you?"

He realized she was making herself available to him, and he stirred. "I'd have to investigate first."

She raised her arms. "In that case, I surrender."

Even with her wet blond hair matted to her face she was beautiful. Hard rain beat on the roof and enveloped them in their own world. It was just them, and only a few feet separated them.

"It's been a horrific day, Sam. No one should have to experience what you saw today. If I can comfort you..."

It was his play. For a moment in time she could help him forget the horror of Wayne's murder.

But she couldn't help him forget Claire. It was too soon. There were too many reminders—not just Claire's blouse, but her smell that still lingered on her side of the bed. The brushes and creams she'd left behind on her makeup table. Even the dog that pined for his mistress.

He took too long to speak, and she said, "I understand."

He shook his head. "I'm a fool, Laura."

"No, you're a good man, Sam."

"Has any man ever turned you down?"

She laughed and pretended to think. "It's possible but I don't remember one."

"That puts me in rare company."

"You're still married. I respect that."

"Have you ever been married?"

"Once. But I married too young. Now I'm a better judge of character."

"But you don't know me."

"I already admired you from what Sylvie told me. When you walked into my house I knew she wasn't wrong."

He was just as flattered as when Claire had expressed her fondness for him some twenty-three years before. He'd been surprised then that a pretty young woman from a prestigious and wealthy family had chosen him over any of the young suitors her family considered more appropriate.

Laura smiled. Her expression showed no reaction to the rejection she had just received. Sam was impressed.

Deep thunder shook the house. He pointed outside. "Can I take a rain check?"

She laughed. "Do you have a piece of paper?"

Sam handed her the notepad Claire kept by the phone.

"Call me anytime," she said. She wrote down her number. "Or come by the shop. Free haircuts for friends." She pulled out a chair from the dining room table. "Starting with this one."

Chapter 16

Across the street from the seawall the Tropicana Hotel stood ten stories tall. The luxury rooms with a view of the Gulf, although commanding a premium price, stayed occupied all year long.

The doorman opened the ornate brass door for Sam, and he entered the extravagant lobby. A huge crystal chandelier hung from the high ceiling, but Sam ignored it and all the other gaudy decorations.

Inside the elevator, the diminutive operator greeted him in his high voice. Jimmy wore his usual red uniform with gold lamé accents. His round, brimless hat reminded Sam of those worn by an organ grinder's monkey. Jimmy had worked at the hotel for as long as Sam could remember and—despite having to wear a demeaning uniform—he never failed to smile or be at his most gracious.

For a moment, he made Sam forget the reason for his coming here: a phone call he'd received earlier in the day from the governor's office.

"They told me to take you all the way to the top today, Sheriff Baker."

"That's right, Jimmy. I'm buying the hotel from Arin Haugen today."

The little man laughed. "You don't say."

"And you're in for a big raise."

"I could use it."

The elevator stopped at the top floor of guest rooms, but Jimmy cranked a lever and the car climbed another floor.

Sam walked into the hallway, his boots sinking into plush carpet imprinted with sailing ships and various sea life. The center of the carpet design featured the pirate Jean Lafitte, who robbed merchant ships in the Gulf long before Germans subs started to torpedo them.

He passed the hotel offices and stopped at a door inscribed with the words *Haugen Shipping Company* in gold-plated lettering. Before he could knock, the door swung open, and he was invited in by the secretary, a woman with a brown blouse and a crooked nose that had probably been broken at one point. Sam had never met her before.

"We heard you were on the way up, Sheriff Baker."

She offered him a drink, and he declined.

"Mr. Haugen will be right with you," she said.

Sam paced the carpeted floor as cool air wafted over him. Arin Haugen had bragged to Sam about the cost of retrofitting the hotel with air conditioning, one of the first in the world with the new system. The sum boggled the mind, but Sam didn't give him the pleasure of seeming impressed.

The inner office door opened. Greta Haugen, Arin's wife, swept up to him. She squeezed his hand with both of hers. "My dear Sam," she said.

Greta was in her late-fifties, a few years older than her husband. She wore a stern wool dress, and her hair had been heavily sprayed into what looked like to Sam to be a gray helmet. Greta's job was to run the Tropicana, and she did it with an iron hand.

"How are Claire and Sylvie?" she asked.

If Sam told her Claire had left him and Sylvie was infatuated with a gangster's son, Greta would exclaim how good it was to hear it.

"Fair to middlin', Greta."

"So good to hear it, Sam," she said. She let go of his hand.

"I'll let you and the other gentlemen discuss your business."

Sam stepped through the door and found Arin Haugen standing at his polished mahogany bar, pouring whiskey from a glass decanter into three glasses.

Three glasses...?

"Sam, I am so sorry about the loss of your deputy," Haugen said, with the accent of his native Norway. "Raymond, wasn't it?"

"McRae," Sam said. "Wayne McRae."

Haugen handed him a glass of whiskey. "Unfortunate business, that."

Sam had yet to hear Wayne's murder described in such lukewarm terms.

"So you got a call from the governor's man."

Haugen never wasted time, insisting on getting down to business immediately. Many people wanted his time, and time was money. He was in his late forties, with an expanding paunch and thinning red hair that exposed orange splotches of freckles on his scalp.

Sam was surprised that Arin and Greta were still in town. They typically went back to Norway in early May to escape Galveston Island's swampy heat.

"His name was Stephen Miller," Sam said. "Called himself the governor's adjunct."

Haugen took a swallow of his whisky. "Probably just some damn underling with less authority than he thinks."

"He read Governor Davis' statement word-for-word."

"Tell me again."

"He said the governor wondered if I wasn't too emotionally involved to properly lead an investigation into my deputy's murder. Because we didn't have a suspect or any evidence, the governor had the right to send the Rangers in to take over."

"Well, do you have a suspect?"

"I can't reveal that."

Haugen pressed, "Evidence?"

"Again, I have to keep—"

"Come on, Sam, this is me."

"Not to anyone, Arin."

"You *are* emotionally involved, Sam. He was your deputy. Maybe a little assistance from the Texas Rangers would help you keep things in perspective."

Sam looked out the wall of windows to the Gulf waters just across the street. The Rangers were a capable force, but no one would hunt Wayne McRae's killer like he would. "No. I'm going to find the son-of-a-bitch that killed him. That's my perspective."

"You've got to solve this quickly, Sam. It's already causing tourists to think twice about visiting Galveston. The hotel's bookings are already down."

"We're making progress but I need you to get the governor off my back."

"What makes you think I have any influence over Governor Davis?"

"You're his biggest campaign contributor."

"And I'm yours, but it's fairly evident today that I don't have much influence over you."

"I've always appreciated your help, Arin, and now I'm asking for it again," Sam said. He walked over and closed the office door.

"Leave it open, Sam. Vince is coming so we can work through these goddamn misunderstandings you and he have."

Sam felt his face redden. "I asked for a private meeting, Arin."

"Sam, your public disagreements with Vince are going to hurt business. That is my top priority today."

A noise came from the outer office. Vince Romano strode into the room. He swept past Sam without a glance and plopped himself onto one of the leather couches. Drago followed closely behind, as though Romano had dragged in a shadow twice his size. He paused to glare at Sam, and then took a position behind the couch where his boss sat. Only then did Romano look at Sam. He shook his head before shifting his gaze out the huge window to the vast Gulf beyond.

Haugen set a glass of whiskey on the glass coffee table. Romano picked it up and downed half of it in one swallow.

"Have a seat, Sam," Haugen said. He took a sip from his own glass. "Aged twenty-one years. Imported from Japan, but don't arrest me, Sheriff. I bought it before the war started." Haugen chuckled dryly at his own joke, but no one else joined in.

Sam locked eyes with Drago. "He can go."

Vince snapped his head around. "No. Drago stays."

"Gentlemen, we will not start our discussion—" Haugen said.

"He's got nothing to add to it," Sam said. Always get in the first punch,   his father had preached. "I'm not sure he can even speak."

Romano snorted. "Don't you think he'll know everything anyway?"

"I'm not going to hurt you, Vince. What are you so damn angry about, anyway?"

Romano half rose from the couch, pointed at Sam. "You threatened me, you son-of-a-bitch."

"You must have misunderstood," Sam said. "I just told you that you weren't taking my perpetrator away."

"No one does that to me."

"Vince!" Haugen barked.

The room grew still. Romano slowly eased back down

onto the couch, the thick leather squeaking as he settled.

Haugen flicked one finger at the door, the gesture quick, meant for Romano's eyes only. After a moment's hesitation, Vince drained the last of his whiskey and nodded towards the door.

Drago kept his eyes locked on Sam as he walked past.

Sam sat down across from Romano and raised his glass. "Here's to us. The merry little band."

"Don't joke, Sam," Haugen said. "We're the men who run this town. The mayor is a drunken slob, and some people say the chief of police is overly helpful to Vince for some mysterious reason."

"Just a fucking rumor, Arin," Romano said. He rose and went to the bar to refill his glass. "Like I told our Sheriff Sam the other day. A rumor just needs a little spark and then..." Vince blew into his palm. "...poof, it spreads its own damn self."

"Is that how you'd spread a rumor about me?" Sam asked. "Just a little spark?"

"You wouldn't know a rumor existed if it bit you on the ass. Your entire life you thought your father was a standup guy until I told you how he could afford to keep his Mexican whore on the side."

Romano leaned against the bar and flashed a satisfied smile at Sam. He downed another slug of whiskey and smacked his lips. "This is damn good stuff, Arin."

Sam felt the same disgust he had for Romano at Madame de Sousa's cathouse. The same roar in his head that made him draw the line in the sand that day almost propelled him across the floor to wipe the smile off the gangster's face. But he held back and managed a dismissive smile.

"That's enough about goddamn rumors." Haugen said, his voice rising. "I want you two to come to an agreement on the issues we have before us now."

"We're talking about it now," Sam said. He got up and casually sauntered over to stand in front of Romano. He watched his expression closely and said, "Here's another rumor for you: Vince Romano had a motive to kill Deputy Wayne McRae."

Vince's mouth opened in disbelief. "You're accusing me of killing your fucking deputy?"

"You don't listen so good, Vince. I said you had a *motive*."

Haugen stood. "Sam, this won't help at all."

Romano slammed his empty glass on the bar. "What motive are you talking about?"

"Maybe you wanted revenge because I stopped you from taking a one-legged man away."

"Sam, you're out of line," Haugen said.

Sam kept his focus on Romano. "Or, maybe you killed Wayne because he got in Drago's face during our little spat."

Vince pointed his finger. "If I was going to kill anybody, it would be you, because you threatened me."

Haugen sliced the space between like a tomahawk. "Enough!" The Norwegian's face had turned as red as his hair. "This is not how I wanted this to go."

"Okay, let's lay Vince's motives aside for the time being," Sam said. "And talk about Phyllis de Sousa."

"Jesus Christ," Vince said. He took a step towards Sam. "I told you I don't know where she is."

"A citizen of Galveston went missing."

"Go find her then."

"People are saying she can't be found without a shovel."

"You know what else people are saying?" Romano said. "Ever since your son was killed, you've gone downhill."

Haugen looked at his watch. "I have an important meeting in twenty minutes, gentlemen. You need to come to a working agreement, like you had previously."

Sam kept his gaze locked on Romano. His reptilian features didn't seem to be shared by his son, Dominick. Not yet, anyway. Maybe it took several years of ruthless ambition before the venom rose to the surface. "While we're at it, Vince, stay away from Madam Peach's joint."

"What do you care about a nigger whorehouse?"

"I care about the law."

"I know who you talked with. That bouncer over there thinks he's so tough."

"He had a right to say no."

"He got physical with my man. Caught him off guard."

"He says different. Leave him alone."

"If there's anybody you'll need a shovel to find, it's him."

"Enough of the threats, Vince." Haugen said. He looked at both of them. "Do we have an understanding there's to be no more public confrontations?"

"Here's what I understand," Romano said. "If I hear a goddamn thing about me in connection with Wayne McRae, the whole town will hear that Sheriff Sam Baker is on my payroll. Just like his father was." Romano pointed his finger at Sam. "Or, one whisper about me and Madame de Sousa…" He blew into the palm of his hand. "and *poof*, here come the rumors."

Romano walked out.

Chapter 17

Sam stared out the jail's front window as the sun dropped lower in the sky. Shadows from a three-story building stretched to the middle of the street. People passed by in the lingering heat but he didn't notice them.

Grace and the deputies tiptoed around him and spoke in hushed tones.

His nerves still bristled from the verbal brawl with Vince Romano and the refusal by Arin Haugen to help him get Governor Davis off his back. He might have been out of line by accusing Romano—even in a roundabout way—of killing Wayne, but he felt he had to take the chance to confront him then. He'd never get the gangster and his bodyguard into an interrogation room.

Just as his instincts had told him the night of the murder, he still believed that Romano wouldn't risk killing a young cop like Wayne McRae because it would be a declaration of war against Sam Baker. He couldn't entirely dismiss Romano's desire for revenge over being threatened by him at Madam de Sousa's cathouse, but he seemed to believe that spreading lies about Sam's corruptibility would remove that particular stone from his shoe.

The less Sam considered Romano as having ordered Wayne's killing, however, the more his son, Dominick, emerged as a suspect. They hadn't been able to locate young Romano since the murder. Even Gus Josie hadn't been able to find him. No one answered the knock at his door, and mail had accumulated in his mailbox.

If he didn't turn up soon, Sam would have to call the FBI to look for him.

Sam poured himself a cup of burnt coffee and sat down in his office. Grace said goodnight to him and left for the day.

Deputy Lowell Turner unlocked the gun cabinet across the hall and pulled out a rifle. Sam looked at the schedule— Turner had a night patrol starting soon, and it took him by the murder site across from the Thirsty Pelican. Sam called to him.

Turner appeared in the doorway. "Yes, sir?"

The young man hadn't yet filled out and had been teased by Wayne and the other deputies about being a beanpole. He wore a black patch over a hollow eye socket—the result of a hunting accident. None of the deputies teased him about that.

"I want you to patrol Avenue B and the seawall. Two more merchant ships docked today. We'll have a lot of rowdy seaman out there letting off steam. Fighting and such."

Turner looked disappointed. "Sir, if I'm not out of line, Deputy Stanton is already patrolling there."

"Let me cut to the chase, Deputy. I can't risk another man out there on that road."

"Sir, I'm familiar with that area. As you know, I interviewed Orville Sessions and three of his neighbors. I'd of course follow any cautions you'd have for me"

Turner had reported that Sessions, the Thirsty Pelican owner, had closed the bar at midnight the night of the murder and would have noticed if Wayne's cruiser had been parked across the road. That information established that it had been left there between midnight and three a.m., when the anonymous caller reported seeing it parked snug up against the thick shrubbery bordering the swamp.

Sam studied Turner's young face. He saw determination to do what he could to catch the killer of his friend and fellow deputy. "Okay, patrol the area but don't get out of the car for any minor accidents or anything that could be a trap," Sam instructed. "Call for backup for anything that looks like a legitimate problem. And Deputy, watch your damn back."

"Yes, sir," Turner said and left.

Besides Orville Sessions' testimony, Sam now had reports from all the deputies he'd sent out to gather evidence. None of them had been fruitful. No one had seen or heard anything, including the Thirsty Pelican's far-flung neighbors.

The only useful update had come from Clyde Hermann, the medical examiner, who said that Wayne had died from a hard blow to the back of the neck, not from the bullet wounds.

That meant Wayne had been shot *after* he was dead.

Sam hadn't been able to speak when he heard that. After a long silence, Hermann said he was sorry and hung up the phone. Sam was now even more convinced that someone had ambushed Wayne when he was out of his car. Maybe even by someone he knew. Maybe Dominick Romano.

The crude medallion found clutched in Wayne's hands only had his fingerprints on it. It had been sent to the FBI for analysis and a possible match to an organization or gang.

But all those setbacks didn't come close to matching the hardest part of the day—meeting with Wayne's grief-stricken parents, Ian and Sophie McRae. Sam and Claire had had dinner with them on a few occasions and had been impressed with how good-natured and down-to-earth they were. Trying to console them had been one of the hardest duties he'd ever had to perform in his life. He wished Claire had been there to comfort them, particularly the inconsolable Mrs. McRae.

In between missing Claire's sympathetic ear and the frustration of the dead-end search for clues, thoughts of Laura Stevens had competed for his attention. The last thing he remembered of the night was crawling under the sheets while she lay down next to him—fully clothed—and whispered softly that everything would be all right.

When he woke up in the early morning, she was gone. All that remained was her lingering scent on the rumpled sheets.

Her fragrance had replaced Claire's.

Chapter 18

Sam finished the bitter coffee and grabbed his hat. He started for the back door but heard Deputy Garza shout for him. In the outer office, a young woman with a thin, pretty face had walked in.

"Sheriff Baker..." she said. She raised her eyebrows. It looked to Sam like she had something to tell him. Something serious.

Sam mimicked writing to Garza, and the deputy grabbed a pad and followed them into the interview room. Sam pulled out a chair for the girl, and she sat at the rickety wooden table. She kneaded her hands together and looked back and forth between Sam and Garza. She stated her name as Debbie Canton. "I graduated Ball High a year before Sylvie."

"I remember you now, Debbie," Sam said. "Your parents own Canton Furniture." Debbie had blossomed from the chubby girl who used to hang out in their store into an attractive young woman on the cusp of adulthood.

"What can I help you with, Debbie?"

"I don't know, Sheriff... It's probably nothing, but I was downtown last week and ran into Wayne. We talked for a few minutes before he had to go." she said. Her voice cracked. "He was always so nice."

Sam gave her his handkerchief. She dabbed her eyes with it. "Wayne walked off, and I could see Dominick Romano coming towards him."

Sam kept silent, not daring to breathe. Garza wrote on his pad.

Debbie took a labored breath. "Dominick waved at him but kept going. Wayne reached out and grabbed his arm."

"In anger?" Sam asked. "He was confronting him?"

"I couldn't tell if he was angry at him or if he just wanted to make sure Dominick stopped."

"How close were you?"

Debbie thought for a moment. "About a half block away."

"Could you hear them?"

"I could hear most of it. Especially after they started arguing."

Sam crossed his legs like he was relaxed and hadn't heard the very thing he'd been hoping for during the past fruitless days of the investigation. "What were they arguing about?"

"Like I said, I couldn't hear every word but there was one they both used."

"What was that?"

"Sylvie."

Chapter 19

Nothing stirred except for a white-uniformed milkman setting quart bottles on the front porch of a bungalow. Car tires splashed through the previous night's rainwater, breaking the silence of the deserted streets. Headlights disappeared into a thick fog. Sam was glad for the shroud that it and the darkness provided.

Sam sat in the front seat as Deputy Eilers drove the squad car. Deputies Robicheaux and Turner sat in the back, cradling their breached 12-gauge shotguns. Both of them were younger than Wayne had been. Sam felt like he and Eilers were taking Boy Scouts on a hunting trip.

And they *were* hunting. Gus Josie, the cabbie informant, had called Sam in the middle of the night with the probable whereabouts of Dominick Romano. Not his own house, either, Gus had said. That bit of information—coupled with Romano's absence from the Indigo Palm and Debbie Canton's testimony that he had argued with Wayne—boosted Sam's case for bringing him in for questioning.

He realized his evidence was circumstantial and flimsy. But Sam had learned through the years to act fast before suspects had time to cover their tracks. As a mob boss' son, however, Dominick would have already acquired an alibi.

Sam looked in the backseat. Robicheaux met his gaze and held it. Unlike the night Wayne had been killed, he now appeared to be resolute and ready.

Turner shared Robicheaux's expression of contained rage. They were all angry, and anger demanded action.

With some reluctance Sam had brought Deputy Eilers along. Despite his many faults, Eilers was a steady hand when things got dicey, and they would if Vince's men were there to protect his son.

The first hint of dawn lightened the eastern sky as Eilers drove into a neighborhood of well-maintained houses. Front yards of palm trees and flowers. White swings hanging from porch ceilings.

A paperboy on his bicycle did a double-take as the squad car passed.

Eilers slowed and stopped across from a one-story house with white porch columns and green storm shutters. According to Gus Josie, the house belonged to Salvatore Longino, a nephew of Vince Romano. No telling who else could be inside.

Sam looked at each deputy in turn. "Are we clear on our objectives?" They nodded. They were ready.

The four lawmen jumped out of the car and trotted to the house. Two cars in the driveway. Eilers ran around to the back.

Sam led Robicheaux and Turner up the porch steps. He pounded on the door. "Galveston County Sheriff. Open up."

He waited, pounded harder. From inside a voice shouted, "Who the fuck is it?"

"Sheriff Sam Baker. I'm looking for Dominick Romano."

"He ain't here."

"Open the door or we'll break it down."

"You do that, you'll answer to Vince Romano."

Sam sized up the door, prepared to kick it in. But the lock clicked and the door cracked open a sliver. Dominick Romano peeked out with one half-opened eye. He wore slacks but no shirt. His dark hair hung down over his forehead. "What's the problem, Sheriff?"

"Let's talk a moment, Dominick."

"What about?"

"Just want to clear some things up. Can I come in?"

The man behind Dominick shouted, "Hell, no! You ain't coming into my house."

Sam could make out a slender man in his late thirties with a protruding Adam's apple and eyes too large for his angular face. Dominick's cousin. *Salvatore Longino.*

"Relax, Sal," Dominick said, not taking his eyes off Sam. "Your father is going to hear about this right now."

"Forget get it, Sal." Romano's eyes darted over to the shotgun-armed deputies on either side of the door.

Sal edged further back. "The fuck you talking about? I don't call him he's going to have my ass."

"I'll take care of this," Dominick said.

The door opened wider. Dominick looked directly at Sam, his expression calm, challenging, like maybe he expected this and had his ass covered.

Sam wondered what Sylvie would think of Dominick now that a lawman—her father—wanted to question her new boyfriend in connection with the murder of her former boyfriend.

Sal Longino stepped closer and looked at the deputies holding shotguns. "I don't fucking believe this. You come to my house—"

Dominick raised a cautionary hand. Longino's rant sputtered to a stop.

Sam wasn't sure what to make of young Romano's coolness in the face of three heavily-armed lawmen standing on the front porch. Maybe he had a clear conscience or—like his father—no conscience at all.

Young Romano pushed the door open and gestured with his head for Sam to come in. He and Deputy Robicheaux entered while Turner kept his post on the porch.

Dominick pulled an undershirt from a chair and slipped it on. Sal wore boxer shorts and an unbuttoned silk shirt over his knobby chest. He muttered a steady stream of cuss words, outraged that two armed cops now stood in his living room.

"Maybe you should put some pants on, Sal," Dominick said.

Sal started to turn, but Sam held out his hand. "I'd rather you stayed here, Sal. We won't be long." He asked him if they could look around.

"Fuck that."

"Be my guest," Dom said. "You won't find anything."

"Is anyone else in the house?" Sam asked.

"Just us."

"Any weapons?"

Sal shook his head in disgust. "Yeah, I got a pistol in the nightstand. Back bedroom."

Sam nodded to Robicheaux, and the deputy disappeared down the hallway. Sam swept his eyes over the living room and looked under all furniture. Nothing seemed out of the ordinary.

"Would it be okay if we took a quick look in your car?" he asked. Dom flashed an amused smile and from his pocket handed Sam a set of keys. Sam passed them to Deputy Turner on the porch.

"Is this about Wayne McRae?" Dominick asked.

Sam looked for a sign of tension in Dominick's expression, but didn't see one. "Just a process of elimination. I appreciate your cooperation."

"I was real sorry to hear about that," Dominick said. "Sylvie was very upset."

The casualness with which the guy said his daughter's name made Sam wonder if he was being baited. See if the father would lose his cool. "Why are you hiding out over here,

Mr. Romano?"

"I'm not hiding. My house is being painted."

"Painted?" Sam said. "You got the night shift over there right now?"

"It smells bad. You know what I mean?"

Robicheaux stepped into the room holding a .45 caliber pistol with his handkerchief.

"Big gun, Sal," Sam said.

Sal shook his head. "You're stepping into some shit, my friend."

"You want me to take it, Sheriff?" asked Robicheaux.

Sam shook his head. The coroner's report confirmed Sam's certainty that Wayne had been shot with his own gun. "Take the clip," Sam said. "Put the gun back and have a look around."

Deputy Turner opened the door and handed the car keys to Sam. "The car is clean, Sheriff."

Sam passed the keys to Dom. "I'd like you come down to the station with us to answer a few questions."

"I didn't have anything to do with Wayne."

"Just a little talk," Sam said. "You're not under arrest."

"This is voluntary?"

"Yes"

"Don't do it, Dom," Sal said. "Your father will blow a fucking fuse."

"Why not?" Dominick said and shrugged. "You already woke me up."

Galveston '44

Chapter 20

Sam pushed open the headquarters door and led Dominick past Grace at the front desk. She kept her focus on her work, as Sam had instructed her to do whenever a suspect was brought in. This time, though, she seemed especially determined to act like it was an everyday occurrence to bring the son of Galveston's mob boss in at such an early hour.

Sam opened the interview room door. "After you."

Dominick stepped in. Sam usually preferred to let suspects sit alone in the windowless room and allow the gravity of their situation to settle down on them before the questioning began. But young Romano hadn't yet shown any visible concern and would probably only be bored sitting alone in a windowless room.

"Grab a seat," Sam said. He sat across the scarred wooden desk from Romano.

Deputy Robicheaux walked in and slapped his notebook on the table.

The room's stale air—which Wayne had believed was saturated with the lingering fear of previous suspects—hung heavy over them. Sam thought of Wayne now and how he might be able to bring him justice this very morning.

Sam locked eyes with Romano. The young man crossed one leg over the other, his white shirt open at the neck where a metal disc hung from a silver chain. It took Sam a moment in the dim light to realize that musical notes had been engraved in the medallion, not skull-and-crossbones.

"Do you know why you're here?" Sam asked.

"Sheriff Baker, I didn't kill your deputy."

"Where were you on the night Wayne was murdered?"

"At Sal's house."

Robicheaux made a note of Dominick's statement.

Sam chuckled. "How convenient for you."

Romano shrugged. "That's where I was."

"Wayne McRae was the boyfriend of the girl you wanted to date," Sam said.

"I really like Sylvie but do you really think I'd kill Wayne because of that?"

"Was he in the way or not?"

"You obviously think that."

"They'd been dating for almost a year. Doesn't that count for something?"

"I suppose it does, but—"

"Did you kill Wayne to eliminate that competition?"

Dominick's expression turned indignant. "I guess this isn't going to be a friendly chat after all."

"Did you get in an argument with him?"

"No."

"You're lying to me," Sam said, raising his voice. "You argued with him two days before he was killed."

Dominick tilted his head. "*Argued* with him?"

"Yes. Outside the Post Office. On the Friday before he was killed."

Romano seemed to search his memory but didn't take his eyes off Sam. "Oh, that… that wasn't a damn argument."

"An eyewitness told us you argued with Wayne McRae," Sam said. He turned to Robicheaux. "What did the witness say, Deputy?"

Robicheaux flipped back a couple of pages in his notepad. "That Dominick and Wayne got into an argument over Sylvie Baker. The witness testified that Wayne said, 'you ain't getting Sylvie into the Indigo without me'."

"What witness was that?" Dominick asked.

"You think I would give you the name of a witness? I know what happens to witnesses in your line of work."

"What line of work would that be, Sheriff?"

"Your father's business. Prostitution. Gambling. A little loan sharking. I could go on."

"I run the Indigo Palm. That's it."

"You don't have gamblers in your club?"

"Yes, but they go down to the casino to gamble."

"You don't have whores in your club?"

"Occasionally but—"

"So, you're a pimp?"

Romano's handsome face began to tighten around the forehead. "No, I'm a music club manager."

Sam was encouraged to see some splintering around the edges of Romano's composure. "Have you heard the phrase 'the apple don't fall far from the tree'?"

Dominick Romano sighed. "Oh, Jesus…"

"Your father taught that you don't let people get in your face."

"My mother and I moved away from Vince when I was four years old. He didn't teach me a damn thing."

"Deputy McRae felt threatened because you were moving in on his girl and he confronted you about it. You didn't like it."

Romano snapped his fingers. "I remember now. We were talking about music."

"You remember *now*?"

"He said he liked big band music like Tommy Dorsey and Benny Goodman. I said I preferred smaller jazz ensembles like Duke Ellington and Thelonious Monk."

"Deputy Robicheaux, please read the witnesses the next

statement. What did our friend here suggest to Deputy McRae?"

"With pleasure, Sheriff," Robicheaux said. "The witness heard you say, 'Let her go, McRae'."

"I told Wayne I would comp him and Sylvie two tickets to see Ella Fitzgerald sing, but he said you wouldn't let the deputies go to the Indigo. I said he should let her go to the show with a girlfriend, not that he should give her up."

"Did you have someone take care of Wayne for you while you established an alibi at Sal's house?"

"Please...," Romano said. He sneered. "Do you think your daughter would associate with someone who would do something like that?"

"Leave my daughter out of this. In fact, I don't want you to see her again."

Romano uncrossed his leg and sat up. "I don't think I can do that, Sheriff."

"That's not a suggestion. Just forget about her."

"She's not going to like that."

"She'll see different when you go to trial."

There was a sharp rap at the door. From the window, Deputy Turner pointed to the front door.

Vince Romano and his men had arrived.

Chapter 21

Sam led Dominick Romano down the hallway to the front door, now barred by a metal rod and manned by Deputy's Eilers. Grace sat out of harm's way in Sam's office.

"You want to take him out the back, Sheriff?" Eilers asked.

"No. Nobody forces us to turn tail," Sam said.

Sam looked out the observation window where Romano stood in the middle of eight or nine men, demanding his son and shouting threats. Drago stood next to him, a smile of anticipation lifting one corner of his mouth.

Three deputies stood guard on the top landing. Turner had a shotgun. The other two held pistols at their sides. No one from Romano's gang brandished a gun, but Sam knew they all were armed.

Something heavy thudded against the door. Things could get nasty.

"Let me talk with him," Dominick said.

"We'll take care of it ourselves," Sam said. He levelled a look at him. "Don't leave town. We have more to talk about."

"Next time it won't be voluntarily."

"Any way you want it."

Sam took off his gun belt and lifted the metal bar from its slot. He opened the door and lunged outside, slipping between the deputies on sentry.

He held the heavy bar horizontal to the ground and pushed it into Romano's chest, driving him back a few feet. Vince was pinned against Drago and his other men. His thin black hair, usually slicked back, drooped off his scalp like he'd just been awakened—probably by a call from Sal Longino.

"Back off," Sam ordered.

"I will rip your fucking face off." Vince's shouted. He tried to reach Sam with his outstretched hands but Sam's arms were too long. Drago reached over his boss. He grabbed the bar with one hand and tried to jerk it free. Sam held on but felt the inhuman strength in those big hands.

"Calm down, Vince. He's free to go."

"You mother-fucker," Vince shouted. Ropy veins bulged on his thick neck. "How dare you arrest my son?"

"I didn't arrest him. He came down here voluntarily."

Vince dropped his voice. He leaned in. "This is going to cost you, Baker."

Sam looked back to the deputies. "Bring him out."

Dominick ran down the steps and ducked under the metal bar. He pushed against his father. "It was just a misunderstanding, Vince."

"What misunderstanding?"

"Let's go," Dom said. "I'll tell you about it."

Vince pointed at Sam. "You and I aren't finished with this."

Drago shoved the iron bar back but Sam braced himself. The big man and the rest of the gunmen followed their boss as he threw his arm over his son's shoulders.

A crowd of onlookers slowly drifted off down the street, probably disappointed that the conflict hadn't turned more heated. Sam hoped they now had a reason to reject any potential whispers that he took orders from Vince Romano.

Sam caught his breath. He watched Galveston come to life in its sleepy, unhurried way. The owner of the café across the street turned the 'closed' sign on his door around to 'open.'

Sam thought he may have made a mistake in bringing

Dominick Romano in without more than circumstantial evidence but at least he had acted.

Deputy Robicheaux joined him in watching the crowd disperse.

Sam didn't look at him. He didn't want the young man to see the doubt and uncertainty he felt. Dominick Romano had demonstrated the kind of grace under pressure that would undoubtedly hold up under even intense questioning in a court of law. On the contrary, would the testimony of Debbie Canton convince a jury that young Romano had argued with Wayne about Sylvie? Any defense attorney worth his salt would discover that Ms. Canton had heard primarily wind-blown snatches of their exchange.

And where was the physical evidence? They had found nothing at Sal's house and probably wouldn't at Dominick's, either. If he had killed Wayne, he would have gotten rid of anything incriminating.

If he didn't know how, his father certainly did.

Sam felt like he'd lost his first boxing match. He had hoped to break young Romano down and at least get him to hesitate in his answers, maybe to even incriminate himself. But he'd been calm, then indignant. In the end, he'd given them nothing.

Other than the untraceable skull-and-crossbones medallion, other than Debbie Canton's thin testimony, he had no other ideas. No fingerprints. No known enemies.

How could he look Wayne's parents in the eye and tell them that?

The McRae's would listen to the empty promise of his words and see in his eyes exactly what he had.

Nothing.

Galveston '44

Chapter 22

Sam felt stiff and warm in his new black suit. Deputy Robicheaux, walking by his side, looked equally uncomfortable in his. Deputies Turner and Garza followed behind them.

He was grateful for the gray clouds as they drifted across the late morning sun. Grateful to be out of the stuffy church after sitting for two numbing hours. Not that Sam begrudged Wayne McRae getting a proper recounting of his short life, but a whole chorus of people had cried during the entire service.

Sam got through his remembrance of Wayne with only having to pause once to tamp down his emotions. He had raised his head in an effort to keep the tears from leaking from his eyes. His gaze had fallen on the crowed balcony where he had been surprised to see a black face in the midst of the white mourners. Henry Jackson had broken the unwritten rule against Negroes—other than the custodian—from darkening the church door.

Sam had been puzzled about Jackson's attendance but the man had shown he wasn't shy about inserting himself in other people's business.

Deputy Robicheaux did well with his eulogy, too. Right at the end, though, his voice broke. His last sentence died on his lips. Sam was proud that Robicheaux spoke about his friend with such unabashed affection and even managed to poke some gentle fun at him. As Robicheaux spoke, it struck Sam that Billy Baker would also have spoken on Wayne's behalf.

If Billy's remains were ever recovered from the Italian battlefield, he and Wayne would share their final resting grounds.

Sam and his deputies merged with a cluster of mourners as they walked on the lush cemetery lawn. The graveyard had the distinction of being the oldest in Galveston County. Legend had it that some of Jean Laffite's pirates were buried under the very ground where they now tread. There were no grave markers proving such rumors, but it made for an entertaining story nonetheless.

Sam stopped at the edge of the open grave. He looked down the chasm to where the polished mahogany casket hung suspended by ropes.

He raised his gaze to the opposite side of the grave where Sylvie and Claire had linked their arms. He had assumed his wife would come down from Dallas to attend the funeral—she loved Wayne as much as Sam did. He had avoided looking at Claire during his eulogy as she sat behind the McRae family. One source of loss was more than enough for one day.

His sister, Missy, stood just behind Claire, dabbing at her eyes with a tissue.

Claire gave him a thin smile and looked away. Sylvie, however, wouldn't meet his eyes. She harbored ill feelings towards her father because he had the audacity to question Dominick Romano about the murder of the man they were burying today. To make matters worse, Sam had had Deputy Stanton question her about what Romano might have expressed in regards to Wayne. But Sylvie said her old boyfriend was a subject they had never discussed.

Sam took Sylvie at her word. The idea that Dominick was the killer took a hit.

Just as the preacher began his graveside service, Laura Stevens stepped to the grave's edge. She linked her arm with

Sylvie's. She looked even prettier in her black dress than the night of Wayne's murder when she had worn Claire's blouse. Perhaps sensing his eyes on her, Laura looked up. She gave him a brief but warm smile.

The four women most important to Sam now stood across from him. One had left him and one wasn't speaking to him. He and Missy had grown distant over the last year but he hoped to repair their relationship. Laura had made her interest in him clear but he wasn't certain he could give enough of himself to her in these difficult days.

Mr. and Mrs. McRae sat in folding chairs and stared down at the casket containing their only son. Sam hoped that Claire had spoken with them because Sam's pledge of finding Wayne's killer had sounded hollow and impotent—because it was.

The preacher finished his sermon and closed the Bible. Stifled sobs broke the ensuing silence.

Sam threw a handful of dirt on the lacquered casket as it descended into the dark grave. Wayne McRae was gone. But Sam wouldn't forget him, just as he would never forget Billy. For his son he could do nothing but grieve. For Wayne he could do more. He could fight to bring his killer to justice or— if he had to—kill him. He would search, and he would never give up, even if it killed *him*.

And that's the only way he would stop.

Galveston '44

Chapter 23

Sam lay in bed and watched the ceiling fan whirl overhead. He picked up his watch from the nightstand—almost three in the morning. He hadn't slept all night from thinking about Wayne's funeral and the great sorrow of the McRae family.

He ran the scene of the murder over in his head, just as he had several times before. What had he missed? He pictured a man hitting Wayne on the back of his neck with something solid. A two-by-four? A baseball bat? Did the killer pull Wayne's pistol from his holster and shoot him where he fell? Or, did they drive him somewhere else—in his own squad car—and shoot him there? Whichever place it was, the killer drove him to the side of the road across from the Thirsty Pelican. Inexplicably, he lifted Wayne's body from the backseat and laid him in the front. Why? And why leave the skull-and-crossbones medallion in his hands?

The last part of the scene Sam pictured was the killer's means of escape. Either the man was picked up by someone or ran on foot in an unknown direction.

No witnesses. No clues. No nothing.

Sam got up and put on his uniform and strapped on his gun belt. It was dead quiet outside, just like that gut-wrenching early morning when he'd gotten the call that had changed everything.

It could be that his sleeplessness had another cause besides grief and frustration. Maybe Wayne had somehow tapped him on the shoulder.

Galveston '44

Chapter 24

Sam cut the squad car's engine. He drifted to a stop just off the edge of the narrow road. A dense wall of shrubbery and trees loomed on each side. The beginning of swampy ground glimmered in the pale moonlight.

A distant owl hooted. Something splashed into the water out in no man's land. He looked down the road to where the killer had driven Wayne McRae's cruiser to a hard stop. He tried to picture the man as he pulled Wayne's body from the backseat and placed him in the front. Nothing formed.

Sam grabbed his flashlight and walked to where Wayne's car had sat. Already sprouts of weeds had filled in the tire ruts. Soon the murder scene would be indistinguishable from any other overgrown stretch of this lonely road.

He looked across the white seashell driveway that led to the Thirsty Pelican. The same rusted remnants of a car sat in front. The bar looked as godforsaken as that night a week ago.

Weariness wrapped itself around Sam like a blanket. He looked at his watch. He could still get a couple hours of sleep before he went to headquarters.

He turned to go but stopped—he thought he'd seen a quick flash of light coming from the bar's front window. He waited but the window remained dark. Probably a quick reflection of moonlight, he thought, just like he'd seen on the night of the murder. Deputy Robicheaux had forced the backdoor open and looked around. No one had been there. The next day. the bar's owner, Orville Sessions, confirmed that nothing other than the busted door lock was amiss.

He walked onto the long drive to look from another angle. Nothing, again. His momentum carried him forward, his boots crunching on the white oyster shells.

He shined the flashlight into the window, over the wooden tables and chairs. Bottles of booze took up the lone shelf behind the bar. All whiskey, no doubt. This was a beer-and-a-shot kind of place.

He rapped on the window but nothing moved inside. He tried the front door without luck. The window around the side of the structure had been nailed shut by rotting boards. Bars with daytime drinkers kept their places nighttime dark. Sam went around to the repaired back door and pulled on the knob. The door squeaked slightly at the bottom but held fast.

That was it, he thought. He hadn't expected anything by coming out here, but the failure of his instincts would probably kill any chance for sleep. He might as well go to the office and drink some coffee.

But his boots stayed anchored to the spot like he'd stepped in wet concrete. He took his pistol out from its holster and set it on the ground. He eyed the middle of the door. Fuck it, he'd pay Sessions for a new one. He reared back with his right leg but in mid-kick the door burst open and sent him sprawling. A man grunted as he leapt over Sam and disappeared around the corner of the bar.

Sam stood and ran. "Stop," he shouted. "Galveston County Sheriff."

He reached the parking lot. He could just make out the man's silhouette as he ran towards the road, his footsteps crunching the seashells.

The man hit his stride on the deserted road, his arms pumping, his head tilted back. He ran out of fear, but Sam ran out of desperation. He kept pace with the man despite the pain in his right leg where the door had jammed it.

A cloud covered the moon. In the darkness Sam lost sight of the man. Had he run into the swampy thicket or had he stopped to aim a pistol at Sam? He pushed harder—trying to call on the daily roadwork he'd done when he boxed, but that was twenty-three years ago.

He yelled again for the man to stop just as a human-shaped shadow flashed past him and disappeared into the darkness.

Sam dug deep but his last hope to catch these men was fading along with his own stamina.

Somewhere ahead, men shouted. Sam came upon them wrestling in the road, grunting with exertion. One man pinned the other man's arms behind him and ground him into the asphalt.

Sam slapped the leather of his holster but the gun was back at the bar. As he reared his leg back to kick the man on top, he caught the reflection of sweat-soaked—and black—arms.

It was Henry Jackson.

"What the fuck are you doing here?" Sam said, straining to speak as his chest heaved.

"Same reason as you," Jackson said, pulling the man's second arm behind his back. "Trying to flush this guy out."

"Who is he?"

"I don't know, but he was hiding in the bar."

Sam squatted and looked at the young man as he grunted from the weight pressed on him. He appeared to be in his early or mid-twenties with stringy, brown hair hanging over his forehead. He had the lean, wiry look of a man used to physical work. Sam was glad to see he hadn't been outrun by someone older and overweight.

The man looked back to see who was on top of him. His expression turned indignant. "Get this nigger off me."

Jackson bent his arm up higher on his back. He yelled in pain. Jackson yelled, too. "You want to say that again?"

Sam let Jackson hold it there a moment. "What were you doing in the bar?"

The man seemed to contemplate what his best answer might be. "I work there."

"Doing what?" Sam asked.

"You know, serving beer. Mopping up. Shit like that."

Jackson shook his head *no* at Sam.

"You're lying," Sam said.

The man thought a moment. "I'm the, you know, the guard. The night watchman."

"What are you guarding?" Sam asked. "Nothing to steal there but some damn beer."

The man looked down the road as if a good story might appear there. His eyes went blank, and he sighed. "Okay. My brother owns the bar."

"What's his name?"

"Orville. Orville Sessions."

"And yours?"

"Horace Sessions."

Sam slapped handcuffs on Sessions and searched his pockets—empty except for a greasy comb. He pulled him up to a sitting position.

Horace Sessions looked at his bloody elbows and hands and glared at Henry Jackson.

"Horace," Sam said. "I'm going to ask you a question. If you lie to me I'm going to hog-tie you and throw you out in that swamp for snake bait. You understand me?"

Horace cast his eyes out to the wet thicket just past the edge of the road.

Sam looked him dead in the eyes. "Did you kill Deputy Wayne McRae?"

"Hell no! I ain't done it."

Sam got in his face. "Bullshit. You're lying."

114

"No! I ain't killed nobody."

"I know you did it, Horace," Sam said. He stood. "I'm going for my rope."

"Sheriff, I swear. I didn't kill your deputy."

"Then why are you hiding in your brother's bar?"

Sessions sighed. "I got an arrest warrant on me in Alabama."

"For what?" Sam asked.

"Breaking and entering a damn liquor store."

"Now here's another question for you Horace, for which a lie—"

"I seen 'em," Sessions said, quietly. He looked down the road at the murder site as if watching the scene unfold again. "A noise woke me up. I looked outside and saw a man pull the deputy out of the back of his car and put him in the front seat. He was a big sumbitch, and he picked up your deputy like he didn't weigh nothin'. Like he was a baby."

Horace Sessions' description fit the scenario that Sam had visualized. "How big?"

"As tall as you, Sheriff, maybe thirty pounds heavier. And it was packed on real solid-like."

Sam and Jackson looked at each other. They knew a man that fit that description, and his name was Drago. Sam had largely discounted Vince Romano and his big bodyguard as suspects, but now the prospect loomed again, and he didn't like it. The only worse suspect than Romano would be one who had fled the state.

"How do you know it was a big man?" Sam asked. "It was dark."

"But the moon was bright. You ought to know because you was there."

Sam was thrown right back to that early morning when the full moon had thrown his worst nightmare into stark reality.

"Would you recognize the man if you saw him again?" Sam asked.

"His face was always turned. But I did see the other fella pretty clear."

"Two men?" Sam said, shouting. "Why didn't you say so?"

"Well, I ain't got to that part of the story yet," Sessions said. "The other fella rolled up in a Lincoln not long after the squad car stopped. He ran over to big man like he was flummoxed by the big sumbitch tossing your deputy into the front seat."

"Flummoxed?"

"Yeah."

Jackson looked at Sam. "Confused. Bewildered. Perplexed."

Sessions looked at Jackson. "Can I ask how the hell you got into the bar without me hearin' you? That door was locked."

"Direct your comments to Sheriff Baker," Jackson said.

Sessions looked at Sam. "We don't have no nigra cops in Alabama."

Jackson faked an expression of pity. "Don't worry. You'll have them someday."

Sam prodded Sessions with his boot. "How do you know the man was flummoxed, as you say?"

"If you hadn't cuffed me I could show you, but he spread his arms out wide like you would when a child misbehaved. Then he shook his head like he was angry at the big guy. Like a father scolding a brat."

"Describe the man."

"Early forties, maybe. Blond hair cut real short. And he looked fit, like an athlete."

"How can you describe him and not the big man?"

"Because he saw the bar and walked up the drive a ways. He got him a real worried look then."

Jackson looked down the road towards the site. "Describe the Lincoln."

"Black. Maybe a '41 model. I think that was the last year they could make 'em."

Sam nodded. Nineteen forty-one was the year American car manufacturers had to shut down production so the steel could be used to make tanks and other war armaments. "Who was first on the scene?"

"An older deputy. Had a good beer belly on him." Sam almost smiled at Session's description of Jim Eilers' most noticeable feature.

"Did you call it in, Horace?" Henry Jackson asked.

"I did," the young man said. "And I don't mind telling you the whole thing shook me up real bad."

"Did you see the license plate on the Lincoln?" Sam asked.

"Nah, I could only see the side of the car," Sessions said. "But when they pulled out into the road I saw the left fender had a dent in it. Headlight didn't work 'cause it was smashed in, too."

Sam felt a ray of hope—a black '41 Lincoln wasn't uncommon. But one with a dented fender and a missing headlight was. If Drago was the killer, though, that meant that Vince Romano was equally guilty. Mob guys like them were rarely prosecuted. That would leave only one way to get justice for Wayne.

And it wouldn't involve a trial.

Galveston '44

Chapter 25

Sam helped Sessions into the back of the squad car and closed the door. He turned and faced Jackson. The man's chin was raised, and his expression was stoic, as always. "What the hell were you thinking?" Sam asked. "You know there's a law against interfering in an ongoing investigation."

Jackson looked at the murder site once more. His face carried a fine sheen of sweat from running after Sessions. "Wayne was my friend." He had said it softly, simply. As if that declaration answered Sam's question beyond debate.

"Wayne never said anything about having a...a friend like you."

"A Negro friend—is that want you were going to say?"

"We were close. Why wouldn't he have told me?"

"I don't know," Jackson said. He shrugged. "He probably thought it wasn't necessary."

"Okay, let's say for the moment that you were friends. The point is you could have chased off this witness."

Jackson laughed sharply. "Chased him off? I chased him *down*. And I blew past you on the way."

"Mr. Jackson, you may have heard that I'm pretty damn good at investigating crimes. Just leave this to me and my deputies."

Henry Jackson looked off. He seemed to contemplate Sam's order. He looked back and shook his head almost imperceptibly. "You think Drago was the big guy Sessions saw?"

Sam sighed. "You know something, Jackson...you're

119

wearing me out."

"There's something else, Sheriff. Romano's men took over Lady Night's joint."

Sam pictured the bright-red, one-story building on the edge of town. The cathouse catered to johns who liked it on the rough side, either as the giver or the receiver.

"How do you know?"

"My sister told me. Madam Peaches, if you remember."

"When did this happen?"

"The day before Wayne was killed. I thought the timing was interesting."

"Maybe it's just a coincidence."

"Could be, but Romano shut the place down as soon as he took over."

"Did your sister say why?"

"She didn't know. But it would be worth looking into."

"I'll check it out later today," Sam said. He reached for the door handle. "Thanks for the information."

"We could go now. It's not far from here."

"Knowing you, Mr. Jackson, you've already been over there."

"Good deduction, Sheriff."

"Did you see any of the ladies around?"

"Not a woman in sight. But I saw a man patrolling the grounds about this time of the morning."

Sam thought that would be a natural precaution on Romano's part if he thought there might be repercussions for taking someone's business away from them. But the main question he had was why would a money-loving man like Vince shut down the place completely. "You think something happened to Lady Night herself?"

"Only one way to find out."

Sam would have to try and track her down. But he thought

they would probably have the same success looking for her as they had for Madam de Sousa, which was none at all. And now his resources were stretched thin because of the hunt for Wayne's killer.

"I ran this witness down for you, Sheriff," Jackson said. "I deserve something for that."

"You turned my money down last time I offered. Kind of hurt my feelings."

"I want to go with you tomorrow."

"I can't drive you around in my squad car, Mr. Jackson."

"I don't recommend a squad car, Sheriff. We should go in your man's taxi."

Sam wasn't sure he'd heard right. No one knew about Gus Josie, not even the deputies. "Describe this man."

"Wears a black fedora," Jackson said. "Hooked nose. He followed Dominick Romano over to Sal Longino's house the night before you raided it."

"How the hell—?"

"I saw Romano get in his car and drive off to Longino's. Your cabbie followed him."

Sam's secret weapon was no longer secret. "Keep that to yourself or you and I are going to have a problem."

"I'm trying to help you, Sheriff," Jackson said. "That's why I showed you that your daughter was involved with Dominick Romano."

Sam studied the man's determined expression. In the dark he hadn't noticed blood seeping down from a gouge in his forehead. Jackson had paid a price in taking the witness down at full speed on unforgiving asphalt. And it was true—Sam wouldn't have caught the younger Sessions without him.

"Okay, I owe you," Sam said. "But forget about being part of my investigation."

Galveston '44

Chapter 26

The morning sun caught Sam full-on through the cruiser's open window, and the glare from passing cars made him squint. He didn't care, though—the first break in the case the night before had buoyed his spirits and made him feel as if he'd slept all night, instead of not at all.

He stopped in front of a seafood restaurant that he and Claire used to frequent back in the days that now seemed so long ago. The owner was a friend of theirs and would keep an eye on the cruiser.

He walked to rear of the restaurant and into a narrow alley hidden by thick palm trees.

Gus Josie was waiting in his taxi. Sam climbed into the backseat.

"Thanks, Gus."

"At your service, Sheriff Baker. Where we going?"

"Do you know Madam Peaches' joint?"

Gus gave him a puzzled look in the rearview mirror. "What you want to go out there for, Sheriff?"

"We're going to pick somebody up and then stake out another joint."

Gus drove on but Sam could tell he had other questions. After a few minutes, Gus said, "Is this fella a colored?"

"Is that going to be a problem?"

"Sheriff, I ain't never had one in my cab before, and I've driving twenty-six years."

"Gus, I'm sure you know that in law enforcement you're sometimes required to do things you wouldn't ordinarily do.

That's the assignment today, and it's a very important one."

"It's just that, well, I kind of hate to break my record."

"You're going above and beyond, Gus, that's for sure.

Gus was quiet a long moment. "Does he live at Madam Peaches' joint?"

"Yeah. She's his sister."

"Now I've heard it all," Gus Josie said.

Sam sat back in his seat. His right leg throbbed in pain from the interrupted kick at the Thirsty Pelican's back door. Both legs had tightened from running after Horace Sessions. He needed to do more road work but he wondered if he was past the point of chasing down younger suspects.

They drove into an area of brick warehouses and a few dilapidated bungalows. Black people walked the pot-holed streets or sat on sagging porches. The taxi stopped in front of a three-story house painted a rich peach color. Its well-maintained condition made it stand out against its rundown neighbors.

Henry Jackson ran out of the house. He joined Sam in the backseat. Sam introduced him to Gus Josie and the cabbie, much to his credit, shook hands with the first black man to ever sit in his cab.

Sam pointed at the bandage on Jackson's forehead. "Looks painful."

"Doesn't hurt at all," he said. "How's your leg?"

"What leg?"

"The one you were limping on last night."

"Nothing wrong with my leg."

"Uh-huh."

Sam turned to Gus, "I assume you know Lady Night's joint."

"Like the back of my hand," the cabbie said, but quickly added, "I mean, I've brought lots of guys there, but I've never been inside. Kinky stuff goes on there, I'm told. I'm like you, Sheriff, I'm a happily married man. I mean, you *were* a happily—"

"That's okay, Gus. I'm still trying to get used to it myself."

Gus drove them past the edge of town and turned onto Old Pelican Road. Sam had him stop at the murder site, and they took off their hats. Across the road, a few cars belonging to mid-morning drinkers were parked in front of the Thirsty Pelican.

"They ought to put up a memorial for Deputy McRae here," Gus said. "But first they should burn that damn bar down."

Sam, however, felt better about the joint now that it had yielded a witness and the first break in the case.

They continued on, past small farms and a one-room Baptist church. Gus stopped the taxi in front of a one-story, bright-red building. Next to the front door, a mural depicting a naked woman and a cocktail glass left no doubt as to its purpose. The cathouse catered to sailors and tourists who liked things on the wild side. But not too wild or the offender would face the wrath of Lady Night and the .45 she kept strapped to her ample waist.

The building stood off the road about fifty yards, with tall pine trees swaying on both sides and the gangly limbs of a Monterrey oak draped over the back roof. Down the road a good distance stood a rickety gray house that looked like the next gust of wind could knock it down.

Sam swept the cathouse with his binoculars. Two black Fords were parked in front. No one patrolled the grounds, but then the midday sun would have made that an unpleasant chore.

"Gus, we need an excuse to be stopped out here," Sam said. "Can you look under the hood like there's a problem with the engine?"

Gus adjusted the black fedora on his head until it was to his liking. He got out and popped open the hood.

Jackson took a turn with the binoculars. "You think the working girls are still in there?"

"I hope not," Sam said. "But maybe someone saw something they shouldn't have."

"It could have gotten messy when Romano's muscle took over the place."

The taxi was beginning to bake. Sam wiped sweat from his brow. "Or, he expects retaliation from Lady Night."

"Was this a regular patrol route for Wayne?" Jackson asked.

"Yeah, twice a week."

Henry Jackson set the binoculars on the seat. "Even if they knew that, they would still have to get him to stop."

"I don't know. It seems too sloppy for Romano. And Drago wouldn't act on his own."

Gus knocked on the cab's fender and began to sing a Gene Autry song off-key. A burly man with a pistol in his belt hurried towards them on the loose stone driveway. Sam and Jackson ducked down low in the backseat. Sam pulled his pistol and held it against his leg.

"The fuck's the problem?" the man asked Gus.

"It overheated," Gus said. "Could I get some water from you?"

"No. There's a gas station about two miles down. Get some water there."

"Listen, a couple of guys want me to bring them here tonight. Is that gonna be a problem?"

"Yeah, it's gonna be a problem because the joint ain't open for business now."

"You gonna reopen soon?"

"Hey, pal, are you deaf?" the man said. "Move this heap on down the road."

The man's heavy footsteps reverberated as he retreated back to the house. Gus slammed the hood and got in the car, cussing the man under his breath.

Sam glassed the house one last time. He wondered how many men were inside. He'd have to come back here with deputies and see if the working girls were being held against their will.

Sam caught movement from the sun-bleached shack down the road. A gray-haired black woman walked out the back door carrying a metal bucket. She pulled out wet laundry and hung it over a single wire strung between two scrawny trees.

"Mrs. August," Jackson said. "She's lived there all her life."

Sam watched her walk back to the house with a slight limp. "Let's pay Mrs. August a visit."

Galveston '44

Chapter 27

While Gus and Jackson watched from the cab, Sam crossed the barren front yard and stepped up onto the rickety porch. Before he could knock, Mrs. August opened the door and wiped her hands on a clean white apron. Her thin face was creased with deep lines, and her hooded eyes gave her the fierce look of a hawk.

Sam doffed his hat. "Mrs. August, I'm Sheriff—"

"I know who you are."

"I'd like to ask you just a couple of questions about the, uh, the place next door."

"Don't know nothin' 'bout it," she said. "I minds my own damn business."

"Yes, ma'am. But I need to know if you saw or heard anything out of the ordinary over there on either Saturday or early Sunday morning."

"It's the same thing every night over there—drinking and carousing and breaking every one of the good Lord's commandments. Shame on you for letting those animals carry on like that."

"I hope I can do something about it, Mrs. August. But first I need to know—"

"Like I told you, I don't know nothin'." She slammed the door. It rattled on its one rusty hinge.

Sam looked over at the whorehouse. He tried to picture a large man or his blond-haired companion—if Horace Session's descriptions were accurate—hitting Wayne in the back of the neck.

If the big man was Drago, who was the other guy?

Maybe Mrs. August hadn't seen anything because there was nothing to see. Or, she had witnessed something and wouldn't cooperate. Negroes had a deep distrust of the police.

Jackson climbed out of the car. "Let me talk to her."

Chapter 28

Jackson knocked on the door and stepped back. Sam stood at a respectable distance behind him. The door swung open hard. Mrs. August stared at Henry Jackson, apparently baffled by the inexplicable association of a black man and a white sheriff.

"Beg pardon, Mrs. August, my name is Henry Jackson," he said, slipping into his other voice—the born and bred drawl of a black man from Southeast Texas. "I'm sorry to bother you again but we got to know what carryings-on you might have seen or heard at that sinful place next to you there."

Mrs. August regarded him with the same suspicion as she had Sam. "What you doin' here with the sheriff? They don't let people like us be no lawman."

"Yes, ma'am, you're right as rain. But you could help us mightily—"

"I don't know nothin'. It's dangerous to know too much."

"I understand," Jackson said. "But anything you tell us won't go nowhere else."

Mrs. August barked out a sharp laugh. "That don't mean a hill a' beans."

"You'd be helping the sheriff close the place down," Jackson said.

"Close it down?"

"If we have the information."

Mrs. August looked over towards the bordello. She hesitated for a long moment. "I promised her I wouldn't say nothin'."

Sam held his breath.

"It was Sunday—maybe midnight or a little after," she went on. "I was asleep but I got woke up by some goldurn car runnin' up and down the road. I looked out and seen it swervin' and runnin' on the side of the road like they crazy. I heard a woman inside the car scream and a man laugh, and they having themselves a good ol' time. Then I heard a loud bang."

"Like a gunshot?" Jackson asked.

"No. Like a car hitting something."

"What kind of car?"

"I couldn't rightly make it out in the dark, but it was a big car, black, if I remember correctly. Had a real shine to it, like it was fairly new."

Mrs. August's gaze drifted out as if she were picturing the scene. "I went back to sleep but got woke up again. Come a noise on my front porch, and I got real scared. I hoped it was just some animal, a coon or a possum. But I heard someone moaning and crying. I peeked out my window and saw a girl lying on the porch. I went out and touched her shoulder and she liked to jump a mile. The whole side of her face was swole up like a balloon. She begged me to let her rest for a minute, then she'd leave."

Sam stepped closer to the porch. "What did she look like?"

"She was kind of honey blond, I guess you'd say. Thin, but not real skinny. And young. Maybe in her late teens or early twenties."

Mrs. August shook her head, remembering. "I helped her inside and laid her on my pallet. I knew some man had walloped her good because her eyes were wild like some poor animal caught in a trap."

"What time was this?" Jackson asked.

"I ain't got no clock but it weren't long after the car smacked into something. She laid there awhile and tried to get up but she couldn't. She could barely tell me her name."

"What was it?"

"Anita. She asked me to call her brother at work, but I don't have no phone. She wrote down his number and name and I ran down to my neighbor's—the Lewis'—and used their phone. About an hour later he drove up. Took the both of us to get that girl into the back seat, she was so torn up. I told Anita God would help her if she asked Him."

"Do you have the number?" Jackson asked.

"I done burned the paper out back with the rest of my trash." Mrs. August said.

"What was her brother's name?"

Mrs. August bowed her head, thinking. "Lord, if I ain't forgot it." She looked off like the name might be written on the wall. She shook her head. "Of late, I been worried about my memory."

Mrs. August whispered names to herself but finally shook her head and gave up. The link to a possible witness to Wayne's murder was locked inside an old woman's brain.

"I can tell you he was 'bout as skinny as his sister," Mrs. August went on. "And he wore a white uniform all covered with flour, like he been baking bread or something. Drove a '32 Ford. I knowed it was because me and my husband had one before he passed."

Jackson pointed at the bordello, shimmering in the heat like a red mirage. "Have you seen any of the women comin' and goin' over there?"

"Ain't seen none of them girls, but yesterday, a couple of men drove up and brought some boxes into the place."

Food, Sam thought.

Sam thanked Mrs. August for the information. He told her again he would try to close the whorehouse down. He hoped to keep that promise but Vince Romano would resist that with all his considerable power.

* * *

They sat in the cab and observed the red building for another moment. Sam hoped to see a woman stroll out and drive off in one of the cars, but nothing moved.

"Looks like a damn prison," Gus said.

Jackson shook his head. "Anita..."

"Yeah," Sam said, sharing his frustration. "Pretty damn common name."

"Mrs. August's description of the car matches what Horace Sessions saw from the Thirsty Pelican," Jackson said. "Black and fairly new."

Sam nodded. "And it hit something. If it was with the left fender then we have a winner."

As Gus reversed the cab back onto the road, Sam took one last look at the whorehouse and its surroundings. Had Wayne McRae been killed there and then driven away in his own squad car? Had the whore named Anita witnessed the murder before she ran?

Sam would return here in the early morning hours and take the place back. He'd kick the back door down and enter fast. Alone. In the war, he'd led soldiers in raids just as this would require. Bringing the deputies would even the odds but he didn't want them getting hurt. And he didn't want the potential chaos that would endanger any captive women.

He'd grab the first man he saw and take him hostage. If the rest didn't surrender or leave, he'd start shooting.

Before Gus could drive off, Mrs. August hurried out and leaned into the backseat.

"Lincoln," she whispered. "The young man's name was Lincoln."

Chapter 29

Sam parked his squad car on the dark street. Two in the morning. No one out other than drunk sailors and broke gamblers. Maybe some bakers, too. Maybe even a skinny one named Lincoln. Two of the deputies were even now scouring bakeries for a man who fit that description.

But *Lincoln?* That could just be a name that had sprung out of Mrs. August's fading memory.

Sam got out and walked over to the jail's back gate and unlocked it. Two cruisers and a few of the deputies' personal cars were parked inside. He unlocked the back door and walked past the lone prisoner—the jail's most frequent guest, Roscoe Petras—sleeping off yet another drunk.

The jail's most important occupant, Horace Sessions, had been transferred to the Mobile, Alabama jail to answer for his burglary there.

Sam peeked inside the front room where Deputy Lowell Turner sat in front of the station-to-station radio, handling calls from the deputies on night patrol. Sam recalled it had been Turner who took the anonymous call from Sessions the night Wayne was killed.

Sam tread softly down the hallway to his office, hoping Turner wouldn't see him popping in at such an odd hour. He closed the door and pulled a leather-sheathed Army knife out of his desk drawer. He'd kept it as a souvenir from the Great War, never thinking he'd actually need it as a lawman. He threaded it through his gun belt and practiced flicking off the thin leather clasp.

He noticed a small package sitting partially covered by the clutter on his desk. He opened it with the knife and the skull-and-crossbones medallion, nestled into tissue paper, stared up at him. For a moment, he thought the killers had sent one to taunt him. But the brief letter inside was from the FBI, detailing their failure to find a connection between it and any person or organization.

He hadn't expected anything more.

Sam slipped the crude medallion into his pocket, went out and quietly slipped a 12-gauge shotgun from the gun rack. When he turned to leave, Deputy Turner stood in the hall, looking at the scattergun and the holstered knife. Turner's forehead creased in confusion.

The deputy had a quick mind and his expression turned from questioning to understanding. "I request permission to go with you, Sheriff Baker."

"Where is it you think I'm going, Deputy Turner?"

"I'm not exactly sure, but I think you're taking a trip back to Lady Night's."

"You have to man the radio."

"Grace can be here in thirty minutes, sir. I'll call her." Turner's dead serious expression and his black eyepatch made him appear older than his twenty years.

Sam couldn't risk losing someone so young, someone who was even a year younger than Wayne had been. But except for Eilers, all the deputies were young. "Nothing to worry about, deputy. I'll call in if there's any trouble."

"Sheriff, if something happened to you, this investigation dies."

That thought had crossed Sam's mind before. Who would take his place as sheriff if he was killed? Eilers was the oldest but wasn't a good lawman. The rest of the deputies had only recently left boyhood and weren't experienced enough to lead an investigation.

Sam nodded. "Grab a rifle."

Turner called Grace and took a Winchester from the rack. Before they reached the back door, Deputy Robicheaux, back from his night patrol, opened it. He looked at Sam and Deputy Turner and their guns—and their resolute expressions.

"We got trouble?" Robicheaux asked.

"Something Deputy Turner and I can handle," Sam said. "Man the radio until Grace comes in."

"Sheriff, I would like to go with you."

Sam hesitated but Robicheaux deserved to be involved in anything having to do with solving Wayne's murder. The young man had had to witness the bloody result of two gunshots to his friend's face.

Sam was proud of his young deputies. He waited until he was sure his voice wouldn't betray him. "All right. We'll take two cruisers. Turner, you go with me."

Galveston '44

Chapter 30

Sam pulled the squad car into a small clearing just down the road from Mrs. August's house. Deputy Robicheaux parked behind him. They climbed out, and a family of raccoons scurried back into the thicket. No car lights appeared on the two-lane road.

Henry Jackson, wearing all black, stepped out from the dense undergrowth. He nodded in greeting. "Sheriff," he said. "I'm glad you decided not to do this thing by yourself."

"I had some persuasive volunteers."

Jackson shook hands with the deputies. Sam had briefed them about the oddity of a civilian being part of the raid. Still, Deputy Turner seemed mystified by a black man materializing from the dark forest at three in the morning.

Sam studied Lady Night's building with his binoculars. It sat dark and quiet, but this time there was only one car parked in front, a gray Ford. Unlike earlier, it sat several yards from the structure and faced the road.

Jackson pointed at the building. "You noticed the car?"

"Yeah. Looks like it's ready for a quick getaway," Sam said. "Any sign of life?"

"Nobody's been outside, but I did see a light in the side window for a couple of minutes."

"What about Mrs. August?"

"She's been gone all day. Got back about seven."

Sam calculated a gap of eight hours when there weren't eyes on the building. He gathered everyone around him. "Okay, we'll run through that stand of trees over there and then separate. Deputy Turner—you take a position in the back behind one of the oak trees there. Do not expose yourself to gunfire. If one of the guards runs out the backdoor, give the order to surrender. If he doesn't comply, shoot him."

"What if it's one of the hookers?" Turner asked.

"Announce who you are and order her to stop. If she runs, chase her down and hold her. We need a witness."

Sam turned to Robicheaux. "You will follow me in through the front door. Stay low. Only return fire if they resist arrest. And make sure it's not one of the girls."

"How are you going to get through the front door?" Jackson asked.

"Kick it in."

"What if you can't?"

"I never met a door I couldn't kick in."

"I can get it open without a sound," Jackson said.

"How?"

Henry Jackson held up two thin pieces of metal, each about five inches long. One had a curved end just wide enough for a finger to slip through. "Took them off a burglar a couple years ago."

"How do you know they'll—"

"I never met a lock I couldn't pick."

Sam remembered Horace Sessions had asked Jackson how he got into the Thirsty Pelican without making a noise and hadn't received an answer...Jackson had picked the lock. "Okay, you get the door unlocked and then get behind that car. Do not follow us in. You got it?"

Jackson nodded but maintained his usual poker face.

Sam asked, "And what do you mean you took a set of lock picks from a burglar?"

"I used to be a cop. A detective."

Sam had to let that sink in a moment. Turner looked as

though Jackson had told them he was from Mars. Robicheaux only nodded.

"A detective?" Sam said. "Where?"

"In Atlanta. I was the second beat cop ever and the first to make detective."

"Why aren't you still on the force?" Sam asked.

"That's a story for another time."

"Deputy Robicheaux. You knew this?"

The deputy nodded. "Yes, sir. He told me and Wayne."

Jackson looked at Sam. "Go ahead. Say something because your mouth is already open."

"Okay. No wonder you're such an arrogant know-it-all."

Sam led them behind Mrs. August's house and through the stand of pine trees. They reached the clearing and ran.

Turner fanned out to the back of the building. Jackson and Robicheaux followed Sam to the front.

A large rusty refrigerator stood at the side of the front door. Sam pointed at it. Jackson shook his head—it hadn't been there earlier in the day. Some warped skillets and broken plates littered the ground on either side of the porch.

Henry Jackson inserted both pins into the keyhole. He worked the top one around until they heard a faint click. He gave Sam a smug look and dropped back.

"Galveston County Sheriff," Sam shouted. He pushed the door open wide. He and Robicheaux rushed in, staying low to the floor, and stopped. Even in the dark they could see there was no furniture. They listened for a moment but heard nothing. Sam swept the room with his flashlight. Piles of trash and broken furniture lay scattered on the wooden floor of the large room.

Sam turned off the flashlight and they advanced. The front window rattled from a gust of wind and echoed in the empty room. The doors of every side room stood wide open. Unless the guards and the women hid in one or more of them—or in the back room—the place had been vacated.

Sam smelled something faint. Gasoline or kerosene. He turned to Robicheaux and sniffed. The deputy shook his head. He hadn't smelled it.

Sam shone the light on the walls and saw something odd—cardboard and chunks of busted wood were piled up against the wall between the open doors. Some of the stacked pieces were lengths of tree branches, set vertically like a campfire. What was under the wood? He'd seen booby traps in the war—usually a German helmet or some other tempting souvenir that, if touched, would set off a bomb.

He decided to be cautious and take cover outside. No one inside would be able to leave, and daylight would allow them and the fire chief to get a better look at the suspicious setting.

He gestured to Robicheaux for them to leave. They had taken a couple of steps towards the door when a faint sound came from the rear of the building.

Sam pointed the flashlight. A man filled the doorway and lit what appeared to be a glass bottle with a lighter. He threw the flaming container, and it shattered in front of them. Flames roared across the wood floor to lick at their legs. Robicheaux screamed. His uniform pants had caught fire.

The man threw another Molotov cocktail. The flames leapt higher, igniting the broken furniture and trash. Sam fired several rounds at him. He pushed Robicheaux down, beat on the flames blackening his pants legs.

They rose, but before they reached the front door one of the piles of wood against the wall exploded into a huge fireball. The next pile exploded and the next in a series that rushed towards them. The walls on both sides of the room burst into flames as high as the ceiling. The room lit up like a giant furnace.

They crawled to the front door and pushed. It wouldn't budge. He and Robicheaux stood and pushed again but gained only an inch. Through the narrow opening, Sam could see that something large and white blocked it from the outside. *The refrigerator.*

They yelled for help and pounded on the door. The flames grew closer. They were going to die here. Images of Claire and Sylvie flashed in Sam's mind. And Wayne—he had failed Wayne.

Shots resounded, loud enough to be heard over the roar of the fire.

A face appeared in the narrow opening of the door. It was Jackson. "Push!"

Sam and Robicheaux pushed as Jackson pulled on the refrigerator. It opened just wide enough that they could squeeze out. They collapsed on the ground, their chests heaving for air.

Jackson kneeled over Robicheaux. With a switchblade he cut away the bottom of the deputy's blackened pants.

Robicheaux grimaced but shook his head. "I don't think it's too bad."

Sam rose on his elbow. He looked at the refrigerator lying against the door where someone had dumped it. He shielded his eyes against the spreading flames and saw a man lying in the shadow of the icebox.

"He's dead," Jackson said. "He ran out from the side of the house and pushed the refrigerator over against the door. They obviously had it ready to go."

Sam rolled him over. He was heavyset, with a flat nose and scar tissue around his eyes. *Maybe a former boxer*, Sam thought. His white t-shirt was stained by a circle of blood coming from his chest. A .38 lay by his hand.

Sam looked at Henry Jackson. "I didn't know you were

armed."

"You didn't ask."

"What took you so damn long?" Sam asked. "It was getting a tad bit warm in there."

"I wanted to wait until you'd be grateful."

"You know what?" Sam said. "I'm going to let it slide this time." Then he remembered... "Turner!"

They ran around to the back of the building where the deputy stood over a man lying on his back. The glow of flames engulfing the structure cast an orange glow over them. "Sheriff, he was shot before he come out the door."

The man was younger than the other one. A black patch covered one eye—just like the one Turner wore. The other eye rolled in pain.

The man who threw the Molotov cocktails, Sam thought. He pulled the man's hands from his chest where blood glistened on his black shirt. He gripped Sam's hand as he fought for breath.

Sam sent Turner to his squad car to call for the fire department and an ambulance.

"Hang on, man," Sam said. "Help is on the way."

"That's a good one, Sheriff," the man said. He coughed. Something rattled in his chest. "That's really rich."

"Who sent you?"

Jackson pointed at the man's right hand which was missing the middle and ring fingers.

Sam nodded. The man was a professional who had lost a couple fingers and an eye while learning his trade. "Did Vince Romano hire you?"

"Never heard of him."

"Your buddy who dumped the refrigerator says it was Romano," Sam lied. "He's in front singing like a bird."

Blood seeped out of the man's mouth. His breathing

slowed. His body relaxed. "It doesn't hurt anymore," he said. A shuddering breath escaped his mouth. His one good eye stared up at the treetops but saw nothing more than the patched one.

Robicheaux made the sign of the cross.

Galveston '44

Chapter 31

The rain that had held off until late morning now drove in at a slant against the cruiser's windshield. Sam parked in his driveway and ran to the house. Rags came to greet him when he walked inside and took off his wet boots.

"Sylvie?" he called, knowing she was gone by the way the little mutt watched him. The profound silence made the house seem larger, emptier. It was like he and Rags lived with a family of ghosts—three of them, by his count. He had hoped to talk with Sylvie for a moment. He had to admit he'd been shaken by the flames licking at his back earlier. They could talk about the damn weather for all he cared. He wouldn't mention the attempt on his and Robicheaux's lives. Or the high probability that Vince Romano—her boyfriend's father—had ordered it.

She would hear about it soon enough. So would Claire.

He didn't know if Sylvie had learned to read his expressions, but Claire could merely look into his eyes and suspect that something serious had gone down. She wouldn't press him too much, caring mainly that he was all right. On such occasions, she'd watch him knock down a shot of whiskey without her usual disapproving look.

Sam took the amber bottle from the kitchen cupboard and poured a shot of whiskey. He set it on the kitchen table and sat down. Out in the backyard, rain had filled in a low spot that Billy and Sylvie used to splash around in until they were covered in mud.

Next to the makeshift pond, water ran off the roof of his

boxing shed. Pounding the heavy bag right now would be the best antidote to his jangled nerves but he needed to get back to headquarters and deal with the firebombing of Lady Night's cathouse. The building had burned to a blackened shell of charred cinder block even before the fire department had arrived.

Right after the fire chief began his investigation of the cause of fire, Clyde Hermann, the medical examiner, arrived to determine the cause of death of the two men lying near the blackened result of the firebombs they had triggered.

Sam could have told the fire chief the cause of the fire was gasoline bombs intended to kill him and anyone else unfortunate enough to enter the building with him. And he could have told Hermann the cause of death of the two arsonists—one bullet each to the chest, one from him and the other from Henry Jackson.

Sam had told Jackson to take off. The mere presence of a Negro on the scene—especially one who had shot a suspect— would shine an unwelcome spotlight on the raid.

Mrs. August had let Jackson hide in her house. She probably hadn't believed Sam when he promised her he would try to close down the rowdy whorehouse. But he hadn't expected to shutter it so soon and so completely.

The tough old woman deserved thanks for her information about the big black car that the probable killer of Wayne McRae had crashed into something with its left fender. She'd also gone out of her way to help the working girl Anita, who the same man had probably punched.

Sam had three of his deputies out searching for her brother. *Lincoln,* Mrs. August had said. Sam could only hope that the name she had unearthed from her fading memory was accurate. He was the only link to the girl, but so far they hadn't been able to locate him. Maybe he wasn't a baker or a milkman after all.

When Sam had driven past Mrs. August's sagging house at first light, he figured the best way to pay her back would be to send a crew of carpenters over there to shore up the sagging house before it collapsed on her.

If Claire were around she could see what Mrs. August needed in the way of pots and pans. Maybe a new pallet and a clock.

But Claire wasn't here, and now he was glad she was safe in Dallas.

Sam hesitated before picking up the phone. He dropped it back in its cradle and picked up the glass of whiskey. Without drinking, he set it down and picked up the phone again.

Galveston '44

Chapter 32

The Whittington's housekeeper, Olive, peeked around the corner of the library entrance where Claire sat reading a book.

"Miss Claire," she said. "You have a phone call from a gentleman."

Regis Underwood, Claire thought. He'd called every day since they'd had lunch at one of the most expensive and, in her opinion, ostentatious restaurants in Dallas. Like her brother, Regis owned a family bank and had a friendly rivalry with him. Regis had been charming and gracious. He was well-read, had travelled the world over. He had asked her to take a trip with him to Hawaii, which, he assured her, would someday become a state.

Claire had been content to let him talk about himself. She hadn't wanted to discuss her separation from her husband or the murder of her daughter's boyfriend. It was the first date she'd had with a man other than Sam since she was twenty-one years old and about to graduate from the University of Texas.

She picked up the phone. "This is Claire."

She heard a man's voice, but the connection crackled and faded. "Regis, is that you?"

"No, it's me, Sam."

She was surprised to hear his voice, and for a moment, she panicked. "Sam! Is everything all right?"

"We're all doing okay, Claire. I, uh, I'm just sitting here with Rags. He seems to have decided I'm not such a bad guy after all."

She heard tension in his voice. Maybe because they hadn't spoken since they'd exchanged a few awkward words at Wayne's funeral.

"You're home at this time of the afternoon?" She felt a surge of hope that Sam had captured Wayne's killer and was calling to tell her. Her desire for justice surprised her. "Does that mean you found the—"

"No, but we're making progress."

"That's what you tell the press, Sam." He had always confided in her before—but that was before.

"We have a description of the car and the two killers," Sam said. "The problem is that one of them could be Drago."

"Oh, Sam..." Claire pictured the huge man—mute, menacing. Trying to arrest Vince Romano's bodyguard would take more men than the Galveston Sheriff's Department had at its disposal.

"I'm not sure it's him. Our witness saw a very large man but no facial features."

"Why would Vince want to kill Wayne?" Claire asked.

"There's a couple possible motives."

She wanted to tell him to quit, to move out of Galveston. But she knew he would never back down from a fight. That was the part of him she'd always had trouble accepting.

"Claire, I hate to tell you this, but earlier this morning we raided one of Romano's joints where we think Wayne was killed. It was empty except for two men who tried to take me out."

"Oh, God—" The sitting room, full of stuffed chairs and couches closed in on her. "Are you okay?"

"I'm fine. Gilbert Robicheaux got burned on his leg but he'll be all right."

"Burned?"

"They tried to trap us inside with firebombs. We, uh, well,

we had to kill two men."

She sighed, deeper than she had intended. "Romano's men?"

"Outsiders, but more than likely hired by Vince."

"Sam, it almost sounds like a war."

"That's why I called, Claire. I want to get Sylvie up there with you in Dallas."

"Why?" She stood. The thought that her last remaining child could be in danger made her stomach clench. "Why would someone want to hurt Sylvie?"

"I just want to make sure she's safe." She heard an undertone of concern in his attempt to reassure her. "I don't know where this thing is going," Sam added.

Olive walked in with the Hoover but left when she saw Claire was still on the phone.

"I'm sorry, Claire. It looks like you got out just in time."

Maybe, she thought. She had left because of the constant dread that her husband would be killed. But she had learned that being a few hundred miles away hadn't lessened that fear.

"Would you ask Sylvie to go up there until this thing blows over?"

"Of course, Sam."

"Thank you," he said. "And Claire..."

He cleared his throat. She waited for him to speak. She knew him well enough to know that he was choosing his words carefully.

"I'm sorry I hung up on you that day."

She remembered the rejection she'd felt the day of Wayne's murder when she wanted to come back to Galveston and help her husband deal with it.

"That's okay, Sam," Claire said. "It was a bad day."

Galveston '44

Chapter 33

The late-afternoon sun cast long shadows from a row of beach houses on the west end of the island. Built on tall stilts, the houses were modest at best, ramshackle at worst. Under one, a scrawny mongrel sprawled. Under another, chickens clucked and pecked for food in a pen built from sun-bleached boards and rusty chicken wire.

A stone's throw away, a tall man stood on the shore and cast his fishing line into the caramel-colored waters of the Gulf. The man didn't seem to be having any luck. Over and over he cast the hook and sinker into the water, only to reel them back in without the reward of a catch. Further down the beach, another fisherman seemed to be suffering the same lack of success.

An early 1930's Chevrolet wheezed to a stop at the edge of the community. A young man wearing a white uniform climbed out. He carried a paper bag and walked as quickly as the soft sand would allow.

The two anglers dropped their fishing poles and ran towards him. The young man scrambled back to his car, but Sam caught him and threw him onto the hood.

He held the skinny man with one arm and with the other pulled his badge out of his pants.

"Galveston County Sheriff."

"I didn't do nothing."

"Are you Lincoln Bragg?"

"Never heard of him," the man said.

Deputy Gilbert Robicheaux ran up and searched the man.

155

He pulled out his wallet and held up his driver's license to Sam. *Lincoln D. Bragg.*

"What does the D stand for, Lincoln? Doughnut?" Sam said. "Tell him about his job, Deputy Robicheaux."

"You make donuts at Supreme Donuts. At least you did until they fired you."

Lincoln's expression lost its defiance.

"What did Deputy Garza think of the doughnuts over there, Deputy?"

"He liked the glazed with chocolate icing, but he didn't cotton to the crullers."

After canvassing bakeries, milk companies, and doughnut shops–any place where employees might wear white uniforms—Deputy Garza had discovered that a man named Lincoln Bragg had worked at Supreme Doughnuts. His former boss only knew that Lincoln lived in a beach house on the west end of the island.

They had surveilled the area for two days and had almost lost hope of finding Lincoln—and by extension—the young working girl whom the killer had punched.

Sam gave a silent thanks to Mrs. August for correctly remembering the man's name.

Sam pulled him off the car's hood. "Where is your sister?"

"I ain't got no sister."

"She's not in trouble. Not with us, anyway."

Lincoln looked down the row of beach houses. "She's going to be mad."

"Let me worry about that."

Sam let him up from the hood. The young man stooped and picked up the paper bag. "How did you know who I was, anyway?"

"How many ex-donut cutters still wear their uniforms?"

Lincoln led them to a weathered house that seemed to list

156

on its stilts. They followed him up the rickety stairs, and Sam rapped on the door. "Anita?"

A young, thin woman with blond hair covering one side of her face appeared behind the screen door. Through the ripped mesh she looked like a mirage that Sam feared would retreat with each step he approached.

"Anita Bragg?" Sam asked. He showed her his badge. "I'm Sheriff Sam Baker."

"Yeah, I know who you are." She unlocked the door and gave her brother a searing look.

Lincoln shrugged. "He looked like a goddamn fisherman."

"A fisherman that doesn't use any damn bait?"

"Have you got a gun, Anita?" Sam asked.

"Yeah. It's in my right pocket," she said, slurring her word like she'd been drinking.

Sam told her to put her hands on her head and turn around. He walked in and took a .32 caliber pistol out of her dress pocket. She folded her arms across her chest and glared at her brother again. "He just cast his line over and over. So did his buddy."

"So next time go out and get your own damn food."

Sam pointed at the door. "Why don't you take a walk, Lincoln."

Lincoln looked like he thought Sam was kidding, then scrambled out the door.

Small beads of sweat dotted Anita's forehead. A squeaky fan on the kitchen counter blew hot air around the one-room house. A pallet with a neatly folded blanket hugged the far wall. A wad of dirty sheets lay crumpled in the corner— Lincoln's bed, Sam figured.

Sam pushed Anita's long hair away from the side of her face. The left cheek was swollen and bruised, with a particularly large lump along the jawline. Sam had seen plenty of broken jaws in his life, both on boxers in the wrong line of work and drunks overmatched in a street fight. No wonder she had slurred her words.

"I think it may be only dislocated," he said. "But we'll get you to a doctor."

She shook her head. "I'm not leaving here."

Sam could see the fear in her eyes. She had run for her life after witnessing the murder of a young lawman. If Mrs. August hadn't taken her in, she might be dead.

"Who hit you, Anita?"

"Nobody hit me, Sheriff," she said. "I fell."

"We spoke with Mrs. August next door to Lady Night's. You fit her description. Your brother's, too.

"There's lots of girls that look like me."

"We'll protect you, Anita. I have a safe house you can stay in."

"The law never did nothing for me."

Sam looked at Robicheaux. The deputy stopped writing in his notebook and said, "That man not only killed a deputy sheriff, Anita, he killed our friend. You're the only one who can identify the killer."

Anita touched the swollen side of her face. She looked out to the Gulf for a moment. "He gave his name as Rumpelstiltskin."

"Anita—"

"I'm not lying. He also said it was President Roosevelt. Then it was Winston Churchill and so on. He thought it was a big joke."

"He didn't say Drago?" Sam asked.

"No. Everybody knows who Drago is."

Sam and Robicheaux exchanged a look. The possibility that Vince Romano's bodyguard had killed Wayne fell away. Part of Sam felt relieved, but that left them without a suspect.

"What happened that night?"

Anita took a deep breath. "When Romano took over the place, they kicked all the other girls out except me and one other. They said we would have a special visitor who liked blondes. So this huge bastard and another guy showed up."

"Describe them."

"The big man was maybe in his late twenties. He had short blond hair and gray eyes. Kind of a square face."

"Any scars or tattoos?"

Anita shook her head. "Nothing like that. But he was kind of small down there for such a big man, if you know what I mean."

Sam stifled a smile. "What about the other guy?"

"Maybe a couple of years older. He was kind of muscular, too, but not like the big guy."

"Why did they clear all the other girls out?"

"They didn't say, but I figured he was some sort of big shot. Somebody important who Vince Romano didn't want anybody to see."

"What happened to the other girl?"

"I don't know," Anita said and her voice quavered. "I hope to god she got out. Her name is Cindy Larsen, if that matters."

"It matters a lot."

Sam nodded at Robicheaux, but he was already writing her name down.

"You went joyriding with the big guy?"

"Yeah, he was driving crazy up and down the road. He hit a damn sign and that's when your deputy showed up."

Sam nodded. The image of Wayne appearing on the scene was vivid—almost too real. "Describe the car."

"It was a blue Lincoln. Pretty new, I think."

"Blue?"

"Yeah, dark blue."

"You're sure?"

"Sheriff, I might be a damn hooker, but I'm not stupid," Anita said. "The car was dark blue."

Sam looked at Robicheaux and knew by his expression that they shared the same frustration—they had been looking for the wrong car. Horace Sessions had described the car that picked up the big man as a *black* Lincoln. But it had been dark across the road from the Thirsty Pelican, he had said.

"Was the car dented when it hit the sign?" Sam asked.

"Yeah, the left fender. And the headlight was smashed in."

Sam nodded, relieved that at least some of their previous information was correct. He signaled for Anita to continue.

"The deputy asked for his driver's license, but the man just laughed and said he had lost it. McRae walked back to his car. I figured he was going to call for backup, but the older guy came out shouting and waving his hands. The deputy walked towards him and ordered him to stop.

Sam's heart beat faster. This was the recounting of the last moment of Wayne's young life.

Anita looked off as if watching the same scene as Sam. "One of Romano's guards ran out carrying a pistol. The deputy pulled his gun and told him to stop. The big fucker came off the car and hit him in the back of the neck. It happened so fast."

Sam felt like he'd been hit in the gut. According to the medical examiner, the cause of Wayne's death was a blow to the back of the neck. A sucker punch powerful enough to break bones in the upper spine.

The endless surf breaking on the beach was the only sound that could be heard in the beach house. Robicheaux had quit taking notes. "The son-of-a-bitch," he said under his breath.

Sam pointed to her swollen jaw. "And then he hit you?"

"Yeah, I started to run, but he backhanded me and I went

down. When I came to they were carrying the deputy to his car. I got up and ran."

"You went to Mrs. August's house?"

Anita nodded. "She saved my life."

"Did you hear any gunshots when you were there?"

"All I could hear was a damn buzzing in my head." Her voice trailed off and she sat down on an unpainted wood chair. Sam filled a glass with water from the kitchen faucet and handed it to her. She would need a doctor for her jaw and a safe place to stay.

Anita's role ended when her brother picked her up. She wouldn't know that the two men drove Wayne's squad car away from Lady Night's with him lying dead in the backseat. The other man followed in the dark blue Lincoln. They stopped along the way and pulled Wayne's body from the car and shot him twice in the head where he lay.

Couldn't they see he was already dead? That was the image that would stay with Sam forever.

But the nightmare went on from there. They threw him in the backseat of the car again before stopping across the road from the Thirsty Pelican. The big man then put him back in the front seat and placed the skull-and-crossbones medallion—the one that now resided in Sam's pocket—in his prayerful hands.

Wayne had come along at the wrong time. He tried to take control of a bad situation, and it cost him his life.

What did Vince Romano have planned that he needed outside professionals for? These men were important enough to him that he chased off every prostitute except for two blonds so their identities could be protected.

Robicheaux snapped his notebook shut and stared at the floor. The deputy, like Sam, now had a clear picture of the last violent moments of their good friend's life.

The big man now had a face and it wasn't Drago's. And the Lincoln was blue, not black.

Anita Bragg had seen the car up close and rode in it with the killer. Dark blue, she swore. And Sam knew who had a dark blue Lincoln.

Arin Haugen.

Chapter 34

The taxi pushed a wake of rainwater across Seawall Boulevard while its headlights struggled to penetrate a misty fog. Gus Josie turned up the volume on the car radio as he and Sam listened to the grim war news. *Nazis troops,* the announcer said, *today massacred over 600 inhabitants of the French town of Oradour-sur-Glane in response to the kidnapping of a German officer by the Resistance. Incendiary devices turned the village into rubble.*

Sam and Gus didn't speak for a while, even after the radio had been turned off. Finally, almost whispering, Gus said, "I hate them bastards more than I got words for."

Sam caught Gus' eye in the rearview mirror and nodded. The bitterness he felt towards the Nazi military machine after Billy was killed already consumed him. The only solace he had these days was in knowing that the tide in the war had turned in the Allies' favor. The sooner it ended the sooner Billy's remains might be identified and returned.

Gus drove the cab past the hotels and restaurants across from the Gulf. Down below the seawall, the storm-driven waves pounded the deserted beach.

They pulled up beside a white '38 Ford parked across from the Hotel Tropicana, looming tall and gray in the dense fog. The driver, Deputy Gilbert Robicheaux, wore a straw cowboy hat pulled low over his forehead. Robicheaux was the only deputy enlisted for this evening's venture, this shot in the dark.

"I didn't see any Lincolns come out of the hotel, Sheriff," Robicheaux said. "But it's getting kind of hard to see with this

163

damn fog."

Sam nodded. "We'll take it from here, deputy. Go get some dinner."

Robicheaux drove off, and Gus pulled the cab into his spot. He flashed his headlights and Henry Jackson, sitting in his black Ford, answered with his. If they were able to spot Haugen or Romano drive off in their respective cars, it remained a long shot that they would lead them to the big man and his older partner.

Romano and Drago were keeping a low profile. They wouldn't have gone underground if Sam had perished in the fire at Lady Night's. Romano knew that Sam would come back after him. By the same token, Romano might try to finish the job.

But, Arin Haugen—how the hell was he involved in all this? It was one thing to pressure the governor to take Sam off the investigation, but another entirely if his car had been used during the killing of Wayne McRae. Yes, the murder wasn't premeditated, but would he really lend the killers his car so they could visit a raunchy whorehouse, one where all the working girls except two had been sent home? And why would he risk his reputation as Galveston's most prominent civic leader and most generous philanthropist?

On one hand, Sam hoped that Haugen's Lincoln wasn't the car in question. On the other hand, if it didn't have a dented fender, they would have to search for one that did. Like looking for a needle in a haystack.

A shiny Bentley drove into the hotel's carriage porch and a uniformed doorman helped an elderly couple out of the car. A bellman pulled their suitcases from the trunk.

Sam settled in for what could be a long wait. Gus adjusted his black fedora on his head and kept his eyes glued on the hotel. His narrow face had the fixed intensity of a junk yard dog when it hears the wind rattle a wire fence.

If he wasn't so eccentric—too much of a round peg—he would be an outstanding detective on someone's force somewhere. He had hinted that he wanted be a deputy, but Sam knew he wouldn't survive the day-to-day duties of a working cop—the rowdy johns, the brawling sailors. The underbelly of the Free State of Galveston.

Rain-streaked cars entered and exited the hotel's garage. Guests walked in and out of the brass doors.

"Sheriff?" Gus said. "I gotta say, I got respect for that Henry Jackson fella. Now I can see how he became the first colored detective on the Atlanta police force.

"He knows his stuff, all right." *Even if he is a little arrogant about it,* Sam thought.

"You ever wonder why he ain't on the force now?"

"Yeah. But I don't think he wants to talk about it."

Time passed and the exiting of cars from the parking garage slowed. Sam thought about how good it would feel to be in bed. He remembered how Claire used to hate when he would be gone all night on a stakeout, worried that he wouldn't come home at all.

He knew that Mrs. Josie—and the one boy still living with them—also resented Gus' absence for the few dollars he earned. Money that came out of Sam's own pocket.

A cream-colored Dodge pulled into the circular drive and stopped just before it reached the doorman. A short man jumped out of the passenger seat. The fog obscured his facial features but Sam could see that he had a barrel chest and the big biceps of a man who lifted weights or worked hard labor. His bald head shone in the light of the bright Tropicana sign.

"Swinging dick?" Gus asked.

"Maybe."

The man took a quick surveillance of his surroundings

165

before disappearing inside the hotel. The Dodge circled the drive and hit the street too fast to see the license plate.

Gus started the car. "He sure as hell was curious about who had eyes on him."

"You recognize him?"

"No, but I would if I see him again."

A cream-colored LaSalle exited the garage. Then a 1940 Ford.

Sam looked at his watch—time seemed to have slowed. He shook his head to stay awake.

Gus pointed. "Sheriff..."

A late model Lincoln filled the garage door opening. Dented left fender. Dark blue.

"Let's go," Sam said.

Chapter 35

The Lincoln hit the street and accelerated. Its tires spun on the wet pavement and gained traction. Headlights from a passing car threw a glint of light on the bald man's head. Jackson eased his black Ford away from the seawall and followed. Gus swung the taxi around and joined the chase.

"The car had both its headlights," Sam said.

"Maybe they replaced the broken one."

Sam caught a glimpse of the Lincoln's taillights before they disappeared into darkness. He didn't see the Ford either, but he knew Jackson would run without his headlights.

The Lincoln and the Ford came into view just as they turned away from the seawall. Gus made the turn, and the cab's tires slid for a few seconds before it regained traction. In the fog a gas station and a string of stores flashed by.

The Lincoln turned again. And again at the next block.

Sam leaned forward. "Either the guy is lost or he's checking to see if someone's following him."

"This is what they call a classic evasive maneuver," Gus said. "Read about it in *True Detective* magazine. Guys will circle around like this sumbitch is doing and come back to the same place they started."

Sam kept his silence in the hope that Gus wouldn't go on about detective and surveillance techniques.

"What caught my eye at the newsstand was the main story in the magazine," Gus said. "Had to do with a boxer and a nymphomaniac. Made me think of you."

Sam's curiosity got the better of him. "Why me?"

"Because you were a boxer." Gus drove relaxed, despite the wet streets and poor visibility. "Title of the article was *'Boxer's Fatal K.O. by a Ravishing Nymphomaniac'*."

"What a way to go," Sam said. He pointed at the two cars ahead of them. "Let's take our turn up front."

Gus accelerated past Jackson's Ford and cut the headlights.

They hit a heavier patch of fog and the Lincoln almost disappeared into the void. They found its taillights again as it turned into a commercial district of car repair shops and fenced-in junkyards. Dim lights shone in only the occasional building.

The Lincoln slowed. Behind them, the vague outline of Jackson's car appeared. All three cars moved at a crawl.

"Gus, if he turns around and comes this way…"

The cabbie looked at him in the rearview mirror until he understood. "You want me to ram his car?"

"I'll get you a new car even if I have to steal one."

"Okay, Sheriff."

The Lincoln pulled into a driveway and stopped at a chain link fence surrounding a low-slung building. The fog obscured the name on the weather-beaten sign. "What is this place?" Sam asked.

"Anthony's Garage," Gus said. "Car repair and salvage yard."

"They chop cars?"

Gus pulled the car over. "That's the talk on the street."

The bald man jumped out of the blue Lincoln. Its headlights cast his shadow against the gray building.

A huge dog behind the fence growled and lunged against the gate.

The bald man shouted something unintelligible at the building, as angry as the dog. A muted exterior light came on.

A lanky man in baggy overalls hurried out and unlocked the gate. He hauled the dog off by its collar, and the bald man drove the Lincoln into the darkness of the salvage yard.

Sam thought about climbing the fence, but realized that several strands of barbed wire ran along the top of it. "I've seen prisons weren't this secure."

"Looks like a Nazi concentration camp."

Sam looked to the other side of the street where Jackson's Ford now sat in front of a small trailer. "I'm going to talk with him," Sam said.

He ran to the Ford and jumped in. Jackson's big hands gripped the steering wheel and his eyes were focused on the garage.

"The fog makes for good cover," Jackson said.

Sam nodded. "You see any more guys than the one who unlocked the gate?"

"Just him and that junk yard dog."

A car came towards them, its tires pushing a small wake in the street water. They ducked down in their seats as the headlights played over the Ford. The car moved on.

"They could already be putting the torch to the car," Sam said. He felt helpless. No way would they open the gate even if he announced himself as sheriff. "If I had my car, I'd crash it through that damn gate."

Jackson looked at him a moment and then fired up the engine. "Hell, I'm game. Only cost me fifty dollars to rebuild this engine."

"Wait—" Sam said and pointed.

Galveston '44

Chapter 36

The lanky man swung the gate open. A car drove out from the salvage yard. The streetlight identified the bald man but he was driving a '41 Chevy, not the blue Lincoln.

The car hit the street at a good clip.

Jackson revved his engine. "Follow or stay?"

"He's in a goddamn hurry for some reason," Sam said. "Let's go."

Jackson eased out into the street, and the taxi followed.

The Chevy took a quick right turn into an area where the modest buildings and houses turned to low-rent hotels and gambling dens.

The Chevy slowed and pulled to the curb in front of a two-story flophouse—a dilapidated joint where street whores brought their johns and where merchant marines rented rooms to sleep off their shore-leave drunk. No matter the purpose of it guests, the darkness under its extended eaves provided some anonymity.

Jackson parked several car lengths down from the Chevy. Gus drove past them and pulled over across the street.

Footsteps echoed on the wooden walkway as a couple—a man in a sailor cap and a woman in a tight black dress—tottered past them and disappeared under the eaves.

The street grew quiet again.

"Do you think he might have been a decoy?" Jackson said. "Lead us away from the garage so they could do their business with the Lincoln?"

Sam shook his head. "I get the feeling he's here for a

reason."

A light from the second story blinked on and a breeze ruffled the curtains of the open window. A hand reached for the shade and pulled it down. The light went out.

A moment later, a gray shadow appeared beside the door and stood ramrod straight, like a sentry settling in.

Sam raised his chin towards the hotel. "You see him?"

"Yeah. Maybe he's waiting there to welcome Mr. Muscles."

"Damn hospitable of him."

A Ford pickup sped past Gus' taxi and slid to a stop on the wet street. The bald man climbed out of the Chevy and ran to the truck. He jumped in and it sped off.

Jackson slapped the car into gear. "We want the bald man or the car?"

"Look, he left the motor running," Sam said. Exhaust rose from the back of the Chevy and merged with the fog. "Let's stay."

The man under the eaves took a step away from the open door and his form grew more distinct. He appeared lean and fit, his body tensed like a runner ready to push off the blocks.

Someone walked out from the doorway and accepted something from the man. The figure—a blond woman in a red dress—emerged from the eaves, her heels clattering on the boardwalk as she passed. Tears glistened on her cheeks.

As if the woman's departure had created a vacuum, the door opened again and another shadow walked out. The two men hurried from the eaves and out into the dim moonlight. The first man jumped behind the wheel of the waiting Chevrolet. The second man climbed into the passenger seat. He had moved quickly but left no doubt as to his size. Just as big as Horace Sessions had described. Bigger than Drago, Anita Bragg had said.

"That's him," Sam said and gripped the dashboard. "That's the son-of-a-bitch."

The Chevy lurched away from the curb. Jackson followed, keeping his lights off.

Gus turned the cab around and followed them, his lights dulled by the curtain of rain that began to fall again.

The white Chevy picked up speed and Jackson pushed the Ford harder, its engine humming without strain. At least they wouldn't be outrun. The Chevrolet turned. It turned again and headed back into the business district. Only a few cars were still out braving the rain and the fog.

The Chevy passed two cars and accelerated. They made another turn and entered the warehouse district. Cotton warehouses flashed by.

"Maybe they're going back to the salvage yard," Jackson said.

But the Chevy turned into another area of older two-story buildings and slowed. Just as Jackson eased up on the gas pedal, the Chevy accelerated again.

Henry closed the distance but a car pulled out of a side street, and he swerved to avoid it. The Ford slid sideways and almost stopped before Jackson could straighten it out. He caught up to a pair of taillights but they belonged to an old panel truck.

The Chevy had disappeared.

Henry Jackson pounded the steering wheel with his fist. *"No!"*

Sam pointed ahead where a pair of headlights came at them fast. "Cut them off!"

Jackson gripped the steering wheel hard, ready to ram the car. But he stopped. "It's Gus."

The cab pulled up beside them. Gus looked distraught. "I couldn't keep up, Sheriff. I'm sorry."

Sam pointed ahead. "Where did you turn onto Wharf Street?"

"Just one block back, Jefferson Street. They didn't come my way."

Sam felt a corrosive bile rise to his throat at the thought that these two men—who had undoubtedly killed Wayne McRae—had gotten away.

Chapter 37

Sam pointed at the larger houses and the commercial buildings on the short block before Jefferson Street intersected Wharf. "They could have turned into one of these places."

"Or, they got past Gus before he got to the intersection," Jackson said.

Sam pointed to the buildings on one side of the street. "What's this?"

"That's a garment factory," Gus said. "And the one next to it, that's an insurance agency." Neither of them had garages.

The three buildings across the street all stood two stories high and were constructed with dark red brick. Like they'd been conceived by the same unimaginative builder. No lights on in any of them.

Gus pointed across the street. "The two on the left are private residences. The last one was a business of some sort. Maybe a furniture maker. Looks closed now."

"The two houses have garages," Jackson said. "Hard to hide a car without one."

Sam checked his pistol. "Okay, you guys sit tight. I'll take a look."

"What do you mean 'sit tight'?" Jackson said. "If these guys are in one of those places, you're going to need backup."

"Mr. Jackson, I don't have a radio, so I can't call the jail."

"I have just as much at stake in this as you, Sheriff," Jackson said. "Besides, I saved your ass from burning up at Lady Night's."

Sam opened the door. Rain soaked his shirt and pants.

"OK. I can't fire you and I can't shoot you. Come on."

They ran down to the first building and Jackson swung the garage door open. Sam stepped into the dark chasm with his gun drawn. Something flew at his head, and he ducked. A gray moth fluttered away. A dark form took the shape of a car. His heart raced until he realized it was a rusty panel truck sitting on cinder blocks.

He closed the door. They ran to the next house. Sam pulled up on the roll-up garage door, but it only lifted an inch. He twisted the flanged lock until the metal dug into his hands.

Jackson nudged him aside and held up a small leather bag. "You're getting forgetful, Sheriff. I have the means of entry."

Henry inserted the metal pins into the lock and probed until the tumblers turned and the lock clicked open.

Sam pulled his Police Special out and nodded for Jackson to raise the door.

The metal slots scraped and creaked as the door climbed higher. The dark space exhaled the salty smell of the Gulf. A small shrimp boat with a narrow pilothouse on one end sat on a trailer. No car at all.

Sam felt hope drain away. The Chevy had disappeared and with it the two killers.

Chapter 38

They closed the garage door and stood under the eaves of the house. Rain pounded without cease. Neither man spoke for a moment as they wrestled with the reality that the two men had slipped away. Out on the street, Gus kept vigil in the idling taxi.

Jackson wiped water from his face. "We had them, goddammit."

Sam pictured the two men hurrying out from the flophouse to the waiting Chevy. He clenched his teeth and agonized over what he could have done differently. But they were quick. They had an escape plan, and they executed it well. If he had to do it all over again, he would have jumped out of Jackson's car and shot the big man right where he sat in the Chevy. It would have been more than justified—the mother-fucker had broken Wayne's neck and shot him twice when he was already dead.

The image of revenge faded and he was brought back down to what was real—him standing with his equally disappointed partner as rain pounded the ground just beyond the short overhang. "Seems like Romano would have cut them loose right after they killed Wayne," Sam said. "Too much heat on them."

"And why is Arin Haugen involved in this?" Jackson said. "He didn't lend his car to those guys out of the kindness of his heart."

Sam pointed at the building next door—the one without a garage. "What if the driver let the big guy out over there and drove off?"

"Could he have done it that fast?" Jackson said. "We weren't all that far behind."

"Won't hurt to look."

"Why not? I can't get any wetter than this."

They ducked their heads and ran through the wet trash littering the yard. The front door and all the windows—first and second floors—had been boarded up tight. A bare patch in the brick showed where the business' sign had hung.

"You couldn't get in here without an axe," Jackson said.

They went around to the far side of the structure where the alleyway butted up against it. The windows on that side were also boarded. A tall wooden fence started at the end of the building and ran about six feet before making a turn at the alley and enclosing the rest of the property in the back.

They looked down the alley where it dead-ended into a tall metal fence. No gate for a car to escape through.

Sam jumped and grabbed the top of the wood fence. He pulled himself up and looked into the backyard. Broken boards and rusty pieces of metal covered most of the cemented area. The next lightning flash lit the back of the building—all the windows on both floors were boarded up.

The light lingered long enough for Sam to catch a glimpse of something odd. A path free of the larger pieces of junk ran from somewhere near the alleyway fence to the back of the building.

Sam jumped down, and Jackson read the curiosity in his face. "What?"

"Probably nothing." They walked down the alley as Sam told Jackson about the curved pathway.

"Maybe they started to clean it up and changed their minds," Henry said.

"But why clean it in a loop?"

Sam stopped at the part of the fence where he thought the cleared pathway began. The wood was lighter in color than the rest of the fence. "This section is new."

Jackson pushed on the slats. "It gives a little here." He tested the boards a few feet away. "But the rest is rock solid."

"I guess it doesn't matter. They couldn't get a car through here without a gate."

They stood as the rain poured down, neither man wanting to be the first to throw in the towel. "Let's get back there," Sam said. He handed his pistol to Henry Jackson and took several steps back.

"What the hell?"

"I'm climbing over."

"You're going to hurt yourself and you're too goddamn big to drag back to the car."

"Then give me a boost."

"No, you give *me* a boost," Jackson said and handed both pistols to Sam. "I'm lighter and you're taller."

Sam realized Jackson was right. "Don't get your ass shot if they're inside."

"I don't see how they could get in. Whoever owns this building didn't want any squatters."

"Wait," Sam said. He kicked at the wet trash in the alley and found a length of wire. He threaded it through the pistols' trigger guards and twisted one end tight.

Jackson's brow knitted. "What the hell are you doing?"

Sam tossed the guns over the fence and slipped the wire between two slats and pulled it down tight. "You wanted your gun, didn't you?"

"I don't need yours too."

"But I do." Sam made a cradle with his hands. "Let's go."

"How the hell are you going to get over?"

"I'm going to fly."

"Your brain must be waterlogged." Jackson stepped one foot into Sam's hands, and Sam boosted him up. Jackson swung a leg over the top of the fence and dropped down.

Sam ran and jumped up and grabbed the top of the slats. He pulled up but his boots wouldn't gain traction on the wet wood. He growled between his teeth and pulled himself higher until he sat on top. He dropped down to the cement yard and gave Jackson a smirk. "I guess I didn't need a damn boost."

Henry Jackson returned his look. "I guess I did it the easy way."

They followed the wide pathway to where it ended at the back of the building. In the dark, Sam hadn't seen that a large section of the exterior wall was made of wood, bordered on each side by brick.

"It's new wood," Jackson said. "Just like the fence."

"Maybe there was a garage here at one time," Sam said.

Jackson pointed up. A row of glass windows ran the length of the wall just before the second story began. "I wonder why they put them so high."

"Security would be my guess."

Jackson traced a finger between two boards in the middle of the wall. "There's a little gap here." He followed the line as it ran vertically up the wall. "What is that? That round metal piece up there."

Sam shielded his eyes from the rain and saw a small circular object inserted high up into the wood. He grabbed a rusted file cabinet and stood on it and saw that a narrow slot ran through the middle of the metal sphere.

"It's a goddamn lock," he said. He felt a rush of adrenaline. "It's a goddamn lock."

He reached up higher and traced a parallel indentation in the wood that ran from the vertical edge over several feet. "You see this?"

Sam jumped down and Jackson took his place on the cabinet.

"Damn," Jackson said. "There could be hinges on the inside. This thing might swing open."

"Open it with your burglar picks," Sam said. They were whispering now despite the cacophony of rain and thunder.

"They don't work on that kind of lock. It has to have tumblers."

Sam felt along the wall where the higher gap ended and found another vertical gap that met the top one. Jackson jumped down and pushed against the wall next to the vertical gap, but it didn't budge.

"The hinges are probably here," Jackson said. "That's why it doesn't flex on this side."

"I'll bet they use that cabinet to reach the lock." Sam pointed at the fence. "There's a gate over there. That's why we missed the sons-a-bitches. They turned into the alley before we got to the intersection."

They looked to the second story where all the windows were boarded except one.

Jackson shook his head. "Why the hell are they going to such extremes to hide these guys?"

A jolt of readiness rippled through Sam from head to toes. He had been given a second chance at Wayne McRae's killers.

He checked his pistol and snapped the cylinder shut. "I'll ask them."

Galveston '44

Chapter 39

Henry Jackson watched Sam stick his gun back in his belt. "You going to call for backup, aren't you?"

"Hell, no. I'm not going to let these fuckers get away again."

"There's no way to get in there."

Sam walked over to where the garage door left off and the brick wall began. Each window had thick planks bolted into the frame and plywood had been secured on the inside of the window.

He prowled back and forth along the wall, trying to will a solution to come forth. He looked up at the dormer windows above the garage door.

Henry followed his gaze. "Not gonna work. You're too big."

"That middle window, it's open a crack." He mimicked making a cradle with his hands. "It's your turn for a boost."

"Sheriff, I don't usually assist in suicides."

"Think positive, Jackson."

"I'm reluctant to tell you what I'm positive about," Jackson said. He laced his fingers together. "What do you want me to do while you're getting yourself shot?"

"What do you want to do?"

"Hide around the corner and shoot them if they try to drive off."

"Sounds good," Sam said. "And, Jackson, don't try to follow me in."

"I don't see how we can both boost each other up."

"You're right as rain." Sam stepped into Henry's hands and rose up. He grabbed the bottom of the metal frame and pulled himself up and pushed the window open a little more with his head.

He felt his wet hands slipping on the metal. His arms began to shake with the strain of holding on. He swung back and forth and threw a leg over the frame and pulled himself up. One leg dangled down into the dark chasm of the garage. The other hung down to where Jackson watched him, his expression concerned.

He heard nothing from inside. Nothing took form.

Sam knew he was a sitting duck. A dead man if someone waited down below for him. Now that he was up here, he realized his plan hadn't taken into account what possible damage might be inflicted on a large man dropping onto a concrete floor. Or would he land on something sharp or an equally unforgiving object?

Sam swung the other leg over the frame and grabbed it with both hands. He tried to ease himself down but his wet hands slipped off the metal.

He plunged and hit hard and rolled. His face hit something solid. Angry dots spun against his closed eyes. His left ankle screamed in protest of the awkward landing. He'd come to rest on his stomach, his face pressed into the cold concrete. He sat up and flexed his ankle. It wasn't broken, but it throbbed inside his boot.

He listened—had the two men heard his fall? Were there other men who had been waiting for the big man and his partner to return?

He heard a noise, close by and rhythmic. His head cleared. He thought he'd only heard the steady drumming of rain. But the sound—a persistent ticking—cut through the roar of the storm.

He pulled the box of wood matches from his pocket, knowing, even as he lit one, that the light would make him an easy target.

Tick, tick. He spun on his haunches, and there it sat, looming above him.

The white '41 Chevy.

Galveston '44

Chapter 40

Keeping his weight off the bad ankle, he stood and felt the hood. Still warm. The engine ticked again as it cooled.

The match's glow lit half the garage's space. Paper trash and busted lumber littered the floor. Metal cabinets stood against the walls. The match burned his fingers, and he threw it down. He pulled another one out, but before he could strike it a beam of light pierced the darkness and sliced the room in half.

Sam ducked behind the car. The dark outline of a man stood in a doorway. He held a flashlight with one hand and a pistol in the other. Lightning flashed outside and lit his features. Short blond hair. Fit, like an athlete—just as Horace Sessions had described him. It was him, the man who had driven the Chevy. The big man's partner who had picked him up in front of the Thirsty Pelican after he had killed Wayne.

The flashlight swept the room, then held steady on the car. Sam could see his own hands pressing against the concrete where he squatted behind the bumper. He reached for the pistol in his belt—*it wasn't there.*

The man stepped closer. The refracted light from his torch caught something dark sticking out from under a crumpled cardboard box. *Sam's gun.*

One more step and his bare feet would kick it. He could pick it up and shoot Sam with his own pistol. Just like they had with Wayne. But the man stepped away, walked around the back of the car and shone the flashlight inside. He continued the circuit, heading to the front where Sam squatted.

Sam duck-walked around to the back of the car, following the man's course. His sprained ankle throbbed in protest at the weight placed on it. He reached the front of the car where he'd begun.

The man spoke but his words were lost in the fury of the storm and the echo of the mostly empty space. Was he speaking to him? Taunting him? Sam's muscles tensed, ready to spring.

But another voice—or voices—joined his, overlapping each other. Then, sharply, a man said, "Carl..."

From the darkness in the back of the garage, the gray shadow of a man's arm rose, pointed up. The man named Carl trained the flashlight beam on the open dormer window and held it there. The men began whispering.

His light swept the big room, back and forth several times. Lightning crackled and lit the room. Sam moved further behind the car.

After a moment, the whispering stopped.

Sam peeked around the bumper as the men turned and walked through a door in the back. The light disappeared. The garage returned to darkness. A creaking sound came from where they had disappeared. Sam realized that at least two sets of footsteps were climbing wooden stairs.

Sam picked up his pistol and followed them through the doorway. The stairs led up to a void as dark as the garage. He held his breath but heard nothing beyond the unceasing rain.

He reached out blindly and just past the foot of the stairs found a closed door. Slowly, pistol in hand, he opened it. Weak light leaked in around the edges of the boarded windows of the cavernous room. Nothing stirred in the semi-dark. A wooden desk listed towards the side of its missing legs. A broken bedframe lay useless on its side.

A small kitchen took up one corner of the open room. But there were no bedrolls or any sign that the men slept downstairs. Sam looked up. That's where they were, just past the tall ceiling of the first floor.

He slipped past the stairs and went back into the garage. He struck a match and discovered a lock securing the garage door to an iron eye bolt drilled into the cement floor. There were no footholds on the door that he could use to climb out the dormer window. And Henry Jackson wasn't there to give him a boost. He was locked in with these men.

So be it.

Galveston '44

Chapter 41

Sam went back to the stairs and eased his weight onto the first step. It creaked and the sound lingered a long moment. He pointed his gun up the stairs, but no one appeared.

Sam eased off the step and went back into the garage. He searched the wooden shelves built into the walls but found nothing more than empty glass jars and dusty coke bottles. A few stubby candles. He lit one with one of his few remaining matches and opened the door of a metal cabinet. Rusty nails and screws lay scattered on the shelves.

He smelled gasoline and blew out the candle. He followed the fumes down to a metal container on the bottom shelf. He unscrewed the cap and sloshed the gas around.

The fumes brought him back to the raid on Lady Night's vacated whorehouse and the flaming Molotov cocktails thrown at him and Deputy Robicheaux.

Sam tried to remember what Wayne McRae had told him about how to make one.

It's like making a cake, Sheriff," Wayne had said. *You just need a few simple ingredients.*

Wayne's instructions came back to him now. He lit the candle and looked over the empty bottles on the wall shelf. All had openings too wide for his purpose but he found another bottle tucked into the corner behind the gas can. The bottle's narrow mouth was what he needed but a long crack in the center of the glass concerned him. Without another option, he poured gasoline into it, and hoped the fumes wouldn't carry upstairs.

The liquid held.

Sam had his choice of rags scattered on the cement floor. He chose one that wrapped around the bottle a couple of turns and left a flap—the wick—hanging loose. Wayne had advised using a cork to seal the opening, but he had to settle for a small piece of rotted wood that he squeezed into the bottle's mouth.

He found a length of electric wire on the floor and wrapped it tight around the cloth. He splashed gasoline from the can onto the loose flap of the cloth and hefted the bottle in his hand to feel the weight.

The device was at least ready to throw. Whether it would ignite and spread fire he didn't know.

He paused at the foot of the stairs. He needed to get higher to make sure the lit bottle cleared the top of the stairs so that the flames wouldn't come roaring down at him. It wouldn't do to have the sheriff burned to death by his own hand.

The images of the people he loved gathered in his mind and looked down at him, their expressions grief-stricken and maybe a little angry.

That crazy Sam Baker. Never was a fight he could turn down.

Lightning crackled and charged the air. He was ready.

He lit the flap of cloth with the candle flame and pushed off with his good foot and charged up the stairs. He reached the floor and threw the lit bottle into the darkness. Glass shattered and flames rushed forward along the path of the gasoline.

Men shouted and someone fired a gun. The bullet smacked into something solid behind him. Flames climbed up the legs of a large table and lit the room red.

Sam fired twice and ran into the other side of the room. He ducked down as they shot back in rapid succession, bullets pinging off walls, the sound echoing in the abandoned building.

"This is Sheriff Sam Baker," he shouted. "Come out with your hands up."

His command unleashed a barrage of gunfire. A man shouted something, but his words were lost in the roar of the fire and the storm outside. The flames crawled over more objects and smoke spread like a cloud, camouflaging the men but leaving Sam more visible. He crawled back further and took cover behind an overturned hutch.

Sam fired. The men shot back. Bullets ripped the hutch and chunks of it splintered away. They knew where he was.

He crawled across the wooden floor to find better cover but a bullet struck him in the upper arm. He groaned and pushed his mouth into the floor to muffle his cry. He crawled to a metal file cabinet, his left arm numb and useless. He shot blindly into the smoke if only to show he hadn't been hurt.

"There are a dozen deputies outside this building," Sam shouted. "There is no chance for you to escape. Give up now."

"I doubt that, Sheriff," a man responded. "They would have already followed you in."

Sam focused on the window side of the room where the voice had come from. A man's outline, tall and broad, appeared. Sam fired. The man went down.

From across the room a man shouted, "Max—!"

Max. The big killer's name was Max, and he had shot the son-of-a-bitch.

The other man—the one someone had called Carl in the garage—shouted again, but Max didn't answer.

Sam checked his own wound. Blood ran down his arm. He knew he would need to staunch the flow soon. He'd never been shot before—not in the war or during twenty-three years as a cop.

A big arm reached up through the smoke and grabbed a

support post. Sam fired but the bullet clanged off the metal.

"Go!" Carl shouted. "Run!"

It puzzled Sam why the man wanted Max to get away while he stayed to be arrested or killed. In his experience, loyalty among gangsters only went so far.

Sam pointed the gun at the top of the stairs, the only escape route available.

Carl shouted again for Max to run, but Sam heard no response. The fire consumed more of the floor and climbed the walls. Burning wood crackled. Sparks shot into the air. Flames crept towards Sam like a grass fire.

"Sheriff," Max shouted from behind the smoke curtain. "We will meet again, my friend. Mark my words."

"Come out with your arms raised."

"So you can shoot me?" the big man said. He fired again. "I'm not a fool like your Deputy McRae."

"Don't you say his name, you piece-of-shit."

"He was so young. So stupid."

Both men, as if planned, fired repeatedly. Sam ducked. When he looked again, the big man was running to the back of the room, away from the stairs.

Sam fired, but Max disappeared behind a wall of fire.

A second later, glass broke. *He's going out the window*, Sam thought, but didn't see how a big man—already wounded—could jump to the ground without severely injuring or killing himself. If he went into the backyard, Henry Jackson would detain him or shoot him.

Sam reloaded his pistol. His wounded arm could barely hold the gun steady.

Carl shot at him rapidly, laying down cover for his partner. Sam fired at the muzzle flash from inside the black smoke. The man ceased shooting.

Sam jumped over a burning desk and stopped behind a

support post. A wall of flames and billowing smoke obscured the back of the building and blocked him from advancing. Heat came at him in searing waves. He angled towards the wall and caught a view of all the windows facing the backyard. Just as he had thought, they were all boarded up. The sound of broken glass had to have come from a side window facing the house next door.

The fire had reached the back wall. Sam steeled himself to run through it, but a section of the burning floor collapsed in front of him, taking the flames with it. Max stood by the broken window, pointing a pistol at him. They fired at the same time. Max staggered and fell back against the wall. Sam felt the sting of a new wound on his calf.

He raised the pistol and aimed—this would be the kill shot. This would be justice for Wayne McRae.

Before he could fire, Carl charged out of the smoke, screaming and gripping a large knife in his upraised hand. Sam grabbed his arm in mid-thrust, and his gun flew out of his hand.

The man's momentum drove Sam against the wall. He saw black but held onto Carl's arm with both hands. Sam slammed his chest into him and shoved him away. Carl brandished the knife again, his eyes wild and confident, despite the dark blood that glistened on his shirt.

"Kill him!" Max screamed from behind the wall of flames.

"Go!" Carl yelled again. He circled around Sam, faking thrusts with the big knife.

Sam picked up a scorched two-by-four and smacked Carl on the shoulder. The board broke in half. Carl lunged forward and stabbed Sam in the chest before he could jump back. Pain radiated out from the wound like he'd been branded with a hot poker.

"Very clever of you to find us, Sheriff," he said,

emboldened by drawing blood. "But now you're going to die."

Carl thrust the knife at him again, but Sam moved to the side and shoved the end of the board into Carl's forehead. The man's head snapped back, but he recovered and stabbed downward. Sam grabbed his arm. They crashed to the floor on a pile of smoldering wood. Sam twisted Carl's wrist and turned the knife blade towards him.

"No!" Max screamed from the corner.

"Go!" the man shouted, growling from the effort to hold onto the knife.

Sam shifted forward. His weight and strength inched the knife point closer to the man's body.

Carl's eyes grew wide. He knew the knife would find a home in his chest.

"I will kill you!" Max said. "I will find you and kill you!"

Sam looked into Carl's face and—transported back to his war battles and the German soldiers he'd killed there—saw his enemy's humanity reflected back to him. But he also saw one of the men responsible for Wayne's death. He plunged the big knife into the killer's heart.

Carl groaned once, low and fading. Sam felt his final breath against his face.

He pulled the knife out of Carl's chest and charged through the flames. He heard the sound of rain and found the open window that Max had broken. A thick rope, tied to the frame, hung to the ground.

Sam grabbed the rope and swung his good leg over the window frame. He tried to push off with the wounded leg, but it had turned numb and wouldn't respond. His left arm was useless. He knew he couldn't shimmy down the rope with only one arm.

He hobbled back to the dead man and searched his pockets

for the key to the locked garage door. He found them empty.
He'd have to find a way out downstairs somehow.

Otherwise, he was trapped in a burning building.

Galveston '44

Chapter 42

Sam limped down the stairs, holding onto the bannister with his good arm. Clouds of black smoke rolled through the first floor. Flames from above cast a reddish glow over the big room. Sam covered his face with his handkerchief and searched for an axe or a crowbar, anything to break the boards nailed over the windows.

He heard a sharp cracking from above and jumped aside as chunks of charred flooring crashed to the floor.

He heard a noise—footsteps behind him—but he saw no one.

"Sheriff," a muffled voice called from the dark.

Sam froze. All he had was the knife. Had Max gotten in somehow?

A shadow formed into a man as he stepped closer. It was Henry Jackson.

"Shit. I thought you were him," Sam said. He dropped the knife to his side. "It's the first time I've been glad to see you."

Jackson looked at Sam's bloody shirt. "Goddamn, Sheriff." He put Sam's arm over his shoulders and helped him to a busted-out window on the neighbor's side of the building.

"Did you see him?" Sam asked. "I shot him, but he got out."

"Which one?"

"The big son-of-a-bitch. His name is Max."

"No," Henry said. "I was busy pulling out boards with Gus' crowbar."

A shot rang out from the front of the building. Then

another.

"Gus!" Sam said.

Jackson helped Sam out and supported him as he limped to the street. Sam pointed at the cab that turned at the corner and disappeared into the fog. "Where the hell is Gus going?"

"Nowhere," Jackson said. He kneeled down. A man lay crumpled in the middle of the wet street, a black fedora next to his hand. Gus Josie, soaked from the rain, stared up at them with lifeless eyes. His head rested on the concrete at an odd angle. Blood soaked his shirt.

"No!" Sam shouted. He dropped to his knees. "Gus..."

Max had pulled Gus out of the cab and broke his neck and shot him for good measure.

Sam thought of Gus' wife and their three kids. He felt ashamed that he'd never met them or remembered their names. The cabbie had given his life for what—a pittance of money and maybe the chance to work on the periphery of his life's dream.

Henry Jackson looked stricken. "I should have stayed with him."

"Not your fault," Sam whispered. "He was my responsibility."

Henry pointed at Sam's shirt. "You're bleeding heavily."

"The other guy stabbed me," Sam nodded. "His name was Carl."

Henry looked at him, questioning.

"He's dead."

They looked at the building where flames licked at the roof. Carl would perish in a funeral pyre.

Rain fell into the cabbie's unblinking eyes. Sam closed them.

"Come sit in my car," Henry said. "You need to get out of the rain."

"I'll stay with Gus. You need to get out of here."

"You'll go into shock."

"No, I won't."

Sirens screamed in the distance. Sam looked down at Gus Josie, pale and drained of life. He took off his wet shirt and covered his face.

It was all he could do.

Galveston '44

Chapter 43

Elmer Smoltz sat alone at a window table in a dark bar. An untouched cup of coffee sat before him. A black medical bag and a small duffel bag sat snuggled between his feet. He wore a black suit that had seen better days.

Smoltz ignored the war news from the bartender's radio, his attention fixed instead on the passing cars as they kicked up plumes of water from Galveston's recent rains. He drummed the table top with long, tapered fingers, of which he was so proud. He considered his hands elegant and his face handsome, despite his thinning black hair and his pasty white skin.

A black Ford pulled up in front of the bar and flashed its headlights.

Elmer took his bags outside and climbed into the backseat next to a beefy man with a jagged scar on his cheek. He let the man tie a cloth blindfold over his eyes and the car drove off.

The driver made several quick turns, designed, Smoltz was sure, to confuse him as to which direction they were heading. Not that he cared.

No one spoke to him. He directed his mind to prepare for the challenge ahead.

The car stopped. The back door opened. Someone pulled Elmer Smoltz out and hustled him inside a structure of some sort. The room was dead silent but Smoltz sensed other people there, watching him. He felt their collective tension and sense of urgency.

The man stopped him and told him to kneel. He obeyed

but in that vulnerable position, and with the blindfold tight around his head, stories of professional execution came to mind.

"Reach back with one foot," the man said.

Smoltz pushed one leg back and felt his foot lose contact with the floor. He sensed a deep chasm behind him and froze.

The man nudged his leg with his foot. "Find the first step."

Smoltz eased his foot down until it found a flat surface a few inches below the floor. The man held onto his coat as he stepped down with the other leg. His hands discovered railings, and he descended until someone below stopped him and eased him down to a landing.

The scent of a woman intermingled with stale air.

A door slammed shut above him. The blindfold was pulled over his head. A woman wearing a nurse's uniform stared at him, her blue eyes almost hidden by a surgical mask covering her lower face, and a rubber cap pulled down low over her forehead. Her gray hair had been tied back in a tight bun.

She led him down to the concrete floor and into a large room lit by a dim light. "Here are the rules," she whispered. "You will put on your blindfold whenever you hear a knock at the door. Stand facing the wall until I have come down the stairs. Do not ask anyone for information of any kind. Of course, you will be allowed to leave when you have completed this job."

The gray walls seemed to close in on Elmer Smoltz and triggered his claustrophobia. *Allowed to leave?* These conditions had never been imposed on him before by this particular client. What made this situation different?

"Most of all," the woman said, her whisper taking on a harsher tone, "Let me impress upon you the need to do your best work here."

"I always do my best."

204

He followed her into the shadows, surprised to see a field operational lamp attached to a tripod stand—the same model used in army hospitals overseas.

The woman flipped a switch. The powerful light fell on a hospital bed made small by a large man lying on it. A single sheet covered all but his massive chest and thick arms, both glistening with a fine sheen of sweat.

Smoltz pointed at the sutures that closed a jagged laceration on his face. "Good job." The woman ignored the compliment and pulled the loose sheet down to the man's bandaged left thigh. Blood leaked around the edges. She dabbed it with a cloth.

"How long has he been losing blood?" Smoltz asked.

"Since last night. Blood will arrive momentarily, but it's been an unacceptably long time." She flashed a look at him.

I got here as quick as I could, he wanted to say. "Is there an exit wound?"

"No."

"Shouldn't be a problem to extract the bullet."

"For the leg, yes, but..." She folded the sheet to the side. A large bandage taped to his side just below the ribcage was soaked with blood. A thin rivulet ran down to the bedsheet and glistened there. If the bullet had hit the gallbladder or kidneys, Smoltz knew the man would die.

Smoltz felt the man's skin and lifted an eyelid. The eye, light-gray to the point of transparency, pulled him deep down to a black mark that reflected the doctor's own face. He drew away, not liking what he saw of himself. "He's not in shock."

"He was lucid when he arrived."

Smoltz had seen few gunshot victims that weren't in shock after this kind of trauma. "You gave him morphine?"

The woman nodded.

"Probably the bullet didn't hit anything vital. The

challenge will be finding it."

The big man rolled over and pointed to a spot on his lower back with his thumb. He locked his gaze on Elmer Smoltz and nodded with a certainty that left no doubt where the probe should begin.

Chapter 44

A languid current under the surface of a clear blue sea carried him along effortlessly. Brightly-colored fish darted between his legs. On a distant shore a man walked barefoot on the pure white sand and adjusted his black fedora to his liking.

Gus, Sam shouted, but the cabbie only turned his face to the cloudless sky and smiled.

Sam tried to swim ashore and join him but his left arm and right leg refused him. His chest throbbed with every useless stroke. His efforts only brought him to the surface where a smiling young woman dressed entirely in white hovered above him.

Daddy, he heard the woman say. A single drop of water fell on his cheek. *Can you hear me, Daddy?*

He blinked against a bright light as Sylvie's features came into focus. "Hi, sweetheart," he tried to say, but the words stuck in his dry throat.

"You're in the hospital," Sylvie said, and squeezed his hand.

A white-uniformed nurse swept into the room. She stuck a hypodermic needle into a bottle and drew the plunger back.

"What's that?" Sam asked.

"Something for the pain."

"Morphine?"

"You just had surgery in three places, Sheriff Baker," she said as she stuck the needle into his arm. "You'll be crawling out of your skin in about three shakes if we don't stay ahead of the pain."

Sylvie kissed him on the cheek and hugged him gently. "I hardly know where to touch you," she said.

"I haven't seen much of you lately," Sam whispered. "If it takes getting stabbed and shot, I'd gladly—"

"Don't joke, Daddy. You could have died." She took a glass of water from the bedside table and gave him a sip.

"Are you still mad at me about Dominick?"

"Only half mad," she said and smiled.

"That's progress." Sam wondered if young Romano had accompanied her here.

"I called Mom after I heard you'd be all right...except maybe for your arm."

"What about my arm?" He panicked and spoke louder than he'd intended. "What did the surgeon say?"

"That maybe you wouldn't have all your strength back in it."

"But the bullet didn't hit bone."

"The doctor said it tore up some muscle."

His first thought was of boxing. He was no longer a pro, but he still had a hunger for it. His second was of the big man, Max, the man who had killed Wayne and Gus. He would need his full strength to hunt him down.

"I know you, Daddy," Sylvie said and patted his hand. "You'll be a hundred percent in no time."

He nodded, grateful for her encouragement. "How did your mom take the news?"

"She was upset, of course."

Claire's worst nightmare, Sam thought. The constant fear he would be killed had almost come to pass. "Did she tell you I want you to go to Dallas until all this blows over?"

"Yes."

"And?"

She nodded out to the hallway where Dominick

undoubtedly waited for her. "I can't do that, Daddy."

The stern nurse wheeled an IV stand into the room and made a shooing motion at Sylvie. "You'll have to leave, young lady. Your father needs to rest."

"Call your mom again," he said. "Tell her...tell her not to worry."

Sylvie tilted her head at him like he should know better. She kissed his cheek and stood. "I'll come back later."

The morphine pulled him down and dissolved all thoughts and images except one—that of Gus Josie lying bloody and dead on the wet pavement. Killing the man named Carl hadn't brought justice to Wayne or Gus. No, the man who had killed them had gotten away. Max could have died from his wounds but Sam didn't think so. Even with at least two bullets in him he had shimmied down a rope and ran to the street fast enough to surprise Gus and pull him from his taxicab.

If the man survived, would Vince Romano and Arin Haugen decide there was too much heat on him and get him out of town? No, he had an idea he hadn't seen the end of Max.

And maybe by now the big man realized he hadn't seen the end of Sheriff Sam Baker.

Galveston '44

Chapter 45

Elmer Smoltz lay on his cot with his shirt off and a fan blowing warm, useless air on his chest. He had come to realize that the ceiling he now stared at, with square wooden beams running across it, also served as the floor of a building. That meant he was in a basement—a hot, stifling basement.

Luckily the room was big or he would have jumped out of his skin by now. His panic at being enclosed in small spaces could only be treated by the calming medication he used for almost anything that ailed him.

Physician heal thyself.

The outsized patient in the hospital bed snorted and cleared his throat. The doctor feared he would awaken. Smoltz just needed a little more peace before the guy woke up and resumed probing his psyche with his pale gray eyes and his incisive questions. Only two days out of life-saving surgery, and he had already discovered Smoltz's vulnerabilities and regrets.

He didn't want to know the patient's name but the man nevertheless gave it, variously, as Hitler or Roosevelt or Jesus, all with an insistence that Smoltz address him by the name of the moment. Earlier in the morning he went by Carl but he said it quietly, reverently.

Smoltz had dutifully called him Carl but the patient shook his head and said, "Don't call me Carl. He was a great man. I could never be him."

Smoltz had begun changing the dressings, hoping to distract him. But his face had hardened and he stared ahead as if he could see something Elmer Smoltz couldn't. "He killed him."

"I'm sorry?" the doctor said.

"The sheriff. He killed Carl and he shot me."

"I don't need to know that. I'm just here to—"

"You knew that. Don't play stupid with me."

"I swear. They didn't tell me anything."

The patient grabbed his arm and pulled the scissors out of his hand. The doctor jerked back, but the man's grip was like iron. "Let's come to an agreement."

Smoltz waited, afraid of what the man might propose.

"We are a team, you and I," the patient went on. "I will help you and you will help me."

"I am helping you," the doctor said. "I dug two bullets out of you."

"Of course," the patient said, waving the scissors around like he was spelling the words in the air. "And for which you are being paid handsomely. Am I right?"

The doctor noticed the preciseness by which the man enunciated his words, the almost formal use of language and the flat accent. "Yes, I am being paid very well."

"That's better," the patient said. "What is your name? Your *real* name."

"Elmer Smoltz. Dr. Elmer Smoltz."

"But you're no longer a practicing doctor."

"That's right."

"Because of your habit?"

Smoltz was taken aback. He'd only injected himself when the lights were out and the patient was snoring.

The man squeezed his arm harder. "Come along, doctor. You're doing so well."

"Yes, I was forced to resign. I have a...a little indulgence."

The man let go of his arm, and the doctor could finally

straighten his back. "Yet, you do very good work."

"I'd like to think so," Smoltz said.

"If not, I'm sure your client, as you call him, would kill you."

Smoltz had always wondered if that could happen. One mistake and he might very well be dead.

"Would you like to know my real name, Elmer?"

Smoltz felt he had no other option than to say, yes.

The man stuck out his big hand. "My name is Max. My real name."

The doctor shook it. His own hand wasn't small, but it was engulfed by Max's.

"Your life is in danger, Elmer."

"Why do you say that?"

"Because of who I am."

Smoltz knew Max was of great value to his employer for a reason he had no desire to know. He had patched up his bullet-riddled men before—but often in squalid safe houses and without the luxury of quality surgical equipment and lamps. And, for the first time, a skilled surgical nurse.

Max tilted his head, silently demanding a response.

The doctor complied, "Who are you?"

"You don't want to know," Max said. "It's enough that you can identify me. And that's your capital crime right there."

Smoltz felt weak in the legs and sat down. He wanted to run screaming from this damp basement and back to his former life, pathetic as it often was. He was surprised to find his instinct for survival to be alive and functioning. There had been times, especially of late, when he had questioned his desire to go on.

"Don't look so glum, my pretend doctor," Max said, slapping Smoltz hard on the leg. "I will help you escape, and you will help me."

"How?"

"You'll know when the time is right," Max said. He brushed Smoltz away with a hand gesture. "Now, let me think."

Chapter 46

A light drizzle fell from gray skies as people exited their cars and walked slowly through the cemetery. Pall bearers pulled the unadorned casket from the back of the hearse and carried it to the open gravesite.

Sam followed behind them, his left arm in a sling and his right arm supported by Deputy Gilbert Robicheaux. He limped heavily. The wounds to his chest and arm throbbed with every step. He had come to show his respects despite the doctor's warning that he was leaving the hospital too soon. But his guilt over Gus Josie's death and his desire to honor the man made missing the funeral impossible.

Sam spotted Mrs. Josie, a thin woman with long red hair. She was supported on both sides by two of Gus' kids—a young man and a young woman in their twenties—as they followed the coffin on its journey to the gravesite. A boy in his late teens who had inherited Gus' angular face followed behind.

Mrs. Josie sagged, and her kids gripped her tighter. Sam's heart pounded and his tongue felt like sandpaper in his dry mouth. He wished Claire were with him. She always had the right words for difficult situations.

He and Deputy Robicheaux caught up with the Josie family.

"Mrs. Josie," Sam said, his hat in his hand. "I'm very sorry about your loss."

Mrs. Josie's facial muscles tightened as if to deflect Sam's condolence. Without a word of acknowledgment, she and her kids walked away. The oldest son glared at Sam in passing.

Sam had heard that people in town blamed him for Gus' death.

Why would the sheriff engage the services of a cabbie when he had several deputies available?

But more shocking to the citizens was the rumor that a black man had been involved in the shootout at the building. Probably someone had seen Henry Jackson come out of the burning building with Sam. Or, they'd seen him drive off before the ambulance arrived.

Sam took another step and his leg buckled. Robicheaux gripped his right arm tighter. "Sheriff, why don't I take you to the house? You done gave your condolences."

"No," Sam said. "I'll see this through."

Sam and Robicheaux stopped at the back of the mourners as the robed preacher extolled Gus Josie's many virtues. The deputy nudged him and gestured with his head to the only black face amongst the mourners. Henry Jackson, as if aware of the eyes on him, turned and nodded.

Jackson had alerted Robicheaux about the bald man leaving Arin Haugen's blue Lincoln at the salvage yard. But by the time Robicheaux and Deputy Garza arrived at the garage, the car was gone.

Didn't have no Lincoln in here, the garage owner had insisted. *Now if you'll excuse me—*

Garza had pushed the man into his greasy office chair and told him that three witnesses saw a man drop off a dented Lincoln the night before. The owner, perhaps more afraid of Vince Romano and Arin Haugen than the law, doubled down on his lie. They charged him with tampering with evidence and jailed him.

Sam felt every one of Mrs. Josie's sobs that carried back to him in the humid air. She sagged in her chair, her arm held by one son as if she could fall out at any time.

Gus had been an invaluable resource for Sam, his unofficial, unseen eyes on the wide-open city called the Free State of Galveston. Sam tried to reconcile his death by thinking he had died doing what he wanted—being a cop, or the closest he could get to it. But, unlike a cop, he hadn't been armed, and he hadn't deserved to die like he had.

"I'll get you home now, Sheriff," Robicheaux said.

"Change of plans, Deputy," Sam said. "Take me to headquarters."

Galveston '44

Chapter 47

Sam shed his suit coat and eased down into his office chair. His shirt was sopped with sweat from the long walk to Gus' grave. His whole body throbbed from his wounds. Now that he was alone, he couldn't block out the sound of Mrs. Josie's sobs or the silent accusations from her family and the other mourners.

Only a heavy bag session would help alleviate the remorse and rage that ran through him. But in his condition that would be impossible. A flask of good whiskey lay in his desk drawer, but he knew one sip would sink him lower than the hospital's morphine.

Grace brought him a cup of fresh coffee and gave him a disapproving look before she left. She thought he should be at home, resting. And she was right.

Sam drained the coffee and, somewhat revived, sketched a diagram of where all his deputies were. He'd sent Robicheaux and Turner in Sam's undercover car to keep an eye on the Tropicana Hotel and follow Arin Haugen if he left. Likewise with the muscular, bald man. It was a longshot, but maybe they would lead them to Max.

Deputies Garza and Eilers were out looking for Vince Romano, still apparently in hiding. Sam had sent Garza with the undependable Eilers to keep him from fucking up. Garza, like Wayne McRae before him, brooked no deviation from a deputy's sworn duties.

Other deputies not on patrol duty were canvassing used car lots on the slim chance the owner of the salvage yard had dumped the dark blue Lincoln at one.

The phone rang.

"Sheriff Baker, I finally got you." The man's voice, thin and grating, left little doubt as to its owner.

"Well, if it ain't Stephen Miller, Governor Davis's assistant."

"Adjunct," Miller reminded him. "Sheriff, you haven't come to Austin to meet with the governor."

"I'm a little banged up right now, Miller," Sam said. "Besides, this investigation takes priority."

"I'm going to do you a favor and not tell him you said that."

"Maybe you heard," Sam said. "One of the suspects is dead and we're looking for the second one."

"Yes, quite a shootout you had there, Sheriff. Unfortunately, you not only destroyed private property, you got a civilian killed in the process. A Mr. Jose."

"Josie. His name was Gus Josie." Sam said. "I thought you fellas over there in Austin knew your letters and such."

"What was this civilian doing with you?"

"That's something I'll discuss with the governor."

"He wants me to gather certain facts before you meet with him tomorrow."

"Spelling the deceased's name right is a good place to start."

"You want to tell me who this other civilian with you was?" Miller went on. "A colored man."

"I'll share that with the governor."

"Fine. He wants you here tomorrow at—"

"I've got a lead to run down right now, Mr. Miller," Sam said. "How about I give you a call when I get a couple hours free."

"Sheriff—."

"I'll be in touch, Mr. Miller," Sam said.
He hung up.

Galveston '44

Chapter 48

A drunken man stumbled out of Vince Romano's gambling den, his head hung low as if on the ground he could find the money he had just lost playing Texas Hold'em or craps. Next door to the joint, a dog barked a warning. The rest of the street had settled in for the night.

Sam caught a whiff of the charred building across the street from where he and Jackson sat in his newly-acquired '34 Ford. Jackson had bought another junker, thinking it best to replace the car he'd driven the night of the shootout. He'd rebuilt the engine till it purred like his former car.

When Jackson had picked him up a couple of hours before, Sam had asked how much he'd paid for it.

"Nothing," he'd said. "I sold the other one for seventy-five. Paid forty for this one and put thirty dollars' worth of junk yard parts into the engine. That's a five-dollar profit, if your math is any good." Henry gave him a smug look designed to challenge. "I got it all done before you got your ass out of the hospital."

"What took you so long?"

Henry nodded. "Good one, Sheriff."

Sam looked at the spot where the big man named Max had broken Gus Josie's neck and shot him twice. That night's rain had washed away the cabbie's blood but nothing would ever cleanse the memory of Gus' lifeless eyes staring up at him. That image would join the one of Wayne lying shot to death in his squad car.

"Let's go," Sam said.

They climbed out of the car and ran across the street. Sam carried a felling axe and Jackson had a crow bar. They passed the front door where the Galveston Police Department had nailed a warning notice. *Stay out. Unstable structure.* The Chief of Police had staked a territorial claim on the crime scene, undoubtedly ordered to do so by Vince Romano.

It was the first time the police department had done anything at all lately except shake down street whores for a free ride.

They stopped at a boarded window on the alley side of the building. They would have preferred to scale the fence and break in from a window in the back side of the building, but Sam was in no condition for that.

Jackson inserted the crow bar behind the boards crisscrossing the window. He pulled but the nails only squeaked and held.

"What's the problem?" Sam asked. "You broke into the window on the other side pretty quick."

"Because you needed somebody to save your ass."

"As you can see, I made out just fine."

"You're about as tore up as a man can be and still walk around."

Jackson placed a foot on the wall and jerked back on the board again. It popped out, and he landed deftly on the ground. He smashed the plywood with the axe and climbed in through the jagged hole.

Jackson helped pull Sam in by his good arm. Sam crouched in the darkness, his wounds throbbing with the exertion.

He felt the other man's hand on his shoulder. "You need a moment?"

"Just took one."

Sam stood and flicked on his flashlight. A large pile of

blackened wood and gray ash lay under a circular-shaped gap in the ceiling. A light blinked from there, and Sam turned off his flashlight. He pulled the pistol from his belt but realized the roof was gone and a solitary star sparkled in the clear sky. He was brought back to the war when he and his men often holed up in bombed-out buildings like this.

He trained the light back on the pile. "I guess this is where they found the bastard."

Not even his mother could recognize him, the medical examiner had said. Despite what the man had done, Sam was glad he was dead before the flames reached him.

"And he told this Max to run?" Jackson asked.

"More like he ordered him to."

Jackson shined his beam up to the remaining ceiling. "Where the hell did you learn to make a Molotov cocktail?"

"From Wayne."

Jackson shined his flashlight around the ash-covered floor. "Trying to find evidence of who these guys were would be messy."

"I'm sure Romano told the police chief to not even look."

They skirted the pile of rubble and went through the door leading to the garage. The car was gone, its vacated space the only area not littered by blackened refuse.

Sam went into the hallway where the stairs now had two boards nailed across the bannister. A handwritten sign warned of the unstable structure upstairs.

Jackson eased past Sam and ducked under the boards.

"Where the hell you think you're going?" Sam said.

"Upstairs to look around."

"You're going to ride this floor down if it gives out."

The stairs creaked as Jackson climbed. "Well, like the cowboys say—yippee ki yay."

"Goddammit," Sam said and followed him up.

Henry stopped and pointed at him. "You're too big. If anything would make the rest of this floor collapse, it's your two hundred and forty pounds."

"Two-twenty."

"That was your fighting weight. Your two-forty might be the straw that broke the camel's back."

Sam kept climbing, each step groaning in protest. "Here comes the straw."

Jackson stopped at the top of the stairs and pointed his flashlight ahead. He whistled in amazement. "You did a good job of torching this place, Sheriff. You better hope they don't make you pay for this."

"So far the owner hasn't come forward," Sam said, "but we did find out which business was in here. Hurley Bed Frames."

Jackson tested the floor with one foot. "Who did Mr. Hurley say the owner is?"

"He didn't know. He pays the rent to the property manager and makes the check out to something called Northland Holding. We're trying to find out who they are but nothing so far."

"Why did Hurley vacate?"

"He said Northland wanted to renovate the place," Sam said.

"You already took care of that," Jackson said. He stepped up to stand on the floor. "I love what you did with the place."

Sam reached the top of the stairs. Yellow moonlight poured in from the charred hole in the roof and lit the surviving edges of the floor. The fight with the two men came back to him in vivid detail. The two most troubling images were of him plunging the fighting knife into Carl's heart and Max escaping out the window.

"Two bullets in him and still he ran," Sam murmured.

He and Jackson shared a look and, perhaps, their guilt over of what the big man had done to Gus Josie. Jackson, for his part, could have protected Gus instead of breaking into the building to help Sam get out. For Sam, guilt conflicted with gratitude over Jackson probably saving his life.

Jackson took a tentative step forward. "He shot Gus after he broke his neck. Same thing with Wayne. Maybe he enjoys it."

"I think he does," Sam said. He pulled the skull-and-bones medallion out of his pocket and handed it to Jackson. "He put this in Wayne's hands."

Jackson shone his beam on the ominous image. "Jesus H. Christ." He felt its heft and studied it from all sides. "Is it from some organization?"

"The Feds couldn't find any connection," Sam said.

"Why didn't you show me this before?"

"I didn't know you were going to butt into my investigation."

Jackson handed the medallion back to Sam. "Yeah, the son-of-a-bitch enjoys killing." He pointed to the other side of the circular gap in the floor. "That's where they were when you came up?"

"Yeah, I'm sure they slept over there," Sam said. "Maybe in the hallway."

Jackson stepped around to the five or six feet of floor beams and planks extending out from the walls.

"Where the fuck are you going?" Sam said.

"I'm going to take a look back there."

"I thought you were worried about falling through."

"That was before you showed me that damn skull thing."

Jackson hugged the wall with his back and shuffled along, looking down at the first floor twenty feet below. Halfway across, the ledge creaked and sagged. He stopped.

Sam pointed, remembering. "Pull up the rope hanging from the window behind you."

Jackson turned and grabbed the bottom window frame. He pulled up the rope and tied it under his arms. "Sheriff, this is going to look bad for you if this slips up to my neck when I fall."

He made it to the other side and untied the rope. He kicked charred furniture and junk aside and disappeared down the hallway that separated the offices. The light from his flashlight danced on the walls as he went.

He returned and waved what appeared to be a magazine. "Found this in a mattress."

"*Under* a mattress?" Sam asked.

"No, there was a slit in the side."

"What is it? A girly magazine?"

"Of sorts."

"Good for you," Sam said. "You can add it to your collection."

Jackson stuck the magazine into the back of his pants. He tied the rope around his waist and stepped gingerly on the sagging ledge and make it back to the floor.

Sam shined his light on the magazine as Jackson flipped through it. The photos were of naked women tied and gagged, their eyes wide with fear. On one page, a man stood over a bound woman with a black whip held over his head.

"One of these guys is sick," Sam said. "My guess is it's the big guy."

Jackson pulled a folded piece of paper out of his back pocket and handed it to Sam. "This was stuck in the middle of the magazine."

Sam unfolded the paper. Someone had sketched a rectangular mechanism with dials and knobs on the front and what appeared to be wiring on the inside. "A diagram of a machine of some sort."

"It's a schematic."

"But of what?"

Jackson shook his head. "Beats me. Something electrical, but it's beyond my pay grade."

Sam stuck the schematic in his pocket. Jackson tossed the magazine down to the ash heap below.

Galveston '44

Chapter 49

They climbed down the rickety stairs to the kitchen where charred paper ash drifted across the floor like blackened tumbleweed. The cabinets contained a few cracked plates and stained coffee cops.

Jackson opened the rusty refrigerator door, but it was barren. "These guys lived here. They must have had some food."

"I'd lay odds our crackerjack police department took it home," Sam said.

Sam shone his light on stacks of cardboard boxes piled on the floor. One box had faint lettering on its side. Sam knocked the stack down and shined his light on the printed logo. A watermark partially obscured the words and it took him a moment to realize he was looking at it upside down. He turned it.

Stinson's Grocery.

"You know this store, don't you?"

"Yes, suh," Jackson said, slipping into his other voice. "But they don' let no colored folk buy they food there."

Jackson's tone of voice was balanced between resignation and resentment. Sam hadn't realized that Stinson's banned Negros, but Claire had done all the grocery shopping.

They inspected more boxes and Jackson found another one stamped with Stinson's name. They examined it closely but, besides the logo, there was nothing remarkable about it.

Jackson started to toss it, but Sam grabbed his hand. "Wait…"

A small piece of paper peeked out from one of the bottom flaps. Sam pulled it free and trained his light on it.

Sal, please bring more steaks next time. M can easily eat two or three at one sitting. I appreciate your attention to this matter. Carl.

"M for Max." Jackson said. "But who is Sal?"

An image of the man formed for Sam. The angular face with outsized eyes and protruding Adam's apple. The blustery tough guy at whose house he and the deputies had found Dominick Romano during the dawn raid.

Vince Romano's nephew.

Sal Longino.

* * *

Dusk eased into a still, humid night that begged for either a cooling rain or a steady breeze, neither of which seemed promising. Sam drove the black Ford down a familiar residential street as he and Henry Jackson swatted at mosquitos.

He pulled over and flashed his lights. A black Dodge pulled away from the curb and parked further down the street.

A moment later, the Ford's backdoor opened and Deputy Gilbert Robicheaux, in overalls and a cowboy hat, climbed in beside him. Wayne McRae had always teased his fellow deputy about his choice of civilian clothes, but tonight they served a purpose.

"I didn't see Sal Longino all day, Sheriff." Robicheaux said. "But he had a visitor an hour ago. Had him a good-sized belly. Didn't get a good look at his face but he wore a black, porkpie hat."

"Somebody let him in?"

"Let himself in with a key. Only stayed a short while and

came out empty-handed."

Sam nodded. "You did good, Deputy. We'll take it from here."

"Yes, sir." Robicheaux climbed out of the car and gently closed the door.

Gray moths crashed into Sal's porch light. A nearby dog barked.

"Maybe Sal went underground like Romano and Drago," Jackson suggested.

"Could be. If he was delivering food to Max and Carl, Vince might want him to lay low."

"Maybe they have Sal along for protection."

"Sal couldn't protect his own skinny shadow."

They climbed out and walked across the street. The dog let loose again. They hurried up Sal's driveway and walked around to the backdoor.

A dim light glowed from behind the kitchen window curtains. Sam put his ear to the door but heard nothing. Henry stuck the two thins rods into the lock and jiggled until the tumblers clicked sharply. The sound echoed in the still air.

Sam pulled his gun from his belt and eased the door open. Metal hinges creaked. They slipped inside a dark hallway and waited, listening. Sam took a tentative step, but Henry grabbed his arm and pointed at his ear. Then Sam heard it—a sharp squeak like someone's shoe on a tile floor.

Sam knew the house's layout and realized that the dim light came from Sal's bedroom where Deputy Robicheaux had found the .45 caliber pistol.

He heard it again, closer. Sam pointed at the kitchen just beyond the short hall. Henry nodded in agreement.

Sam lunged forward, flattened on his belly and pointed his pistol at the dark room.

Jackson did the same. Sam aimed his pistol but he heard

the sound again—the unmistakable chirp of a small bird.

Sam fought to suppress his laughter. Almost had it clamped down, too, until he heard Henry's stifled laugh. He turned on his flashlight. A birdcage sat on the kitchen table. The green and black parakeet walked across its perch to get a better view of the strangers.

Sam peeked around the doorway to the master bedroom where a small lamp burned. He checked under the bed and the closet. The room was empty.

Jackson emerged from the second bedroom and shook his head.

They searched the living room and returned to the kitchen. Sam flicked on the overhead light and the bird chirped again.

"Cheep," Sam said. He and Jackson laughed hard. Sam wiped tears from his eyes. "I damn near blew Tweety Bird away."

"Me, too. I'm surprised my gun didn't go off."

Sam caught a whiff of something burnt. "You smell that?"

Jackson sniffed and nodded. "Maybe the guy Robicheaux saw smoked a cigarette before he left."

Sam followed the scent to the kitchen counter where a thick clump of burned paper lay at the bottom of the porcelain sink. Only the very tops of the papers had escaped total disintegration. Sam lifted up the singed papers and gingerly laid them on the tile counter. The bottom portion crumbled into charred airiness. "Must have been something important if the guy came here to destroy it."

Sam shined his flashlight on the remnants of each page. Someone had written something very small on the top of a middle sheet. He squinted and read, "Catholic Sisters for, hell, the rest of it's just chicken scratchin'."

"Let some young eyes take a look," Jackson said. He leaned closer. "War Orphans. Catholic Sisters for War

Orphans."

"War Orphans? How many kids could have lost both parents in an overseas war?"

Sam went to the roll top desk in the living room and found a phone book. No listing for Catholic Sisters for War Orphans. He searched the rest of the desk and found nothing but unpaid bills and two perfumed letters from a woman in Brooklyn. She called him 'my silly Sally'. Not what most gangsters would want as a nickname.

"Sam," Jackson called.

Sam found him standing by a stack of boxes in the kitchen pantry. *Stinson's Grocery* was stenciled clearly on the sides of each one, not blotted by firehose water like the box they had found at the Wharf Street building.

"My guess is Sal bought the food at Stinson's," Jackson said. "Then he put it in plain boxes before taking it to Carl and Max."

They tore open all the boxes but found nothing else. It didn't matter. They had discovered a connection between Sal Longino and the men hiding at the Wharf Street safe house. And, by extension, Vince Romano and Arin Haugen.

"You want to stay until Sal comes back?" Henry said.

Sam frowned. "I don't think Sal is coming back."

"You don't know that. Have a little faith, man."

"I have faith," Sam said. "I have faith that Sal ain't coming back."

They almost made it out the back door when the parakeet chirped again. The bird leaned against the side of the cage and didn't move when prodded by Sam's finger. It screamed weakly.

"He doesn't have any water," Sam said. He opened the cage door and took the water bottle and filled it at the faucet. He put it back and the bird scooted over on his perch and

235

drank.

Jackson pointed at the open door. "You're going to let Sal's bird fly away."

"He's in no shape to fly."

"Maybe he'd be better off if we *had* shot him."

"He's going to die in here," Sam said. He cursed and picked up the cage by its carrying handle.

Chapter 50

Sam walked past a '37 Mercury flatbed truck with *Stinson's Grocery* painted on the yellow cab. In the hot sun, two muscular black men unloaded boxes from the truck, their white undershirts soaked with sweat.

Sam climbed the loading dock steps and walked past the *Employees Only* sign. Smells of fresh produce wafted from the stacked crates and boxes. In the humid air flies swarmed the fruit.

Sam knocked on a door marked *Private* and entered.

Claude Stinson looked up from the *Galveston Daily News* and dropped his feet from where they had been propped up on the desk. "What the hell?"

Stinson, a rotund man with a bristly head of gray hair, stood and squinted at Sam through thick eyeglasses. An unlit cigar stub lay in an ashtray, fouling the stale air. "You gave me a fright, Sheriff."

Sam closed the door. "Catholic Sisters for War Orphans…"

Stinson's forehead wrinkled in puzzlement, either real or feigned. "What is that?"

"Think, Claude."

"Oh, yeah, the War Orphans people," Stinson said, suddenly remembering. "Come to think of it, I ain't seen them in a couple of weeks or so."

"Who was it that set up the account with you?"

Stinson thought a moment. "It was a bald fellow. Lot of muscle on him. Had a tattoo of a naked woman on his left arm." The grocer chuckled. "It was done real good, too."

"What was the name?"

"Of the woman?"

"No, Claude," Sam said. "The bald man."

"Shoot, don't make me lie to you, Sheriff. I don't recall."

"Let me see the paper work."

Stinson opened a metal cabinet and shuffled through files. He handed a manila folder to Sam.

The first invoice was dated June 23rd, 1944. About two weeks before Wayne was murdered. An invoice existed for every few days, but the last one was dated a day before the shootout in the Wharf Street building. Maybe since then they found another source of food for Max. Or—the scenario Sam most hoped for—Max was dead and wouldn't need any more damn steaks.

Sam noticed that the bald man had signed each invoice as 'John Smith.'

"John Smith," Sam said to Stinson. "You didn't think that name was a little common?"

"I didn't pay no attention to it, Sheriff."

"These war orphans sure ate a lot of expensive steaks, Claude." Sam said. "How did this guy order the food?"

"By phone. Then he came and picked it up."

And brought it to Sal Longino's house, Sam thought. Sal then put the food in plain boxes and delivered them to the two men. Good way to break the link between the man picking up the food and the man delivering it. Probably something devised by Vince Romano. "How did he pay?"

"Up front with a big wad of cash. There's still money left in the account."

"Call me if he comes back," Sam said. But he knew Stinson's Grocery had seen the last of the bald, muscle-bound man.

Chapter 51

Sam paced the plush carpet of a waiting room hung with portraits of famous Texas men—Sam Houston, James Bowie, Davy Crocket. But he wasn't sure he recognized the oil painting of one beaming man. He pointed it out to the young receptionist. "Is this Frank Simons?"

The girl said it was and turned away to hide her smile.

Above the portrait a sign in gilded letters spelled out Simons Realty.

"What's keeping him?" Sam asked her, irritated that he'd been kept waiting almost half an hour past his appointment time. "He must have an important client in there."

The girl looked embarrassed and stammered that she didn't know who was in his office.

Sam opened the office door and found Frank Simons staring out his window. The man shot him an indignant look. "Uh, Sheriff, a knock would have been more polite."

"Not keeping me waiting for nothing would have been more polite."

Simons wore a three-piece suit, and his puffy face failed to meet the spruced-up rendition of him on the wall. The realtor hooked his thumbs into the side pockets of his gray vest. "What can I do for you, Sheriff?"

"The building at 716 Wharf Street. Who's the owner?"

"Oh, yes, the one you burned down after you broke in."

Sam closed the door. "Mr. Hanson at the bed frame company said they made the rent check out to Northland Holding Company. Who is that?"

"Unfortunately, I'm not at liberty to divulge that."

"This is in regards to the murder of Wayne McRae," Sam said. "You'll give me the information one way or another."

"You don't have any call to threaten me."

Sam locked the door and propped a chair against the doorknob.

Simons lunged for the phone on his huge oak desk. Sam grabbed him and pushed him down into his ornate chair. Simons' face turned livid. "I'll have you arrested, Baker."

"Why did you kick Hanson Bed Frame out of the building?" Sam demanded.

"Hanson was behind on the rent. Northland wanted them out."

"That's not what Hanson says."

"Hanson is a drunk."

"You allowed two wanted men to hide out there."

Simons' hesitated a beat. "Those men were squatters."

"They had a key to the garage."

"Bullshit."

"The door was locked and their car was inside."

Sam detected a fine sheen of sweat on Simon's forehead. "Where did you send the rent check?"

Simon reached for the phone again. "I'm going to call my lawyer now, Baker. So if you'll just get the fuck—."

Sam tipped the heavy desk over. It pinned the realtor by the neck on the polished wood floor. Sam knelt by him. "Simons, I'm asking for the last time: what is Northland Holding's address?"

"They use a P.O. box in Seattle."

"What is their phone number?"

"I don't know."

"We were doing so well here, Simons," Sam said. He pulled the desk down tighter against the realtor's neck.

240

"Where is the file?"

Simons pointed to his file cabinet against the wall.

Sam stood and opened drawers until he found the Northland file. It contained only the typed agreement between the company and Simons. The letterhead listed a P.O. Box in Seattle.

Sam tapped the paper with his finger. "Where's the phone number?"

"They didn't give it to me."

Sam found the rolodex on the floor. "Frank, if I find it in here, we're not going to be friends anymore."

"I'm not lying," Simons insisted.

"How did you meet them initially?"

"They called me."

"They called you out of the blue?"

"Yes, just that one time," Simons said. He had to take a labored breath before he could speak again. "Then they sent me a letter instructing me to evict Hanson Bed Frames. That's the only two contacts I've had with them."

"Are they still paying you a commission?"

"Yes. By mail."

"Who signs the checks?"

"It's not legible. Look at the signature on the agreement."

Sam found scribbled writing that reminded him of Sylvie and Billy's first attempts to sign their names. He knelt back down by Simons.

"This didn't seem damn suspicious to you?"

"Yeah," Simons mumbled. "I guess."

"I might have to charge you with aiding and abetting murderers, Frank. That's a serious offense. It would be a shame to have to give up all this. Big office. Pretty secretary."

Simons nodded.

"Frank, if you're still lying to me..."

"I swear, Sheriff. That's all I know."

Sam locked eyes with him and saw fear and capitulation. "I want you to keep cashing the checks they send you. If you find out anything else about Northland, I want you to tell me immediately. Got it?"

"I will. I promise."

Sam lifted the desk. It landed with a dull thud on the plush carpet. He unlocked the door and walked past the secretary.

She looked at him, concerned. "Is everything all right?"

"Frank had a lot to get off his chest."

Chapter 52

The sun hung low in the sky but with still a couple of hours to go before it dropped into the horizon beyond the Gulf. The beach was full of people frolicking in the foamy waves and building sand castles.

Sam jogged in the sand while doing bicep curls with his injured arm. He had made progress with strengthening it but still had a ways to go. The knife wound in his chest made him wince if he ran too hard. The calf—the least serious of his wounds—was almost completely healed.

Townspeople waved to him as he passed, but the tourists didn't recognize this big man with the angry red pit in his arm. It felt good to work his body and break a sweat. When he had boxed, roadwork had always helped him heal and get stronger.

He and Claire had rarely visited the beach after Billy and Sylvie reached their teens and preferred to go with their friends. He remembered watching Billy—young but fearless—body surfing the Gulf waves. He and Claire would each take one of Sylvie's hands as she laughed at her brother and kicked at the shallow water.

To catch his breath Sam slowed to a fast walk. A shapely blond woman wearing a white sun hat and a tight blue swimsuit walked the beach. He shielded his eyes from the sun, and she caught him looking.

Laura smiled. "Sam!"

She hugged him, pressing her firm breasts into him. He held on a long moment, in no hurry to let go of her warm body.

She stepped back and lightly circled the mangled gash in

his arm with one finger. "Oh, Sam," she said. "They hurt you bad." She placed the palm of her hand over his heart. "Sylvie told me they stabbed you here."

"Somewhere in the neighborhood," he said. He felt a stirring.

"I was so scared."

"I look worse than I feel," he said. "But maybe that's always been true."

"Same old Sam," Laura said and laughed. "I visited you in the hospital, but you were asleep. I wanted to stay, but the nurse chased me out." She took off her sunhat. The breeze blew her blond hair free of her bare shoulders.

Two younger men eyed her as they passed. Other people lounging on the beach watched them—the tall sheriff and the striking young woman with her hand on his chest.

"Why don't you come over for a friendly dinner?" she said. "My cooking is good for what ails you. Remember?"

The places she had touched vibrated with something that felt like healing and desire. He couldn't deny what he felt for her physically, and he couldn't help but be flattered by the attention from such a young, pretty woman. But right now he couldn't give anything of himself. Every thought and action went into finding Wayne and Gus' killer. That obsession wouldn't leave room for anything or anyone else.

"I'm going to do you a big favor and beg off," he said. "At least for now."

She shrugged her shoulders and smiled. "I understand, Sam. I got carried away by seeing you again."

He kissed his finger and touched her nose. "I almost got carried away, too."

Chapter 53

Sam set little Rags next to the birdcage so he could watch the parakeet walk on his perch and chirp. It usually calmed him, but the dog had picked up on Sam's frustration and wouldn't be distracted by his new feathered friend.

Sam had just hung up with the private investigator, Herbert Marlowe, he'd hired to find out who owned the torched building on Wharf Street. A P.O. Box for Northland Holding and a scribbled signature on a property management agreement was all Sam could give him. Deputy Garza had worked the phones for two days but had only come up with the name of the man, Torg Andersson, who had opened the checking account at the Seattle bank. *Probably an alias*, Sam thought.

He had called Herbert Marlowe on Henry Jackson's recommendation. The Atlanta Police Department had hired him back when Jackson worked as a detective, and the man had done good work in quick order.

Over the phone call, Sam had expressed skepticism about the gumshoe's last name.

"It's the handle I was born with," the man had assured him in his high-pitched voice. "Marlowe's the name and investigation's the game."

Sam impressed upon Marlowe the urgency of discovering the people behind the facade of Northland Holding because it would help solve the murder of a young deputy sheriff.

"Could be difficult, Sheriff," Marlowe said. "People with something to hide usually create several layers around them.

It's like peeling an onion—eventually your eyes tear up and you quit."

* * *

Sam sat at the kitchen table and petted Rags. The little bird seemed to take comfort in his two companions and chirped out the melody of a Jimmie Rodgers song Sam had been singing.

Sam thought about the low odds Herbert Marlowe had given for discovering the people behind the façade of Northland Holding. They hadn't surfaced after their building had burned to the ground, yet they continued to pay a commission to Frank Simons every month.

Reaching an apparent dead end had him thinking about knocking back a quick shot of whiskey. Instead, he took a deep breath and dialed the phone.

After several rings he figured the housekeeper had retired to her quarters for the night. Finally, a man answered. "Who is it?"

"Hello, David."

"Well, well, he lives." Whittington's tone was as caustic as when he'd first learned that an ex-boxer would become his brother-in-law. But Sam detected something additional in his voice—a touch of triumph. "More bad news from Sin City?"

"No. We're the same paradise we always were."

"Uh huh," Whittington said. "Well, you just missed Claire. She's out for the evening with a good friend of mine. He owns one of the biggest banks in Dallas."

Sam's breathing missed a beat, but he gathered himself. "I'm sure she won't hold that against him."

"Actually, they're discussing their upcoming trip to Hawaii over a nice dinner."

Hawaii? Sam's mind whirled with images of Claire

walking on a white sand beach with a rich man. She had never been impressed with high-society men in three-piece suits, but like she had told him before she left—she was tired of being a sheriff's wife. "I hear it's nice there," he finally said. "Just have her call me."

"I'm not sure she's coming home tonight, Sam."

"Anytime she wants. It's not an emergency."

Whittington mumbled a vague promise and hung up. Sam held the receiver a long moment before dropping it in its cradle. He had wanted to show her that she was on his mind, that he hadn't given up on them. But, as usual, he'd waited too long to share his feelings.

He looked in his wallet and found the piece of paper with the phone number written on it. She answered on the first ring.

"It's Sam. I hope I'm not calling too late."

"No, I'm a night owl, Sam," Laura said. Her tone was bright and welcoming, despite his decline of her invitation on the beach this morning. "I'm making seafood gumbo. One of my specialties. Want to come over for some?"

Galveston '44

Chapter 54

Dominick Romano walked slowly between the tables in the Indigo Palm, each one full of people turned expectantly to the bandstand. An electric current ran through the nightclub. Everything was ready. Everyone had a drink, and the staff scurried to bring them more.

U.S. Navy sailors wearing dress uniforms occupied one table. Dominick had made a point earlier of introducing himself to them as the manager of the joint, just in case they got too high-spirited. Sometimes people thought him too young to manage a nightclub of the stature of the Indigo Palm, and he had learned to establish his authority early on. Of course, sharing the last name of the owner, Vince Romano, didn't hurt.

Dom smoothed the front of his dark blue, double-breasted suit and smiled in passing at a table of four young women. A well-built blond grabbed his arm. "Join us, good-looking. We want to buy you a drink."

"If I wasn't working, I would," Dom said. "Nothing would give me greater pleasure."

"*I* could give you greater pleasure," the blond said. Her friends covered their mouths and tittered. Dominick now knew where potential trouble lay in his club tonight. He would tell their waitress to water down their drinks—this was not the night for a bad scene.

"With your permission, I'm going to send over some shrimp and crab appetizers," Dom said. "On the house." He wanted some food in their bellies to soak up the booze.

Dominick looked towards the entrance, just as he had throughout the early evening. This time she was there. He missed a breath, as he always did when he saw her. She looked radiant in a simple black dress. Already several men were turning towards her.

Sylvie saw him and smiled. He hoped the excitement of seeing Frank Sinatra perform would at least temporarily distract her from her losses of the last year—her brother, Billy, and Wayne McRae.

As if their deaths hadn't been enough, she had been deeply shaken when her father was seriously wounded in the shootout with the two murder suspects. Her parents—her role models and her only remaining family—had separated. Sylvie's world had turned upside down. Dom wanted to make everything all right for her, but he knew there was only so much he could do. It would take time. He was patient. She was worth it.

Dom hurried over and took Sylvie's hands in his.

"Hi," she said. "Reservation for one, please."

"I'm sorry, Miss," Dom said. "I'm not sure if I can let you into the club tonight."

"You'd better have a good reason, mister. I'll have you know the manager of this establishment is a friend of mine."

"The only available table is just four feet from the stage. Once Mr. Sinatra gets a look at you, he's going to forget the lyrics to the songs."

"If he looks at me, I'm going to forget my own name." Sylvie took his arm and he escorted her to the front of the club. "Dom, the place is packed."

"If we can't sell out for Frank Sinatra, then we got problems." He pulled her chair out for her and she touched a bouquet of yellow roses on the table. "Oh, Dominick, for me?"

"I don't know," he said. "Why don't you read the card?"

Sylvie pulled a note out of the envelope and read, "Hi,

Sylvie. I like you. You real pretty. – Frank Sinatra."

"He can't write too well, but he sure can sing."

She pointed at the note. "You know, it's funny. Frank's handwriting is a lot like yours."

"Must be because we're both Italian." Dom said, and smiled. "Distant cousins or something."

Sylvie took a pen from her purse and crossed out Frank Sinatra's name and wrote Dominick below it. "Now I have it on record that you like me."

"Where's my proof?" he asked. She tilted her head back, and he kissed her. "I like that proof."

"Me, too."

He left to make a final check, skirting the table where the suggestive blonde and her friends were eating shrimp appetizers. They barely noticed him.

Everything was perfect.

Galveston '44

Chapter 55

Sam and Laura sat at her kitchen table eating shrimp gumbo and drinking beer. She'd been in high spirits all night, touching his hand for emphasis as she told funny stories about her pampered clients at the hair salon and about her eccentric family back in England.

Sam laughed, glad to be distracted from the news that Claire and some fat cat banker were going to Hawaii together. And Laura *was* distracting. She wore a low-cut white blouse with a blue stone pendant hanging just above her cleavage. Loose strands of her blond hair hung over her forehead. Without thinking, he pushed one out of her eye with his finger.

She took his hand in hers. "I'm so glad you're here, Sam."

They looked at each other a long moment. "Laura, I want to be fair to you," he said. "Right now, I can't give you much of myself. I—"

She put her finger against his lips. "I'm not asking anything from you, Sam," she said, smiling. "I understand you've only been separated a while. And I know you're going to hunt that man even if it kills you. And it might." She pushed up the shirt sleeve of his left arm and gently touched his bullet wound. "I will be here any time you want to see me. Just tell me what you want...shrimp gumbo...beef stew...me." She took his hand and placed it on her breast.

He pulled her onto his lap and kissed her.

* * *

Sam and Laura lay tangled together in the sheets. Her bare breasts rose and fell and glistened with a fine sheen of sweat where he had pressed his body into hers. He started to roll off her but she wrapped her legs around his back. "Stay a minute, Sam. Please."

"I'm not crushing you?"

"No. Did I hurt your chest or your arm?"

"No," he said. "I guess they passed the test."

"Jesus, Sam." She laughed, her breath on his neck. "You passed the test, too."

"Didn't know I was auditioning."

"You weren't. You had the role the first time I met you."

It seemed like a long time ago when he'd come to Laura's house in his filthy uniform to be with Sylvie. They had all been in shock from Wayne's murder, yet Laura had served them a resurrecting meal and cleaned his bloody tunic. She'd cut his hair and offered her body for comforting.

She was younger than Sam but old enough to be Sylvie's mentor, to be someone her daughter looked up to. If there was any woman who could take Claire's place in Sylvie's eyes, it would be Laura.

By all rights he should want to stay in her bed forever, to move in here and let Claire have the house she had left him with. She would see how lonely it is in a big house haunted by the loss of Billy and by the inevitable loss of a daughter who was hardly at home and would eventually leave it for good.

Unless the Dallas banker took Sam's place, both in the house and in her heart, she would only have a furry mutt to welcome her home.

But Sam didn't wish loneliness for Claire. Even as he lay in the arms of a beautiful young woman who seemed to adore him, he wished the best for his wife. Even if she divorced him, he couldn't betray their years together as a couple who had raised two admirable kids.

No, Laura wouldn't replace Claire in his heart. He had hoped she could salve the pain over his wife leaving him and finding a new man so quickly.

He rolled off Laura and looked up at the ceiling. He felt he had used her.

She turned his head to read his expression. Her brow furrowed. "Sam, what?"

"I'm sorry, Laura."

He got up and dressed in the semi-dark. She watched him, frowning. She had failed to make the connection she wanted. Yet, she managed a brave smile. "Please don't be sorry."

"You're incredible, Laura," he said. "And I *am* sorry.

He kissed his finger and touched her nose. And left.

Galveston '44

Chapter 56

Sylvie sipped her soft drink and ignored the looks from the sailors at the next table. She hoped they had witnessed Dominick kissing her so they would get the idea and leave her alone.

From her periphery a man's arm waved emphatically. Over the charged atmosphere of the club she heard her name called.

A huge man stood in the shadows beyond the side of the bandstand. It was Drago. She couldn't imagine what he would want with her. They'd never spoken before, and she was glad for that. The man gave her the creeps. She looked back to the stage where a technician adjusted the height of the microphone that would soon amplify the silky voice of Frank Sinatra.

A big shadow fell across the table and she looked up to see Drago's large head looming over her. His eyes reflected the red light from the glass candleholders. "Vince wants to talk with you," he said.

She couldn't imagine what Vince Romano would want to talk with her about. She was the sheriff's daughter, he was a gangster. Besides, her father had asked her—almost begged her—to go to Dallas because of the increasing conflict between him and Romano.

Sylvie smiled. "Please tell Vince that Dominick and I will talk to him after the show." She looked at her watch. "It's about to start."

Drago wrapped a big hand around her arm and pulled her

out of the chair like she was a rag doll. He hustled her through the side door and into the backstage area. Music stands and open instrument cases covered the floor. Plain wooden shelving held towels and supplies for the dressing rooms.

Vince had his back to them but turned when the door closed. He looked puzzled, as if Drago had brought him the wrong Sylvie Baker. "Sweet Jesus if you ain't grown into a fine woman." He lit a cigarette and inhaled sharply. "Does my son know how goddamn lucky he is?"

He looked older than when she'd seen him in passing just a few months before. Deep lines creased his perpetually sunburnt face, and his forehead couldn't be any more tightly furrowed.

Sylvie tried to free her arm but Drago held her firmly. Vince pulled deeply on his cigarette. He stared like he was deciding her fate.

"Mr. Romano," she said, keeping her voice level. "The show is about to start. Dominick will be looking for me."

A smile broke out over his leathery face. He held out his hands to her. The chameleon changing colors. The cigarette held between his lips bounced as he spoke. "Sylvie, my dear. Thanks for giving me a few seconds of your time."

Drago pushed her towards Romano, and he took her hands in his. "I asked you back here because I want to talk about you and my son."

"Wouldn't it be better if Dom were here, Mr. Romano?"

"Please. Call me Vince."

"I don't know what Dom told you, but we've only been dating a short while. We haven't discussed any plans at all."

"You know how Dominick is. He don't tell me shit." Vince let go of her hands and jabbed the cigarette at her a couple times. "But I got eyes. I see him and you together, and I think to myself, you make a real handsome couple."

"Maybe in a year we could have this—"

Vince snorted. "A year? Hell, a lot can happen in a day. Forget about a fucking year." He paced the floor. "Sylvie, as you know, sometimes your father and I have our differences. Am I right?"

"He doesn't tell me his business."

"That's good," Vince said. "That's smart. And I wouldn't tell you mine. What I will say is that if you and Dom become a couple, you will have to decide on which side your bread is being buttered."

"I'm not sure what you mean."

"It's simple, sweetheart. Your father has caused me some fucking ass aches lately that I didn't need. He accused me of some bullshit I know nothing about. He burned down a joint of mine and that cost me money." Romano pointed his cigarette at her again. "And *nobody* fucks with my business."

"Mr. Romano, I'm afraid I don't know—"

"Let me finish." He held up a hand to silence her. "I need to know right now. If you and my son become an item, whose side you going to be on?"

Sylvie decided not to argue with this foul man. He seemed to be smoldering inside from some consuming pressure. Let him have his say. Then smile and answer: *Of course I would betray my father and be some damn mob doll, Mr. Romano.* Then she could escape back to the table and put on a brave face for Dominick. Pretend nothing had happened, at least until the show was over.

Let him enjoy his successful evening, his triumphant booking of Frank Sinatra. Then she would tell him.

Galveston '44

Chapter 57

The Indigo Palm hummed like a well-oiled machine. Sinatra's manager had said they were ready. The curtain would rise and the big band would launch into a jazz instrumental before the star hit the stage.

Dom arrived at the vacant table where Sylvie's soft drink sat almost full. He hoped she would hurry back so they could share the excitement when Sinatra hit the stage.

A sailor got his attention and pointed at the side door.

* * *

The orchestra ripped into the first song as Dominick stepped through the backstage door. Vince stood close to Sylvie, and his hard gaze shifted from her to his son.

"What are you doing, Vince?"

"I'm having a talk with little Sylvie." Vince made a shooing gesture. "Go manage the club."

Dom looked down at her arm where red marks stood out against her fair skin. He softly brushed her arm with the back of his fingers as if to make Drago's handprint go away. "Are you all right?"

She smiled and nodded, but her eyes said the opposite.

He turned to Vince. "You have no business to conduct with her."

Vince pointed at his own chest. "This is my club. I do what I want here."

"You heard me," Dominick said. He looked at Drago.

"And if anyone ever lays a hand on her again, they're going to pay."

Drago nodded once to accept the challenge. No one spoke as the new reality sunk in.

The silence was broken by voices coming from the hallway. The door opened and Arin Haugen stepped inside. "Here you are," he said to Vince.

Dominick was surprised to see the shipping and hotel magnet inside the Indigo Palm. He and Greta travelled in a loftier realm and would probably cause a stir in the society column if they were seen visiting the club or, especially, the casino. Dominick had only met him on one occasion and had come away feeling he'd been quickly assessed and dismissed for having no ability to bring him more money.

Vince kept his eyes on Dominick. "Give us a minute."

"Let's go, Vincent," Haugen said. "We have a meeting with the new guy."

"I know we got a goddamn meeting with the new guy."

"Don't be cross, Vinny. He's got something for you." Haugen walked out.

The mobster shouted after him, "Better be the whole fucking thing this time."

"Vince," Dominick said. "I'll see it through to the end of the show, but that's it for me. I quit."

"Too late. You're fired." Romano's eyes went dead, like black curtains drawing closed. "Don't let me catch your punk ass around here." He turned on his heels and walked out. Drago gave him a last look and followed.

Dominick took Sylvie's hands and felt them tremble. "I am so sorry, Sylvie."

"It's not your fault." She kissed his cheek. "You were here for me."

"Always." He wanted to tell her he would give his life for

her, but that would be the last thing she wanted to hear. "What the hell did Vince say?"

"He wanted to know whose side I would be on if, you know, you and I became a committed couple. His or my father's."

"That's crazy." Dom shook his head. "I don't like you that much."

She laughed a little. But only a little.

* * *

Dominick and Sylvie stepped out of the backstage room and into the darkened hallway. The red glow of his father's cigarette followed him as he walked towards the casino at the end of the long pier.

Drago, standing in the shadows, opened the door for him.

Arin Haugen sat a blackjack table, his fingers drumming the green felt like an emperor awaiting his tardy subjects.

A man in a leather jacket paced the floor behind him. Late-thirties or early forties. Thick neck and a square jaw. The *new man*.

"Kind of odd for someone to wear a coat in this heat," Sylvie said.

Drago shooed them away with a wave of his big hand.

But Drago didn't need to threaten him to leave. He was already gone.

Galveston '44

Chapter 58

The bedside phone rang and woke Sam from a troubled sleep. A man's high-pitched voice gave his name as if Sam should know it. "Who?"

"Marlowe is the name, and private investigation is my game."

"How could I forget?"

"Sorry to wake you but you said to call anytime I had news about that building's ownership. The one on Wharf Street there in Galveston."

Sam sat upright, fully awake now. "Go ahead."

"I found out that Northland Holding Company is owned by International Sea Lanes, Incorporated."

Sam's irritation rose. He had been awakened about a corporate smokescreen, another blind alley. "Let me ask you something, Mr. Marlowe," Sam said. "If I wanted to shoot somebody at International Sea Lanes, where would I go to do that? Brazil? South Africa?"

"You wouldn't have to go anywhere, Sheriff Baker. They're right there in Galveston."

"International Shipping Lanes is here?"

"Yes, sir. And so is the man who owns that company. And that company owns the building you burned down."

"I don't suppose you got any names to go with that company?"

"Just one," Marlowe said. "Arin Haugen."

* * *

A glossy green LaSalle drove into the parking lot of a white colonial building. Thick support columns reached to the top of the tall overhang. Massive chandeliers hung from the ceilings, but the smoked glass windows obscured the identity of the well-heeled attendees inside.

An older couple—he in a black tuxedo and she in a long ivory gown—exited the car and walked to the building.

"Is that a LaSalle?" Sam asked from the passenger seat of Henry Jackson's Ford.

"A 1940 model. Last year they quit making them."

"Who needs a car that expensive?"

"They were cheaper than a Cadillac."

"How much they go for?"

"About fourteen hundred."

"That's cheap?" Sam said. "They could have donated that to the charity these people are supposed to be supporting tonight."

"Catholic Sisters for War Orphans?"

"Beats me. I just hope Arin Haugen is attending."

A parade of formally-dressed people entered the event center. None of them were Haugen.

"He could have skedaddled back to Norway," Jackson said. "No way he doesn't know there's heat on him now."

"He owns the governor, so he won't give a shit. He and Greta think they're untouchable."

The stream of people into the charity ball slowed to a trickle. With each minute the odds against Haugen showing up grew. Sam and Jackson had already cased the Tropicana Hotel without luck, and now two deputies were there keeping a lookout for him.

A boisterous group of sailors passed by. Sam pulled his straw hat down over his forehead. Time ticked by.

Jackson yawned. "Any other ideas?"

"Go home?"

A gray-haired woman in a flowery silk dress walked outside. Jackson raised the field glasses. "Greta Haugen."

"I'll be damned. They must have got there early."

Greta hurried to the street, a gold-colored clutch in her hand.

A red Cadillac roared out of its parking spot down the street and braked hard in front of her. She jumped in the back and the car sped off.

"Where the hell is Arin?" Sam said.

"Could have been him driving."

"But why would she get into the backseat?"

Jackson let another car pass before easing the Ford from the curb. He gradually picked up speed but stayed behind red Cadillac. At Avenue K the Cadillac turned and pulled to a stop in front of the opulent Bellaire Hotel. Its rooms didn't allow a view of the Gulf, but it was just as stately as the Tropicana.

"Don't tell me she's giving business to the competition," Jackson said.

"Knowing her, she's there to burn it down."

Jackson turned the car into the parking lot and stopped where they had a good view of the Cadillac. A man, bald and muscular, jumped out and opened the back door.

"Look at this," Sam said, adrenaline already rushing to his head. "It's our friend, the car delivery man."

"He's a regular jack-of-all-trades."

The man scanned the area before climbing back into the red Cadillac and driving away. Jackson followed. They travelled several blocks before the car made a quick turn. Jackson stayed with him. He looked into the rearview mirror. "Somebody's behind us."

Sam looked back, but the car seemed to be slowing.

The Cadillac gained speed and turned sharply.

"He's on to us," Sam said.

Jackson downshifted and turned. The red Cadillac took a hard right, and a hubcap blew off a tire and rolled away. It was a now a race. Jackson pushed the pedal to the floor and the well-tuned engine roared.

The Cadillac hit a long street but couldn't pull away. It turned hard and slid and hit a parked car broadside. The bald man jumped out and ran.

Jackson slammed the brakes. Sam jumped out and sprinted after him. The man ran down the street and looked back once and ducked between two buildings.

"Stop! Galveston County Sheriff," Sam yelled. With every stride, he gained on the shorter man.

The bald man turned into an alley and ran out of room. An iron fence loomed. He jumped up onto the first cross beam, but Sam grabbed him before he could throw his leg over the top. They fell to the hard ground. Sam dug a knee into the man's back and pulled one of his arms behind him. "I'm Sheriff Sam Baker. You're under arrest."

"What for?" the man croaked.

Jackson ran up and grabbed the man's other arm. Sam cuffed him and pulled a .38 caliber pistol from his waistband. They pulled him up into a seated position. The bald man stared in surprise at seeing a Negro in partnership with a white sheriff.

He bled from scratches on his face, but it was him—the guy who had not only brought the white Chevy to Max and Carl at the flophouse, but the man who had picked up food for them at Stinson's Grocery and delivered it to Sal Longino.

Henry searched his shirt pockets and pulled out a pack of cigarettes and a book of matches.

"I'm going to ask you a couple of questions," Sam said.

"And I'm going to know if—"

"You can take me to the damn jail first." The man sneered. "I got my rights."

"Oh, you're going to jail all right, my friend. But I'll have the truth right here first. You get my drift?"

Henry pointed to the street. "You want me to get the stretcher, Sheriff?"

"Let's see how cooperative he is first."

The man looked at the dark walkway that ran between two shuttered buildings. Nothing but overgrown bamboo and a couple of scraggly palm trees, brown fronds swaying in the light breeze. "They said you were a hard ass," he said.

"Who said that?" Sam asked. "Was that our friend Arin Haugen? Or maybe Vince Romano?" He searched the man's front pants pockets and came up with a folding knife and a few coins. He tossed the knife into the bushes.

Sam shoved the coins back into the man's shirt pocket. "What's your name, friend?"

"Campbell," he said. "Freddy Campbell."

"That better be your name, Freddy."

"It's what's on my driver's license."

Sam pulled Campbell's wallet from his back pocket and shuffled through the contents. "Three dollars, Freddy? Arin Haugen ain't paying you so good, is he?"

His driver's license, issued in California, confirmed his name.

Nothing remained in the main compartment of the wallet. Sam slipped a finger in the smallest pocket and pulled out a folded scrap of paper. Jackson picked up the matches and struck one. Someone had drawn a rough map of four nameless streets with an X marked on one. Three numbers written at the bottom. A long mark next to the numbers had been torn off.

"What is this map of, Freddy?" Sam asked.

Campbell shook his head. "The road to hell, Sheriff."

"Is this where Max is?" Henry asked.

"I don't know any Max."

Sam pointed at the torn mark. "Is this a number or a street?"

Campbell sneered and looked away,

"You're going to tell me, my friend. Believe me," Sam said. He looked at the map again. "I wish Gus was still with us," he said to Henry. "He might be able to make sense of this."

"Amen on that."

Out of the darkness came the sound of heavy footsteps. Flashlights blinded them. Men shouted.

Vince Romano, Sam thought. He reached for the pistol in his belt, but strong men grabbed him from behind and pinned his arms to his sides. Sam wrenched one free and elbowed a man in his stomach. Another man jumped on his back. They wrestled him to the ground face first on the rough concrete. Two sets of hands pulled his arms behind his back and handcuffed him.

He looked up to see not Vince or Drago, but several uniformed Texas Rangers.

"Stand him up," a voice commanded. Two Rangers lifted him by his arms and stood him next to Freddy Campbell. Jackson lay still on the ground, his eyes closed. Blood ran down his face from a cut on his forehead.

"What the fuck are you *doing*?" Sam shouted. "I'm Sheriff Sam Baker, and you're interfering with a murder investigation."

The Rangers breathed deeply from their brief exertion. They stared at him as if he were some exotic animal. Their curious expressions seemed to be mixed with some respect.

Sam held their gaze, amazed at their size. One man was as tall as him.

A pudgy man in a white dress shirt broke through their ranks. Mid-thirties. Receding hairline. "Sheriff Baker," the man said. "We finally meet." The man's voice quavered like someone much older.

Stephen Miller. Governor Davis's adjunct.

"You should have come to see the governor, Sheriff. You could have saved everyone a lot of trouble."

Sam nodded at Freddy Campbell. "As you can see, Miller, I've been pretty busy."

"Do you always go around without your uniform, Baker?"

"I'm undercover, Mr. Miller. Maybe one of the Rangers can explain that to you."

Miller looked down at Jackson, still unconscious. "Is this the colored you've been working with?"

"I deputized him," Sam said. "He was a detective in Atlanta."

Miller cocked his head at Sam as if he hadn't heard correctly. "Atlanta. Atlanta, Georgia?"

A couple of the Rangers exchanged doubtful glances. Sam stifled the urge to kick them in the balls. Miller's, too. He said, "We're close to catching the killer of Deputy Wayne McRae."

"That's not my immediate concern, Sheriff. The governor sent me here to carry out his orders, and I think you know what those are."

Sam indicated Freddy Campbell again. "There's a strong probability this man knows where the killer is hiding."

"That's a goddamn lie," Campbell said. "I work for Greta Haugen. She'll vouch for me."

Sam decided not to reveal that Arin Haugen had been hiding the killers in one of his buildings and supplying them cars and food. It was doubtful he would be believed.

"What do you say about that, Mr. Baker? He says he works for one of the richest men in Texas."

"This man aided and abetted murder suspects."

"Your successor can look into that because you are no longer Sheriff of Galveston County. By order of the governor."

The Ranger captain stepped forward. "With all due respect, Sheriff, you've made a mess out of this investigation. Do you have your badge on you?"

"Back pocket."

The captain pulled the badge out of his pocket and handed it to Miller.

"You can take these cuffs off, and we'll be on our way," Sam said.

"So you can cause more trouble?" Miller said. "No, Sheriff, you're going to spend the night in your own jail."

Chapter 59

Raspy snoring reverberated from across the narrow corridor. A steel door clanged shut somewhere. Gravelly voices came and went.

Sam covered his head with a musty pillow but the noises cut through. He rolled over on the hard mattress. Pain from his arm and chest wounds, aggravated from the tussle with the Texas Rangers, brought him fully to consciousness. Now that he'd experienced the jail's impossible sleeping conditions from the perspective of an inmate, he wondered why they— and the smell of sweat and vomit—weren't more of a deterrent to crime.

He sat up on the saggy mattress and looked at the source of the guttural eruptions in the cell across from his. Old Jaspar Jones was sleeping off yet another drunk. He frequented the jail so often that the deputies liked to joke that he got his mail there.

Two cells down, Freddy Campbell lay on his own cot. Sam had urged the Ranger captain to bring him in for questioning, despite the order by Stephen Miller to cut him loose. The captain, a thick-set man with a mangled ear, had held up an arm to silence Miller.

When they got to the jail, the captain took Sam into the interview room—the very room where he had questioned hundreds of suspects over his twenty-three years as a cop— and looked him in the eyes for a long moment. "How did this Freddy Campbell, as you claim, aid and abet murder suspects?"

"He delivered a car to them. He was involved in bringing food to—"

"What evidence do you have that he brought them a car?"

"I witnessed the exchange myself. So did the man who was with me. Henry Jackson."

The captain shook his head. "Mr. Baker, right now you're a man without a lot of credibility. And as far as a colored man's testimony goes, well, you know what that's worth around here."

Sam asked about Henry's condition. Had they taken him to someone who could examine the bloody gash on his forehead?

"He'll be all right," the captain said. "Colored men have hard heads."

Sam's anger flared. He decided he wouldn't divulge the evidence that Arin Haugen was somehow involved in protecting Max and Carl. That his car had been driven by them the night of Wayne McRae's murder. That his building had hid them. He would keep to himself the role Freddy Campbell had in buying food for them and delivering it to Sal Longino.

His accusations would undoubtedly be picked up by Stephen Miller who would pass them on to the governor. And the governor would warn his largest campaign donor, Arin Haugen, that the former Sheriff of Galveston County had incriminating things to say about him.

No, Sam wasn't about to show his hand and let Haugen and Vince Romano ship Max someplace safer. No one in authority was going to believe him anyway. He didn't have Haugen's Lincoln—it was long gone now. Gus Josie, another witness to Freddy Campbell swapping the blue Lincoln for the white Chevy, was dead. And, like the captain had said, the circumstantial testimony from a Negro would be given little credence.

"What am I charged with?" he had asked the Ranger.

"Let's start with abuse of the office of Sheriff. Dereliction of duty. Arson of two buildings. And maybe even the murder of the man you burnt to a damn crisp." The captain had told him to settle in, that this would be his home for a while.

When the Ranger left, Jaspar Jones, his hair even whiter than the last time Sam saw him, leaned unsteadily against his cell door. "Hey Sheriff. Did you rob a bank?" He cackled and slapped his leg.

Quick footsteps echoed in the hallway. Deputy Robicheaux slapped Jasper's knuckles with a short length of rubber hose.

Jasper howled and grabbed his hand. "You broke my fingers."

"No, they ain't," the deputy said. "But I'll break your filthy neck if you don't shut up." He turned to Sam. "Sorry about that, Sheriff Baker."

"You don't need to call me sheriff anymore, Gilbert."

"I can't believe it," he said. He looked both ways down the corridor. "I'm about as confused as a fellow could be. How could they do this to you?"

"I rubbed somebody powerful the wrong way."

"Arin Haugen?"

Sam nodded. "And his buddy, the governor."

"That ain't right. You were just tryin' to find Wayne's killers."

"Who's the acting sheriff?"

"It's Deputy Eilers." Robicheaux shook his head. "He ain't fit to be dogcatcher."

Gilbert nodded at Freddy Campbell's cell and whispered, "He didn't tell Eilers or the Rangers anything about where that Max is. Just keeps saying he works for Greta Haugen."

"He had this on him," Sam said. He pulled the crude paper

map from his pocket and showed it to Robicheaux. "Do you know these streets?"

The deputy held it to the dim light and turned it to various angles. "I reckon that's the street in question with the X on it. But these numbers at the bottom, is that first one a number four? Or maybe it's an H. That last one where it's ripped could be anything."

"He might have that torn piece on him. Maybe in his wallet."

"All I know is they're going to call Greta Haugen in the morning to confirm he works for her." Robicheaux pursed his lips, an expression Sam noticed he did when he was puzzling something out. "That's an interesting connection. This son-of-a-bitch and Greta Haugen."

"I just found out that Arin Haugen owns the building where they were hiding."

Robicheaux shook his head. He took a moment to take it all in. "Did you tell the Rangers that?"

"They weren't interested in what I had to say. The Ranger captain told me my successor could look into it. So did Stephen Miller."

"Eilers don't know how to conduct a damn investigation." Robicheaux spoke in a low growl and looked down the hallway at the back door. "Wayne deserves better than that. He needs your help."

Sam held his breath as the young deputy, his expression tight with bitterness, seemed to be making some life-changing decision. He looked at Jasper, asleep on his cot and snoring like a buzz saw. "Fuck it," Robicheaux said. He stuck the cell key into the lock.

"Wait a minute, Gilbert. You let me out and you'll not only be out of a job, you'll be breaking a serious law."

"I owe it to Wayne, Sheriff." Robicheaux unlocked the

cell door. Sam slipped past Freddy Campbell and out the back. Dark clouds blocked the moon. Everything was still, quiet.

Robicheaux unlocked the security gate and swung it open. He ran to his squad car and pulled out a Winchester rifle. He gave it to Sam along with his pistol.

"You'll have to run," Sam said.

"I figure I'll go back to my family in Louisiana," Robicheaux said. "They'll never find me in the swamp."

"You're a hell of a man, Gilbert," Sam said. "I thank you for this."

"Just find that son-of-a-bitch, Sheriff."

They shook hands. Robicheaux got in his Ford and Sam jumped in Robicheaux's squad car. Sam fired up the engine and drove out of the gate. He hit the street and drove away from his former life.

Just like Max, Sam was now a fugitive from the law.

Galveston '44

Chapter 60

The taped ball of medical wrap rolled across the concrete floor and thumped against the leg of Smoltz's cot. He kicked it back across the room, but it went wide of its target.

"You kick like a girl," Max said, standing in front of his improvised goal. "I'm beating you nineteen to one. Don't you have any pride?" He retrieved the makeshift soccer ball and threw it at Smoltz's head. "Next time I expect a little more competition."

The big man walked in a square around the dank basement, starting the exercise routine he'd begun a few days before. His recovery over the last few days had amazed the doctor. Smoltz had stopped advising his patient to stay in bed. It did no good and it agitated him.

"I am ready to fuck the next woman I see," Max had informed Smoltz while eating a large steak and several eggs for breakfast.

The next woman he would see, of course, would be the gray-haired nurse who brought their meals. Smoltz didn't think she was who Max, probably in his late-twenties, had in mind.

Smoltz lay back on his cot, nauseous from the withdrawal of his medicine. Max had made him hand it over and would only allocate a small amount at a time, not even enough to fill half the spoon. He had stuffed the glass vials under his mattress along with one of the doctor's surgical scalpels.

"You've got to be clear-headed when the time comes," Max had said. As of yet, he hadn't explained when that time would be or what would be required of him.

Smoltz had a small allocation of heroin he had managed to stash for when the vomiting and tremors started. The doctor had kicked twice before, and the sleeplessness and seizures had almost killed him. God forbid he would become irritable and anxious. That kind of behavior would not go over well with his fellow underground denizen.

Max pumped out several pushups and sit ups. He wiped sweat off his massive chest with a towel and lay down in his bed. Barely a minute had passed before the first deep snore reverberated around the basement.

Smoltz couldn't wait longer. He got up and fixed a bit of the white powder and spiked it into his veins. A sharp knock sounded at the upstairs trapdoor, and he scrambled to hide his rig. Two more knocks followed a pause. Smoltz tied the blindfold in place and stood against the wall.

The door opened, and footsteps clattered on the wooden steps.

Smoltz jumped when the woman grabbed his arm and guided him to the stairs. She had never touched him before, and he found the human contact not unpleasant.

The maintenance fix of his medicine hit his brain and he wobbled. The woman steadied him while his foot found the first step. He began to float up to a faint white light above him. *Overdose,* he thought. But why would heaven open its gates for a sinner condemned to fry in hell with an oversized killer?

Below him the woman whispered. "Reach for the floor." Smoltz returned to earth.

His hands found a level surface. He swung his leg over and stood. Fresh air wafted over him, cooler and drier than the dank basement.

The woman gripped his arm and eased him forward. A light source seeped around the edges of the blindfold.

Sunlight! That meant daytime. Down in the pit, day was night and night was day.

The doctor's hopes soared. With Max's rapid improvement they might pay him and send him home. Or, like his big patient had warned, they would shoot him because he knew too much about the man who held such great importance for them.

The unmistakable aroma of steak drifted to him. Probably their next meal. But a competing whiff of sweat overtook that of the food. A floorboard creaked and the smell came closer. Someone—a man—breathed heavily though his nose. Maybe it was the man who would pay him and take him back to the bus terminal...or kill him.

The man—and the smell—passed by him. The creak of footsteps on the floorboards ceased. The basement stairs began to groan as the man climbed down.

The woman steered Smoltz forward a few more steps and helped him sit on something soft. A sofa or a chair. He relaxed and spoke to the woman for the first time since her assistance during Max's surgery. "Is the job over?"

"Shhhsssh," the woman said.

She sounded close, maybe across from him in a chair. Did she have a gun? Probably. These people wouldn't risk leaving her alone unarmed with a man. They knew their business. Everything had been run like clockwork for the last few weeks. Food was abundant and medical supplies were always top quality.

The phone rang, shattered the silence. "Don't move," the woman whispered.

She picked up the phone. "Yeah, he's here. They're meeting now."

The phone clattered onto its base. The seat cushion whooshed as the woman settled back into her seat. Somewhere a clock ticked. Then voices, increasingly strident, rose from below. Max and the new man shouted, but their heated words were distorted beyond comprehension by concrete and distance.

Elmer Smoltz wondered if the new man had been warned of Max's volatility, his disturbing ability to penetrate into your mind and discover your innermost secrets and weaknesses. He had entered the lion's den and he'd better possess more than a whip and a chair.

The woman cursed. She crossed the floor and the trapdoor slammed shut with a bang. Silence resumed.

After a few minutes, a fist pounded on the trapdoor. The woman rose again. A lock clicked and the door creaked back on its hinges. Evidently, it only opened from the floor side.

"I know," the woman said, apparently agreeing with something the man had silently communicated. He sighed and zipped something together forcefully. Smoltz guessed it to be a leather coat because it creaked with each step the man took. Smoltz also owned one, but he wore his in the Houston winters, not in the Galveston summers.

With a deep sigh, the man walked away. Somewhere, a door slammed shut.

The woman grabbed Smoltz' arm and pulled him from the sofa. His hopes rose. Surely she would now take him to the Galveston bus station while he wore the blindfold. Instead, she pushed him forward and opened the trapdoor.

A sense of foreboding gripped him. He couldn't go back down into the hell hole with Max. He didn't know how much more he could take. Especially if the big man was riled up by the argument with his malodorous visitor. Smoltz had to try one last time.

"In my professional opinion, the patient needs no further medical care. My work here is done."

"Down you go, doctor." The woman pressed the persuasive barrel of a gun into his back.

Galveston '44

Chapter 61

The eastern sky glowed red with the first hint of dawn. A stiff wind rustled palm tree fronds and pushed tall pines into a slow, swaying dance. Sam carried Robicheaux's rifle as he trotted along a dark street pitted with pot holes. The deputy's pistol rode snug in his belt.

He passed a small liquor store and a beauty shop, both with 'closed' signs hanging on their unpainted doors. Gray shotgun shacks lined both sides of the street.

He approached a house where black men knelt on the narrow porch, their backs bent over a flickering candle. Other men stood outside the circle, passing around a bottle of wine. Dice clattered sharply on the wooden slats, and men shouted their approval or cursed their luck.

Sam crossed to the other side of the street and tried to hide the Winchester against his side. A wiry man paused with the wine bottle at his lips. "What the fuck…?"

Every head snapped around and stared at Sam. Not only was he a big white man, he carried a goddamn rifle. And why was he running and, *hey*, isn't that the fucking sheriff? They wouldn't know he'd been stripped of his badge just hours before, but it wouldn't make his invasion any less threatening.

One hefty man walked off the porch into the barren yard and shouted at Sam to stop. He tried to pick up the pace but his legs burned after covering four or five miles since ditching the squad car in the woods. He looked back, but no one dared follow.

The street began to look unfamiliar and he feared that he'd

made a wrong turn somewhere. A bright porch light broke through the darkness and guided him to a three-story, peach-colored house. The large, well-maintained property seemed almost as much an anomaly in the neighborhood as did Sam.

Muted lights shone in a few windows. Three cars were parked in front.

Sam stashed the rifle and pistol behind some bushes and rapped on the front door with the brass knocker. He had the feeling someone watched him from the round peephole in the door. He wiped sweat from his face and tried to look nonchalant and non-threatening. What he couldn't do, however, was change his skin color.

The door swung open and a sturdy black woman in a peach-colored robe pointed a pistol at his head. "Well, if it ain't the sheriff."

Sam raised his arms. "I assume you're Madam Peaches."

"Maybe. What business you think you have up in here, Sheriff? Or, should I say *ex*-sheriff."

"I'm looking for your brother."

"He ain't here." She started to close the door, but Sam stopped it with his foot.

"I just want to know if he's all right."

She pointed the pistol at his face. "Let go of my door."

Sam didn't relish going back down the same street. The dice players might be more prepared for him this time. "Would you give your brother a message for me?"

"Just let him be. You gone get him killed."

Sam removed his foot, and the madam closed the door. He looked back down the dark road, the only one out of the neighborhood. He went to the bushes and retrieved the guns.

The front door opened. Henry Jackson stood framed by the yellowish light behind him.

"Nice of you to drop by, Sheriff."

"I was in the neighborhood."

"They let you out already? You weren't in jail but a few hours."

"Somebody left the back door open."

Jackson thought about that a moment. "Robicheaux or Turner?"

"Robicheaux." Sam stepped closer to look at Jackson's forehead. Several stitches held a swollen gash together. "You already went to a doctor?"

"My sister is the doctor. She had a lot of practice stitching me up when I was a kid."

"I'll bet you got a good headache."

"There you go again with that keen analytic mind of yours," Jackson said. "So, what are we going to do?"

"You haven't had enough fun already?"

"I figure it's just starting. Any ideas?"

"I was hoping you could tell me," Sam said. "I don't have a badge, and they're going to be looking for me. The only idea I have is that they're going to release Freddy Campbell soon."

"Yeah, Arin Haugen won't let him sit there too long."

"I'd like to greet our bald friend when he gets out."

Jackson swung the door open, and Sam followed him into the house. Stained glass lamps glowed with a mix of bright colors. Overstuffed sofas and chairs filled the anteroom. Two young black women wearing peach-colored nighties sat smoking cigarettes, sleepily waiting for the next john to show up. They stood, startled by the big sweaty man.

Peaches rushed out, her hands on her hips. "Henry, what the hell you doin'?"

"Sam needs to rest a minute, Sis. We'll be out of here in a flash."

"I don't care if Wayne was your friend," she said. "You cross into their world again you gon' get tore to pieces. Just like in Atlanta."

"You know I have to do this."

She squeezed his jaw with one hand, but tenderly. "Ever since you little, you stubborn."

"I know. It runs in the family."

Jackson led them into his room in the back of the house where a single bed took up one corner. A schoolroom desk abutted one wall, shelves of books above it.

Sam pulled a book out. "*Native Son* by Richard Wright. Any good?"

"You can borrow it, if you want."

"Sure. Unless you have a good western."

"Fresh out of westerns."

Sam squeezed into the snug bathroom and splashed his face with water. The sink and tub were a sparkling white. The only blemish in the room was a long crack in the mirror glass that split his face into mismatched halves. The side away from the light was in shadow, just like his long-time identity as a lawman.

The clearer side was who he was now—a criminal on the run.

Chapter 62

Rags whined as he watched his mistress pace back in forth in the living room. Sylvie looked out the front window. Gray clouds had blown in from the Gulf, ready to drop rain when the heat of day arrived.

The whoosh of car tires came from the street. A black Ford turned sharply into the driveway and accelerated past the side windows.

She looked at the clock. Dom couldn't have gotten here in the few minutes since they'd spoken on the phone. She had called him when she got the news from Deputy Turner that her father had been arrested, only to escape a few hours later. She looked out the back door window. The strange car had stopped in front of the garage. She couldn't see the driver.

Sylvie found the key hidden under the hutch and unlocked the bottom drawer. She reached under a pile of papers and pulled out a Police Special. She hurried back to the kitchen window and looked out.

The driver's side door swung open and a black man climbed out. She opened the door when she saw it was Henry Jackson. "Henry, what the—"

Jackson put his finger to his lips and whispered, "Are you alone?"

"Yes."

He waved his arm at the car. Her father, wearing a big straw hat, jumped out and ran inside.

"Daddy!" She set the pistol down, and they hugged for a long moment. "Is it true?"

"Afraid so, sweetheart. But don't worry, everything's going to be fine."

His attempt at reassurance rang hollow. The pain and anger in his voice were evident. He'd given his all to serve the people of Galveston County, risking his life and wearing out the patience of his wife.

"I take it you know Henry."

"I do," she said and hugged him. "But what are you doing with my father?"

"Trying to keep him out of trouble. As you can see, it's not working."

"Henry is helping me with the investigation," Sam said. He went to the living room window and looked out.

It all clicked together for Sylvie. "You're the Negro people saw coming out of that building on Wharf Street."

"Just a vicious rumor," Jackson said.

"Right," she said. "Could have been any Negro in Galveston who just happens to be a former detective."

Jackson shrugged and smiled. "Could have been any of us."

Sylvie pointed at the stitched bump on his forehead. "What happened?"

"This is from last night. Courtesy of the Texas Rangers."

A car's squeaky brakes sounded from the street. A '38 Dodge pulled to a stop in front of the house.

"It's Dominick," Sylvie said. "I called him when I heard the news."

"It's best if he doesn't know I'm here," Sam said.

"Daddy, you can trust him. He doesn't even work for his father anymore. He quit last night."

"Why?"

"Because of what Vince said to me."

"What?"

290

"We'll tell you what happened," she said.

Her father nodded. She opened the door, and Dom stepped in. His move to embrace her was aborted when he saw Sam and Jackson. He recovered quickly and displayed the same presence of mind and confidence as when Sam had interrogated him at the jail. "I didn't know you had special guests," he said to Sylvie.

"You never know who's going to drop by."

He turned to Sam. "Sheriff Baker, I'm sorry to hear about what happened."

"It's just Sam now," he said, and shook Dominick's hand. "I hear you quit the Indigo."

"It's been a while in coming," Dom said.

Sylvie slipped her arm through Jackson's. "Dom, this is Henry Jackson. He was Wayne's good friend."

Dominick shook his hand. "Sylvie has told me good things about you. About Wayne, too."

Henry nodded. "He was one of a kind."

"Amen," her father said. He looked at Sylvie. "Tell me about last night."

She told them how Drago had pulled her backstage, and Vince had demanded to know whose side she would be on—his or her father's—*if the shit hit the fan.*

"Tell me if I'm wrong," Sam said, "but I thought we were already throwing it pretty hard."

Dom said his father had been extremely agitated lately over the conflicts with Sam. Also, about some new Las Vegas hotel he was trying to buy into. He told Dominick he needed to raise a good chunk of money before the opportunity slipped away. "I kept telling him, I didn't want to know about anything that wasn't related to the Indigo, but he couldn't stop talking about it."

"Here's the kicker, Daddy," Sylvie said. "Arin Haugen

showed up when we were dealing with Vince. He was with some man he called the 'new man.' Arin told Vince that this guy had something for him."

"Vince told him it better be the whole thing this time," Dominick said.

Little Rags pushed against Sylvie's leg, and she picked him up. "With a nice cuss word tossed in."

"What did this guy look like?" Jackson asked.

"I'd say around forty," Sylvie said. "Thick neck, kind of a square jaw. We thought it was strange because he wore a leather coat."

"That is strange, in this weather." Sam checked the street again. "We need to get out of here before the Rangers come calling."

Her father turned to her and paused. She knew the look and what he was going to say before he said it. "I don't want to go to Dallas, Daddy. I'm going to stay at Aunt Missy's."

Sam thought about that a moment and nodded. "Okay."

From the kitchen came a chirp from the parakeet. They went in, and it scooted over on its bar for a better look at them.

Dominick looked inside. "It's Sal's."

Sam nodded. "Henry and I went to his house. The bird was dying."

Dom ran his hand over the cage's iron grid. "He loved this bird."

"Maybe he'll be back for it," Sylvie said.

Dominick shook his head. "He won't be back."

Chapter 63

The throaty rumble of a big engine cut through the sticky night air before the red '40 Plymouth glided by them. From inside Jackson's car, Sam caught the dim outline of four men. Vince Romano and Arin Haugen would want the maximum amount of manpower while still leaving room for Freddy Campbell.

A second car, a white '39 Chevy, followed closely behind the Plymouth. Four more men.

"It's a damn parade," Jackson said.

"Mr. Campbell is getting a nice welcoming party."

The cars drove past the jail and stopped across the street in front of the café, now closed for the night. Their headlights blinked off, and the street returned to darkness.

Jackson swatted at a mosquito on his arm. "I hope they're getting bit up as much as we are."

"Eight men," Sam said. "Not the odds I was hoping for."

Two of the men got out of the Chevy and looked inside the cars parked along the storefronts across the street.

"I'd lay odds they're looking for you, Sam."

The men crossed the street and looked inside a rusty panel truck. The driver, maybe not liking the looks of the men, started the engine and drove off. That left about ten cars to search before they reached Jackson's Ford.

"We could circle the block," Jackson said. He reached for the ignition keys, but the jail door opened and Jim Eilers walked out.

"Well, if it ain't the new sheriff," Sam said.

293

Eilers walked over to Romano's men and pointed at the jail. The men nodded.

"They seem pretty damn chummy," Henry said.

Eilers joined the two men in searching the cars. They came closer to Sam and Jackson. It was too late to run.

Sam checked his pistol's cylinder. "I should have fired Eilers when I had the chance. Now I might have to shoot him."

Chapter 64

Sylvie sat in Missy's bay window and watched for movement in the dark street. She didn't think Vince Romano knew she even had an aunt, and much less that Sylvie was laying low there. But her father had told her to keep an eye out for unwanted visitors.

Rags sat next to her on the cushion, his muscles tensed under his wiry coat. He was usually relaxed at Missy's house but he had picked up on his mistress' unease.

Aunt Missy slept on the couch, her .38 caliber pistol within reach on the coffee table. She began to snore. Sylvie smiled for the first time since she'd seen her father early this morning.

A car engine broke the night's silence. She watched as it drove past. The street grew quiet again.

Rags whined. She told him not to worry but he wasn't buying it.

She wasn't, either.

Galveston '44

Chapter 65

Sheriff Eilers and the two Romano enforcers walked within twenty feet of where Sam and Henry sat low in the car seat. Sam pulled the hammer back on his pistol.

A pudgy man opened the headquarters door and stepped out on the landing. Tan slacks, white shirt, receding hairline. Stephen Miller, the governor's errand boy, apparently had unfinished business beyond removing Sam from office.

Miller said something to Eilers and pointed to the back of the jail. Romano's men trotted back across the street and Eilers disappeared inside.

The red Plymouth drove away from the café and down the side street that flanked the jail.

"They're going to pick Campbell up around the back," Sam said.

Jackson nodded. "Fewer eyeballs."

The white Chevy's high beams lit the street, but it didn't move away from the café.

"Looks like they're going to keep watch until the Plymouth drives off," Sam said.

"They could take him the other way out, and we wouldn't know it."

Sam thought about their options—none good unless the Plymouth drove out the way it came in. And if the Chevy followed, they would have to trail behind a caravan of eight armed thugs—nine, counting Campbell.

"What do you think?" Sam asked. "The only ideas I have are loco."

"I have some suicidal ones myself, but talking with Campbell is probably our last chance."

Headlights flared from the side street. Jackson started the engine. "Here they come."

The Plymouth drove out past the jail and turned. The Chevy stayed.

Every muscle in Sam's body tensed as the Plymouth got further away. "Come on—shit or get off the pot."

"Let's hope they're just trying to flush us out."

The Plymouth turned again and disappeared. Now the Chevrolet drove away from the café and accelerated in its direction.

Jackson followed. He turned the corner, and they caught sight of the Chevy. At Seawall Boulevard it turned. Several cars travelled the wide street, but none of them were the Plymouth.

"They could just be a decoy," Sam said.

Jackson sped up, and they flashed by the Tropicana Hotel. The Chevy slowed as it ran close to another car—the Plymouth.

Sam relaxed his grip on the dashboard as the three-car caravan settled in at the speed limit. As the seawall diminished in height, the wind picked up and buffeted the car. White-capped waves from the Gulf reflected the full moonlight.

The Plymouth and the Chevy cruised to the end of the seawall and drove down the concrete ramp to the beach road.

"Jesus," Jackson said. He cut his headlights. "Are they going to take a swim?" He pulled the Ford to the curb to let the two cars gain some distance. From atop the seawall they looked like two metal ants as they snaked slowly around piles of driftwood and seaweed.

"Maybe they're going to hide him in a beach house," Sam said.

"Or a tent," Henry said. "There isn't much out this way."

Jackson drove down the short ramp and onto the hard-packed sand. The occasional rut in the road jarred the Ford. They kept pace with the other cars and skirted the same piles of kelp and tidewrack as they had. Jackson gunned the engine to pull out of a patch of soft sand.

Beach houses and bait shops became less frequent.

Henry rounded a rotting shrimp boat and braked to a stop. Ahead the Chevy sat still. The driver and a big man jumped out. They looked back down the road they had just come down.

"Good God," Jackson said. "Is that Max?"

"Not big enough."

"Have you considered that Romano and Drago could be in one of those cars?"

"Of course," Sam said. "As usual, I'm way ahead of you."

"Except when you run," Jackson said.

"Have you considered, they might turn around and go back?"

"I'll back up behind the shrimp boat," Jackson said. "We can take cover there."

"And ambush them?"

"If you want to call it that."

Sam had led men in an ambush of German soldiers, and it took a degree of cold-blooded resolution. Even though he heard that resolve in Jackson's voice, he didn't think his friend had been through a real battle before. He had killed a man to save Sam and Robicheaux from certain incineration at Lady Night's whorehouse, but this was four against two. These thugs cared not a damn about a fair fight. About mercy. Only by accepting those rules of engagement would they have a chance to find out if Freddy Campbell had the rest of the crude map on him.

If not, they would have to persuade him to lead them to the big killer he was protecting.

"You're a good cop, Henry," Sam said. "But this ain't going to be detective work. This is war."

Jackson's stoic demeanor softened. "I've been in a shootout, Sam. In Atlanta." He looked out to the crashing surf of the moonlit Gulf. "We were on a raid Three detectives and two plainclothes cops. We'd had a positive ID on a couple of murder suspects inside a house. I jimmied the lock and was first in. But instead of two men there were five. They were ready for us and started shooting. I returned fire, but I was alone, the other cops had stayed outside."

"Jesus..."

Jackson pulled up his shirt. A milky-white surgical scar ran the length of his stomach, with a gnarled knot protruding from the middle. Sam had seen more of the aftermath of bullet wounds and surgery in the Great War than he cared to recall. Jackson had been gut shot.

"The men ran out the back, and the rest of the cops came in. They let me lie there bleeding for a while before they called for an ambulance."

"White cops? They set you up?"

Henry nodded. "I was so pissed I refused to die."

Sam didn't know what to say. Could he apologize for every white cop, or his whole race? Maybe all he could do was be different, be better. "I can see why your sister didn't want you to get involved in this."

"Neither did your wife."

The two men jumped back in the Chevy and drove on. Jackson's chin lifted, and his lips tightened with a tinge of bitterness. Of resolve. He slapped the car in gear and followed.

Chapter 66

No lights had come on in Sal's bungalow in the hour that Dominick had sat in his car watching it. It was past midnight and nothing on the street had moved.

He ran across the street and unlocked the door with the key his cousin had given him. He stepped inside and waited. He heard nothing other than gusts of wind outside. He padded down the hallway to Sal's bedroom. Everything was in order, as if Sal would soon come home, happy to pour his cousin a nightcap and explain where he'd been.

Dominick took Sal's .45 caliber pistol from the nightstand and felt its considerable heft. His stepfather back in Indianapolis had one, and they used to take target practice with it when they weren't working at the family's nightclub. The gun had a hell of a kick, but Dom preferred shooting his Remington rifle. Neither of them went hunting, preferring to blast beer bottles than shoot wild animals.

The last thin hope he had was that Sal had to run for his life and left everything behind. But he knew deep down what had happened. A couple of days before the Sinatra show, he had confronted Vince about his nephew's whereabouts.

"Fuck if I know," his father had said.

"Why haven't you asked me if I knew where he was?"

"Because he's a useless piece-of-shit."

His father had walked out. Dom knew then that Sal had fucked up in some way, or he posed a risk to Vince somehow. Either way, he would never hear the truth about his cousin.

In the living room Dominick searched the secretary desk.

Galveston '44

He picked up an unpaid electric bill—five days overdue. Soon the lights would be cut off, and Sal's house would be darker than the black pall that hung over it now.

Chapter 67

The taillights from the white Chevy bobbed and danced as the car bumped along the rutted beach road. Sam's eyes burned from staring at the two red dots on the journey to some unknown destination. He rubbed his eyes and looked out to the moonlit Gulf.

Down the beach a light undulated like a candle bent by a breeze.

As they approached, the light grew until they were certain—Romano's men had built a bonfire banked against a sand dune. Orange and red sparks showered the beach, and the red metal body of the Plymouth reflected the flames. The white Chevy pulled to a stop next to it.

Jackson stopped behind a wide sand dune, the last cover between their car and the bonfire. They jumped out, and Sam trained his binoculars on the men as they threw more wood into the flames. "I don't see a beach house."

Jackson shook his head. "There's nothing down this far except sand crabs and dead jelly fish."

"I count ten men. One must have been there to get the fire started."

Men drank straight from whiskey bottles and passed them around. Bursts of laughter and shouting mixed with the crackling of burning wood.

Two men walked out of the shadows behind the fire, and the men howled and hooted. Even without the field glasses, Sam recognized the muscular build and bald head of Freddy Campbell. "There's the guest of honor." Sam focused the binoculars and saw that Campbell's hands were tied behind his back.

"What the hell?"

The big man grabbed Campbell by his shirt and shouted something that was carried away by the swirling breeze. Campbell answered but the man shook him and shouted louder, *"What did you tell them?"*

Freddy Campbell shook his head and responded. The man slapped him and pushed him into another man who pushed him into another. Campbell fell. A burly man pulled him up and pushed him close to the fire. Frenzy took over the gang as they pushed Campbell again and again near the flames, pulling him back just in time.

Sam said, "Haugen and Romano must think he told the Rangers something."

"Or, they just want to make sure."

Two men held Campbell while another waved a piece of burning driftwood in front of him. His shirt caught fire, and they threw him in the sand to smother the flames.

"Goddammit, they're going to kill him," Sam said. "Doesn't matter if they believe him or not."

"Romano won't take any chances if Campbell knows where Max is." Jackson pointed out to the sand dunes to the left of the bonfire. "I could circle around from the dunes and you could drive to the other side. Catch them in a crossfire."

"Too much moonlight," Sam said. "If they spotted us before we got there, we'd be caught out in the middle with no cover."

Campbell screamed as they pushed him into the fire and pulled him out. He lay still in the sand, the remnants of his clothes charred black. The big man stood over him and shouted a question again.

"Once more and he's dead," Sam said. "I'm going to get

behind them."

"You going to fly over there?"

"So to speak," Sam said. He climbed behind the wheel of the Ford.

Jackson grabbed his shirt. "Sam, they're going to shoot you before you get around them."

"I'm not going around them."

Jackson looked back at the bonfire and saw a man kick Campbell in the ribs. He grabbed his rifle from the backseat. "Okay, I'll cover you."

Sam drove around the sand dune and floored the accelerator, aiming for a narrow opening between the fire and the sand bank. The car gained speed and bounced over driftwood and debris. Romano's men startled and scattered. One man picked up a rifle from the sand and fired. Others fired pistols and the windshield exploded into pieces. Two men dropped to their knees in the car's path and shot repeatedly. A bullet whizzed by Sam's ear and blew out the rear window.

The men rose but before they could scramble, the car hit them dead on. One man flew over the roof. The other disappeared into the fire.

Sam cleared the side of the bonfire but found a car dead in front of him. He swerved and clipped the car and spun out into a sand bank. He was facing the bonfire but the flames faded in and out of his vision. Something wet flowed down from his forehead.

He wiped the blood out of his eyes as a man charged at him, firing his gun. Sam shot through the busted window and the man fell back. He grabbed his rifle, dove from the car and took cover behind it. Bullets slammed into the metal. More glass shattered. Men fired from the other side of the bonfire, their figures silhouetted in red.

A figure ran behind a black Dodge before Sam could get

off a shot. The man rose to shoot. A shot rang in the distance. He dropped his gun and fell to the sand.

Jackson had shot him.

Another man ducked low to the ground and ran. Sam fired and missed. The man disappeared from the light behind a pile of driftwood.

Trying to outflank me, Sam thought. If the man circled around behind him, he'd be exposed—an easy target behind the Ford. But there was no other cover nearby, and he was under heavy fire.

Sam's mind went back over twenty-five years to the Battle of Belleau Wood, when his platoon had been pinned down by a curtain of German machinegun fire. *I could die here*, he had thought back then. He had the same feeling now, but this time he knew his wife and daughter would never know what happened to him. His body would join Freddy Campbell's in the funeral pyre. Maybe Jackson's, too.

He propped the rifle on the trunk and sighted out into the darkness where the man had disappeared. He caught a fleeting movement from the darkness. The man shot twice and ran. Sam fired and dropped him.

Jackson's rifle crackled in the distance, and a man screamed.

Sam trained his gun on the bonfire but saw no movement beyond the swaying of the soaring flames. He tried to count how many men were left. Maybe one or two.

A dull metallic sound broke the silence, and Sam tensed for more shooting. An engine fired up, and the Plymouth accelerated around the beach side of the bonfire, throwing off sand and gaining traction. Sam shot into the darkness where it had disappeared. He jumped in the Ford and turned the key but the motor wouldn't crank.

The whine of the Plymouth's engine trailed away in the

distance. Jackson's rifle fired repeatedly. Sam hoped he had stopped the car.

Except for the roar of the bonfire and the whistling of the wind, the beach took on a new silence. Sam wanted to shout for Henry, but didn't want to draw fire if another man lay in wait. Maybe the car had left as a ploy to get him to leave his cover. Were they that smart? These men looked like the dregs of Vince's goons—the enforcers—but maybe one of them had some brains.

A faint moan came from the other side of the fire. Someone in pain. Or someone faking it.

Sam shouted. "Henry?

"Yo!"

"You all right?"

"Yeah. You?"

"I'm okay," Sam said. "You hear that?"

"It's Campbell. They shot him."

"See anybody else?"

"Nothing's moving."

"Cover me."

Sam dropped down and crawled through the sand, the rifle cradled in his arms. He drew nearer the bonfire. The moans grew louder.

Sam pulled his pistol from his belt and eased around the fire. Several gunmen lay scattered in the sand. The one Sam had hit with the car lay blackened in the fire. Only his booted feet had escaped the flames, and they appeared disembodied from the rest of him. The smell of burning flesh sent Sam back again to the French battlefields. He looked away but the grotesque image would join those already seared in his mind.

He waved out into the dark. "All clear, Henry."

Jackson emerged from the darkness and took in the carnage. "Lord have mercy..."

They squatted down to Freddy Campbell. The blackened remains of his shirt lay in tatters against the sand. His bare chest had already blistered into a white leathery sheen. But his burns were the least of his problems. With every labored breath a dark hole in his chest bubbled with blood.

A sense of recognition passed over his face. "You mother fuckers again ...?" His raspy voice trailed off.

"We're going to get you some help, Freddy," Sam said.

"Your help is killing me."

Sam pulled Campbell's wallet from his pants pocket and found the torn piece of paper. He took the other part of the map from his shirt pocket and held them to the light. The new part had only a solitary letter or number written on it, made indistinct by the jagged tear.

Sam held the paper in Campbell's line of vision. "What is this mark? Is it a letter or a number?"

Campbell smiled. "It's my shopping list."

"Does the X show where Max is? What's the street name?"

Campbell chuckled and shook his head. "Haugen said you were smart, but I'm not seeing it."

Henry pointed at the paper. "It looks like there could be a number that goes in front of the seven-seven-eight. "Maybe a zero? Or, an 'O'?

"Don't you get it, man? You found Max once, but it won't happen again."

Campbell coughed and gasped for breath. "You dumb fuckers have no idea what's coming your way."

"Tell me, Freddy," Sam said. "What does Haugen have planned?"

"Gonna be big." Campbell looked up into the night sky as if he could see something up there that they couldn't. "Things are about to change, and you're on the wrong side of the line."

308

Campbell coughed, and blood bubbled out from his mouth.

Sam patted him on his shoulder. "Hang in there, Freddy. We'll get you to the hospital."

Jackson ran to the black Dodge and climbed in.

Campbell moaned once, and a wet rattle escaped from his chest. His last breath eased out of him and with it went the last chance to make sense of the crude map. Sam shook his head at Jackson. Neither man spoke. They had found what they came for—what they had killed several men for—but it hadn't brought them closer to discovering Max's hiding place.

Sam grabbed his hat from Jackson's car and slammed the door shut. Sam pointed at the car. "They could trace it to you."

Jackson got out of the Dodge and took the keys out of the Ford's ignition. He opened the trunk and took out a large can of gasoline and poured some on the front and backseats. From the fire Sam brought a long piece of burning log and tossed it inside. He ran back as the seats burst into flames. The car exploded into an orange fireball.

"The Chevy, too," Sam said.

Henry doused the white Chevy's seats and the hood and set the can on the front floorboard. Sam threw another piece of burning wood inside. Flames shot out the open windows and doors. A moment later the car blew up, and metal fragments showered down onto the sand.

The flames from the bonfire and the two cars—along with the full moon—illuminated Romano's gunmen lying sprawled in the sand next to their guns.

The beach looked like the aftermath of a battle scene staged in a war picture. And Sam knew war is how Vince Romano and Arin Haugen would respond to it.

Galveston '44

Chapter 68

Hushed, urgent voices hummed from the far end of the room.

Elmer Smoltz sat on the sofa and tried to cipher what the gray-haired woman and the leather-coat man were discussing so early in the morning. *Max*, more than likely. Just the day before, his big patient had told him that he refused another demand by his caretakers to move to another safe house.

We're going to get out of here, he had said. *You're going to help me, and I'm going to save your sad life.*

Smoltz had been brought upstairs by the woman after she'd awakened him by covering his mouth with her hand. He'd been dreaming about the two goldfish he had left behind in his Houston apartment as he hurried to leave for this hellish assignment. The fish were undoubtedly now floating lifeless on the water's surface in their glass bowl. He'd grown fond of the little guys, and would give them a proper burial when he returned home.

If he ever did.

Smoltz struggled to keep his eyes open as the conversation hummed just beyond earshot. He thought about his powdered medicine that Max kept under his mattress and decided he'd sneak a little out when they sent him back down to the basement. It was risky, but he was nauseous and his joints hurt. If he didn't get a shot soon, he'd be too sick to eat or get up from the cot.

The voices ceased, replaced by the squeaking of floorboards. "Doctor," the man said, his rank breath only inches from Elmer's face. "Tell me, what has he been talking to you about?"

He started to tell the man that Max planned to escape the basement and take revenge against the sheriff, the man who had killed his friend Carl. *And* that he would take Elmer Smoltz with him to help in the search. But he held back, betting that leaving the basement with Max would be his only chance at survival, no matter how horrific his plan might be.

"He talks about how he feels," Smoltz said. "How he's healing. Things like that."

"Bullshit," the man said, irritation rising in his voice. "He's back to normal. He exercises for hours every day."

Smoltz tried to think of what else Max had talked to him about—something true but not something that would be a betrayal. His mind was muddled, though, made sluggish by his withdrawal. Finally, he remembered. "Women. He's always talking about women. Philosophy, too. I was surprised he had read Jean Paul—."

"Fuck that," the man said. "Why won't he leave the basement?"

"I don't know. I thought he was waiting for some assignment or something."

Smoltz felt the cold barrel of a pistol press against his forehead. "Last chance, doctor."

The prospect of imminent death cleared Elmer Smoltz's mind. He knew he had to double down on his lie. "He doesn't confide in me about anything else," he said. "I swear."

He could hear the man breathing heavily through his nose, as if weighing the likelihood of Smoltz's lie. After a long moment the man removed the gun, and Elmer could breathe again. Sweat dripped from his scalp. The malaise returned, and he drifted off to a troubled sleep.

After what seemed like only seconds the woman grabbed his arm. "Let's go," she said.

Elmer didn't protest. More than the fresh air and a comfortable couch, he needed his medicine.

Galveston '44

Chapter 69

A dull silver light in the eastern sky marked the beginning of dawn as Jackson drove the Dodge up the beach ramp and onto the start of the seawall.

Neither of them had spoken during the trip back. There wasn't much to say. They had tried to save Freddy Campbell and find out from him where the man named Max hid. But he'd given them nothing except veiled warnings: *Something big coming your way.*

Maybe he knew that Romano had plans to come full-force after him and Henry. Or, maybe the threats were just hot air from a dying gangster.

Sam thought that this could be the end of the hunt for Max. The torn piece of the map from Campbell's wallet hadn't helped them and they had no other clues or ideas to follow. And he no longer had the badge and the resources to effectively pursue the killer of two innocent men.

Instead of the hunter, he was the hunted.

Sam pressed his handkerchief to the throbbing bump on his forehead. For the first time since he'd seen Wayne McRae lying murdered in his own squad car, he felt a tamping down of the fire that had driven him to find justice for his deputy. Anger had given way to exhaustion.

From the sagging of Jackson's shoulders and the lowering of his chin, Sam knew he felt the same loss.

They passed the Tropicana Hotel. Sam imagined Arin Haugen looking down from his fortress on the top floor and laughing at the two fools who had dared to find the killer he was hiding.

Jackson turned onto a side street and pulled to the curb. Seagulls cried in the dark sky overhead and light mist began to dot the windshield. Finally, Jackson broke the silence. "You'll have to get the hell out of Texas, Sam."

"Yeah, Mexico, maybe."

"You speak any Spanish?"

"Just cuss words."

"Well, that's a start."

"What about you?" Sam asked.

"*Hablo un poco.*"

"No, I mean what are you going to do?" Sam asked. "Romano would love to catch you out somewhere."

"It's easier for a Negro to hide than a tall, ex-sheriff."

"I wish Gus was still with us," Sam said. "He'd know someplace where I could hide out. Bring me food, too."

"I wish he was here to look at that map. He's probably the only one that could make sense of it."

Sam took the two pieces of Campbell's map from his shirt pocket and squinted at them in the dark. Henry shined the flashlight on the rough drawing of intersecting lines and scrawled numbers or letters

Sam pointed at the X marked on one line. "Maybe Freddy was playing tic-tac-toe and got distracted."

"Then he'd have the last laugh on us."

"I still think the last number could be a four. The first number, too."

"What if it's an 'H'?" Jackson said. "Look, there's a faint line coming down on the side of it."

"I don't see it."

"You've got old eyes."

"Maybe so, but no street address begins with a letter."

"*Unit* H, maybe?"

"What if the first mark *is* an H," Sam said, "and the second is an O, not a zero?"

"But the 0 is so much smaller than the—"

"H O 7 7 4."

"That's a telephone number. Not a street address."

Sam pulled out his wallet and found the slip of paper where Laura had written down her phone number. *H O-774.* He held it next to the map and they studied the similarities in the numbers.

A car approached quickly from behind, and its headlights swept the interior of the Dodge. Jackson cut the flashlight off, and they ducked down in their seats.

The car drove past, and the street returned to darkness.

Henry clicked on the light again. "Whose phone number?"

Sam hesitated to speak her name. There was no way that she—an attractive woman with a thriving business—would harbor Wayne McRae's killer. And if she was, she wouldn't invite to her bed the very man obsessed with finding him.

"Her name is Laura Stevens."

He told Henry how he came to have her phone number and the one time he'd used it.

But he didn't say *why* he'd called her, that he'd been hurt by Claire and had used Laura in a failed antidote to his jealousy and pain. "I was at her house the night Wayne was killed," Sam said. He shook his head at the recalling of the shock they'd all felt that night. "She was as upset as anyone."

"Probably not her number," Henry said. "Besides, the first and last mark could almost be anything." He pointed at the X on the map. "Is her house close to the end of a street, like this?"

"I don't know."

"Maybe it's a dead end."

"Sounds like our kind of lead."

Galveston '44

Chapter 70

A steady wind blew into the open window of the car and ruffled Vince Romano's silk shirt. Out in the Gulf choppy waves crashed on the shore, the sound masked by the rumble of his Cadillac's motor as Drago drove the car as fast as the soft sand would allow.

Romano had never been to any of Galveston's beaches before. He couldn't see the point in swimming or building a goddamn sandcastle when he could be out making money.

Romano turned to the backseat and locked his eyes on the young punk who sat sandwiched between two big men holding rifles. The kid's broad face was pitted from acne and he looked scared. Headlights from the backup car lit the kid from behind like he wore a halo. He was no angel but Vince might make him one. He hadn't decided yet.

Drago swung the big car around a sand dune. A bonfire loomed ahead in the darkness. Two smaller fires flickered next to it.

"Wait a fucking minute," Vince said. He turned to the kid. "Why three fires?"

"We only built the one, Mr. Romano. Just like you said."

A vein throbbed in Vince's neck. He had issued simple instructions: find out what Freddy Campbell had told the Texas Rangers about the safe house where the big fucker was recuperating from his gunshot wounds. And more importantly, what had he told Sam Baker and the colored man before the Rangers found them?

Drago pulled the car to a stop a safe distance from the

bonfire. Charred wood and gray ash formed a large base above which burned thicker timbers. The blackened shells of two cars flickered with smaller flames. Bodies lay scattered in the sand.

"Son-of-a-whore," Vince muttered. He ordered his men out and they took cover behind the car. Five heavily-armed men in the other car joined them.

Vince turned to the young kid. "You sure there were just two guys?"

"Pretty sure, Mr. Romano," he said. "One of the fuckers drove right at us and took to firing from the other side. That's his car burning back there." He pointed to the sand dune behind them. "There was somebody shooting from over there that we couldn't see. They caught us in a damn crossfire."

Vince tried to picture the fight in his mind—the gunfire, the chaos. He'd been in shootouts before, but this looked more like a military battle.

"Don't know if you can see that poor fucker in the fire," the kid said. "But the man hit him with the car when he drove at us."

"Who the fuck drives a car into a man?"

A thin smile cracked Drago's lips. He knew.

Vince did, too, and he wondered if he was out there with his black buddy, waiting to ambush them from behind the sand dunes. He pointed to the kid. "Walk over there."

The young man got out of the car, walked to the fire and stood still, as if not wanting to be noticed. After a long moment, Vince gestured. They got out of the car, and his men spread out and advanced with their guns drawn. Like a cautious general, he brought up the rear.

The man in the fire's leather boots had melted around his feet. Vince flinched. He'd seen a lot of dead men—many terminated by his own hand—but he'd never seen a man burnt beyond recognition.

"Campbell? Which one is he?"

The kid pointed to the bald man lying in the sand. "He swore on his mother's soul he told the sheriff nothing. Even when we were burning his ass."

Maybe he didn't, Vince thought. Jim Eilers had told him last night that Campbell hadn't revealed anything useful to the Rangers. The new sheriff was proving to be as cooperative as Sheriff Jim Baker—Sam's father—had been. The chief concern he and Haugen had, though, was that Campbell had given up the safe house location to Sam Baker. The ex-sheriff had an intimidating presence that rattled even strong men.

Now, if they could just convince Max to move to a safer hideout, he and Haugen could breathe easier. They were so close to finishing the job that Romano could taste the money. But he needed it now. His partners in the Las Vegas casino wouldn't wait much longer for him to pony up his share.

He pointed at the kid. "Throw these mother-fuckers in the fire. The rest of you get more wood." Before full daylight, the dead men would be as unrecognizable as their cremated buddy.

Romano grabbed the man by his booted feet and swung his legs further into the fire. One skinless, blackened hand stuck out of the coals as if begging someone to pull him free. Vince stared at him, searing the image in his mind. He wanted to remember this scene and the inconvenience and worry its perpetrator had caused him.

He couldn't remember wanting to kill someone as badly as he did Sam Baker. And when he was done he wanted him to look like this burnt-up mother-fucker.

Galveston '44

Chapter 71

Elmer Smoltz's hip hurt, and he rolled over on the hard cot to give it some relief. After returning from upstairs the maintenance shot of his medicine had only slightly relieved the persistent pain in his joints.

Unfortunately, he only had one glassine left which he had to save in case Max reduced his allotment even more.

Smoltz drifted back to a fitful sleep but was soon awakened by floorboards creaking above him. Maybe the woman was up to fix them breakfast, but it seemed too early in the morning for that.

The trapdoor opened and a man climbed down the ladder to the landing. The dim light reflected the dull sheen of his leather coat as he tossed it and a crumpled wad of sheets to the basement floor. A pair of shoes followed. With a key he unlocked the landing gate and locked it behind him as he descended to the basement floor.

He looked up, listening.

Galveston '44

Chapter 72

Sam raised his hand to knock for the second time, but the front door opened a crack. Laura peered out cautiously. She threw the door open. "Sam!"

The dawn sun played over her naked body. She spread her arms as if to afford a better view. He willed his eyes to meet hers but saw no apprehension or guilt. She smiled and pulled him into her arms. "I was sleeping," she said. Her bare breasts pushed into his body but he kept his arms at his sides.

"You're hurt," she said. She reached for the swollen gash on his forehead.

He brushed her hand away. "Things have been crazy."

"You live a crazy life, Sam Baker," she said. "Why don't we crawl into bed, and you can tell me all about it."

"I'm not here for that."

The smooth skin of her face creased in confusion. He hated to be the cause of that but he had to follow their only lead, if nothing else to eliminate the possibility that the last number on Freddy Campbell's map was a 'four' and the first mark was an 'H.'

Laura opened the blinds. The morning sunlight outlined her shape. "I don't see your car."

"I'm parked on the road," Sam said.

"What for?"

"A quick getaway."

She smiled. "You mean after a hit-and-run?"

"You're too good to me, Laura." He looked around the

living room but saw nothing different from the last time he'd been there.

Sam walked into the kitchen. A few bowls and plates sat in a wooden drainer. He opened cabinet doors and found them stocked with canned food and bags of flour.

The refrigerator, too, was full of food of all types.

"Lots of vittles," he said. "Are you expecting company?"

"Sam, I think you're jealous. Did you come by early so you could catch me fucking another man?"

"That's none of my business."

"If you don't mind, I'm going to put something on."

Sam followed her into the bedroom.

Laura took a red, silk dressing gown off the bed post and slipped it on. She looked no less enticing than before.

The bed was unmade. There was only one indentation where she had slept. He saw no evidence that a large man had been in this room. Probably it just wasn't her phone number on Campbell's map, and he was destroying whatever goodwill they still had between them.

He opened the closet door. Nothing but women's clothes and shoes. A large suitcase.

"What are you looking for, Sam?"

He went out into the hallway and looked in the closet there. He searched the other two bedrooms while Laura trailed behind him. She took his arm. "This isn't like you, Sam. I'm worried what they're saying is true."

"What are they saying?"

"That you've gone crazy looking for a murderer who is probably long gone. You were arrested for burning down two buildings. You forced a deputy to help you escape."

Laura came close. They stood looking at each other. "You're breaking my heart, Sam."

"I got a message for you from Freddy"

He watched her eyes, but he could only read the hurt in them. Either he'd made an unforgiveable mistake in coming here, or she—like Vince Romano—could lie without giving herself away. She could have been warned that he might be coming. The man who had escaped the shootout would have had time to call her.

"Please, Sam, stop."

But he couldn't. He had nothing else. Just this one slim hope.

"Freddy says he can't bring you any more supplies."

Galveston '44

Chapter 73

Smoltz lay still on his cot, ready to close his eyes if the man should look his way. His panicked descent into the bowels of the building had charged the dank air with expectation.

Max slipped on his pants. "What happened, Charles?"

"We have a visitor."

"Who?"

Charles hesitated. "I don't know."

"Who would visit her this time of the morning? Is it a man?" Max asked. He walked over to Charles, towered over him. "It's a man, isn't it?"

"Be quiet," Charles hissed. He slipped on his leather coat, perhaps hoping it would give him authority over the big man.

The floorboards creaked and groaned. They all looked up. Smoltz wondered if it could be the same man who had visited the woman a few nights before. He figured the visitor had to have been big, not only because of the pressure exerted on the floor, but because of the heavy rocking from what undoubtedly was the woman's bed. Middle-aged women weren't his cup of tea, but obviously someone had found her to their carnal liking.

The vigorous fucking hadn't woken Max. He'd exercised three hours during the day and snored his way through the whole thing.

"I know who it is," Max said. "It's the fucking sheriff."

Charles pointed his finger at Max, an act Smoltz considered risky. "Let me worry about who it is."

Max moved a step closer to the smaller man. "Is he

329

alone?"

"What makes you thinks it's him?"

"He came to fuck her, or he suspects I'm here."

"There's no way he could find you here."

"Don't be stupid," Max said. "He found me and Carl at the other safe house when it was supposed to be impossible."

From above, heavy footsteps moved across the floor.

"I'm going up," Max said.

"There is no need to kill him."

"He killed Carl," Max said, his voice rising.

Charles pulled a pistol out of his leather coat and stepped back. "He died for you, Max. He died because you have more important things to do."

Chapter 74

Laura followed Sam out to the redwood garage at the end of the long drive. A '42 Ford sat on the concrete floor. A few garden tools hung on the unpainted walls. There wasn't an attic or anywhere else to hide a big man.

"Freddy can't bring any supplies?" Laura said and crossed her arms over her chest. The flimsy nightie ruffled in the wind. "You're talking nonsense, Sam."

He scanned the deep backyard but there wasn't another structure. If the X on Freddy Campbell's map had actually marked Laura's house, there was no sign that she was hiding Max. Her expression showed nothing more than confusion and disappointment. He felt the same. He had come to another dead end and had destroyed a relationship for the slim possibility that she harbored the killer of Wayne McRae and Gus Josie.

"I'm sorry, Laura," he said. "But I had to know if—"

"Leave, Sam," she said and pointed out to the street. "It's time for me to get on with my life."

* * *

Sam and Jackson carried their rifles into a stand of pine trees flanking a stone cottage. They'd been surprised to find another house further down from Laura's because the road's asphalt had ended and deeply-rutted mud had begun. The road dead-ended at a barbed wire fence fifty yards down from the cottage.

Behind them, a couple hundred yards of swampy woods obscured Laura's house. Sam tried to shove what had just happened out of his mind but it clung to him. He wished they'd come to this house first—maybe the bad scene with Laura could have been avoided.

Henry had tried to reassure him. *You did what you had to.*

The ground turned soggy, and a black snake slipped under the water's surface. Sam glassed the house with his binoculars. A gray '39 Ford sat in the driveway. A well-tended garden took up most of the side of the house. Other than the gentle swaying of the pine trees, nothing stirred.

They waited and slapped at mosquitos. Sweat dripped down Sam's face but, once again, only small beads of moisture dotted Henry's upper lip. "Why don't you sweat?"

"Maybe because my ancestors were from Africa."

"Which part?"

"The hot part."

"Kind of like jumping from the frying pan to the skillet, ain't it?"

"It's not like we had any choice in the matter."

Sam thought about that a moment. "I guess you got a point there."

Jackson took the binoculars and scoped the house. "How long do you want to wait?"

Sam slapped at a mosquito on his neck. "I've got to move soon, or there won't be nothing left of me."

Jackson pointed at the house. The front door swung open. A plump, white-haired woman walked out with a watering can and tipped it over a row of flowers in the garden.

"Doesn't look the type to harbor a killer," Henry whispered.

Sam grabbed the glasses and trained them on her. "Ermine Brady," he said. She had been a good church friend of his

332

mother's. Mr. Brady, too, until he died a couple years ago.

"I've known her my whole life," Sam said. "Ermine was the first one to bring over a covered dish when Billy was killed."

A medium-sized brown dog scampered out of the house and snuffed at the trees and the flowers. He suddenly froze, his tail pointed, and barked in their direction. Mrs. Brady spoke to the dog, but it only barked louder and ran to the edge of the trees.

"There goes our cover," Sam said. "I might as well say hello."

"You sure? You're a wanted man."

"I'm starting to not give a shit." Sam said.

He handed his rifle to Henry and moved closer. "Mrs. Brady?" He waved his arm. She turned and dropped her watering can.

"This is private property, mister," she said in a quavering voice. "You best go or I'll get my squirrel gun."

"It's Sam Baker, Mrs. Brady."

She shielded her eyes from the sun and squinted.

Sam took a step out into the clearing. The dog backed off.

"Lordy, Sam Baker," she said and looked at him like he'd just risen from the dead. "Son, they're looking for you. I heard it on the wireless."

"Yes, ma'am. I guess they are."

He walked over to her, and she hugged him. "What are you doing sneaking up on me like that?"

"I didn't know you lived here, Mrs. Brady."

"Are you hiding in the woods?"

"No. To tell you the truth we're still looking for the man who killed Wayne McRae."

"We?"

"Me and my..." Sam searched for the right word to call

333

Henry Jackson. "My partner."

Sam waved at Jackson and he walked into the clearing. Mrs. Brady's mouth dropped open at the sight of a black man with two rifles emerging from her piney woods. Sam introduced them, and she began to regain her composure.

Sam pointed in the direction of Laura's house. "Mrs. Brady, have you ever seen any suspicious goings-on next door? Maybe a really big man walking around."

"No. Only time I ever seen it up close was when Buster here chased a 'coon over there, and I had to go get him."

"You see anyone other than a young blond woman around there?"

"Didn't see nobody because they were still building the thing and the workers had gone for the day."

"When was this?" Jackson asked.

Mrs. Brady looked off, thinking. "Well, it hadn't got hot yet so it must have been five or six months ago."

Sam thought about the time frame, but it didn't strike him as odd. He looked at Jackson but the man shook his head. They were out of questions for Mrs. Brady. The irony that the hunt for the killer of Wayne McRae and Gus Josie had dead-ended on this dead-end road was not lost on Sam. He had come away from the manhunt with nothing more than Max's skull-and-crossbones medallion, which now weighed heavily in his pocket. It would always be a reminder—his cross to bear—of his failure to avenge Wayne's death.

"Ya'll look ragged," Mrs. Brady said. "Come in the house 'n let me fix you some vittles."

Chapter 75

Smoltz hated guns, and not thirty feet from him Charles pointed his at Max's big chest. He stood from his cot and moved further out of firing range.

"Last warning, Charles," Max said. He held one hand out. "Give me the fucking gun."

The trapdoor opened, and the woman climbed down to the landing. She flicked on the ceiling lights, and they illuminated the standoff between the two men. "What the fuck are you doing?"

Smoltz recognized her voice, but now she had blond hair, not the bluish-gray when she'd assisted during Max's surgery. Not only was she young and pretty, she wore a short camisole that didn't leave much to the imagination.

She unlocked the gate and climbed down the stairs a few steps. "Max, back off!"

"You're not going to shoot me, Charles," Max said. "Without me, you're nothing."

The woman turned to Smoltz. "You don't have your blindfold on."

"He came down so fast I didn't have time to do it." He grabbed the blindfold from where it hung on the cement wall.

"Too late now," Charles said with a quick glance at him. "That's a fucking shame, doctor."

Max slapped the gun out of Charles' hand. It clattered across the cement floor. He pulled Smoltz's scalpel from his waistband and thrust it deep into Charles' abdomen. He grabbed him by the throat and twisted the scalpel like he was gutting a live fish.

Charles gasped, looked down in surprise at the blood already soaking his white shirt.

"No!" the woman screamed.

Max tossed Charles aside like a rag doll.

* * *

Laura stumbled up the stairs and slammed the trapdoor shut. Before she could turn the key, the door flew open in her face.

She ran to the bedroom, stuck her hand under the mattress, found the gun. She stood, but Max snatched the pistol and slapped her. She fell back on the bed. The room swam around her in black circles.

Laura staggered from the bed and ran out the open front door. In between the trees, she caught a flash of Max running down the long driveway. But thick shrubs blocked her view of the road. She found herself hoping Sam had gone. It wasn't hard to admire him. He was smart and relentless and he had somehow come to suspect that she was hiding Max. But she had played her role of the rejected mistress to perfection. Yes, she was a surgical nurse and—maybe—a whore. But also a trained actress. And, despite that training, didn't a good actress sometimes develop real feelings for her leading man?

She ran down to the basement. The doctor kneeled over Charles, applying pressure to his abdomen with a bloody towel. The leather jacket supported his head.

Smoltz looked at her and shook his head. *Not good.*

She took Charles' limp hand, and told him he'd be all right. But she knew better. She smelled piss and shit and couldn't detect a pulse from his wrist.

Max clambered down the stairs and picked up Charles' pistol from the floor.

"Was he there?" she asked him. Max ignored her. She hadn't heard any shots, but the basement would have muffled the sound.

Max pushed Smoltz away from the man. "Can't you see he's dead?" He stuck both guns in his waistband. "Get ready to go."

Galveston '44

Chapter 76

Sam drained the last swallow of his coffee. Jackson ate the last bite of the four eggs Mrs. Brady had cooked for him. She took his plate. "You want more eggs or grits?"

"No, ma'am," Jackson said. "But thank you for your hospitality."

"Not at all. Any friend of Sam Baker's is a friend of mine." She put the plates in the sink and looked out to the woods. "I just wish I could tell you more about that house over there."

"How far along were they in building it when you saw it?" Sam asked.

"Not very. They had big stacks of lumber around a hole in the ground. Lots of iron rebar, too."

"A hole in the ground?" Sam asked. "How big?"

"Deep and wide. I reckon they were building them a basement."

Galveston '44

Chapter 77

Smoltz pushed off from the top of the basement stairs and stepped onto the wood floor of the house. His hands shook from witnessing the horrific gutting in the basement. Countless times he'd performed surgery on the bloodiest and most critically injured people, but he had never before seen the inhuman acts that brought them to the hospital.

The woman emerged from the back of the house carrying a large suitcase. She had changed from the sheer nightie into black pants and a simple white blouse.

She and Smoltz shared a look. Two witnesses to unspeakable savagery. Down in the basement Smoltz hadn't noticed the red swelling on her face and the blood trickling from her lip.

Max scrambled up the stairs and grabbed her arm. "Show me where the rest of the guns are."

"You have my only gun."

"I'll break your fucking arm."

She stared at him without blinking. "I have some fighting knives but no more guns."

"Get them," he said. "Your car keys, too."

"You can't leave me here," she said. "Sam could come back."

"I'll drop you off somewhere."

"She took the keys from a glazed bowl on the entryway credenza and tossed them to him. "Look behind the books. Top shelf."

Max went to the built-in bookcase and swept the

knickknacks and books to the floor. He pulled a flat wooden box from the shelf. He opened it and took out a long knife with a black, ridged handle. He tested the knife across his thumb and drew blood.

"What about our objective, Max?" the woman asked. "What should I tell the others?"

"Nothing changes. We go on as before."

"Not if Sam Baker kills you. Not if you get caught killing him."

"He won't know what the fuck hit him."

Smoltz followed Max out to the yard. The woman followed behind, carrying her suitcase.

For the first time in weeks his feet tread soft ground. Nearby a bird trilled with the sound of freedom. He had finally escaped the hot pit.

The only problem? His jailer came with him.

Chapter 78

Jackson drove the Dodge into Laura's tree-shaded drive. Tentacles of shrub branches scraped against the car.

Sam pointed at the empty garage. "She's gone."

Jackson slammed on the brakes. They jumped out and ran to the front door. Sam turned the knob, but it was locked. "Can you pick it?"

"No, that's a high-security lock."

Sam found a thick branch lying in the yard and swung it against a window. Glass shattered. Jackson squeezed inside and opened the door for Sam. Both men pulled their pistols.

Inside, books lay scattered on the floor. The house felt abandoned. Sam went into Laura's bedroom and found her red nightie hanging from a bedpost. Clothes littered the floor and a gray wig nestled among them like a sleeping cat.

In the living room, Henry tested the floor with his weight. The wood creaked slightly. "What the hell does a basement door sound like?"

"Hell if I know." Sam pulled the leather chair and the area rug away. He pushed against the big sofa, but it barely budged an inch.

"Where's that famous Sam Baker strength?" Jackson said. He got down on his knees and lifted the sofa's leather skirt. A foot from the side of the couch, two rubber wheels were bolted into the frame. A metal flange pressed against the front side of the wheel. "It's a brake." He pushed it up and freed the wheel.

Sam did the same on the back wheel. "Pretty goddamn

343

clever." He pushed the couch and it rolled away in a semi-circle. They felt between the wood slats in the floor but no gaps were larger than the others.

Sam went out to the car and returned with the flashlight. He focused the light close to the floor and something caught his eye. A thin seam ran perpendicular to the rest of the slats. Four feet away they found a parallel line, barely visible.

Sam tried to get his fingernails under the seams, but they were too tight. "This reminds me of the garage on Wharf Street."

He shined the light closer to the wood and found another perpendicular seam inside the larger rectangle. A small box within a larger box, about six inches squared. Sam pulled out his pocket knife. When he tried to pry it up the blade broke off. "Goddammit. I liked that knife."

Jackson pushed and prodded on the area between the lines. "It's kind of spongy right here." He pushed straight down on one side of the small square. It popped up on its hinged side. Like a hidden jewel, a metal pull lay snuggled just below the surface. A slotted keyhole took up the center part of the latch.

Henry pointed at it. "I think I can pick that." He pulled out his metal pins and inserted them into the keyhole. He prodded, and the lock clicked open.

Sam eased the trapdoor back on its hinges and peered down into a black hole. They heard nothing. He trained the flashlight on the stairs and the landing and down to the concrete floor.

A musty smell wafted up. Sweat and dampness and something worse. Sam heard only his own breathing. He crouched lower and directed the flashlight further into the room. Something took shape—a foot, barely visible and not moving.

"Hey," Sam shouted. The man lay still. "Hey, you!"

Sam smelled death, like he had many times in the Great War.

"I'm going down."

Jackson pointed at the landing. "Light switch," he whispered. They climbed down and Jackson flicked it on. The room flooded with light.

"Jesus, God almighty..."

The man lay like an island in a red lake of his own blood. A bloody towel covered his lower stomach, and a folded leather coat supported his head. Sam pushed the towel away with his boot and had to avert his gaze when he saw the bulge of the man's innards through the ripped shirt.

The man was around forty. Broad face, square jaw. The leather coat completed Sylvie and Dominick's description of the man who had met with Romano and Haugen at the casino.

The new man.

Jackson shook his head. "The shit people do to each other."

"I don't get it," Sam said. "They sliced him open and then tried to stop the bleeding."

Sam looked around the sparsely-furnished room. A canvas cot with rumpled sheets. A side table with rolls of bandages and tape. Dominating the room was a large bed with surgical lamps on either side of it. He pictured Max being operated on there, recovering there.

Had he been down in this dank pit when Sam made love with Laura upstairs just a few nights before? He wanted to believe she had been forced somehow into hiding Max, that she'd been blackmailed by Romano and Haugen for some trouble she'd gotten into. Gambling debts, or something.

That absurdity faded before he could construct a face-saving scenario. The truth was he'd been fooled by a con artist who had played to the hilt the role of the infatuated younger woman. She'd been hired to get close to him, to find out what he knew about whatever large-scale grift or heist they were up to.

His face burned, and he couldn't look at Jackson. He questioned the intuition and ability to read people he'd always taken pride in. "I was like putty in her fucking hands."

"She's a damn professional, Sam," Jackson said. He pointed to the dead man. "Let's just be glad you didn't wind up like this poor bastard."

Jackson reached under the bed and drug out a duffel bag and dumped the contents on the bed. A huge brown shirt. An equally large pair of pants. A book titled *Circuit Theory and Design*. "Our boy might be an electrical engineer."

Sam thumbed through the book and a sheet of paper fluttered onto the bed. It was the same drawing of the square contraption with the array of wires they had found at the Wharf Street building. He picked it up. "Schematics."

"You remembered the word."

"I always knew the word." He turned it over. A phone number had been scrawled at the bottom of the sheet. "Let's make a call."

Chapter 79

Elmer Smoltz drove Laura's car as Max sat in the backseat and checked the cylinders of the two pistols for bullets.

The doctor's stomach had cramped, and he feared he would vomit. The pain in his joints now extended to his knuckles. He had told Max he badly needed a fix—just a small one to help him function normally.

I'll tell you when, Max had replied.

Max caught his eye in the rearview mirror. "Where's the jail?"

"I guess downtown."

"You guess?"

Smoltz thought better of reminding Max that he lived in Houston—a mosquito-ridden town just north of this mosquito-ridden town. *A place you can get lost in.* The image of his humble apartment waiting for him brought a stab of homesickness.

The buildings grew larger and displayed the names of businesses on their facades.

"I may have to ask directions," Smoltz said.

"No. Don't talk to anyone."

Smoltz made a turn onto a wide street. After a few blocks he saw the jail, but said nothing as he passed it.

"You missed it," Max said. He slapped him on the head. "Are you blind?"

"Sorry. I was watching the road."

"Pull over a couple places down," Max said. The doctor swung the car around and parked in front of a barber shop.

Inside, a man sat with his head tilted back as a white-coated barber shaved his neck with a straight razor. Smoltz knew how he felt.

The doctor jumped when Max pushed the pistol against his head. "I'm going into the jail and send the fucking sheriff to hell. When I come out, you pull the car up fast. You hear me?"

"Yes," he said. His heart beat faster than he thought possible.

"If you're not here when I come out, I will find you. It doesn't matter if you're in Houston or in Mexico or in hell. I will find you, and I will skin you alive and eat your fucking heart. Do you believe me?"

"Yes," the doctor said. He knew Max could find him. *Would* find him. He had discovered his habit—his need for his medicine—in the first minutes of their initial meeting. Smoltz felt like Max had looked deep into his psyche and seen his weaknesses, his shame of losing his medical license. Of losing his wife to divorce.

But mainly, he felt sick from withdrawal and couldn't part from the man who held the promise of relief. Smoltz now understood that Max had planned it that way.

He would stay.

Chapter 80

Max walked up the three steps to the sheriff's office—his big shirt pulled over the two pistols stuffed into his belt—and opened the front door.

Just two people in the front area, a skinny older woman at the receptionist's desk and, at a desk behind her, a fresh-faced deputy talking on the phone. The sidearm strapped to the deputy's leg didn't concern Max. Neither did the fact that they both stared slack-jawed at him. His size always caught people by surprise. And even if they recognized him as a suspect, so what? He felt no fear, no trepidation. He would be victorious today. He had the element of surprise and something even greater on his side—the sense of righteousness.

Max flashed his best smile and let his arms dangle loosely at his sides. Just a law-abiding citizen come to call on the sheriff.

The deputy continued to stare. Maybe he was trying to reconcile Max's likeness to the big man they were hunting. If the deputy came at him, though, it would be his final act.

"Can I help you, sir?" the woman asked in a syrupy twang.

Max made note of the brass name plate on her desk. "Hi, Grace," he said, his voice low and calm. "Is Sheriff Baker in?"

"I'm sorry, but Sam Baker is no longer the sheriff of Galveston County."

The woman spoke with such a deep drawl that Max thought he must have misunderstood her.

"I'm sorry. I wish to speak with Sheriff Sam Baker."

"You must not have read the newspaper," Grace said. She

lowered her voice. "It's all anybody's talking about."

"This can't be true."

"We all feel the same way."

Max wanted to call her a liar and strangle her skinny, wrinkled neck. *Sam Baker no longer the sheriff?* Anger wiped the false smile from his face.

The young deputy hung up the phone and looked at Max again.

He felt an urge to pull a pistol on these two hicks and get some relief for his rage. But he resisted—only by killing Sam Baker would he revenge the death of his friend Carl.

The woman ran her fingers through her thin, gray hair. "Is there something Sheriff Eilers can help you with?"

"No. I want to thank Sam for helping my mother when her car broke down."

"Sheriff Baker was like that," she said. "Sure enough."

"Can you tell me where he lives?"

She smiled. "I'm afraid I can't give you that information."

The young deputy stood. Max bowed slightly to Grace and mumbled his thanks.

* * *

Smoltz sat in the car and listened for gunshots to come from the jail. He hoped Max would be gunned down in his attempt to assassinate Sheriff Baker, and he could just drive away a free man.

But Max casually stepped outside of the jail's front door, whistling an off-key tune. Smoltz pulled the car forward, and Max climbed in.

"Drive slow," Max ordered. He stared out the window, his mouth set tight and his eyes turning dark gray. They went several blocks before he said, almost to himself, "He's not the sheriff now."

"Was he killed?" Smoltz wouldn't wish that on the man, but if he was dead there would be no reason to look for him.

"Shut up and drive," Max said.

Smoltz drove aimlessly while Max talked under his breath. It eventually became evident that he was debating the pros and cons of various courses of action.

"We have to find his house," Max said. "How can we do that?"

The doctor stroked the stubble on his chin and made a show of thinking. Max didn't like when he failed to respond to his questions in a positive manner. "We could ask someone."

"I told you to forget about talking to people," Max said. "Where can we find a phonebook?"

"Maybe at a store of some kind. I'll go in and look him up."

"No, I don't trust you," Max said. "Bring me the fucking book."

Galveston '44

Chapter 81

Sam picked up Laura's phone and gave the switchboard operator the number written on Max's schematic. Two rings later a man answered with a cheery voice, "Fontainebleau Hotel."

Sam gripped the phone tighter, his mind whirling. Then he remembered who they had seen going into the luxury hotel after Freddy Campbell had dropped her off.

"Yes, I'm bringing some papers to Greta Haugen today, but I forgot the room number."

"Uh, I'm afraid I don't have anyone by that name staying at the hotel, sir," the clerk said.

"I know she has a room there."

"Sir, I'm afraid you're mistaken."

Sam heard the hesitation in the clerk's voice and asked for his name.

"Ralph," he replied.

"Ralph, do you have a list of people who are privy to that information."

"Uh, yes, sir, actually, I do. Your name?"

Arin Haugen? Vince Romano? Sam thought Ralph might recognize their voices. A longshot came to him. "Stephen Miller. Governor Davis' adjunct."

"Yes, Mr. Miller," Ralph said, sounding relieved. "Room 436."

Galveston '44

Chapter 82

Vince Romano paced back and forth in the dockside cotton warehouse and observed the dozen hard-bitten men gathered before him. Muscle from Houston and Corpus Christi. The best Arin Haugen's money could buy on short notice. Romano approved. Their scarred gravity lay in sharp contrast to the men whose bodies they had disposed of earlier that morning.

Vince had no sympathy for them. They had greatly outnumbered the two men who had taken their lives—even if one of those men was Sam Baker.

It turned out the ex-sheriff didn't need a damn badge to continue to look for Max. Arin Haugen's idea to have the governor remove him from office had backfired. Now the gloves were off. Baker was fighting bareknuckle, and they'd better do the same.

Romano walked in between the knot of armed men. They parted to let him pass. He went to the back of the cavernous warehouse where five cars flanked a large box truck like tugboats ready to escort a freighter. The truck was empty except for thick chains that hung from each of the interior walls.

They were prepared on their end. He'd done his part despite the broken promises made by his unknown partners. Haugen promised he'd get the rest of his money. They had had it ready before, but it had burned up in the fire Baker set at Haugen's building. The man Baker had killed there had been replaced by the man in the leather coat who had given him another small payment and promised the balance would come this evening.

But if the truck left with its cargo after his men had loaded it and sent it on its way, Romano would take his payment out of someone's flesh.

Only, he wouldn't know exactly who to be pissed at. Haugen claimed he was just the go-between, and he wouldn't reveal what his freighter had brought or where it had come from.

Vince thought it was probably some large antiquity. Arin and Greta collected shit like that—valuable art and antiques. Haugen had showed him a yellowed book of Shakespeare's plays and told him it was worth hundreds of thousands of dollars. Vince wondered what fool would pay that much for some damn stories you couldn't even make sense of.

He'd heard that the chaos of the war in Europe had made invaluable works of art vulnerable for the taking. Arin knew his way around that continent—why couldn't an enterprising and ruthless man like him snatch something priceless and bring it to Galveston, Texas?

If that was the shipment, though, Haugen had lied to him—there were no silent partners directing him. He was the ringleader, and he had Vince's damn money.

Above the murmur of the hired men Vince heard his name called. Drago, standing by the truck entrance door, gestured for him. The big man pushed the black cloth away from the window and peered out. "Black Cadillac."

"License number?" Vince asked. He knew who it was, but he had insisted on strict security procedures. Drago called out the plate numbers. Vince gave him a thumbs up. One of the other men helped him lift the heavy garage door just high enough for the Cadillac to slip inside.

Arin Haugen killed the engine and climbed out. "Vince," he said as he passed by him.

"Arin, we need to talk."

"Sure. But not now." Hands on hips, Haugen studied the strongmen he'd paid for like he owned them. And he did. In a way, he owned Vince Romano, too.

Haugen waved at his Cadillac, and the passenger door swung open. A young blond woman climbed out, holding a cloth against the swollen side of her face. She walked past Romano without a glance. It had to be her—the pretty woman Haugen had brought in to get close to Sam Baker and find out what he knew.

Apparently, she hadn't been too successful because Baker was still out there looking for Max—and killing Romano's men.

Galveston '44

Chapter 83

Smoltz pulled Laura's car into the gravel parking lot of a small grocery store. His big passenger fumed about Sam Baker not being at the jail, and seemed to take it as a personal affront that Baker had been replaced as sheriff.

The doctor's entire body ached. He'd had his first hallucination—a huge bat hurtling out of a black thunderhead directly at the car's windshield.

Smoltz climbed out of the car and walked unsteadily into the store. The bearded clerk greeted him with a nod. A petite, red-headed woman inspected the produce.

"Could I take a look at your phone book?" Smoltz asked the clerk.

"You don't look so good, amigo," the man said.

"It's, uh, it's damn hot out there."

The man slapped the coverless book on the counter. Smoltz looked under Baker, but the only listing was for a Melissa Baker. Max would not be pleased.

"My eyesight is bad," Smoltz said and took the book closer to the windows. He quietly tore out the page and stuffed it in his pocket.

"I was looking for Sheriff Baker's address," he said to the clerk. "Do you know where he lives?"

"Ain't you heard? Sam Baker broke out of jail. He ain't likely to be hiding in his own damn house."

Smoltz thought for a moment that the man was joking. "I, I knew that. I just needed to put some legal papers in his mailbox."

"All I know is he lives on the west side," the clerk said.

The red-headed woman pointed out the window. "It's on Jackson Street. Two doors down from State Avenue. Light green color with a big white porch."

* * *

Smoltz drove Laura's car down Jackson Street as a light mist dotted the windshield, the drops sparkling in the late afternoon sun. *"Two doors down from State Street,"* the woman in the grocery store had said. *"Light green color and a big front porch."*

Max spotted the house first and ordered Smoltz to pull over across the street. "There's a car in the garage," Max muttered under his breath. "It could be his, but if he broke out of jail, would he come back to his house?" He checked his pistol once again and snapped the cylinder closed.

Smoltz let his hands drop from the steering wheel as another wave of nausea rolled over him. His eyes closed, but Max slapped his shoulder. A blue Rolls Royce turned into the Baker's driveway. A portly man in a gray suit and a pretty, red-headed woman climbed out. The man pulled three suitcases from the trunk while the woman unlocked the front door.

Chapter 84

Sylvie and Aunt Missy watched Dominick ladle steaming pasta onto three dinner plates, his movements quick and efficient. He added thick red sauce and pulled garlic bread from the oven.

Little Rags stood sentry at Missy's front door as if he knew that his main mistress, Claire Baker, would soon join them. Sylvie had called her when she learned her father had not only been arrested for some inexplicable reason, but had escaped from jail.

"I'm on my way," Claire had immediately said. "Stay inside and don't talk to anyone."

Sylvie felt relieved. Her mother's strength and steadfastness were sorely needed. She took the two black pistols—Missy's .38 and Dom's .45—from the dining room table and put them on the kitchen counter.

Missy set the plates on the table. "This is enough food to feed an army."

"Dom's stepfather taught him to cook in his nightclub," Sylvie said. "That's why he cooks such big quantities."

"Great. He can cook for those four kids you're going to have."

Sylvie laughed. "Slow down, Missy."

"Listen, girl. Your Uncle Edwin looked like Ichabod Crane, and he couldn't even boil water. If you got yourself a handsome man who can whip up something this good, I'd latch on real quick."

Sylvie smiled at Dominick. "It might have crossed my

mind a time or two."

* * *

Hot, stale air hung heavy in the dark living room. Claire listened for signs of life but knew there wouldn't be any, not even from Max. Sam's ghost had joined Billy's, and Sylvie had been forced out due to concerns about her safety.

David Whittington set her suitcases on the wood floor. The dull sound echoed in the room. "Place could use a good airing out, Sis."

"That'll have to wait." She hurried into Sylvie's room and grabbed the clothing she had been asked to bring to Missy's. Her daughter had put on her brave voice when they spoke on the phone, but Claire had detected a deep concern for her father.

Claire hadn't been able to disguise her own dismay. *Sam Baker on the run after being arrested and thrown in jail? Why?* He was an honest man, and had served the people of Galveston well, often risking his life to do so. She knew him better than he knew himself. There had to be some kind of mistake.

She brought Sylvie's things out and packed them into a suitcase. David reached for it. "I'll take it out to your car for you."

"I can take it from here, David," she said. "Thank you for driving me down."

He shook his head and seemed reluctant to leave. "I just wish ya'll would come back to Dallas. You and Sylvie."

"I need to be here now."

David hugged her and kissed her cheek. She couldn't remember the last time he'd done that.

B.W. Peterson

Galveston '44

Chapter 85

The chubby man walked out of the house and drove away in his Rolls Royce. No sign of the woman. Max figured she was Baker's wife, and maybe—as risky as it would be for a fugitive—he was inside waiting for her. Maybe the cops thought it unlikely as well because none of the few cars parked on the street had anyone in them surveilling the Baker house. Max scanned the street, but none of the neighbors were out. The drizzle had probably chased them indoors.

This was a sign, he thought. Not only was the weather in his favor, he'd arrived at the very moment the sheriff's wife had come home from some trip. The man in the three-piece suit had gone. And, most importantly, there was a chance Sam Baker was inside. If not, he would take care of the woman. Make her suffer first until she told him her husband's whereabouts.

Max snatched the car key from the ignition and stabbed Smoltz in the neck with it. "Be here when I get back."

He stuck both pistols in his belt. At that moment a white '38 Dodge backed out of the driveway and into the street. The woman straightened the car and drove away.

Even better, he thought. *She'll lead me to Baker.*

He handed the car key back to Smoltz. "Follow her.

* * *

Smoltz felt his mind floating somewhere out into the drizzle as he followed the white Dodge. From the backseat, Max

365

chanted what sounded like a petition to the gods of revenge.

Smoltz, in turn, prayed that Baker had fled Galveston Island and Mrs. Baker would have to drive a long ways to join him.

The woman turned off the county highway and drove into a community of Spanish-style houses. Smoltz silently urged her to keep driving, but the Chevy stopped in front of a one-story house with an orange-tiled roof. It reminded Smoltz of the home he and his wife had in Galveston before his dismissal as a doctor and the fracturing of his marriage.

"Back off," Max ordered.

Smoltz let the car drift to a stop several houses down.

Mrs. Baker climbed out of the car and opened the trunk. The door to the house flew open and a pretty young woman with raven hair ran out and threw her arms around her. A young man with equally dark hair walked out but hung back as the two women hugged a long moment. *Mother and daughter,* Smoltz thought.

The young woman seemed to introduce Mrs. Baker to the young man and they shook hands.

A heavy-set woman, about the same age as Mrs. Baker, walked out and joined them. She wore a pink apron and carried a small white dog that squirmed out of her arms and jumped into Mrs. Baker's.

To Smoltz it looked like a family reunion where no one had to travel very far. The women talked all at once and laughed, oblivious to the swirling mist.

The young man grabbed Mrs. Baker's suitcases and followed the women inside.

Max squeezed the back of the front seat with a death-grip, and his acrid breath fogged the windshield.

"Where the fuck is Sam Baker?"

Chapter 86

Blue spotlights lit the rain swirling around the Fontainebleau Hotel. Guests scurried from their cars to enter the luxury hotel through its ornate doors.

Gusts of wind rocked the stolen Dodge where it sat in the parking lot. The motor idled, and the windshield wipers slapped a steady rhythm. On the drive over, Sam and Jackson had brainstormed about how to slip into the lobby and up to Greta Haugen's room without anyone identifying the fugitive ex-sheriff.

Sam pushed his cowboy hat back on his head. "Getting up to Greta's room might be the least of our problems if she has some sort of security."

"You know what the biggest problem we have is, don't you?"

Sam raised an eyebrow. "We're dirty and we smell?"

"Speak for yourself," Jackson said. "No, as a Negro walking into a hotel like this, I couldn't draw any more attention than if I were a jaguar."

"Good choice of color."

"The metaphor was intentional."

Sam looked in the backseat for some idea to jar his mind but the two rifles lying there offered nothing. He pulled the car keys from the ignition and got out and opened the trunk.

Split pieces of firewood were stacked to the top. *The Dodge owner's contribution to the bonfire on the beach,* he thought. He tossed several pieces onto the wet asphalt and saw something yellow lying at the bottom. A canvas golf bag.

He pushed the bag aside to search further, and a few golf clubs slid out. Snuggled in between them was the black barrel of a 12-gauge shotgun. He pulled it free and broke it open. Two shells in the chamber.

Sam dumped the bag and the clubs into the trunk and a pistol grip 12-gauge clattered out with them.

"Henry..."

Jackson climbed out and looked at the weapons. "Damn. Romano's guys were loaded for bear."

Sam unzipped the bag's pockets and pulled out four boxes of shotgun shells. "How's your golf game?"

"You know they don' allow no blacks on th' green, Mr. Baker, suh," Henry said. "Unless you the caddy. Then they need yo' strong back."

That's it," Sam said and snapped his fingers. "You're my caddy. You walk in behind me carrying the bag."

"But they might recognize you."

"I'll wear my hat," Sam said. "We'll walk in like we own the place."

"That hat just makes you look taller."

"You got a better idea?"

"No," Jackson said. "Let's go."

Sam shoved the golf clubs back into the bag and slid the shotguns in between them. "Goddamn, I hope we don't need these."

Jackson put the rifles in the trunk and slung the golf bag over his shoulder. They ran and caught up to two men wearing yellow raincoats. A Cadillac drove under the extended overhang of the entrance. An older man and woman got out and the uniformed doorman pulled their luggage from the trunk.

They merged with the two men and entered the brightly-lit lobby. A bellhop carried a suitcase in each hand, and two guests followed behind him. Several people stood in line at the front desk.

Sam walked ahead, the hat pulled low over his head. Henry trailed behind, carrying the golf bag. The clubs and the shotguns clattered against each other, and the desk clerk looked at them. A heavy-set man with a newspaper tucked under his arm watched them pass. *A hotel dick*, Sam thought.

Sam pushed the button for the elevator, and the brass arm of the wall dial slowly counted down the elevator's descent.

A formally-dressed couple walked past them and disappeared inside the restaurant.

The elevator doors jerked open, and they stepped inside. An older black man—dignified despite the ornate gold uniform and shiny gold hat—bid them good evening and asked for their floor. The man eyed the golf bag slung over Henry's shoulder and nodded at him in understanding.

"Fourth, please," Sam said.

The elevator climbed slowly and stopped. Sam and Jackson stepped out and walked down the carpeted hallway. They paused at room four thirty-six. Across the hall, a door swung open and a pug-nosed man wearing a rain slicker walked out of the room. The man nodded at them. "Looks like your game got rained out."

"It came down when I was on the third fairway," Sam said. He had never golfed in his life and hoped it sounded appropriate.

"It's a hurricane," the man said. "In case you hadn't heard."

"No kidding? I thought it was just a regular Galveston squall."

"I don't know why we didn't get a warning. I just now heard it on the radio."

Sam knew that merchant ships in the Gulf couldn't

transmit radio warnings about storms for fear it would signal their presence to German subs. "Is it coming right at us?"

"Apparently, so," the man said. "But we're just getting the leading edge right now."

The man walked to the elevator and got in.

Jackson whispered, "Why don't I knock on the door. Say I'm from room service. They open the door, and we blow in."

Sam nodded and took the golf bag from Henry. He gripped the stock of the pistol grip shotgun.

Henry knocked. "Room service."

No one answered. He knocked again and a woman's voice, loud and irritated, came from inside the room. "I didn't order room service."

"Yes, ma'am," Henry said in his Southern drawl. "Room four thirty-six."

"Goddammit, I said I didn't order anything. Go away." It was definitely Greta Haugen's deep, raspy voice.

"Beg pardon, ma'am. It say here it was ordered by a Mr. Arin Haugen."

The lock clicked, and the door swung open. Jackson charged in and grabbed Greta in a tight hug and slapped a hand over her mouth. Her scream died abruptly. Sam rushed in with the shotgun, and kicked the door closed. No one else in the front room, but the rest of the large suite disappeared in darkness down a narrow hallway. He walked back to the bedroom and flicked on the light. Empty. So was the closet.

He pushed the bathroom door open and pointed the shotgun inside. No one there and no men's toiletries sat on the shelf above the sink.

In the living room, Greta kicked at Henry's shins and fought to free herself from his grip.

"Good evening, Greta," Sam said. "I guess I'm the last person in the world you wanted to see."

370

Sam opened the door and pulled the golf bag inside. He found a spare sheet in a closet and tore long strips from it. Greta watched his every move. "Put her face down on the bed," he said.

Jackson flattened her on the bed. Her shouts died in the mattress.

Sam looped the strip of sheet over her head and pulled it into her mouth. He tied it behind her head, and Greta cursed into the gag. With a second strip he tied her hands behind her back. They sat her on the edge of the bed. Her eyes blazed and her gray-streaked hair hung in disarray. "Greta," Sam said. "I want to know one thing, and if you lie to me, I'll know it." She stopped cursing and looked at him.

"Where is Max?"

Galveston '44

Chapter 87

A gust of wind rattled the kitchen windows. Hard rain drummed the roof. An occasional bolt of lightning flashed across the black sky.

Dominick and Aunt Missy sat at the dining room table drinking coffee and chatting. Sylvie washed a skillet, and Claire wiped it dry and set it in the drainer next to the two pistols. She didn't like guns but was now comforted by their presence. Missy could shoot almost as well as him, Sam had told her. You didn't grow up in Sheriff Jim's house without learning to handle a firearm. Dominick's stepfather had taught him to shoot as well.

Being around the young man for the first time, Claire decided he wasn't at all like Vince Romano. His disdain for his father was evident as he told her about how he had grilled Sylvie backstage during the Frank Sinatra show. *Whose side are you going to be on when the shit hits the fan?*

Claire said, "Sam told me that Vince and Arin Haugen were protecting the man who killed Wayne."

"He told us that, too," Sylvie said.

"It's hard to believe Arin would get involved in something—."

The back door blew open and slammed against the wall. Window glass shattered on the kitchen floor. Sylvie screamed.

"Damn this door," Missy said. "I thought I had it fixed after the last squall we had." She closed the door, and they pushed the big dining room table against it.

Claire put her arm around Sylvie. "You okay?"

"I'm just a little jumpy."

"We all are," Missy said. "Let's take our coffee into the living room and try to relax."

Claire bent to pick up the shards of glass, but Missy shooed her away. She joined Dominick and Sylvie in the living room and smiled to see them share a quick kiss.

Just as she set her coffee cup on an end table, the front door exploded into pieces and flew open.

A huge man lunged into the room. He punched Dom and knocked him into a tall hutch. Sylvie's scream was cut short as Max grabbed her around the neck with one big arm. In his other hand he held a long-barreled pistol.

Claire jumped on his back, but the big man sent her flying with a twist of his hips. Like a dog shaking off water. He dragged Sylvie into the dining room.

Missy fired her pistol high into the wall above him. He shot back, and she ducked behind a counter.

"Where is Sam Baker?" he shouted.

"He's not here," Missy said. "Let her go!"

Max put the pistol to Sylvie's head. "Tell me right now, or I'll blow her pretty face away."

"He's out looking for you, you son-of-a-bitch!" Missy rose and fired and the bullet ripped out a chunk of wall close to his head.

Max shot back and dragged Sylvie back into the living room, past Claire and Dom where they lay on the floor. He threw the girl over his wide shoulder like a bag of flour and ran out the door.

Claire struggled to her feet and stumbled after them. Max disappeared into the gray curtain of rain with Sylvie hanging limp over his shoulder.

Chapter 88

Thunder rattled the hotel room's rain-streaked windows. Lightning lit the sky and cast a gray hardness on Greta Haugen's defiant expression where she sat tied to a chair.

Sam sat on the bed. A heavy weariness had settled into his bones. He tried to think how long since he and Jackson had slept. Several times they'd heard footsteps in the hallway, but they were never followed by a knock at the door from Arin Haugen, or anyone else.

They had tried to pry information out of Greta, but she hadn't said one word other than to curse them. They had threatened her with torture, but she saw through that. Neither he nor Jackson had that in them, and she knew it. Wayne wouldn't want that, either. But if Haugen showed up, Sam would wrench from him the whereabouts of Wayne and Gus' killer with whatever means it took.

Sam picked up the phone and gave the operator Missy's number. After one ring a woman answered, her voice so rushed and overwrought that he barely recognized her voice.

"Claire?"

"Sylvie's gone, Sam!" Claire said, between sobs. "He got Sylvie!"

"Calm down, Claire," Sam said. But Claire could only repeat her panicked refrain. "What happened?"

"Sam." It was Dom, sounding amped, but his voice was steady. "Max must have followed us. He kicked the door open and knocked me flat. He grabbed Sylvie and drove off."

Sam cursed as the room spun in a circle. "No!"

"I'm sorry, Sam. He came in so fast I didn't have time to grab my gun."

Not his little girl. *Not Sylvie.* Sam's hands trembled as he pressed the phone hard into his ear. "Describe him."

"He was a big man, short blond hair," Dominick said. "And Sam, he asked for you. He wanted to know where you were."

Jackson watched him, his brow knitted with concern. Sam was vaguely aware that Dom was asking him what they should do. The blood rose in his chest and down into his fists. He turned to Greta, her expression curious and pleased. She fed on his distress, whatever the cause might be. He grabbed her by the throat and pulled his fist back. She stared back as if welcoming the blow, her cloth gag expanding and contracting with her rapid breathing.

Jackson grabbed his arm. "No, Sam."

Sam pushed him back. Fire roared in his head.

"Easy, Sam." Jackson pulled him away from Greta. "What happened?"

They stepped out of earshot. "He got Sylvie."

"What the fuck!"

"Max broke into my sister's house and grabbed her. Dominick said he was looking for me."

Sam realized then that Greta didn't know where Max was. Even if they tortured her, she could only lie about his whereabouts. Max, like Sam, sought revenge. He wanted retribution because Sam had killed his partner and shot him before he could escape. "I think he's gone rogue."

Jackson thought a moment. "Maybe he's the one who gutted the guy in Laura's basement. He tried to get out when you were there."

Sam picked up the phone. "Dom?"

"I thought I'd lost you, Sam."

"You need to get out of there in case he comes back."

"Please, Sam," Dominick said, his voice rough with anger and fear. "I want to help you look for Sylvie."

"There's a hurricane out in the Gulf, Dom. Ya'll would be safer here at the Fontainebleau. We have Greta Haugen here." Sam told him to bring Claire and Missy and get a room on the fourth floor as close to room 436 as possible. "Then you come alone to 436 and knock twice, then twice again."

"Got it," said Dom. "We're on our way."

Galveston '44

Chapter 89

Max stood inside a phone booth as wind rocked it and rivulets of rain ran down its sides. He kept an eye on Smoltz where he sat behind the steering wheel of Laura's car, his head in his hands. Max had taken the car keys, but the doctor was too sick to run off anyway.

The Baker girl lay in the backseat bound hand and foot, gagged with Laura's clothes he had found in the trunk. The pretty girl was the next best thing to finding Sam Baker himself.

Max knew he would look for his daughter.

The phone rang twice and someone picked up on the other end without saying anything. Just as he had expected.

"Give me Mr. H."

A moment later a man said, "Mr. H."

"It's me," Max said.

"Where the fuck have you been?" Haugen sounded angry and relieved at the same time.

"I just had to pick up something."

"What do you mean? Did you find Sam Baker?"

"No."

"We thought we had lost you, Max."

"I'm still with you. Don't worry."

"The ship has docked, my friend," Haugen said. "It got here just in time because there's a hurricane approaching."

Max looked out to the road where passing cars cut through the curtain of rain. "Won't that make it difficult to move the cargo by truck?"

"We still have a window of opportunity. But we have to move *now*."

"When can I see it?"

"Soon as you get here. But hurry."

* * *

Max unlocked the car's trunk and opened the back door. The girl raised her head and looked at him, her eyes wet and imploring.

"Please..." she said into the gag. He had left a little slack in the cloth because he liked to hear her beg for her life.

She undoubtedly made Sam Baker proud, and that made Max angry. He hoped he'd have time to rip her clothes off and make his mark on her. Use her up and slip a skull-and-crossbones medallion in her flawless hands. Carl hadn't approved of him leaving one with the deputy. Yes, killing him had been unavoidable, but the gift he'd given him was unnecessary. It was the only time he'd ever disappointed his mentor. After that Max had strived even harder to please him—like a repentant son—until the sheriff had stabbed him in his heart and left him to burn to ashes in the fire.

He opened the trunk and pulled the girl out of the backseat. He dumped her into the trunk, her head thumping against the metal bottom. He listened to her cry while the rain soaked her, then slammed the lid shut.

Chapter 90

Sam paced the floor in front of Greta Haugen. He felt like he could explode out of his skin. But he kept his expression neutral. He wouldn't let her feed on his anger and panic. She probably didn't care what had caused it, only that he had suffered a loss of some sort.

Jackson pushed off from the wall where he'd been watching her gloat. He pulled a strip they'd cut from a sheet over her eyes and tied it behind her head. Now she was mute and blind.

"You're ready for execution now, Greta," Jackson said. "Would you like a cigarette first?"

Sam knew Jackson was also shaken by the crushing news. Wayne, too, would be horrified that his killer had kidnapped the young woman he had loved so much.

All that mattered to them now was finding Sylvie. Though Sam knew that finding her also meant finding Max. He clung to the hope that Max would keep her alive as bait. He wanted to lure Sam to him.

And Sam wanted to find *him* more than anything he'd ever wanted before. The problem was that he and Jackson didn't know what to do if Arin Haugen or one of Vince Romano's goons didn't come to check up on Greta.

They could drive around in the approaching hurricane, looking for a huge man with a young woman. But the odds were worse than finding a needle at the bottom of the Gulf.

Someone knocked on the door twice. Sam and Jackson pulled the shotguns from the golf bag. Two more knocks followed. Sam opened the door to let Dominick in. A swollen gash spanned the width of his chin.

"Damn," Sam said. He turned the young man's head to the light. Blood seeped from the cut but his eyes were clear.

Dominick shook his head, distressed. "I'm really sorry, Sam. He kicked the door down—"

"Not your fault, son."

Henry walked over to Greta and pulled the blindfold off. "Say hello to our guest of honor."

Dominick crossed the room and stood before her. She couldn't hide her surprise at seeing Vince Romano's son. "Does she know?"

"She only knows what their plan is," Henry said. "Not where Max is."

Sam gathered them together out of Greta's earshot. "We're hoping Arin will come see why his wife hasn't been answering the phone," Sam said to Dominick. "It rang twice."

"So if you get Arin, he could lead you to Max?"

"If he'll talk.

"Otherwise?"

Jackson shook his head. Otherwise, they had nothing.

"Did you bring your gun?" Sam asked.

Dom lifted his shirt to reveal the .45 in his waistband. "It was Sal's."

"What room are Claire and Missy in?"

Dominick pointed. "Four-forty. Two rooms down.

Jackson pointed at the rug on the floor. "We're going to roll Greta up in that and put her in the other room."

"I saw a laundry basket down the hall," Dom said. "Wouldn't look so odd that way."

Sam nodded. "That's better." He opened the door slowly and waved Dominick out.

Jackson tied Greta's feet together and untied her from the

chair.

Dominick pushed the laundry basket inside. Greta screamed muffled protests as they picked her up and set her inside and covered her with sheets and blankets from the bed.

Dom wheeled her out and Jackson followed behind.

Sam stayed alone in Greta's room. Weariness weighed on him. He tried to hold onto his last thread of hope, but it was unraveling fast. He thought of Claire, just two doors down. In the weeks since she'd left him all her worst fears concerning his safety and his soul had come to pass. And now her beloved daughter—her last remaining child—had been kidnapped.

* * *

Two knocks came from the door, followed by two more. Sam opened it, and Jackson and Dominick slipped in.

"How is Claire?"

Jackson shook his head. *Not good.*

Sam slipped out and knocked on the door of the other suite. Missy opened it, and then Claire was in his arms. He held her tight as she cried into his chest. He took her into the bedroom, not wanting Greta to feast on their pain.

"I'm sorry, Claire," Sam said. "It's my fault."

"Only one thing matters now."

"I thought I had to keeping looking for him because I owed it—"

She put her finger to his lips. "He asked for you. He wants to find you."

"I'm praying he does."

Galveston '44

Chapter 91

Lightning crackled overhead and shot a sliver of light around the edges of the pitch-black trunk. Over Sylvie's head rain drummed against the metal lid.

Each panicked breath brought her closer to the edge of blacking out. She inhaled slower and deeper and began to gain some control. She had to be alert if somehow she found an opportunity to escape the big son-of-a-bitch—the man who had killed Wayne.

The man her father hunted. The man who hunted her father.

Max, that was his name.

Somehow he had found them and busted in. She could still hear the sharp crack of his fist slamming into Dominick's face. She feared for Dom and her mother and her aunt. She didn't know what happened to them because Max's chokehold had brought her to semi-consciousness. The only thing she could recall was hearing gunshots and him demanding her father.

The image of her father came to her now in the darkness. She felt his strength, his love for her. She knew he would try to find her.

The car's brakes squealed, and she felt it slowing. Were they stopping? If she got the gag off she could scream for help. She reached back for the knot behind her head but her bound wrists made it almost impossible to pick at it. She gritted her teeth and worked the knot again. And again.

* * *

Laura walked around the perimeter of the semi-darkened warehouse, aware of the appraising eyes of the gunmen that followed her whenever she left the cramped office to stretch her legs. The only one who didn't pay attention to her was the man named Drago who never took his deep-set eyes off the smoldering gangster—Vince Romano—as he prowled the cement floor.

Laura was surprised initially to find such a large group of hard-bitten men gathered together in the cotton warehouse. It went contrary to Arin Haugen's instructions to keep a low profile. But she began to hear snatches of talk about a man who could be a potential wrench in the plan.

It all made sense when she heard Romano spit out the word *Baker*. They feared Sam Baker, and had fortified their number because of him.

But not even Sam Baker could find his way here. She ran a mental inventory of every room in the safe house and knew it was clean. There was not a shred of information left there that could point him here, the final stage of the operation. She had done her job precisely, as her superiors ordered. Keep a close eye on the sheriff. *Fuck him,* they said in so many words. Find out if he had suspicions about Vince Romano or Arin Haugen.

Then, after Max killed Wayne McRae, find out how his hunt for him was going. But he never told her anything useful, even when they were lying in her bed in the afterglow of sex.

Haugen had told her that her superiors thought she had failed in her duties. *They had expressed disappointment,* he had said. She hadn't gained the confidences of the sheriff, and Max had fled. But how the hell was she supposed to stop a big ape bent on revenging the death of Carl Strabo?

She strolled to the front of the warehouse where the

windows, covered by thick carton for privacy, rattled in the fierce wind blowing in from the Gulf.

Two of Haugen's new men, armed with shotguns, kept guard by the entry door. One man noticed her approach and nudged the other man. But she didn't know if they stared because of her looks or because one side of her face was swollen from Max's slap.

A light from outside leaked around the drawn shade of the entry door. Laura pulled part of the carton aside from a window and looked out. A car idled a few feet from the first garage door, its headlights illuminating the heavy rain that fell before them. She couldn't make out who the driver was but she'd recognize the car anywhere. It was hers.

Romano ran to the door. The hired men surged forward like troops on the attack, rifles and pistols ready.

"It's Max," Laura said.

* * *

A current of excitement ran through the warehouse as though lightning had struck it. The feral pack of gunmen had retreated back to the box truck, shaking off the false alarm like guard dogs dropping their hackles. All eyes were fixed on the large newcomer.

The wayward son.

Max met their gaze with his steely gray eyes until they found it prudent to look elsewhere. Laura could tell by the furrowing of his brow that he was as perplexed by their number as she was.

As if he could hear her thoughts, he turned and found her. The corner of his mouth lifted in amused contempt, perhaps at the swollen result of the hard slap on her face. Unlike the murderous expression when he had killed Charles with the scalpel, he appeared calm and at ease. He turned away and locked eyes with Drago, standing, as always, next to Vince Romano.

Lightning flashed outside and lit the front area of the warehouse. Laura detected the bulge of a pistol against Max's wet shirt. Had he extracted his pound of Sam's flesh with it? Or, with one of the fighting knives he had taken from her?

That possibility—that she would to a certain degree be an agent of his murder—turned her stomach. She hoped that Sam was alive, and Max had just come to his senses and returned to the mission.

Romano skirted Drago's broad back and stood before Max. "Bring your car in. We don't want to attract attention."

Max towered over the gangster. "I only take orders from Arin Haugen."

"Do you see Haugen here?" Romano said and swept his arm around the room. "And where the fuck is the money man? If I don't get my money, this truck won't make it out of here."

"Word of caution, little man. Don't make threats you can't back up."

Max turned his cold-blooded gaze from Romano to Drago, but neither the bodyguard nor the gangster said anything.

He walked over to Laura. "Take me to the ship."

Thunder and wind gusts shook the garage door. Laura peeked out the window at the slanted rain pounding the dock between the warehouse and the churning Gulf.

"Get one of those goons to do it. They won't say no to a big gorilla like you."

Max slapped her on her swollen cheek. Not as hard as the first time but the pain brought tears to her eyes.

"Orders from Haugen. Let's go." Max took her by the arm and opened the driver's side door of a black Cadillac.

Romano scurried over. "Hey, that's my car."

"She's coming back," Max said. He turned to the guards at the garage door. "Open up."

Laura started the Cadillac and drove out as rain lashed the windshield and wind rocked the car. Max followed behind in Laura's Chevy. Vertical lighting stabbed the bay waters and lit up the dock. Laura looked in the rearview mirror. She thought she saw two figures in the trailing car. If so, Smoltz would be the other. And that might mean that Max had retained his quest for revenge against Sam Baker.

She might have been mistaken about what she had seen—the lightning had been brief and darkness had once again descended—but either way, she wouldn't tell Haugen. Let him figure it out his own damn self.

Galveston '44

Chapter 92

Laura drove Romano's Cadillac over the dock's black timbers. She passed a row of cotton warehouses where squares of plywood had been nailed over the windows.

Only a few cars and trucks drove the wharf with her, all headed for the exit. She turned straight into the stiff wind where Haugen's cargo ship loomed ahead, lashed to the dock by several taut lines. Such a large vessel for just one piece of cargo, she thought.

Laura swung the car around to point in the opposite direction and stopped. Max pulled up close to the lowered gangplank. He jumped out of the passenger side door and in long strides ran to it.

That meant someone else had been driving.

* * *

Max walked down the narrow corridor towards a small light flickering somewhere ahead. It appeared near and far away at the same time. The cramped confines of the ship transported him back to the long voyage to Galveston on another freighter with Carl Strabo. In whispered conferences, his mentor had made him feel valued, important. With the older man's steady guidance and encouragement, he had begun to believe in himself again. To be reborn.

Carl had assured him that the glory of his impending sacrifice would redeem his many mistakes of judgement.

As Max walked toward the light, Carl Strabo's face

appeared in front of his eyes. But it couldn't be him—Carl had died fighting the sheriff. He had saved Max so that he could carry on with his critical role in the mission. Max hoped his murdered friend would share the righteousness of his new objective. It was ordained. Baker would find him one last time. The bound daughter in the trunk of Laura's car guaranteed it. And this time Max would be ready.

More than ready.

But as he took another step the light disappeared, blocked by the gray outline of a large man...the sheriff had found him before he was ready. Max pulled his pistol and fired several shots at the shadow.

He squatted and listened but heard nothing except the muted roar of the storm outside. Then a guttural moan echoed against the passage walls.

"No!" Max screamed in his head. This wasn't how the sheriff had to die. This would be too easy for him and wouldn't honor the great man he had killed. The son-of-a-bitch had to suffer.

And he had to die knowing that his daughter would also die.

Max crept forward in the dark and squatted beside the man. He was older and had Strabo's broad nose and short blond hair. For a panicked moment he thought he had killed the very man—somehow no longer a hallucination—for whom he sought revenge.

But a white officer's hat lay next to the man. He had shot the ship's captain, the man who would grant him entry to the cargo hold. His cry of relief drowned out the man's groans. Of course, the dying man wasn't Carl. He must control the thoughts that his adored friend had somehow come back to life.

The captain handed something metallic to him. *The key to*

the cargo hold.

Max knew then that providence still smiled on him. It still sanctioned his obligation to revenge Carl Strabo's murder in the only fitting manner possible. Joy surged in him.

Max left the man and hurried towards the dim light guiding him like a lighthouse. He climbed down the metal stairs to the cargo holds. His hand shook in anticipation as he unlocked the heavy door with the key and swung it open. A light from the far side of the hold illuminated a large wooden crate resting on a four-foot high steel base. Thick chains encircled the crate, ready to pull it out of the two-story hold. Chain tightening tools and smaller chains hung from hooks on the walls. The room had everything he needed.

Max pulled himself up to the crate and placed his wide palms reverently on the rough wood. He could feel the ungodly power of its contents. He reached in between the narrow slats with one finger and touched the metal housing.

A gentle caress from a devout admirer.

With the key Haugen had given him, he unlocked a hinged section near the middle of the crate and swung the wooden cover aside. With a second key he unlocked an interior metal panel, exposing an array of color-coded buttons and dials arranged in precise rows. He flipped one of the switches, but left the others alone. The sequence wasn't that difficult, but he'd been drilled by his trainers like a child to the point where he felt insulted and disrespected.

Yes, he'd made grave mistakes in his personal life but he was an intelligent man—more so than most of his so–called superiors.

Max jumped down from the base and grabbed a long chain from the wall. He climbed back up and threaded it through the links of the thicker chains. He stood back, satisfied the hanging chain would serve his purpose.

393

Galveston '44

Chapter 93

Smoltz jumped each time the sheriff's daughter kicked the trunk. He thought he'd heard her scream but how could that be possible with the gag in her mouth and the howling wind and clatter of rain on the car roof? Maybe his withdrawal from heroin had him hallucinating again.

If he survived this horror, he would never touch the stuff again. Sure, he'd promised himself that before, but this time he would stay clean. He'd change everything—his powerful habit, his so-called friends, his shitty apartment near the Houston ship channel.

He'd get a job in a medical clinic performing whatever tasks they asked of him. He could no longer treat patients, but he'd change the dirty sheets and mop the floors if he had to.

But how could he live with himself if he allowed something to happen to this girl who was guilty of nothing more than being Sam Baker's daughter? He still felt bound by the solemn oath he had taken many years before as a medical school graduate. The girl was in grave danger. They both were. The doctor knew he had served his usefulness to Max. He had patched him up and drove him around as he hunted the sheriff. And he'd been compliant, too sick to take action when he could have.

The Baker girl kicked the trunk lid again. Smoltz jumped out into the rain and unlocked the trunk. The young woman looked up at him in sheer terror. The gag lay loosely around her neck and her bound hands were clasped as if in prayer. Her legs were still shackled together; she'd been hitting the trunk lid with a tire tool that lay at her side.

"Please help me," she cried.

Smoltz tried to loosen the strips of clothing Max had tied around her wrists but they held fast. He gave up on the wrist bindings and fumbled with the sheets around her ankles. He panicked. Time was running out for them both. Then he remembered Max gutting the man named Charles in the basement. He looked in the backseat and let out a cry. Max had left the scalpel. He grabbed it and cut the girl free.

"Run!" he said. She thanked him and scrambled out of the trunk and ran into the rain.

"Smoltz!"

Max looked down at him from the ship's railing as lightning shot across the sky and lit him like a feral dictator about to address his subjects from on high. The doctor cursed and ran on shaky legs in the opposite direction of the Baker girl.

Smoltz thought he heard Max's footsteps thundering behind him on the wooden planks, but he dared not look back. A howling gust of wind blew him off his feet and onto the rough timbers. His knee screamed in pain. Headlights lit him up, and a car stopped just feet from him. His hopes sank. Now he would die.

"Hey, buddy!" A voice broke through the rain and thunder. A man looked down at him from his panel truck window. "Are you okay?"

The man wore a hat emblazoned with a company name. White hair stuck out from under it and matched his bushy moustache. "Looked to me like you were trying to outrun the hurricane."

Smoltz looked back but didn't see Max.

"Come on," the man said. "Get in before you blow away."

Smoltz hobbled to the truck and climbed in.

"Where you headed?" the man asked.

"Anywhere you're going," Smoltz said, trying to catch his breath.

Wind rocked the truck as it pulled away. "You looked like you were running for your life."

Smoltz tried to smile but he knew the sheriff's daughter was running for her life, too. He looked out into the wet darkness but in the pounding rain couldn't see her or Max's car. A piece of hard debris struck the side of the truck.

"Jesus, Joseph and Mary," the man said and sped up.

"I'd be grateful if you could you slow down a little, mister," Smoltz said. "There was a young woman running out here, too."

Smoltz kept vigil out the side window. Once or twice he thought he saw movement, a flash of something, but the rain and flying objects made it difficult to trust his eyes.

The man tapped the brakes again. "Here she is."

The Baker girl ran ahead of them, her feet splashing up rainwater illuminated by the truck's headlights. She looked back at them, her face a mask of terror.

"She thinks it's him," Smoltz said.

The man looked at him. "Who?"

Smoltz rolled down his window and shouted. "Miss Baker! Get in!" She didn't slow or look back. Probably hadn't heard him in the storm. He cupped his hands to his mouth. "Miss Baker, it's me. I let you out of the trunk!"

The driver's forehead creased in confusion. "Wait a fucking minute. What do you mean you let her out of the trunk?"

"Miss Baker!"

Sylvie stopped and turned. The truck stopped, too, its headlights spotlighting her like an actress on a horror movie set. Her black hair lay plastered to her head, and her chest heaved. She studied them, distrustful but hopeful.

"Get in," Smoltz said. "You're going to be all right. Max didn't come after us."

Sylvie smiled, relief washing fear from her face.

"Who the hell is this Max?" the driver demanded. He looked past Smoltz, startled by something. A car shot out of the darkness and slammed into the truck's front fender and shoved it aside.

Max jumped out and fired his pistol at them. The windshield shattered and glass rained inside the truck's cab. He shot again. The driver slammed the gearshift into reverse and backed up into the headwind. More bullets took out the remaining shards of glass and smacked into something metallic in the back of the truck.

The driver stopped when they were out of pistol range behind a warehouse. "Who the *fuck* was that?

Smoltz felt a numb pain in his shoulder. Blood flowed and mixed with his wet shirt. So, this was what it felt like to be shot.

Chapter 94

Sam kept his ear pressed to the hotel room door, attuned to the slightest sound coming from the hallway. The howling wind and the rumble of thunder drowned out all but the loudest passing conversation.

Jackson and Dominick sat on the hinged side of the door. Time ticked on. No one spoke.

Weariness pressed down on Sam, and he pulled up a chair for a quick rest.

Someone knocked at the door.

With his pistol drawn Sam pressed his back against the wall on one side of the door. Jackson and Dominick covered the other side. The soft knock at the door had been so quickly absorbed by the storm that Sam wondered if he had heard it coming from across the hall.

The second knock was louder. A man called softly, "Greta?"

Sam jerked the door open, but no one was there. He bolted into the hallway as a red-headed man ran toward the stairs. Sam sprinted after him and tackled him on the carpet. Arin Haugen tried to shout, but Sam clamped a hand over his mouth. He and Dominick dragged him into Claire's room.

They threw Haugen on the bed. Henry pushed his face into the mattress. Sam gave Claire his knife, and she cut long strips from a sheet. Sam tied Arin's hands and feet together. They gagged him and set him in a chair across from his wife.

"Nice of you to drop by, Arin," Sam said. "Look who beat you to the party."

Arin looked at Greta as though she had been spit out of the howling wind and landed, bound to a chair, in an unfamiliar room.

Missy looked back and forth between them. "Ya'll don't look so goddamn almighty now."

Jackson searched Haugen's pockets and threw the contents—a few coins, a fat wallet and some car keys—on the bed. He opened the wallet. "Damn, Haugen, you got enough cash in here to choke an elephant." He threw the money on the bed and searched the wallet but found nothing that would lead them to Max and Sylvie.

"Maybe you ought to wait in the other room," he said to Claire. "We're going to get some information one way or another."

"Let's do what we have to do," Claire said. "We can ask for forgiveness later."

Sam told Jackson to get behind Haugen with his pocket knife and slice his throat open if he said anything above a whisper.

"With pleasure, Sam."

"Let me do that," Dom said. He took the knife from Jackson and pressed the blade against Haugen's fleshy throat. Haugen's eyes widened. Sweat dripped from his orange-freckled scalp.

Sam untied his gag. "I'm going to ask you some questions, Arin, and I want the truth and I want it quick."

"Fuck you, Baker."

Sam slapped Haugen hard, and his head snapped to the side. Tears welled in his eyes, but his expression of defiance returned. Sam had never taken Arin for a tough guy. A ruthless businessman, yes, but his eyes seemed to burn with fervor for something.

"Arin," Sam said. He leaned into his face. "Max broke

away from whatever you and Vince have cooked up, didn't he?"

"As usual, my dear Sam, you don't know shit."

"Greta told us."

"I doubt that, or you wouldn't be trying to beat it out of me."

Sam realized that Haugen was going to be as tight-lipped as Greta. "Maybe you're tough, Arin, but can you take seeing your wife hurt?" He started towards Greta with his hand raised to strike her. Missy stopped him as though to protect the woman, and then wheeled around and slapped her hard. Greta's head lolled on her shoulders. Blood trickled from her lip.

"I don't care what kind of bullshit you and Vince and your damn wife have planned between ya'll," Sam said to Haugen. "I only care about one thing—the whereabouts of my daughter."

Haugen looked perplexed. "Sylvie? How the hell would I know where she is?"

Claire stood in front of him. "Max broke into Missy's house looking for Sam. He took Sylvie."

A smile pulled up a corner of Haugen's mouth. "I haven't seen her, Claire. And that's really your problem, isn't it?"

"Here's your problem," Claire said. She slapped him hard. His head hung down for a long moment before he could raise it. He sneered at her.

"You know you're going to jail, don't you?" Sam said.

Haugen shook his head. "When this is all over, Greta and I will be protected from any harm."

"We know your car was used during the murder of Wayne McRae," Jackson said. "We know you supplied another car to Max and the man Sam killed. They were hiding in your building."

"None of that matters, my friend. In fact, in a matter of a couple days America will be in total chaos."

"How?"

Haugen laughed. "Afraid I can't tell you that. But the likes of you will be rounded up and put in camps."

"The likes of me?"

"Sub-human people from Africa, of course. You'll be sleeping on the floor with Jews and faggots."

"I don't think so, Haugen," Jackson said. "You're going to be sleeping on a piss-stained bunkbed with a murderer for a cellmate."

Dominick's mouth widened in disbelief. "You're *Nazis*?"

"Of course. Too bad you're not on the right side, young Romano."

The room grew silent as each absorbed Haugen's revelation.

"The Germans are done, Haguen," Sam said. "They're recruiting young boys and old men to fight."

"What we have coming right here in America will turn the tide," Haugen declared. "You can kill me and Greta, but that won't stop it."

Greta shouted into her gag. Her eyes burned brighter. She and Arin shared a fervent look that told Sam this was their mission, not some spectacular heist or the theft of priceless art.

Claire whispered in his ear. "Whatever we have to do. I just want Sylvie back."

Sam agreed. They were running out of time. The hurricane was building strength and would soon make it impossible to drive the roads, even if they did know where Max and Sylvie were.

He pulled his knife and pressed the blade against Greta's cheek. "Arin, your wife is never going to look the same unless

402

you tell me where Max is."

"You're bluffing," Haugen said, but a note of concern had entered his voice.

Sam drew the knife across her cheek. Blood seeped down her jaw and dripped on her white blouse.

Haugen tried to yell, but Jackson clamped a hand over his mouth.

"Here's what's going to happen, Arin," Sam said. He pressed the knife against Greta's other cheek. "You're going with us to find the son-of-a-bitch. If we can't, Greta is going to bleed to death right in this hotel room."

Haugen shook his head, *no*.

"Death of a thousand cuts." Sam sliced Greta's other cheek, deeper than the first one. Blood flowed, covering the lower half of her face. Greta screamed into the gag and thrashed against her bindings. Sam held the knife against her throat, and she held still. "So help me, God," Sam said to Arin. "I'll kill her right in front of your eyes."

"Please! Stop!" Haugen's expression fell. He looked at Greta as if asking permission. Or forgiveness. "Max is either at my ship or at a cotton warehouse on the docks."

"What's on your ship?"

"That's where the weapon is. An extremely powerful bomb. It's going to Washington, D.C. When President Roosevelt gives his speech on Friday, the bomb will be detonated. He will be killed along with the congressmen and cabinet members sitting behind him. In fact, this bomb will kill everyone within several hundred feet. Without leaders, America will be like a chicken with its head cut off."

"*Jesus, God,*" Claire said.

"Max will take the bomb?" Sam asked.

"Yes. He's the one who will detonate it."

"What about the warehouse?"

"That's where the transport truck is. Romano and about ten men are there to help load the bomb into the truck. And they're armed to the teeth. "

"What does the truck look like?" Sam asked.

"A large box truck. D.C. Catering Company is written on the side."

Sam turned to Missy. "Call the F.B.I. about the truck."

Sam huddled with Jackson and Dominick and Claire. "We need to get into that warehouse. It's the only play we've got left."

"How do we get in?" Dom asked.

"You don't have to do this, Dominick," Sam said. "Like Haugen said—there will be several gunmen there. Your father, too."

"Sam, I couldn't live with myself if I didn't try to get Sylvie back."

Missy hung the phone up. "The lines are down."

Everyone was silent, trying to think of a way to get into a warehouse with a chance to survive a gunfight.

"I know a way," Jackson said. "Trojan horse."

Chapter 95

Laura sat in the cotton warehouse's back office and watched through the grimy window as the gunmen checked and rechecked their weapons. They had grown restless and undoubtedly itched to shoot somebody.

Vince Romano paced the floor, waiting for Arin Haugen to return. Waiting for the new handler to show up and pay him his money. Except there wouldn't be a new handler—Sam had killed the first one, and Max killed the second. There wouldn't be any more money.

Laura, too, wondered why Haugen hadn't returned by now. As time ticked away, the wind and rain increased their fury. Something had to give soon.

* * *

"Trojan horse," Jackson repeated. "It's the only way."
Thunder rattled the hotel room's windows. The lights flickered off and came back on.

Sam knew what he meant. They would have to sneak into the warehouse somehow without being detected. A direct assault against gunmen who were waiting for him would be suicidal.

"Haugen won't just show us where the warehouse is," Jackson went on. "He's going to take us inside. You in the trunk and me and Dominick in the back seat."

Dom pulled the blanket off the bed. "We can cover ourselves with this."

"If he alerts them…" Jackson said. He pushed his finger into the back of Haugen's head like a gun barrel. "It will be the last thing he ever does."

Missy took the knife from Sam. "Arin, if they don't come back with Sylvie, you know what will happen to your wife."

"Sam," Haugen said. "Let us go, and I'll give you three hundred thousand dollars cash. It's in my office safe."

"Your money is worth nothing compared to our daughter," Claire said.

Dominick nodded. "Less than nothing."

"Let's use the rug," Sam said.

They untied Haugen from the chair, and rolled him up in the rug.

Sam held Claire for a long moment. There was nothing he could say that would give her reassurance or even hope that he'd bring Sylvie back safe. Instead, he told her he loved her, and walked out.

Chapter 96

Rain poured into the windowless panel truck, drenching Smoltz and the white-haired driver. They waited several warehouses away from where Max had crashed into them and shot the windshield out.

"You hurt bad?" the man asked.

Smoltz shook his head. "The bullet hit the fleshly part of my shoulder. It's not bleeding real heavy."

"You reckon that son-of-a-bitch is gone?"

"Probably," Smoltz said. Max had recaptured the girl—his bait to lure Baker—and wouldn't bother with a couple guys who were just trying to help her. The big man wasn't crazy, just insane.

* * *

Rain pummeled Haugen's Cadillac faster than the windshield wipers could clear the water. Gusts of wind buffeted the big car as Sam drove it through flooded streets. Most traffic headed in the opposite direction—out of town.

In the backseat Haugen sat between Jackson and Dominick. The shotguns and rifles lay on the floorboards. They all had pistols and plenty of ammo. Enough firepower, not enough men.

All eyes were focused straight ahead, on the uncertain fate that awaited them. The silence reminded Sam of the reflection he and his fellow G.I.'s shared when they prepared to battle the Germans in France. Often, they knew in advance they were

407

Galveston '44

outnumbered, and the dead quiet on those days—like now—
was unlike any other.

Chapter 97

Car lights played across the cardboard covering the warehouse windows. Romano looked outside but the car went on. The traffic leaving the dock area had dwindled to a trickle. He was about to climb out of his skin. Haugen should have been back by now. Max, too.

And where was the new handler and the rest of his damn money?

He looked into the glass window of the warehouse office where Laura sat watching him like a cat that wanted to scratch his eyes out. He wouldn't admit it, but she rattled him. He had never worked with a woman in any operation like this. Especially one so goddamn pretty.

A horn blared. Headlights filtered in through the covered garage door windows. Vince hoped Haugen had finally arrived, but it was Max, barely visible through the rainwater lashing his windshield. The gunmen advanced, but he waved them off. Vince nodded and the guard unlocked the garage door and swung it open.

The car entered, dripping water on the concrete floor. The entire left fender was caved in, something Vince hadn't noticed before.

Max gunned the engine and drove to the back of the warehouse. He jumped out and made a show of sticking a pistol in his waistband. He snapped his thick fingers and pointed in Vince's direction. "Where's Haugen?"

Vince briefly considered saying something sarcastic, but thought better of it, even with Drago there. "Not back yet."

Max gestured at Laura to join him. She touched the bruised side of her face and ignored him. He shouted something in German. She got up slowly and strolled to the car. He opened the trunk.

Laura looked down—her mouth open in disbelief—as Max pulled a young woman by her arm out of the dark cavity. Her wet black hair stuck to her face and her soaked clothes clung to her body. Max held her up by one arm like a rag doll that might otherwise collapse. Laura took her other arm.

Vince and Drago hurried over. The woman's head hung down. One side of her face was red and puffy, but Vince recognized her. "What the fuck are you doing with Sylvie Baker?"

Max brushed him aside as he and Laura half-dragged Sylvie into the office. Vince felt Drago's presence behind and felt emboldened enough to grab Max's big shoulder. "Don't you know Baker will come looking for his daughter?"

Max and Laura set Sylvie down in a chair. She dropped her head, and her shoulders shook as she sobbed. Laura patted her back.

Romano entered the office. "Are you fucking crazy? Do you know who you're dealing with here?"

With one quick shove Max pushed him out of the office. Drago lunged forward, but Romano stopped him. Shooting the key man in the operation would guarantee that he wouldn't get his money.

Romano stood, dumbfounded. At least he had said his piece to Max. Now Haugen would have to deal with the lunatic giant. Vince knew Sam would look for his daughter, come hell or high water.

And it was getting higher by the minute.

Chapter 98

Sam kept a hard grip on the steering wheel and drove the Cadillac onto the Galveston docks, its big wheels bouncing over the uneven timbers. The hard wind rocked the car from side to side. He headed for slip number seven, where Haugen's ship—its sole cargo a powerful German bomb designed to kill President Roosevelt and members of Congress—had docked.

Over the years Sam had dealt with a lot of different crimes in Galveston, everything from petty theft to bank robberies to first-degree murder, and he never imagined a day when he would be up against Nazi assassins.

Haugen pointed ahead at the dim outline of the moored freighter, gray against the black sky. The gangplank had been lowered, but no car was parked in front of it.

"He's not here," Haugen said.

Sam turned to the backseat. "Arin, it's way too fucking late to start lying."

Haugen shook his head. He looked exhausted, defeated. "He'll be in the warehouse. I swear."

Henry cut the strips binding Haugen's hands and reminded him to drive in as close to Romano's men as possible.

Sam had them repeat what each man's role would be. Jackson would lie on the backseat and Dom would scrunch down on the floorboard. They would cover themselves with the blanket and hope Romano didn't discover them before Sam jumped out of the trunk and opened fire with his shotgun. That was their signal to come out shooting.

"What about me?" Haugen asked.

"Duck and pray," Sam said.

"Let me remind you again, Haugen," Jackson said. "If you alert them in any way, your brains will be all over the windshield."

"I won't say anything," Haugen muttered. "I just want to protect Greta."

Sam looked at Dominick. "You all right?"

The young man gave a confident nod. "I'm okay. I just hope to God Sylvie is there."

Sam reached into the backseat and shook hands with both men. "Good luck." He jumped out into the rain, and Haugen took his place behind the steering wheel.

Sam climbed into the trunk and held the lid open a crack. Rainwater flowed in. He cradled the shotgun to his chest. He was more than ready for battle, despite the odds of three men against ten or eleven.

The car moved forward.

Chapter 99

Just outside of the office, angry voices spoke in German. Sylvie wasn't familiar with the language, but she recognized her own name when Laura said it.

But Laura? How could her salon boss, her friend, be involved with Vince Romano and this bunch of armed men? She wanted to believe that Laura's swollen face meant she had also been punched and kidnapped by Max. But the more she heard her argue with him, the more Sylvie realized she was part of Vince's operation.

Romano paced the floor near the front door, constantly looking out a gap in the window covering. His thin lips moved as he either muttered to himself or spoke to Drago.

Laura walked into the office and set a glass of water in front of her. "I cleaned it as well as I could," she said. "Everything in this dump is filthy."

Sylvie thanked her and pressed the glass to her swollen cheekbone where Max had slapped her before throwing her back in the trunk. She had been so close to freedom, so close to escaping this huge monster who had killed Wayne and now wanted to kill her father. Probably her, too.

Sylvie looked fully at Laura, who met her gaze. Her expression seemed to sympathize with Sylvie and, at the same time, repel any inquiry. She seemed to be a different person now—harder, tougher. The pretty salon owner had been an act, a cover for who she really was—a criminal of some sort. One who spoke German. Was she a saboteur? "You fooled me, Laura. I guess I was pretty dumb to not figure you out."

"You're not dumb, Sylvie," Laura said. "I genuinely like you. Your father, too."

"What are you and these men—"

Laura shushed her and looked out the office window.

Max walked across the dusty floor. A knot of the armed men parted to let him pass. He climbed into the cargo truck and started the engine.

Vince threw up his hands. "What the fuck are you *doing*?"

Max's response was to rev the engine several times before shutting it down. A cloud of gray exhaust drifted across the floor. Romano shook his head and looked out the window again.

Sylvie caught a look of contempt in Laura's expression as she watched Max climb out of the truck. "How did he find you?" Laura asked.

"At Missy's house," Sylvie said. "He kicked the door in like it was made of cardboard. He wanted my father. No telling what he would have done to us if Missy hadn't shot at him."

Laura looked out the window and nodded like she was picturing the scene in her mind. She reached into her purse and handed Sylvie a folding knife.

"Use it if you get a chance," she said. "Stick it in his eye."

* * *

Romano strode into the office and gestured into the main room of the warehouse with his thumb. "Take her out," he said to Laura. "I got to call the hotel again, see where the fuck Haugen is."

Laura stared at Romano a long moment. "I just called the hotel. Phones are down."

A scar-faced gunman ran up to the office and pointed to

the front of the warehouse. "Mr. Romano."

Max looked out the window. "It's Haugen." He turned and walked back towards the office, his sunken eyes fixed on Sylvie.

Galveston '44

Chapter 100

Sam lay in the dark pit of the trunk as Haugen's Cadillac bumped over the rough timbers of the dock. The car moved steadily forward. Sam felt a familiar calm brought on by the inevitability of what lay ahead. Like the last moments before climbing into the boxing ring. Or, awaiting his commander's order to climb out of their muddy trench and charge the Germans.

Nothing else to do but do it.

The car stopped. He listened for voices but the roar of the rain and wind drowned out everything, even the rumble of the car's idling engine. More time ticked by. They should have been let in by now.

Had Haugen warned them after all? All it would take would be a hand gesture or a nod of the head towards the backseat.

Sam pulled one of the hammers back on the double-barrel shotgun and waited for someone to appear at the rear of the car. Lightning crackled overhead. Adrenaline pumped through his veins. What the hell was taking so long?

The car moved slowly forward, climbed over a slight bump and levelled off. The clatter of rain quieted.

They were in, but just barely.

Voices sounded all at once. Sam picked out Romano's as he cursed Haugen for making him worry.

Through the gap in the trunk lid Sam caught a glimpse of a man with a pistol in a side holster walk past the side of the car. He pulled the garage door down, just barely clearing the

417

rear of the car and leaving little space for Sam to jump out.

Sam shoved the trunk up and levelled the shotgun at the man. He fired. The blast blew the man off his feet. Sam scrambled out of the trunk and shot another man as the latter raised his rifle.

Dominick and Jackson jumped out of the back doors, firing the rifle and the other shotgun. Men screamed and clutched their bodies and fell back. Others pulled their weapons and returned fire. Bullets shattered the Cadillac's windows and ripped into the body with a drumming metallic percussion.

The fuselage forced them to squat behind the passenger side of the car. The wall close behind them protected their rear but not their flank. When a man appeared there, Jackson shot him with the rifle.

Romano and his men fell back and fired from behind their cars and steel support posts.

"Keep an eye out for Max," Sam told Jackson and Dom. He saw Drago leave his cover and shoot at him. Sam fired back but missed.

* * *

Gunshots reverberated through the spacious warehouse as Max calmly walked away from the firefight. A stray bullet kicked up concrete off a support post near his head, but he didn't flinch. He carried himself like a man not concerned or even curious about a gun battle that raged nearby.

Sylvie looked out the office window, but the big truck and a stack of broken pallets blocked her view of the fight. A moment later a man staggered back from it, holding his chest. Another bullet took him off his feet.

"*My God,*" she said. "Max said it was Arin Haugen who

drove in. Why would Romano fight with him?"

Laura stood next to her, witnessing the madness. But instead of sharing Sylvie's sense of confusion and horror, her ex-boss' smile seemed to express amazement, even admiration.

"Let's take a look," Laura said.

Sylvie followed her out into the main room—staying low—and they took cover behind a wooden crate. Romano's gunmen rose and fired and ducked back down. Sylvie could only catch a glimpse of the men shooting back from behind a black Cadillac. "Who is it?"

"Why do you think Max brought you here?"

Laura met her gaze and held it until she got the message. Sylvie inhaled sharply. "My father?"

She stood for a better look, and Max appeared and grabbed her arm. Oddly, his expression had softened, and he gave her a brief smile.

"Our guests have arrived," he said. "And they're here for you."

Galveston '44

Chapter 101

Sam squeezed off a shot. A man dropped to the floor. A new wave of lead came back at them, shattering the last of the window glass in the Cadillac.

Jackson yelled between clenched teeth and clutched his calf. He fell, and Sam rushed to him and lifted his pants leg. A bullet had ripped away a chunk of his calf and blood flowed from the wound. Dominick pointed to the concrete floor. "Bullets are ricocheting up from under the car."

"*Damn,*" Jackson said, pain etched in his face. "Don't tell my sister I got shot again."

"Hell, no."

"Help me up."

Sam took his hand and pulled him to his feet.

"Hey, Baker!" It was Vince Romano. Sam peeked but couldn't spot him. Romano shouted at his men to stand down. The warehouse grew quiet. "Looks like we got one of your guys. Was it the nigger?"

"Don't know anybody by that description over here," Sam shouted. "But thanks for asking."

"Told you I'd get that mother-fucker someday."

"Looks like you're going to have a change of plans, Vince," Sam added. "That bomb isn't going anywhere."

"You're too late. It already left."

"The truck is still here. Haugen told us all about your plan to kill the President."

"Arin's a liar," Vince said. "Besides, we got you outnumbered."

"Looks like we evened up the odds quite a bit, if my arithmetic is right. At this rate we're going to get you, too."

"You're going to die right where you stand," Vince shouted, anger creeping back into his voice. "Maybe I'll let you and your colored friend go if you throw down your guns."

Sam looked at Dominick. "What about my other friend?"

Dominick cupped his hands. "You sold your country out, Vince."

"Dominick?"

"It's a shame you won't be able to spend your dirty money."

"You ungrateful piece-of-shit," Romano said. "You want to kill your own father?"

"If Sam doesn't beat me to it."

"You're on the wrong side, son. You best turn around and walk out through that door or you're going to die."

"We'll make you the same deal, Vince," Sam said. "You give us Sylvie, and we'll leave."

"You're in no position to offer that, Baker. I got eight good men here. Plus Drago, and he counts for two."

"You got four at best, and I'll bet they're wondering what the hell they signed up for."

Vince's laugh was harsh and dry. "They're here to kill you."

Sam caught a glimpse of Drago as he rose and fired at them. The rest of his men opened up, too. Sam sighted his pistol through the car's broken window until Drago exposed himself again. Sam fired. Drago clutched his chest and dropped behind the car.

"Drago!" Vince yelled.

"Now you have three men," Sam said.

"You son-of-a-bitch!"

Sam cupped his hands. "Sylvie!"

"Daddy!" It was her voice, and it came from the back of the room.

Dominick half-stood. "Sylvie!"

A man stepped away from behind a car and fired with a rifle. Dom fell onto his back and lay still.

"Dominick..." Sam said. Blood ran from a hole in his chest. Sam pressed his hands to the wound. The young man's eyes fluttered once and closed. "Dom, stay with me."

Jackson shot several rounds in response and then stopped. "I see them."

Sam stood. Max held Sylvie in front of him as they walked deeper into the warehouse.

"Daddy!"

Max waved at Sam, mocking him. He pulled Sylvie back by her throat, and they disappeared into the dark recesses of the room.

Sam crept to the front of the car, staying low but keeping an eye on where Max and Sylvie had disappeared. Bullets flew around him as the gunmen saw him move.

"Sam," Jackson said. "Stay down,"

"Cover me. I'm going to run back there."

"They'll cut you down."

"He'll kill her."

"You won't be any good to her if you're dead." Jackson fired his rifle and ducked back down. "Our best bet is to finish these guys off first."

Dominick moaned. Sam squatted down to him. "Sylvie's going to be with us soon. I promise." Dominick's eyes fluttered open and looked at him for moment before closing again.

Sam reloaded his pistol and fired. "Hey Vince!"

"Looks like that worthless son of mine got hit."

"He'll be all right," Sam said. "He just needs a minute."

"Bullshit. It's down to just you."

"You're bad at math."

"Nigras don't count," Vince said. "Besides, he's shot up, too."

Jackson rose and fired. "Never felt better, Vince."

From the dark shadows a powerful engine roared to life. The cargo truck lurched forward and slammed into the rear of a car and shoved it from its path. Romano and a man with a rifle were exposed and ran. Jackson fired once and Romano fell.

The other man stopped and shot back. Jackson dropped at Sam's feet. The man ran for cover, and Sam shot him.

The truck accelerated. Sam aimed at the cab, but Max held Sylvie by her neck and pushed her face against the windshield. He had to hold fire.

"Sylvie!"

Another gunman jumped from his cover and aimed his pistol at Sam. Max ran him over with the truck just before it slammed into the garage door and ripped it wide open.

Sam ran around to the driver's side of the Cadillac, keeping his back to it and his pistol ready. But no one fired. Everyone was dead or dying—including Jackson and Dominick.

Vince Romano and Drago, too.

Sam opened the car door and pulled Haugen's bullet-ridden body from the front seat. He heard the sharp click of a pistol hammer behind him.

"Baker…"

He turned his head. Drago stood unsteadily—like a thick oak tree waving in the breeze—and pointed his gun. Blood ran from his head and covered his face. A triumphant smile pulled at one corner of his mouth.

"I didn't know you could actually speak, Drago."

"Listen to this," Drago said. He took a step closer. "It will be the last thing you ever hear." He held the pistol with both hands and aimed dead at Sam.

A shot rang out. Sam dove and rolled on the floor. He scrambled for his gun as another shot reverberated through the cavernous room.

Drago swayed, his gun held at his side. Another shot. The big man pitched forward and slammed hard into the unforgiving concrete.

Behind him, Laura still aimed her gun.

Sam and Laura looked at each other a long moment. "He took her to the ship," she said. She pointed outside. "*Go!*"

Galveston '44

Chapter 102

Laura watched Sam drive the bullet-riddled Cadillac through the shattered garage door. She feared for him and Sylvie. Max could have killed Sam during the gun battle, but had chosen to lure him to the ship where he would have revenge on his own terms—and that probably didn't involve a quick, merciful death.

She found Vince Romano, dead from a gunshot to the head. A man moaned, barely audible over the roar of the storm. Dead and dying men lay scattered on the floor like on a battlefield.

A black man rose slowly, using the wall for support. He had to be the Negro who was helping Sam. Sylvie and Wayne's friend, she had told her...Henry something.

Laura went to him. Blood had soaked his shirt. "Please," she said. "Let me take a look."

"Where'd they go?"

"To the ship."

He pointed his rifle at her. "You're going to take me there."

"Let me see your wound. You're hurt bad."

"Let's go," Jackson said. "I hear it's good weather for a boat ride."

"You'll die," she said.

"I'll die there."

Laura heard the moan again. Dominick Romano lay on the floor with his bloody hands over his chest. Jackson squatted by him. "Dominick..."

The young man opened his eyes. In a bone-dry whisper, he said, "Henry."

Laura kneeled and pulled his hands away from his chest. She pressed her hand on the bullet hole where the blood oozed out.

Dominick tried to lift his head. "Sylvie..." Laura eased him back down.

"Sam went to get her," Jackson said. "Don't worry."

Laura slapped Dom's face and told him to stay with her. She was surprised he wasn't in shock yet. Maybe because of his concern for Sylvie.

She stood and whispered to Jackson. "He's going to die unless we get him to a hospital."

"Would you take him?"

"Of course."

She found a car with the keys in it and drove it close to the wall. She slipped her hands under Dominick's armpits. Jackson gritted his teeth against the pain and helped her lift him into the backseat.

Chapter 103

Slanted sheets of rain poured in through the busted windshield as Sam drove over the wharf. Violent gusts of wind threatened to stop Haugen's Cadillac in its tracks. The rain and darkness swallowed the twin beams of its headlights. He knew the docks lay somewhere ahead, but he couldn't see the ships tied there. He feared running into a stalled car. Or, into the rising waters of the Gulf.

He turned where the dock narrowed between the warehouses and the docks. The cargo truck sat dead ahead, one headlight pointing at Haugen's freighter like a beacon—like an invitation.

Sam grabbed the shotgun and jumped out of the car. He leaned into the howling wind and inched his way to the cab. He threw the door open, but they were gone.

He ran up the gangplank to the deck where two doors led inside the ship. One was open a crack. He slipped inside to the darkness of the narrow passageway. The sounds of the storm diminished, replaced by the muffled bumping and grinding of the huge ship against the dock.

After several steps, he stopped. Somewhere ahead a light flickered, dancing like a candle.

He could make out metal doors with porthole windows from which he could be watched. Max could step out as he passed and shoot him in the back. But Max seemed to have something more elaborate planned. And he feared it involved Sylvie.

After a few steps he heard a moan, low and brief. *Maybe*

the ship protesting the force of the wind, he thought. But it came again, right below him. He took a step, and his foot found a white captain's hat. A few feet from it, a uniformed man lay on his back. Blood shone on his uniform shirt. Sam knelt. The man took his hand and said something in German that sounded like a prayer. The captain's grip weakened, and he gave out.

Sam had no doubt that Max had killed him, joining the murders of Wayne McRae, Gus Josie, the disemboweled man in Laura's basement.

Sam set the captain's hat on his chest and went on. The dim light—an electric bulb in a glass sconce—grew closer and lit the intersection of two converging hallways. Both directions were ink-black like cave openings. He had no idea which to choose.

* * *

Pain shot through Jackson's chest like he'd been poked with a hot iron. His calf had gone numb except for the sensation of blood filling his boot.

Fierce wind shook the car like a toy as Laura turned towards the docks. A shard of lightning struck a metal warehouse and sparks shot sideways, carried away by the wind.

"It's like the goddam world is ending," Laura whispered.

In the backseat, Dominick's breath came slow and shallow. Jackson reached back and patted his shoulder. "Dominick, tell us where you're going to take Sylvie out next time."

Dom tried to speak, but words died on his lips. Jackson took off his shirt and laid it over him.

The massive freighter loomed ahead like a floating castle.

The cargo truck and Haugen's Cadillac faced the port side of the ship.

Laura pulled up close to the gangplank. "Max will be ready for you."

"So be it," Jackson said.

They looked back at Dominick, pale from the loss of blood.

"I'll get him to the hospital," Laura said, dropping her voice. "But it doesn't look good."

"Where you going after that? Back to Germany?"

"I don't think so," she said. "Maybe I'll get lost in America."

Galveston '44

Chapter 104

The storm hammered the ship into the dock with a steady rhythm. The metal floor vibrated like an electric current running up through Sam's boots and into his chest. He had placed his ear against every door in every passageway but heard nothing besides the creaking and groaning of the steel structure.

He had explored a short distance down both passageways that intersected the one he had come from. He had no idea which one to continue on. Other than the dead ship captain, Max hadn't sprinkled any more breadcrumbs.

He looked ahead where another speck of light quivered in the distance. Was it there all along, or did someone just turn it on? He ran, hoping to catch Max by surprise, but tripped and fell to a sliding stop on the floor. He crawled back and found his shotgun next to a young sailor, his hands thrown behind him as if surrendering. Blood leaked from a dark hole in his forehead.

Max had left him a trail marker after all.

* * *

Jackson stepped into the dark passageway. The roar of the hurricane had softened. Rainwater mixed with blood dripped off his bare chest and plinked on the steel floor. He felt the same deep weariness and draining of life force he'd experienced a year ago in Atlanta. If he made it out of here alive, he would hear Viola scold him: *Damn, brother. You went and got your ass shot again!*

He walked forward, the rifle ready. He hadn't gone far before he saw the dead man on the floor with the captains' cap on his chest. Jackson squatted and touched his face. Still warm.

He sat and leaned his back against the passage wall. He just needed to rest a minute before he went on. Just for a minute.

Chapter 105

Sam stepped off the last rung of the spiral stairs and onto the lower level. A wall sconce cast a sliver of light against large metal doors. He was below in the cargo holds. The floor hummed louder here than on the first level, like angry bees chased from their hive.

Like a warning.

He went to the first hold and slowly opened the iron door. He stared into a silent blackness and knew the huge room contained no cargo. Same thing at the next hold. He understood then that the only cargo on the ship was the German bomb.

A faint light crept out from under the next door. He lifted the door handle and leaned his weight against it. It creaked open. This time the sound didn't echo back to him.

There was something in here.

He crouched low and took a step inside. An unseen light illuminated the closest side of a large wooden crate. It rested on a wide metal base four feet tall. Thick chains wrapped the crate, ready to hoist it out from the cargo hatch three stories higher. This was undoubtedly the bomb, but it wasn't going anywhere now. Not without Vince and his men there to offload it and protect it. Not without Haugen to give instructions.

Max had blown up their assassination plot. He'd chosen personal revenge over German victory.

The ship swayed and on the other side of the crate the chains clinked together. Sam crawled with the shotgun cradled in his arms and stopped at the end of its metal base. He realized the light came from behind the bulwark to his right and exposed him to anyone waiting in the dark side of the room.

Sam started to inch forward but stopped. A sound separate from the storm came from the other side of the crate. Possibly someone breathing. Or someone wounded and moaning.

He edged further in until he could see some of the room behind the bulkhead. Large iron tools and cargo chains hung on the wall. A coiled rope lay on the floor. But no big man with a gun.

Sam reached the corner of the metal base. The muffled cries became louder, more urgent. They seemed to come from everywhere all at once.

The time had come. He took a deep breath and lunged into the room with his finger on the shotgun's trigger. Shadows danced in the darkness, but none presented themselves as human. Then the voice broke through again. Right behind him.

Sam wheeled around and almost shot his daughter.

Above him Sylvie hung from the side of the wooden crate, suspended by chains that wrapped under her arms and crossed behind her back before finally looping through her legs. Lengths of rope tied her to the chains and forced her arms straight out to the side, as if she had been crucified. One side of her face was swollen. Her white blouse had been stained with blood from a cut lip. A cloth gag forced her jaws apart.

Sam's blood pulsed with rage. But *she was alive!*

Sylvie shouted something urgent into the gag and looked up above her, as if to draw his attention there. Forty feet up, a metal walkway rimmed part of the hold. A faint outline in the wall marked the entrance door.

But Max wasn't there.

Sam climbed up on the base platform and reached behind Sylvie. Multiple knots tied the gag to her head but none would loosen. He reached into his pocket, and realized he'd left his knife with Missy back at the hotel.

He followed the tangle of rope and chain down and found a small wood door open next to her knees. Inside the door rows of dials and switches populated a metal control panel. This was the reality of Michael's drawings they'd found in both safe houses. *Schematics*, he could hear Henry say. What they hadn't known then was that they diagrammed the control unit attached to a German bomb.

A small red light glowed from the center of a round dial. It ticked, ticked again. It was a timer. The minute hand pointed to the number thirty. *Thirty minutes until the bomb detonated?*

Was this Max's revenge? Let Sam suffer for thirty minutes while he tried—and failed—to free his daughter?

Sylvie's eyes darted up again. A gunshot cracked and echoed in the hold. Sam felt the bullet scream by his ear and clang against the bomb's metal housing.

On the iron walkway Max stood and pointed a rifle down at Sam. The light from below cast his shadow high up against the cargo wall, making him look impossibly large. Even the rifle looked small in his hands.

"Congratulations, Sheriff Baker," Max said. "I knew you would come for your daughter. How do you like the way I prepared her for you?"

Sam looked down at the shotgun where it leaned against the metal base, just out of his reach.

The pistol tucked into the back of his waistband was his only hope, but even reaching for that would take too long. "Let my daughter go, and you can do what you want with me."

"My dear sheriff, I'm going to do with you what I want. You can count on that."

"She doesn't have anything to do with this."

"Sure, she does. She's the fucking prize. If you win the contest, you can come back and free her before the bomb goes off."

"In thirty minutes?"

Max leaned forward to look at his watch, and the dim light reflected the feral intensity in his deep-set eyes.

"Twenty-nine minutes before it detonates, to be exact. And Germans *are* exact. The plan had been to take it to Washington and kill your president. But when you killed Colonel Strabo, I had to make some changes."

"That sounds pretty goddamn insane to me," Sam said.

"Strabo was like a father to me. My own father was a drunken piece-of-shit. He beat my mother and me until I got big enough to return the favor. I buried him in our backyard next to the rose bushes."

"That's a very touching story."

Max fired the rifle. The bullet ricocheted off the back wall. "I just wanted you to understand why you have to die. Your pretty daughter, too." He gestured with his rifle. "Dump the shotgun shells."

Sam stepped down to the floor and broke the shotgun open. The shells clattered on the hard floor, and he set it down.

"Now turn around with your hands up."

Sam turned, knowing that the bulge of the pistol in his back would be visible.

"You came prepared, Baker," Max said. "Pull the pistol out with two fingers of your left hand and unload it. Do it slow."

Sam took the pistol from his waist band and thought again about taking his shot while he still had the chance. But with Max's rifle pointed at him he knew he would die here and lose his chance to free Sylvie. He dumped the bullets from the cylinder. "Hardly seems a fair fight, Max."

"You're going to get every chance that you gave Carl," Max said. "Throw me the shotgun."

Sam climbed down from the base and tossed the 12-gauge up to Max. He caught it with one big hand like it was a toy.

"Now the pistol."

Sam threw the gun up to him. He felt naked, powerless to help his daughter. He turned to her. "I love you, Sylvie."

She returned his declaration, muffled by the gag, but understood. Tears filled her eyes.

"That's very touching." Max said. "You should say goodbye while you're at it."

"Come on down here, Max. She can watch me take you apart."

"No, this room doesn't have the right...shall we say...ambiance.

"Don't worry," Sam said to Sylvie. "Plenty of time left." He turned away, afraid she'd see through his false confidence.

"There's not as much time as you think," Max said. "Didn't you did see the lock on the chains?"

Sam stepped up on the base and found a heavy lock looped through three chain links.

Max held up something small between two fingers that caught a slight shine from the light below. "This is the key," he said. He slipped it into his pants pocket. "If you can kill me, you know where to find it." He barked out a laugh like a boy eager to play a game. "It'll be fun. Don't you think?"

"You know what I think? I think you're sick."

"Thank you for that. I'll take even more pleasure in killing you." Max pointed up. "I'll be in one of the rooms on the main level. I'm sure you can find me one last time." He disappeared through the door.

Galveston '44

Chapter 106

Sam ran into the dark hallway and bounded up the stairs. He didn't fear an ambush. What Max had planned would be more elaborate than that, more twisted. He climbed up the second set of stairs to the main level and flung open the first door in the passageway. It was a galley, empty except for a row of ovens and a metal prep table.

In the next room a black anchor sat on a metal cart. He picked up a short piece of iron rebar from the floor. Better than nothing. The next room contained bunk beds. So did the next.

Time ticked away.

He opened the next door, but the room was a workshop. He took a step inside to look for a weapon, and a thick arm grabbed him from behind in a choke hold. He tried to pry Max's big arms loose, but they were locked on tight. White dots began to swim in his vision. He gasped for air.

Max dragged him down the hallway and kicked open a door. He threw Sam inside, and he slid across the metal floor. The room blazed with red. Overturned desks and chairs and piles of wood roared with flames four feet tall.

"This is the best I could do with limited time," Max said, his face lit red by the flames. "Does the fire remind you of something?"

Sam breathed in smoke and gasped. "You've seen one fire you've seen 'em all."

"Try to have some imagination, Sheriff. Or, should I say *ex-sheriff*?"

Sam stood and moved away from a burning pile of wood.

441

Max had recreated the hideout where Sam started the fire with the Molotov cocktail. Where he had killed Carl Strabo and shot Max twice. Where Sam had almost died from a knife wound near his heart.

Sam tensed, ready to rush Max, but the big man pulled out a large knife. "Not so fast, Sheriff," Max said. "Don't you want to play a little while?" He looked at his watch. "Maybe another twenty minutes or so?"

"There's only one thing you left out here, Max," Sam said. "Where is my gun so I can shoot you again?"

"No guns, my friend. Don't you know they're dangerous?"

Sam hoped Max wanted to fistfight. The man was bigger than any heavyweight he'd ever fought in the ring, but a bare knuckles brawl would at least play to Sam's strength. "Put the knife down. Let's settle this man-to-man."

Max flipped the knife and caught it without taking his eyes off Sam. "All debts will be settled. Since you killed Strabo with a knife, you will die by the knife."

"An eye for an eye?"

"And a tooth for a tooth."

"Are you the only one who gets a knife?"

"No, we'll have identical ones. Guess who they're from?"

"Humor me."

"Your friend, Laura." Max said. "Don't you find some irony in that?"

Sam could almost hear the seconds ticking away. "Why don't you shut the fuck up and give me a knife."

Max threw something, and it bounced off his chest. A skull-and-crossbones medallion lay next to a burning desk and reflected a red glint from the flames. Sam pulled its twin from his pocket—the one he'd found in Wayne McRae's clasped hands—and threw it off Max's shoulder.

"How touching that you kept the souvenir I left for your deputy," Max said. "He was a stupid son-of-a-bitch to turn his back to me. But what do you expect from a hick lawman?"

Blood rose to Sam's face as he pictured Max hitting Wayne in the back of his neck and shooting him twice. But he kept his voice level. "If you don't give me a knife pretty soon, I'm going to think you're afraid to fight."

Max smirked. "That's the spirit." He slid a knife across the metal floor to Sam.

Sam picked it up. He fit his fingers into the knobbed handgrip. He'd never been in a knife fight before—not even in the war—but he'd better learn quickly.

Max turned his back to Sam and looked out the porthole window, as if the lightning strikes and the surging waves were of more interest to him than a man who badly wanted to kill him.

Sam knew he needed to shake up the big man's confidence, get him to react somehow. "Your dead friend Carl...I drank his blood."

Max turned to face him. "What the fuck are you talking about?"

"I drink the blood of all the men I kill," Sam said. "It's something I learned from another soldier when we destroyed Germany in the Great War. My sergeant, actually. Meaner than a goddamn rattlesnake. He said if you drink the blood of your enemy after you kill him, you'll be protected from retribution."

Boredom fell from Max's expression. He took a step towards Sam. "Tell me you didn't do that!"

"Carl's blood tasted like maggots on a dead rat. I guess that's because he was a fucking Nazi sent to babysit a sick mother-fucker."

Max clasped the knife in a fighting grip and feigned a

lunge. "Your retribution is coming."

Sam circled him, the knife ready. "Three years of fighting Germans and I never was wounded. And, in the warehouse just now...every man dead or dying, but do you see a scratch on me?"

Max moved to one side, quickly reversed himself and stabbed Sam in the side. He never saw it coming. The big man moved faster than any agile boxer he'd ever fought. He wasn't sure how deeply he'd been cut, but the red-hot pain was the same as when Carl Strabo had stuck the knife in his chest.

"Now you have a scratch on you," Max said.

Sam managed a smile. "You'll have to do a lot better than that." He lunged at Max and slashed him on his forearm.

"Thank you," Max said, matching Sam's smile. "I want you to fight for your life like Strabo did."

Sam thought of Sylvie chained to the bomb. He knew he had to force the action. He changed his stance like he often did in the ring and slashed Max's cheek. But before he could jump back, Max stabbed him in the upper chest. He sagged but tried not to show pain.

The big man bounced on his toes, his expression exultant. He kicked a pile of burning wood at Sam and faked a stab at his face. He laughed...playing with him now.

Blood from Sam's chest soaked his shirt and mixed with that from the stomach wound. A dull ache took over his left arm, still weak from the shootout at the safe house. The room rolled under his feet, and he knew it wasn't from the storm.

In his short career as a boxer he'd never had to come from behind. Rarely took a punch so hard that he needed to clinch and hold. But now his legs felt rubbery and disengaged from his body.

Max tossed his knife again. Like a cat playing with a half-dead mouse, he would finish the job at his leisure. He looked at his watch. "You only have a few minutes to live, Sheriff," he said. "In the meantime, I want you to think about your failure to save your daughter. Your failure to avenge the death of your deputy. And that stupid cab driver—he was asleep when I pulled him out and broke his skinny neck."

Max faked a thrust at his chest and stabbed him in the thigh. He roared in triumph, tossed the knife in the air and caught it.

Pain spread through Sam's leg. He wanted to shout out for Sylvie. Tell her again that he loved her. *Why hadn't he told her that every day of her life? And Billy and Claire, too? You keep things inside you and time goes by and then it's over.*

Sam gripped the knife hard and bent low and hoped Max would get careless.

The big man laughed and mimicked Sam's move. "Good. The sheriff wants to go out fighting." Max circled around. The light from the fire reflected red in his eyes. No more laughter.

The time had come.

Blood from Max's shoulder wound had soaked through a large patch of his shirt. He hugged his left arm tight against his side. As a boxer, Sam had looked for weakness in his opponent, and he hoped this was one. He switched the knife to his left hand and faked a quick thrust. Max lunged forward with his knife, and Sam punched him hard with a straight right hand to his chin.

The big man's knees buckled. Sam drove the knife deep into his stomach.

Max gasped, and his eyes opened wide in surprise.

Sam pulled on the knife handle, but Max grabbed his wrist with one hand and slashed him across the cheek.

Sam smashed his elbow into Max's face and drove him back. The fight was now more his style, and a reserve of strength shot through him. He hit Max with another hard right, and he dropped his knife. Sam kicked the knife into the outer edges of the flames. The blade buried in Max's stomach glinted in the light from the fire.

Just as Sam took a step towards him, Max pulled the knife out of his stomach and lunged at him. Sam jumped to the side, but the knife ripped his arm. Max wheeled, ready to attack again. He held his hand against his stomach wound, but appeared revived.

"Looks like I've got an unfair advantage, Baker."

"You're bleeding out, Max."

"Fuck that. We're all going to die here anyway."

Sam scanned the floor for Max's knife. Something metallic reflected the light from the fire—the skull-and-crossbones medallion called to him like a beacon. He bent to pick it up—keeping his eyes on Max, but his hand found something else. The knife.

Max attacked with his knife, but he was slower now. Sam dodged and stabbed him in the side. And again—deeper—grunting with each thrust.

Max swayed. The knife slipped out of his hand and clanged on the metal floor, now slick with blood. He nodded at Sam, as if acknowledging defeat. Sam waited for him to fall, but he turned and staggered to the starboard wall. He dug his hand in his pocket and pulled the porthole window open.

"No!" Sam shouted.

He grabbed Max's arm just before he could throw the key out into the churning waters. He pulled Max's arm behind his back and took the key from his hand.

Sam kicked him in the back of his knee. Max collapsed to the floor.

Chapter 107

Sam ran down the dim corridor. The roll of the swaying ship and the cuts on his legs made him feel like he was running in quicksand. He climbed the stairs and slipped on the last step. He stood and ran as the ticking of the clock pounded like his heart.

He ran into the cargo hold and climbed onto the metal base. The timer showed four minutes to go. He reached behind Sylvie for the lock and pushed the key against the keyhole.

It didn't fit!

He turned the key over. It went in and the lock clicked open. Sylvie helped Sam free her from the chains. They climbed down from the crate and started for the open door.

They stopped. Max blocked their path and pointed a shotgun at them. His shirt and pants were dark with blood, and he swayed like a pine tree in the wind. But his gray eyes shone with triumph.

"Say it, Baker," Max said. "Tell me you're ready for your retribution."

"Fuck you, Max."

Max pumped a shell into chamber and lifted the gun to his shoulder. Sam covered Sylvie with his body. A gun roared—but not Max's. His body jerked. He dropped the gun and turned to face his assailant.

Henry Jackson stood behind Max, blood gleaming on his dark torso. Both men stood slack, as if their puppet master had cut their strings.

Max lurched forward. Jackson shot him again. The big

447

man fell back onto the hard floor, his vacant gray eyes staring at the cargo doors above. Jackson shot him again. Blood spread out on the floor from under Max's body.

Sam looked at the timer–less than two minutes to go.

Chapter 108

Jackson dropped the rifle and sank to his knees. Sam and Sylvie lifted him and dragged him out of the hold.

Sam led them to the long corridor leading out of the ship. "Run!"

They pushed open the entrance door and emerged out into the fury of the wind and rain. Jackson stumbled on the wet gangplank and slipped from their grasp. They picked him up and staggered down the ramp, past the Cadillac, to the rear of the truck.

"Get under!" Sam shouted. He and Sylvie pulled Henry under the truck bed.

The wind calmed for a solitary second, and the storm—and time—hung in suspension.

The bomb exploded.

The blast sounded muffled and deep, then piercing and deafening as the ship imploded. A huge, fiery hole blew out of its port side. The captain's wheelhouse and the cargo cranes and the guts of the ship launched out into the dark sky. Mooring chains busted loose from the dock bollards.

They huddled together as flaming metal smacked against the truck and rained down around them. The shower of metal slowed, then stopped. They looked up to see a huge crater in the middle of the deck with flames roaring up from inside. Like Hell unleashed.

Unmoored, the ship began to slam into the dock. And then—rapidly—to sink.

Sam let out the deep breath he'd been holding, seemingly,

for months. He hugged Sylvie, and told her again he loved her.

Then Sam remembered. "Dominick…"

Sylvie read his concern. Tears sprung to her eyes. "Tell me he's alive."

"I don't know, sweetheart," Sam said. He couldn't bear to tell her that the young man had been bleeding heavily from a bullet to the chest.

"Dominick…" Jackson whispered.

Sylvie leaned closer to him. "What happened to him?"

Jackson raised his hand and pointed. "Hospital…Laura…" He passed out.

They lifted him into the cab of the truck, and Sam drove them away, the wind at their back.

Chapter 109

A brisk wind blew dust across the gravestones of the All Saints cemetery. Wispy, white clouds floated past the afternoon sun. A flock of geese flew in formation in a southerly direction.

A dented '34 Chevy passed through the iron gates and lumbered into the gravel parking lot. The car stopped, brakes squealing. Viola Jackson, wearing a black dress with a peach collar, climbed out from the driver's seat. Henry Jackson opened his door and stood, wincing in pain. He wore a black suit with a white shirt and a blue tie.

"Now, Henry," Viola said. "You wait and let me get them crutches."

He reached for the back door but his sister was quicker. Jackson fitted the crutches under his arms and looked up at the deep blue sky. He filled his lungs with air. "There's a touch of fall in the air today, Sis."

"'Bout time."

Jackson moved forward, favoring his wounded leg. "It's a good day to be alive."

Viola followed behind. "You fall, I'm gonna be mad at you."

"Aren't you already mad at me?"

"You shouldn't even be here. You ain't healed by a long shot."

"It's the right thing to do," Jackson said. "Didn't you always tell me to do the right thing?"

"I told you the sheriff was going to get you shot. That's

what I told you."

"See how smart you are?"

"No, you the smart one," Viola said and laughed. "You answer every question with a question."

They reached the edge of the tree-shaded cemetery where the rough asphalt turned to soft grass. People strolled between rows of grave markers and spoke in hushed tones.

A portly, mustached man waved his hand and hurried towards them. He wore a brown shirt with sweat marks under the arm pits and a chest patch bearing the cemetery logo. "I'm sorry, folks. This ain't your area of the cemetery."

Henry stopped and rested on the crutches. "We're here by invitation, sir."

"Don't make no difference," the man said, and pointed off into the distance. "All the coloreds are buried in the south corner."

Viola jammed her hand on her hip. "Ain't people all the same when they turn to dust?"

"Hey!" The shout came from a tall man hurrying between pine trees and granite mausoleums. It was Sam, hobbling on a cane but still imposing in his black suit.

Claire trotted behind him, holding the hem of her black dress off the ground.

Sam pointed his cane at the man. "What's the problem?"

"I'm afraid the rules don't allow these people to enter this section of the property."

Claire took Sam's arm, and he lowered the cane. "Sam, if I could just..." She smiled at the man. "Sir, I know the cemetery has its rules, but we are laying a loved one to rest today and this man..." Claire pointed at Jackson, her voice cracking with emotion. "This man saved my husband and my daughter's lives. If not for Henry, I would be burying three loved ones today instead of just one."

"It was you killed that German fella?" The man looked at Henry Jackson as if he'd appeared suddenly out of thin air. "The newspaper didn't say you was colored."

"Born and bred."

The man looked at his crutches and nodded slowly, beginning to understand. "Okay, you folks can come on in," he said.

Galveston '44

Chapter 110

Sam led them down the sun-dappled path towards a sizeable group of people standing around an open grave. A pink-faced preacher in a black clerical shirt and white collar nodded as they approached.

Sam and Claire took their place next to Missy at the grave's edge. He pulled Henry and Viola to their side.

Every few seconds Sam and Claire looked over their shoulder in the direction of the parking lot. The minister smiled patiently, holding a bible in his hands. Everyone waited quietly, alone with their thoughts.

Claire turned again and smiled. "Here they come."

Down the path, Sylvie pushed Dominick in a wheelchair, flashing in and out of the sunlight like flickering images on a movie screen. The mourners smiled at the sight.

Sylvie looked radiant in a simple black dress. Dominick wore a black suit and seemed embarrassed, perhaps because he had to rely on his girlfriend for mobility. Sylvie stopped the wheelchair and helped Dominick walk the last few yards. They took their place next to Sam and Claire.

"Sorry we're late," Sylvie whispered. "The hospital took their sweet time getting Dom released."

"We would have waited all day," Claire said.

The minister smiled and cleared his throat. "We are gathered here to celebrate the short life of a brave young man—Billy Baker. The Bakers, as you know, only recently received their son's remains from Italy, where Billy gave his life over a year ago while fighting the Germans. The Bakers decided not to have a military funeral and the accompanying twenty-one gun salute because—as Sam so elegantly phrased it—we've heard enough damn gunfire for a while."

The preacher went on to extol the highlights of Billy's short but admirable life. Afterwards the coffin was lowered into the grave. They tossed handfuls of dirt after it and smiled at each other.

Billy was home.

Chapter 111

Sam broke away from a group of Billy's friends who had pressed him for more details than the newspaper had revealed about the shootout at the cotton warehouse and the fight on the ship. But he begged off. The F.B.I. had told him not to discuss it until the investigation was completed.

Sam had received a letter of commendation from them for stopping the bomb plot, but he had given it to Henry. Sam's only intention had been to save his daughter, and he didn't feel much like a hero.

Greta Haugen—the only survivor of the plot to kill President Roosevelt—had been arrested. Her great wealth would not help her in prison.

Jim Eilers had been arrested for aiding and abetting fugitives from the law, ending his brief tenure as sheriff of Galveston County. He awaited trial in the same jail cell from which Sam had escaped. Sam appreciated the irony of that.

He spotted Henry at another section of the cemetery where he leaned on his crutches, his eyes cast down. Sam picked up a bouquet of flowers—Billy had far more than he would have approved of—and limped over to stand beside Henry.

He set the flowers against the granite headstone. The engraved inscription read:

Wayne McRae. Born 1922, Died 1944. He loved people almost as much as he loved horses.

They stood in silence for some time. A bird in a nearby tree trilled, and another one in the distance answered it. A cool breeze blew the first leaves of fall across the grave.

The End

Thanks for reading *Galveston '44*

Reviews are everything!

If you enjoyed this book, I would really appreciate it if you would go to Amazon and/or Goodreads, rate the book and write one or two lines about what you liked about the story.

B.W. Peterson

ACKNOWLEDGEMENTS

A thousand thanks to my great friend Ed Daniels for his steadfast support and encouragement. Every writer would find invaluable a similar believer in his or her work, a cheerleader who will urge them to carry the book across the marathon's finish line. Additionally, his original idea for the book cover design, sparked by his photographer's eye and familiarity with the story's elements, was ultimately brought to life by the cover designer.

Special thanks to my editor, Carolyn V. Hamilton, for her hard work in making the book as error free as possible, and for her patience with my incessant rewriting. She also brought the final touches to the book cover with her eye-catching design of the title and fonts.

I am grateful to the talented graphic designer August Kovach for his evocative book cover design that accurately captures the time and tone of the story. He must have been exposed to a lot of noir—film or novel—in his life.

I want to acknowledge Ed Daniels, Marianne Schroeder, Jennifer Snare and Fay Binning for reading earlier drafts of the book, and for their constructive and helpful comments.

Heartfelt thanks to Marianne Schroeder for taking the author photo. You had a difficult assignment in making your subject look presentable.

AUTHOR BIO

B.W. Peterson is a former travel and article writer turned crime fiction writer. He is a serial ex-pat, a lover of living in foreign locales.

He now lives high in the Andes Mountains of Ecuador where he enjoys studying Spanish and eating warm banana bread.

Stowing away in his mind as he moved to his new home high in the Andes Mountains of Ecuador was a trigger-happy cast of characters in cutthroat conflict with each other.

When he isn't wrestling these characters and their story onto the page, he enjoys learning Spanish and eating warm banana bread.

Made in the USA
Coppell, TX
09 October 2020

39511408R00256